I0788571

The Beginning

Book Three - Eight Realm Series

Entertainment Enterprise
Entertainmententerprise.net

Frist Edition March 2025

The publisher is not responsible for websites (or their content) that are not owned by the publisher.

ISBN 978-1-947040-04-5

Printed in the United States of America

The Beginning

Book Three - Eight Realm Series

Catherine Sitz

Catherine Sitz

Chapter One

The Beginning

"She's an elder?" Dak asked in surprise looking at Leiya.

"Her ancestors were," Egon explained.

"I don't understand," Leiya said, looking back and forth between Dak and Egon as they all stood at the foot of Sierra's and Dak's bed.

Pointing to his chest Egon said, "I'm an Elder. I thought most of my people were dead. You are proof that my people settled in a new world and prospered," Egon said, his voice filled with emotion. "I'm very pleased to meet you my dear."

Leiya took Egon's hand between hers. "I don't know what to say. If this is true, you should come visit my home."

"I would love that."

Dak glared at them in frustration. "If a Willow-Wisp has Sierra, how do we rescue her?" Dak asked, changing the subject back to Sierra.

"She can escape them at any time," Egon said.

"Will they hurt her?" Egon asked Leiya.

"I don't think so. They are curious about her," she said.

"They did approach her before, asking her questions," Lazrus said, his head occupying the space where the wall should be.

"At the moment, there is nothing we can do for Sierra. She can handle the Willow-Wisp," Egon said. "We need to continue helping the Muricks, Dragons and Phoenix, so they will be ready to return home when they are able."

Dak threw his hands up in frustration. "So, we do nothing? I don't accept that."

"I can't make a gate to their world. I'm sorry son, but I don't know how to help her. She's the strongest person I know. I'm certain she'll be fine," Egon said. "If I didn't believe this to be true, we would tear their forest apart looking for her."

Dak knew he spoke the truth but was frustrated there was nothing he could do, except wait.

Sierra glared angrily at Lisha. "I appreciate your offer, but I'm not interested."

Lisha and the other Willow-Wisp frowned. "It isn't often that we ask anyone to join us," Sasha said stepping forward. "This is an honor."

Sierra blinked to focus on the nearly transparent woman. It was disturbing to be able to see the lush green forest through her.

"Why do you decline our most generous offer?"

"For one, I have a home that I'm eager to return to and secondly, you stood by while the people of this world were stricken with a horrible disease, and you did nothing to help them."

"We observed and learned from it," Elissa said.

"What good does knowledge do if you don't use it?" Sierra asked. She felt like something was crawling beneath her skin. She cast a protective spell on herself and instantly felt better.

"What did you do?" Sasha asked, growing angry.

"I cured them," Sierra replied.

"Not that. What did you just do?"

"Nothing," Sierra said.

The lights in the darkness grew dimmer and angry.

The Willow-Wisp whispered among themselves, while glaring at Sierra.

"You insult us by refusing our offer," Lisha said.

"And you insult me, by kidnapping me," Sierra said.

"What is kidnapping?" Lisha said.

"Forcing me from my home."

"I thought you'd be honored to join us."

"Well, I'm not. So, take me home."

"I can't do that," Lisha said.

"You will learn to like it here and become one of us," Sasha said.

"Like hell I will," Sierra said. "And what is that irritating noise?"

She tried to ignore the noise but was unsuccessful. She wanted to know what was hiding in the darkness, so she created balls of light to dispel the darkness.

"What are you doing?" cried Elissa. "Put them out."

Before they could extinguish the lights, Sierra saw a grey mass of something, it was the source of the humming noise.

"Why did you do that? The light hurts him."

"Him?"

"The keeper of knowledge."

Sierra sighed. She felt like she was in a twisted 'Land of Oz.'

"While I appreciated your offer, I must decline and now I will be going," she said eager to leave.

"Going isn't an option," Sasha yelled surprising the other soft-spoken Willow-Wisp.

Sierra grew angrier by the second. She was exhausted and irritated and allowed her anger to shine through and her entire body started to glow.

The Willow-Wisp shielded their eyes from the glow, until the darkness grew even darker. Sasha took a step toward Sierra. She put up her hands to stop her and nothing happened.

"Your magic won't work on us," Sasha said in triumph.

"Interesting," Sierra said. "But it does work on the world around you."

Vines grew out of the ground and wrapped around the Willow-Wisp, anchoring them in place.

She sent orbs of light to light up the entire forest.

"Now, let's see what you're hiding."

The vines covered their mouths preventing them from speaking.

Sasha fought violently against her bonds.

Sierra parted the vines and bushes heading toward the grey blob that still emanated a soft humming noise.

She touched it with the tip of her booted foot and the humming stopped.

She reached out to it and discovered that it wasn't exactly alive. It seemed to be some sort of fungus.

She shrank it down to the size of a pea and the humming stopped.

She turned around and looked at the Willow-Wisp.

Sasha had stopped struggling.

Sierra briefly considered leaving them tied up, but she loosened their bonds as she opened a rip and entered her bedroom in Pandora.

She smiled, pleased that she'd been able to open a rip and actually travel to where she'd intended and didn't end up in nothingness.

Dak raised up in bed, where he'd been trying to figure out a way to create a new gate. He let out a yell as he threw back the bed covers and lunged at Sierra, wrapping her in his arms.

"Miss me?" She laughed.

"What took you so long?" He teased.

"Hey, I wasn't gone long."

He released her, pulling her down next to him on the bed. "What happened?"

"The Willow-Wisp invited me to join them."

"By force?"

"Pretty much."

"What did you do to them?" he asked kissing the top of her head.

"I taught them the error of their ways."

"Are you all right?"

"I'm fine. I just need sleep, then I'll be as good as new."

"Promise?"

Sierra smiled as she pulled three gates out of her pocket and sent them to the safety of the gate room, along with the mysterious glob.

She waved her hand in front of her and transferred her black leather pants and teal shirt, for silky white pajamas.

She kissed Dak softly and climbed beneath the cool sheets and was soon fast asleep.

Chapter Two

The Muricks

Sierra had Jinks, Leiya, and Adam stayed to train with the fairies while she met with Egon.

Egon and Lazrus were pleased yet surprised to see Sierra striding toward them smiling up at Dak.

Egon greeted her with a kiss on her cheek. "Are the Willow-Wisp still standing?" He asked teasingly.

"Yes, but I'm certain that I left them extremely pissed."

Egon frowned.

"Upset," Dak explained.

"Well, they were insulted that I didn't embrace their offer to join them, and I sort of took something of theirs with me when I left."

"Sort of?" Dak said.

"I shrunk some grey blob that was humming. They called it the Keeper of Knowledge."

Dak, Egon and Lazrus stared at her.

"What? I'm not kidding," she said.

"Maybe we should inspect the blob," Dak said, curiously.

"He's right," Lazrus said. "If it's the Keeper of Knowledge, the Willow-Wisp will come for it."

"They could be a little detained," Sierra said innocently.

"What did you do to them?" Egon asked.

Sierra smiled. "I sort of tied them up with vines. My powers didn't work on them, so I had to improvise."

Lazrus snorted a puff of smoke and laughed.

"Your magic didn't work?" Dak asked.

"That's interesting," Egon said. "We should check out the Keeper of Knowledge before they try to take it back."

Sierra called the shrunken mass from its hiding place in the gate room.

It passed through the glass, and through the wall and across the yard where she gently sat it on the ground in front of them.

She grew it to its full size and cringed when the humming filled her head.

"What is that noise?" Egon said.

Dak frowned. "What noise?"

"You don't hear it?" Sierra said, pointing to the grey mass. "It's humming."

"I don't hear anything," Dak said.

Sierra tried to block out the noise. When she blocked the humming, she could hear the creature talking. It didn't really make any sense. It muttered incoherently.

Egon seemed to be listening to it too.

The creature's tone changed, and Sierra heard her conversation with the Willow-Wisp. She smiled. "It repeats whatever it hears," she said.

"Interesting," Egon said. "But how?"

"I believe it is the moss," Lazrus said. "I've seen this before, but not in such a mass as this."

"I think we should return it to the Willow-Wisp and make certain that they understand it will be a mistake to come to Pandora uninvited again," Sierra said.

"You three take care of the Willow-Wisp while I check on all the refugees and organize their return home," Egon said.

Sierra raised one perfectly arched eyebrow as Egon walked away toward Pandora's new town. "Shall we return the glob?" she asked.

"Sure, let's go scare some Willow-Wisp," Dak said, smiling.

"First, I need to cast a spell to alert me if the Willow-Wisp s up uninvited again," Sierra said, as she raised her hand and waved it in front of them, satisfied that she wouldn't be surprised by them again.

She opened a rip and stepped through it followed by Dak and Lazrus.

The Willow-Wisp forest was dark and quiet. Sierra placed the blob on the ground and returned it to its former size.

Its hum filled the forest, echoing off the trees. Lisha and Sasha appeared before them.

"Why have you returned?" Lisha asked.

"I brought back your knowledge thing," Sierra said, and to make sure that you won't be returning to Pandora."

"I thought you would be honored to join us. Few are asked."

"You didn't ask. You tried to force me."

Lisha stared at them silently.

Dak shrugged. They were definitely weird. "Okay then," he said. "Let's go before this gets any weirder."

The humming grew louder, and Sierra blocked out the noise.

Sasha appeared next to Sierra and put her pale hand on Sierra's arm.

"You've returned," she said.

"Only to return what belongs to you," Lazrus said, coldly growing irritated with the tiresome Willow-Wisp.

The light seemed to be sucked out of the dark forest. Uncomfortable with the darkness for the first time in his life, Dak created four balls of light to dispel the darkness. The balls floated around them, surrounding them with their light.

The Willow-Wisp shrank away from the light. Sasha removed her hand from Sierra's arm and shrank into the forest, just out of the range of the light. Lisha moved next to her.

"Why are you here if you have no desire to join us?" Sasha asked, angrily.

Sierra exhaled softly. "I took something that didn't belong to me, so I've returned it."

Dak glanced at Sierra and said, "It's obvious they aren't interested, and I don't really see them being friendly, so let's make certain we understand each other. You touch my wife again and I'll come back and burn down your depressing forest."

Lazrus exhaled a small flame to press Dak's point.

Lazrus winked at Sierra, as she tried to hide her smile.

"Well, okay," Sierra said.

The Willow-Wisp remained quiet as they stared at Sierra, Dak and Lazrus, with abject hatred.

Sierra opened a rip and before they stepped through, she made the balls of light brighter, lighting up the entire forest.

The Willow-Wisp vanished as Sierra, Dak and Lazrus stepped through to Pandora.

"Well, that was fun," Sierra said.

"I doubt we've heard the last of them," Dak said.

"I believe I'll join Egon," Lazrus said before taking flight, heading toward town.

Lazrus landed in the center of town. Egon was surrounded by the Muricks and Dragons. He was giving them words of encouragement and assurances that it was safe to return home.

"What if we don't want to return home," Salarus, a weary old Dragon asked. "Is there a chance we can stay here if we choose?"

"I will speak to Sierra about the possibility," Egon assured him. "Are you certain that's what you want?"

"Some of us would like a fresh start. Too many sad memories at home. Most of them we'd like to forget."

"I understand, my friend," Egon said. "Pandora is a place for starting over," Egon said.

The Muricks were eager and more than excited to return home.

Sierra and Dak entered the village and were immediately surrounded by the grateful Muricks. All at once they were thanking them for rescuing them.

Sierra opened a rip and the Muricks hurried through excited to return home.

They were surprised to see their town completely rebuilt. They walked around the town in wonder. Sierra had talked to Nodrik, so she could recreate their home for them, as they remembered. She wanted everything to be perfect for them, after everything they'd been through. The look on their faces reflected their happiness.

The Muricks were in awe. Everything looked exactly as they remembered.

The town was small, but quaint, surrounded by small colorful cottages. A tree-lined road led out of town to numerous farms that kept the villages well fed.

Murmuring in excitement, they split up and headed to their new homes.

Sierra linked her fingers with Daks. "This feels good," she said.

"What about the Willow-Wisp? I don't want these poor people hurt again."

Sierra tightened her grip on Daks' hand and waved a protection spell around each and every Murick.

She reached out across their world and opened up the entrance to the underwater world. She also sent out a message to the Wyaliians to let them know the underwater world was open and so was the entrance to Jinks' village.

She encouraged them to reach out to the others.

She created small gates and sent them to each village and city so they could contact her if they needed anything.

"So, what now?" Dak asked.

"We leave them alone unless they need us."

"You don't want to expand Pandora here?" he asked.

Sierra studied his smooth handsome face and smiled. "You're brilliant," she said.

Dak grinned. "I'm aware of that, but why am I brilliant this time?"

"We expand Pandora City into the far corner of the world. That way we can be a part of both worlds."

"Just brilliant," he teased." So, what far corner do you have in mind?"

"The place where we found the creature. I think we turn that lovely place into something good,"

Dak frowned slightly. "I'm not sure how I feel about Pandora being opened to this world."

"It won't be open. I will restrict who can enter Pandora. I will allow them to see into Pandora, and we can see them, but they will need permission to enter."

Sierra opened a rip into what would be Pandora Two. Hand in hand, they stepped through. Shuddering at the memory of the creature, she decided that the colorful flowers of the meadow needed a little more color if they were going to resemble Pandora.

She gently closed her eyes, taking Dak's hand as she lifted her hands.

Mountains appeared in the distance with a gentle river running between them.

Across the meadow, she created a smaller version of their home.

Near the front of the house, she placed a shimmering gate. You could see the village of Pandora through it.

A small town appeared at the base of the mountains. It was unnaturally quiet. There were no birds or animals anywhere.

"The creature scared away or changed everything in this part of the world," Dak said.

"It's a little creepy deserted, isn't it?" she said.

"Just a little," he said smiling.

Sierra bent down and put her hand flat on the smooth green grass. She could feel the life beneath her fingers.

Soon the sky was filled with birds. The meadow began to fill up with life as foxes, deer, rabbits, and squirrels raced toward them.

To their surprise, six of the black dogs they'd seen before slowly approached them, taking human form.

"I am Asher. We heard your call and wish to relocate."

"Welcome Asher. If your pack doesn't mind," Sierra said.

"It is our desire to develop a kinship with others, especially those like us."

"We would like that as well," she said as she created the trees they slept in on the edge of town near the forest. "I believe you will find accommodations to your liking, just beyond the town."

"Thank you, my lady," Asher said, returning to a fluffy black dog as he raced toward the trees.

"I thought they hated us," Dak said.

"I did too."

Movement to his left caught Dak's eye and he turned to see a dozen or more people climb from the river and walk toward them. When they reached Sierra and Dak, they bowed slightly at the waist.

A young blond woman stepped forward nervously. "Queen Kallam gave us her blessing to relocate to the waters beneath this land. I request your permission to do so," she said.

"We would be delighted to have you," Sierra said. "Please let me know if there is anything you require."

"If we may use materials here to build a city."

Sierra smiled. "I can do better than that," she said reading the woman's thoughts, seeing the city she imagined. Sierra created the city she dreamed of building in the deepest depths of the river, just before it entered into the underwater ocean.

"I believe you will find everything you need below the surface," Sierra said, putting the image in her mind of the blue and white palace she'd just created for them.

"How did you do that?" she asked in wonder.

"My world has magic," she explained.

"I don't know what to say except, thank you."

"You are most welcome, and please thank Kallam for me. I hope she will visit soon."

"I will let her know. Thank you, again."

She turned and rejoined her friends, excitedly telling them about the castle.

"Let's go home," Sierra said.

I can't wait to tell the Dragons about this place. It's not the home that they remember, but it is their world.

"I bet they will love it," Dak said, leading the way to the gate that would take them home.

Chapter Three

Return to Normal

Sierra was so glad to be home. She looked around the bustling city of Pandora and smiled. Pandora City was something out of a dream. It was a mixture of old and new. The city sported an old village atmosphere with the wooden sidewalk that framed the many shops and buildings, while having a modern hospital, bank, library, and coffee shop. They had accomplished so much in such a brief time.

She reached out to all the Dragons asking them to meet her on the castle lawn.

She could feel each one of them as they took flight, their powerful wings slicing through the warm air.

She sent them images of the new Pandora and soon dozens of magnificent Dragons landed on the lush green lawn. Lazrus and Raziel took their places next to Dak and Sierra.

"It's your home. Only better if you want it. You are welcome to stay here, or in the new Pandora, the choice is yours," Sierra said.

Gorreth, an old, very wise Dragon stepped forward and bowed his head in honor and respect to Sierra and Dak.

"My people will serve you, my lord and lady, but returning to our home world is more than we hoped for."

"I know that you didn't want to return to your home after everything you'd been through, but this would be home, yet different," Sierra said.

"That is most thoughtful," Garreth said. "Most of us are eager to return, but there are those that would like to stay in Pandora."

"We are glad to have them. If you're ready, I can show you your new home. The gates between the two

Pandoras will remain open for you, so you can travel freely between the two."

"Thank you, my lady."

Sierra followed them through the gate to Pandora Two.

The Dragons looked around their new home before taking flight toward the cliffs.

She could feel their relief and joy as she passed through the gate, entering Pandora Two. It was similar to Pandora, yet different. She hoped that it would allow her to be a part of this new world and form strong friendships.

Dak pulled her into his arms and kissed her softly. "Another catastrophe averted."

Sierra laughed, "Until the next one."

"Shh, don't say that too loud," he teased. He looked over Sierra's shoulder and saw her mother, Erin heading their way waving her arms excitedly. "I think the next one is on its way," he groaned.

Sierra buried her face in his chest.

"I'm sorry to interrupt sweetheart," she said as she looked around at the new city laid out before her. "But Bree contacted me, and she thinks that you may have missed some of the infected."

"Why does she think that?" Dak asked.

"She said people were really acting crazy. She wants you to come home so she can show you."

"Now?" Dak asked.

"I'll get Egon, and we'll go check it out," Sierra said.

Erin kissed Sierra on the cheek. "Sorry darling. I wouldn't have bothered you if she hadn't been so sure."

Sierra forced herself to smile. "You think there's a chance we missed some infected?"

"I guess we could have but we have to check it out."

Sierra reached out to Egon, telling him of their latest problem.

He quickly replied that he was on the way.

Sierra smiled when he appeared a few moments later in front of her.

"Bree wouldn't have reached out to us unless she was certain something was wrong," Sierra said, convinced that it was true.

"While we are there, I'm going to try to locate the Elders that were sent to watch Ben and the other exiled Elders," Egon said. "It's time everyone came home."

Sierra hugged him. "I agree. You find your friends. We will deal with the infected."

"Thank you my dear, just one thing before we go. Can you show me how to open a rip?"

Sierra laughed. "I would be glad to." While she opened a rip, she showed Egon and Dak how to feel the energy and concentrate on reshaping the energy while directing it where to go.

After multiple failed tries they were able to open a small rip.

Sierra opened a rip inside her old bedroom, and they stepped through. She looked around wistfully. Her life was so much simpler before she discovered Mags was so much more than a pet. She picked up the phone from its charging station and dialed Bree's number.

Bree answered on the first ring. "Thank goodness. I'm so glad you're here. I don't know what's going on, but it's beyond weird. Like Pandora weird."

Sierra laughed. "Breathe and tell me what's up."

"People are changing. I don't know how to describe it. But I can show you. I'll be there in five," she said, hanging up.

Sierra returned the phone to its cradle. "She's on her way."

Egon patted Sierra and Dak on the shoulder. "Good luck. I'm going to try to locate my friends."

"Bring them home safely," Sierra said.

Dak shook Egon's hand. "What she said," he said.

"Take care of my granddaughter," he said.

"Always," Dak promised.

"My magic is limited in this world so I will not be able to keep in touch with you. I will see you at home once I locate them."

Sierra nodded. She wished she could help him, but she knew this was something he needed to do.

Egon smiled and vanished into a puff of smoke.

The front door banged open, bouncing off the wall, as Bree stormed inside, racing up the stairs.

Sierra and Dak met her at the top of the stairs. Bree hugged Sierra briefly. "I'm so glad to see you," she said glancing at Dak. "You too," she added.

Dak smiled slightly. "Good to see you too," he said.

Bree grabbed Dak and hugged him. "I'm sorry. It's good to see you too. I've just been so damned scared," she said thrusting her phone in front of them touching the play button.

They watched as a group of teens came into view. They were pale and looked like they were on drugs by the way they moved so slow and jerky.

The video ended and Sierra looked at Bree. "Are they going to a goth event?"

Bree rolled her eyes. "No, that's David Lewis, Randy Stone, and Stan Cast."

Sierra's eyes widened in shock. "No way."

"Yes, way. They've stopped going to class. Their parents are worried to death about them."

"Could they be on drugs?"

"You know them. I don't think they would do drugs. We need to find them and see for ourselves."

"Sounds like a good plan. Let's go," Sierra said.

Dak followed the two women walking with their arms around each other, down the stairs, and out of the house to Bree's sports car parked in the driveway.

Bree opened her door and pushed the seat up, waving to Dak to climb in the back seat.

Dak frowned, rolled his eyes heavenward and silently climbed in the back seat.

Sierra hid her smile as she climbed into the car.

The rock music blared as Bree started the car.

Dak leaned forward. "I realize that you call this music, but it's splitting my brain in two."

"Whatever," Bree said, turning the music off. "You are such a big baby."

Dak bit off his retort and sat back in the seat watching the cars go by. There was a different feeling in the air than the last time he'd visited this world. Something was definitely wrong here.

His gaze drilled into the shadows, seeking out the young men that might take refuge in the darkness.

Sierra tapped Bree's arm and pointed to a group of young men huddled together between two buildings.

Bree turned into the parking lot and Sierra was out of the car before Bree put the car into park.

Dak lunged over the seat to follow her.

Sierra slowly approached the young men. Their eyes raked over her appreciatively. She could smell the sickness on them. How could this have happened? They'd had a tracking spell on the infected. It had been weeks with no sign of the sickness. Thousands could be infected now.

Dak slowed his pace and waited for Bree. He didn't want to scare them away.

"Stone is that you?" she said sweetly as she moved closer.

Randy squinted to get a better look at her. He tried to clear his fuzzy mind but wasn't able to shake off the sickness.

"Don't tell me you don't remember me," she said stopping next to him, touching his arm.

Randy managed a slight smile. His body was burning up. She noticed they were passing around something that looked like clear rock candy.

Using her magic, she took one of the rocks without anyone noticing and slipped it in her pocket.

"What are you guys doing?"

Bree and Dak strolled toward the front of the convenience store.

"Why aren't we going with Sierra?" she hissed.

"She's got it handled."

Sierra felt their fear and confusion. She knew they were about to bolt.

She slowly calmed them as she cast a spell on them, keeping them rooted to where they stood. She called silently to Dak to come help.

"Come on," Dak told Bree.

Bree quickly followed him.

"They are definitely infected, but I'm not sure how. It looks like they may be taking a drug. I need to test it to see if it has anything to do with the infection."

"Will the cure work on them?" Dak asked.

"We're about to find out," she said as she plunged a needle in Randy's arm.

Randy's body jerked and he collapsed on the asphalt moaning as his body thrashed. His color returned to normal as the sickness left his body.

Sierra removed the spell she cast, and Dak helped him to his feet.

"You okay buddy?" he asked.

Randy struggled to stand. He frowned when he recognized Bree and Sierra. He looked around in confusion. He noticed his friends and frowned. "What's wrong with them. How did we get here?"

"You don't remember?" Bree asked.

"No. Last thing I remember was being at a party out by the lake."

The lake? They didn't check to see if the fish had been infected. They messed up.

"What is this?" Sierra asked holding up the clear crystal rock she'd taken off them.

Randy squinted at it. "It looks like rock candy. Why?"

"You were passing them around like a drug," Sierra said.

"I don't do drugs," He looked at his friends again. "What's wrong with them? Can you help them?"

"Yes. We'll help them. One by one Dak and Sierra gave Randy's friends the cure. Like Randy, they collapsed on the ground, thrashing as the sickness was driven from their bodies.

Dazed and confused, they stood up, wondering what had happened to them.

Bree called them a cab and instructed them to go home and stay away from the lake.

"Dak, you, and Bree keep tracking down the infected and give them the cure. I'm going to see if I can rid the lake of the infection."

Dak kissed her briefly. "Be careful," he said.

Sierra vanished in front of them and raced toward the lake. She dove into the water and felt the sickness surround her and immediately put a protective bubble around her. The fish that swam near her were disfigured, hardly resembling fish at all, more like something out of a horror movie.

She created the cure in the water, keeping the water back as the cure grew in size. Satisfied that it was big enough, she released it into the water. She watched the light blue cure as it spread through the water. As fish swam through it, they twisted and changed. Sierra stayed in the water until she no longer felt the sickness.

Bree and Dak continued to drive around town looking for the infected. Dak was relieved that his magic worked well enough to hold the infected while creating the cure.

Bree pulled to a stop next to a bowling alley. There were a dozen men keeping to the shadows.

Dak put his hand on Bree's arm. "I need to incapacitate them before we approach them. There are too many for us to safely approach them."

Bree nodded.

Dak drew on every bit of strength he possessed. This world limiting his magic frustrated him. Every spell moved in slow motion.

He cast a binding spell on the men. Then created a dozen smoke bombs, threw them, and lit them in midair.

The men vanished in the purple smoke.

Dak climbed out of the car with Bree by his side and they slowly approached the men seated on the ground, confused, and bewildered.

Satisfied that the lake was free from infection, Sierra disappeared in a cloud of white smoke and raced through the forest, through town toward Dak and Bree.

Dak created syringes and started injecting the confused young men to make certain that all traces of the disease were gone.

Sierra appeared a few feet away distracting Dak long enough for one of the infected to reach up and bite him on the arm.

Dak dropped the syringe and grabbed his arm. He immediately felt the disease race through his blood.

Sierra watched as he dropped the syringe and reached for it. Their eyes met as the disease gained control and Dak vanished in a cloud of black smoke and was gone.

"No," Sierra cried out.

Bree looked over at her in alarm. "What's wrong?" she asked.

"Dak's infected," she cried.

Chapter Four

Repaying The Giants

Ambro was out on the field training with his soldiers when a hummingbird flew in front of him dropping a missive in his hand.

He tore it open and was surprised that Aswaa was requesting his aide. He wondered briefly what it concerned, then answered that he would be along at dusk. He also sent a missive to the witch, Minerva, to please join him in traveling to the giant realm.

He waved for his people to continue without him.

Ambro strolled back to the castle, meeting Minerva on the way. "So, what do I owe the honor of your summons?" Minerva asked.

Ambro laughed. "I believe I asked you to join me," he said.

"I know, but it was much more fun when we were enemies."

"I'll try to make you angry at least once while we're gone."

"I doubt you'll have to try," she teased.

Together, they vanished into smoke and headed toward the gate, passed through it, and entered the deserted-looking giant village.

They retook their human form and knocked loudly on the massive door of the giant town hall.

Aswaa threw open the enormous wooden door, frowned when he didn't see anyone, then looked down and smiled when he saw Ambro and Minerva standing there.

"Come in, come in," he said. His booming voice echoing off the marble walls.

Ambro and Minerva entered a room the size of their entire village.

Aswaa sat cross legged on the floor next to them. "Would you like refreshments?" he offered.

Ambro smiled thinking that if he accepted the cup, it would be taller than him. "No thank you," he replied.

"Thank you for coming so quickly."

"What can we do for you?" Minerva asked.

"It has come to our attention that the other realms have set up shops and are trading with one another."

"That's true," Ambro said.

"I hear that your town has prospered under your guidance, and we would like your assistance in setting up shops so we can begin trading with the other realms."

Ambro smiled. "We would be delighted, on one condition."

Aswaa's face fell. He wondered at the condition. Maybe he was wrong to trust Ambro. "What's that?" he asked.

"We get the first option to trade with you."

A grin spread across his face. "That's a deal."

"Get your shop keepers together and meet us in the town square. Minerva here's going to give your town hall a little more appeal."

"I am, am I?" Minerva said.

Ambro rolled his eyes at her. "Keep in mind that many of your potential clients are much smaller than you. So, craft items with that in mind."

"I will gather my people and meet you in the square," Aswaa said excitedly.

Outside, Minerva turned to Ambro. "This is a good thing you're doing. I didn't know you had it in you."

"I've been telling you for months that I'm a changed man."

"Right. I've got my eye on you."

"Which one?"

Minerva frowned. "What do you mean?"

"Which eye? I want to stand on the opposite side of you so you can't keep an eye on me." he said laughing.

"I can turn you into a toad," she said glaring at him.

Ambro laughed. "Work your magic on this town."

"As you wish," she said. A dozen stores got a new coat of paint, and shiny new signs.

The steps and walkways were repaired, and half a dozen new store fronts popped up.

Aswaa and his people watched transfixed as their town came back to life. They clapped in excitement that echoed like thunder across the revitalized town square.

Minerva didn't stop there. She gave the homes and office building a new coat of paint as well.

The shops consisted of a market, bookstore, crafts, diner, vegetable market, clothing and accessories, tavern, furniture, and the empty shops were ready for a new shopkeeper.

Aswaa bent down to Minerva. "We are in your debt my lady," he said.

Minerva winked at him. "Make me a new bed and we'll be even. I've heard that you used to make the best mattresses in all the realms."

"You heard right. My very first bed shall be yours."

Minerva smiled. "Send me a missive if we can be of further help. Not that he did anything," she said glancing at Ambro before disappearing.

Ambro stayed with the giants to help them set up their new shops and to learn the art of trading. The giants were excited and eager to learn, ready to start a new phase in their lives.

Chapter Five

Egon's Search

Egon used every ounce of magic he possessed in this world to search for any trace of the Elders, with no luck. Saddened, he wondered what could have happened to them.

Frustrated and upset, he remembered Leiya and decided that it was a good time for him to visit her in Wyalii. Maybe he would find the answers he was seeking there.

Concentrating, he tried to open a rip. It took multiple tries, but he finally succeeded in opening one large enough to step through.

Light blue skyscrapers loomed in the distance. He immediately felt the presence of Elders. His heart raced with excitement at the thought of seeing them. He smiled to himself as he slowly strolled toward the city.

He saw a young girl as he entered the city and greeted her. "I'm Egon, friend to Leiya. Can you tell me where I can find your city's leaders?"

The young girl smiled. "I'm Misha, please follow me," she said warmly.

Egon studied the pale blue city and the pale blue clothing everyone wore, and wondered why there were no other colors.

He followed Misha into one of the pale buildings that looked like an office. He could feel the presence of Elders, but he also felt something different.

Misha led him to a comfortable blue room.

"Would you like something to drink?" Misha asked politely.

"That would be wonderful," Egon said.

Misha smiled, leaving him alone. He looked out the window overlooking the impressive modern city. Were these his people, he wondered in excitement.

Misha returned with a refreshing lemonade in a frosted pale blue glass.

She handed it to him and left. Iesha entered as she left.

She smiled warmly at him. "Misha said that you are a friend of Leiya's."

Egon took a sip of the lemonade and smiled. "The lemonade is wonderful. Thank you for your hospitality. I met Leiya when she accompanied my granddaughter Sierra to Pandora." he said warmly.

Iesha's smile widened. She eagerly approached Egon taking his hands with hers. "Your Sierra's grandfather? I am so delighted to meet you. Please sit down and tell me what brings you to Wyalii."

Egon sat across from her on the plush blue couch. He took a slight breath and said, "Years ago my people fled our home after a long and terrible war. I believe you and your people are descendants of those people."

Iesha thought for a moment and frowned slightly. "I recall the history of our people. They came from a faraway place after a terrible battle between family and friends, dividing them."

"That sounds like my friends," he said sadly. "Are any of them still alive?"

"How can they be your friends? You are still a young man while they are old," she asked in confusion.

"There is magic in my world. It makes us age slower," he explained.

"One of our Elders just returned to us and a few others are still with us. I will invite them to join us. They will be so happy to see someone from home."

"Not nearly as delighted as I am to see them," he said wiping a tear from his eye.

"Tell me of your home. It must be wonderful."

"You should visit. It is very different than your city. You have grown and appear very prosperous."

"We have two cities. The other is much smaller than this, but there are about five thousand of us."

"That is amazing. Do you possess the magic of your Elders?" he asked.

"I didn't know they possessed magic. That would explain how the two cities were built so quickly."

Misha re-entered the room and Iesha asked her to gather their Elders including Angus and arrange a celebration in the great hall.

Misha tried to hide her surprise before she hurried from the room.

"Because of the war, our people discouraged differences. That is why our city and clothing are all very similar. We try to ward off envy and jealousy," she explained.

Egon frowned. "May I speak freely my dear? After all, we are family."

"Of course."

"By striving to be the same, you may have lost your creativity as well as your ability to perform magic."

Iesha frowned, lost in thought.

"I will have to give this more thought. I hope you will stay with us a while. I trust that we can learn a lot from you."

"Thank you. I would be delighted."

Linking her arm with his. "It's time for a reunion," she said excitedly.

Egon couldn't wait to see his old friends and family.

Pushing open the frosted glass door, Iesha escorted Egon into the great hall. Pictures of his friends lined the light blue walls. He studied the faces of his friends, memories of the past flooding back.

He blinked back tears, trying not to cry. He looked toward the end of the room where a dozen elderly people stood smiling. He didn't recognize them, but he could slightly feel that they were Elders, and smiled warmly.

When they reached the end of the room, they surrounded him, saying his name and patting him warmly. Angus stepped forward, tears streaming down his face. "Hello brother," he cried throwing himself at Egon, hugging him.

Egon embraced him warmly, tears flowing down his face. "I feared I'd never see you again."

"Time has been good to you," Angus said.

"Where is everyone?" Egon asked.

"They have passed brother. Come sit with us and we will explain."

Iesha smiled at the change in Angus since his return. She followed Egon and the Elders, eager to hear their story.

"When we left our world to watch over Ben after you exiled them, we stayed close to them without their knowledge. As the years passed, they stayed out of trouble. When we discovered a portal to this world we decided to relocate. We didn't want to return to a world we'd helped destroy, so here we are."

"I waited for you to return," Egon said sadly.

"We didn't have a way to reach you, and the portal closed so we couldn't leave if we wanted to. We settled this world, building two cities like those on the world you exiled Ben to. We poured our magic into this world so we wouldn't repeat the same mistakes."

"Your city is wonderful," he said.

"We have missed our home. We'd all love to see it again before we die."

"I can take you home. But it is quite different than the world you remember. Many beings came to be as a result of our war."

"What of Ben and his followers?"

"They have recently returned. They have changed and are eager to make peace."

"And you believe them?"

The others murmured loudly, still not trusting them.

"I do and they have proven themselves and have rebuilt our home."

"I wish to see this," Ela said wistfully, lowering her head.

Egon looked at Iesha. "Do you mind if I take them home?"

"If that is their wish. I would like to visit your world if that is all right. I feel that we can learn much from you."

Chapter Six

Revenge Part Two

The Sylphs moved unnoticed through the star lit night sky in a misty cloud form. They hovered above Mags' glistening castle waiting.

Lorilie stepped from the pond, dry and determined, dressed in a soft green dress that flowed as she walked. She was followed by dozens of Water Fairies. She looked up and nodded to the Sylphs and a light rain-like substance fell from the clouds, coating the castle in a sparkling sheen.

The Water Fairies cast a spell on the rain as it fell and watched the water shimmer and sparkle.

Satisfied, Lorilie smiled, before her and her people turned and vanished beneath the depths of the pond that now connected to a waterway in the fire realm.

The Sylphs returned to Windspell without anyone knowing that they'd ever left.

Lorilie and her followers swam through the green water, returning to the underwater castle. Sitting on her throne, a sly smile turned up the corners of her mouth as she imagined what tomorrow would bring to Brisslewood.

As the sun rose over Brisslewood, its rays hardened the fine sheen that covered the castle. The sun baked it, causing a green fog to emanate from it. The fog rose and drifted across the realm infecting everyone it passed.

Sores immediately broke out on their skin, making them itch. When the residents of Brisslewood scratched the sores, they spread, making them miserable.

Thomas was out tending his garden when the unknown mist passed over him. A large sore appeared on his arm.

He immediately scratched it, and it spread up his arms and onto his face.

As the poison from the sore raced through his body, he cried out as he collapsed onto the ground, his cheek resting against the cool dirt in the garden. He felt paralyzed.

From the kitchen window, Elanor saw him fall and raced outside to him, kneeling down next to him.

She placed her hands above him and tried to cure him, but her magic caused the sores to spread even more. Using magic, she moved him inside and laid him gently on his bed.

She raced to the kitchen and created a poultice that her grandmother had taught her how to make decades ago.

She simmered the foul-smelling liquid and poured it into a bowl, carried it upstairs and sat it on the wooden table next to the bed. She dipped some clean white cloths into the smelly brown liquid and covered every sore with them.

Thomas frowned as she covered him nearly from head to toe and she watched as the sores slowly began to shrink.

Thomas appeared to relax, and Elanor was certain that he would be all right if she left him alone, so she raced from the house and up the slight hill to Mags' castle.

Inside, the castle was chaos. Elanor tried to take everything in at a glance, but all she could focus on was Mags, lying on the floor covered in sores, just the way Thomas had been. "Stop using magic," she screamed. "It only makes it worse."

Rhys and Slade looked up at her, fear evident on their faces.

"Take all of the infected into one room," she ordered. "Send guards to the gates. Don't let anyone in or out of Brisslewood."

"Yes ma'am," Rhys said hurrying to do as she instructed.

"Carry my daughter into the throne room along with all the infected. Tell them not to scratch, it only makes it spread."

Slade gently scooped up Mags and carried her into the throne room where Rhys already had people putting up temporary beds for the sick. He laid Mags on one of the beds near the window when he noticed the sun shining off the castle in an unusual way. Suddenly it appeared as if the castle was alive as insects the size of kittens with hard shells appeared on the castle walls. He slammed the windows shut and ran from the room.

"Don't use magic," Elanor called after him unaware that they had a new problem to face. She raced toward the kitchen to brew her grandmother's poultice, while Slade ran through the castle ordering everyone to shut all the windows and to not use magic to kill the bugs.

Slade then ran outside with a piece of wood used for the fireplace and began smashing the grotesque creatures as they scurried toward him.

Soon the castle grounds were full of soldiers smashing the insects, covering the grass with their smelly remains.

Iera and the butterflies flew around with tiny buckets dumping water on the remains, trying to wash them away.

Slade looked around satisfied that his men and women were taking care of the insects. He motioned Iera to come to him.

She flew to his side carrying her small bucket. "Tell lady Elanor that something is covering the castle. We need something to wash it away. She's in the kitchen cooking up something for the infected."

Iera nodded, dropped her tiny bucket, which Slade caught before it hit the ground, and raced to find Elanor.

She located her in the kitchen stirring a terrible smelling liquid in a giant pot.

"Lady Elanor," said Iera. "There is something on the castle causing this. Mister Slade says we need something to wash it away."

"Thank you my dear. Let me think on it. I don't possess the magic that my daughters do."

"What about the strong soap we used to keep the castle walls clean. It has enough chemicals to kill just about anything," Iera suggested.

"It is worth a try. Get a team scrubbing the walls. I can create a cloud to wash down the top of the castle,"

Elanor said, "I will join you outside as soon as I get this poultice on our sick."

Iera raced away as fast as her wings could carry her. She located what was left of the cleaning crew that hadn't been bitten or infected and they made tubs of soapy water to clean off the castle.

Elanor, followed by a dozen men carrying steaming buckets of the poultice and towels followed her into the throne room filled with the sick.

She first tended to Mags, covering her sores with the poultice drenched towels, and instructed her helpers to do the same to the rest of their patients.

She then hurried outside. Soldiers were still smashing insects while others scrubbed the castle walls.

Elanor created three small clouds and filled them with the soapy liquid and rose them above the castle.

They floated over the castle like large sponges washing away the film that covered the castle.

The soap ran down the walls helping to wash it away.

Before the soap could do its job, flies began to form on the areas still covered by the film.

The soap washed over many of them, killing them instantly, but far too many of them managed to escape, biting anyone they came into contact with, raising large whelps on their skin.

Elanor raced back inside to the throne room and grabbed a bowl of the poultice and a clean rag and hurried back outside, where she covered the bites with the smelly liquid.

The soldiers went from smashing insects to swatting flies.

Chapter Seven

Dak's Infection

Sierra vanished in a puff of white smoke, leaving Bree standing alone in the parking lot. She raced after him, over buildings, between cars driving down the highway.

Dak wove in and out of them trying to lose Sierra.

Sierra reached out to him begging him to stop. He blocked her out, determined to escape.

He flew over a semi-truck and dove to his left and around a convenience store and into a grove of trees.

She went over the truck and lost him. She couldn't tell which way he went.

Frantic, she reached out for him and felt nothing. She reached out for the infected, and there were too many of them to distinguish Dak from them. She sadly turned and headed back to Bree, finding her sitting in her car. She retook her human form next to the building, so she was out of sight and there was little risk of her being seen. She raced to the car and threw open the door, joining Bree in the car.

"Did you catch him?" Bree asked, concerned.

"No, and there are too many infected for me to find him," she said sadly, fighting tears. "We've got to cure more of them at one time."

"How?"

"I'll make it rain the cure on the entire town and put the cure in the water supply. Then it should be easier to track the rest of them," she said.

Bree looked at her best friend in amazement. "Is it scary to have so much power?" she asked.

Sierra smiled. "It's scarier to have so many depending on you to always fix things," she said.

"You seem to know what to do."

"But what happens when I don't? I'm not always going to be able to take care of everything. We are growing so fast, and I can't take care of everything. I'm scared."

"I know you are honey. You will find Dak. Everything will be all right."

"I'd still love for you to live in Pandora. You can bring your entire family. You would all be such a big help in what I'm trying to achieve."

"I'll let you talk to my parents about that," Bree laughed.

"Let's get out to the water treatment plant, and once the rain starts, I'll talk to your parents."

Bree took a deep breath and said, "You are going to blow their minds."

Sierra laughed. "It won't be the first time."

"True."

Bree drove to the outskirts of town and stopped across from the water treatment plant.

Sierra climbed out of the car and crossed the street. She noticed the security cameras all over the property.

"Watch," she said raising her arms and pointed the cameras away from them. She created a large cloud of the cure and floated it toward the plant.

Inside, a technician was hurrying to relocate the cameras back to their original position. Seeing the cloud moving toward the plant, he said, "What the hell?" He raced from the room toward the exterior door.

Sierra passed the cloud through one of the tanks and turned to Bree. "Let's go."

They drove away, just as the technician emerged from the building.

"Where to now?" Bree asked.

"The lake. It's isolated so hopefully no one will see us."

"So how do you just create something out of nothing?"

Sierra turned to look at Bree and said, "I concentrate on what I want to appear and then it appears."

"Could I learn to do it, if I move to Pandora?"

"I don't know. Not everyone can do magic."

"Why can you?"

"My real father was from the Eight Realms. James isn't my dad, but please don't tell him. My mom doesn't remember what happened. I don't know what happened. Only my biological father does, and I haven't asked him."

"Holy crap. You've had to take on way too much in such a short time."

"It doesn't seem to stop."

"Are you going to be, okay?"

"I will be when I get Dak back."

"We'll find him."

Sierra took Bree's hand and squeezed it. "I know. Thanks for helping me."

Bree laughed. "I haven't done much. I'm just the driver and here for moral support."

"You've done way more than that."

Bree pulled the car to a stop at the edge of the lake, her headlights shining across the smooth surface.

They climbed out of the car. Sierra took Bree's hand lifting them up together, creating rain clouds over the lake. Bree could feel the energy through Sierra's hand. It was like nothing she'd ever felt.

"That's amazing," Bree said.

Sierra felt Dak trying to probe her thoughts and reluctantly pushed him away. She didn't want him to know what was coming.

The cloud grew bigger and darker. Sierra filled it with the cure, growing it in size. Lightning flashed inside of the cloud, brightening up the sky.

Sierra exhaled and pulled Bree to her, hugging her, pushing back the tears. She never thought there would be a time that she'd have to push Dak away. "Thanks," she said.

Bree returned the hug. She knew Sierra was in a dark place.

The cloud rose and burst open, and Bree and Sierra raced to the car, climbing in just as the rain gushed from the sky.

As the rain fell, Sierra could feel it as the number of infected dropped. She prayed that Dak would be one of them.

Dak stood in the darkness, beneath an underpass watching the rain. A thirst like nothing he'd ever felt burned inside of him. He huddled against the stone wall, knowing the rain would hurt him.

Bree and Sierra ran from the car through the rain to Bree's house.

Bree's mother, Amy, frowned at them as they dripped puddles on her tile floor.

Bree burst out laughing at her mom's expression. "Mom," she said. "Sierra has something she wants to ask you."

Sierra glared daggers at Bree, which made Bree laugh even harder. "I'll get us a couple of towels. You get comfortable," she said and left Sierra alone with Amy.

"What is it dear?" Amy asked, leading her by the hand to the living room.

Bree tossed a towel over Sierra's head and sat down next to her. "Well Mom, it's like this, Sierra lives in another world called Pandora. We can travel there by gates, which I happen to have one in my room. She wants us to move the entire family there so we can help her. Oh, and by the way, she can do some kick ass magic," Bree blurted out.

Sierra and Amy stared at her in shock.

Sierra shrugged like she had no idea what Bree was talking about.

"Are you on drugs?" Amy asked Bree in alarm.

"Go on, tell her," Bree said.

"You're doing all the talking," Sierra said.

Bree leered at her. "Fine then. Would you like to see the gate?"

"Bree, stop this. It isn't funny."

"I'm being perfectly serious. Come on, I'll show you the gate." Bree jumped up. Sierra followed her with Amy slowly following her up the stairs to her room.

Bree threw open her closet door and there stood the simmering blue gate.

Amy gasped. She could see Pandora shimmering behind the gate. "This joke has gone too far," she said.

"It's not a joke," Sierra said.

"Bree shouldn't have blurted it out the way she did, but what she said is true."

"You're both crazy or on drugs. This can't be real."

"It is. It's where my family moved."

Amy sat down on Bree's bright red comforter and stared at the gate. "But how? And why do you want us to move?"

Sierra bent down in front of her, taking her hands between hers. "You've always been like family, and I'd love to be close to you again. We have established a town with a hospital, and we could use a doctor, and Bree wants to be a nurse, and you could teach."

"How do you know that would even be possible?"

"It's Sierra's town," Bree said.

"What? How?"

"And she can do magic."

Amy slid her hands out of Sierra's.

"Magic?"

"There is magic in this world and things and people like you've never seen. It's magical," Sierra said.

"Show her some magic," Bree urged.

Sierra frowned but created the tiny cloud like she did for Adam and let it snow.

Amy watched it with a mixture of horror and wonder. "This can't be happening," she said.

"I know it's a lot to take in, mom."

"You've been there? When?" Amy demanded.

"When Sierra got married."

"Married? You're married?"

"Yes ma'am. And he's in trouble and I have to find him."

"Trouble, what kind of trouble?"

"He has an infection that has made him not quite himself."

"That's what the rain is for," Bree said. "It will cure him and everyone else that's infected."

"I'm sorry. I don't follow. This is too much to take in, let alone believe."

Sierra waved her hand and stopped the rain.

"She did that." Bree said.

"You stay here with your mom. I've got to find Dak and the other infected. If it's all right, I'll come back after I've found him."

"Go. I'll explain it all to mom."

"You can't just walk…"

Sierra smiled and vanished in a puff of smoke and left, leaving Bree to explain.

Amy looked as if she were about to faint.

Sierra tracked the infected, curing dozens upon dozens of people.

Every once in a while, she could feel Dak, then he was gone. Damn him for being so good at hiding.

She reached out farther for any sign of the infected and was fairly certain that Dak remained the only one.

As soon as the rain stopped, Dak exited his hiding place beneath the underpass. It didn't take him long to locate a bewildered young man who'd recently been cured.

Dak quickly approached him, grabbed him and sunk his fangs into the tender flesh on the young man's throat. As the warm blood filled his mouth, he let down his guard giving Sierra a clear view of what he was doing and where he was.

"Damn it," he said, pushing the young man away. Turning into smoke, he quickly raced away.

Sierra was on the young man in seconds, healing his wound and curing him of the infection once again.

Sierra didn't try to follow the trail of the infection. This time, she followed the scent of blood.

She was horrified by what she'd seen, but it wasn't Dak. He couldn't control what the infection was making him do. She had to find him and stop him from infecting others.

She was worried how this would affect him once he was cured. He would remember the stories she'd told him and that she'd called bloodsucking Vampires monsters.

Dak tried hard to mask his trail, but the disease made it hard to concentrate. He retook his human form. His face was pale, and his eyes were wide and blood shot. He'd located another victim, this time, a young woman emptying the trash behind her apartment.

He grabbed her so quickly that she didn't have time to scream.

His fangs sank into her soft flesh.

Sierra immediately picked up his trail and raced toward him.

As her blood entered his body, he felt euphoric. It was the most amazing sensation. He was so lost in the experience that he didn't notice Sierra until it was almost too late.

He caught the dart that she threw at him and dropped the semi-conscious woman. Sierra eased her down on the soft grass never taking her eyes off Dak.

Dak threw the dart on the ground, watching Sierra intently.

Sierra cast the cure in smoke and Dak easily blew it away. He almost caught the second dart before it pierced his skin, but it imbedded itself in his thigh.

Sierra released the cure, but Dak pulled it out before she could release all of it.

He hurled the dart at Sierra, growling in anger and lunged at her.

Caught off guard, Sierra tried to push him away, but he put his arms around her, pinning her arms to her side.

Sierra looked into his eyes and couldn't see any sign of the man she loved. Her eyes filled with tears.

A trace of the cure worked its way through Daks' body. His mind cleared for a moment, and he hated himself for what he was doing, and released her. "Sierra," he cried.

"Dak," she said in desperation.

She latched onto the cure inside of him and made it spread.

Feeling strange, Dak looked longingly at her and vanished.

Sierra didn't try to follow. She held onto the cure moving it through his system, wiping out the infection.

Saddened to her soul over the encounter with Dak, she slowly walked back to Bree's.

Dak tried to shake off whatever was making him feel weird. He found a homeless man and sank his teeth into his neck. When his warm blood touched Dak's tongue, it made him feel sick and he spit it out in disgust, releasing the man.

The man scurried away in fear.

Dak returned to his spot beneath the underpass and worked his way into a tunnel in the side of the hill. Resting his head on the dirt wall, he fell asleep.

Sierra knocked on Bree's front door and when Bree opened it, Sierra fell into her arms crying. Amy rushed down the stairs to see what was wrong.

"Did you find him?" Bree asked.

Sierra nodded.

"Well, where is he?"

"I don't know. I managed to get a little of the cure in him, but now I wait to see if it was enough."

Bree hugged her. "I'm so sorry. I know that must have been awful."

"You have no idea," she said sadly.

Amy hugged her tightly. She wasn't a woman running a city right now. She was just a heart broken young girl.

Dak woke just as the sun set. He was filled with anger and confusion. He vanished into a puff of smoke and tore through town, encountering a party. Weaving in and out of the party goers, he appeared and fed on several of the young people, appearing, then disappearing in a puff of smoke, only to reappear again to feed again.

Angry and frustrated when it didn't give him the ecstasy that he got from the first couple of feedings, he vanished into smoke and headed towards Sierra.

She was going to undo whatever she did to him.

He flew beneath the front door and quickly searched her home, furious that she wasn't there. Opening his mind, he reached out to locate her.

Sierra felt him immediately. He was on her in a second appearing in front of her as smoke before taking his human form.

He cast a spell at her, which she reflected just in time.

"What are you doing?" she cried.

"What was in that shot?" he yelled.

Hearing them yelling, Bree entered the room to see what was happening.

Dak grabbed Bree, pulling her close with his arm around her neck. He smiled wickedly at Sierra as he ran his finger down Bree's smooth cheek. "If you don't want your friend to get hurt, undo what you did to me."

Sierra looked at Bree, then at Dak. She couldn't believe the effect the disease was having on him.

"I don't know how to undo it, but I can cure you completely," she said.

Dak bared his fangs, "I don't want to be cured," he yelled, his eyes wild with the infection.

Sierra blocked her mind from him and created the cure inside the air conditioner, releasing it through the vents.

Dak lowered his head with the intent to bite Bree, but Sierra hit him with a spell throwing him backward, slamming him into the wall.

Bree wasted no time, running next to Sierra.

Dak pushed away from the wall smiling. "So, this is how it's going to be?" He fired off four spells, two at Bree and two at Sierra.

Sierra instantly created a protective bubble around them.

One of the spells went through the bubble. Sierra ducked out of the way, but Bree wasn't as lucky. She collapsed at Sierra's feet.

"I knew you'd do that," he said smiling.

Furious, Sierra collapsed the bubble angrily, slowly approaching Dak. She pulled power from the elements surrounding them as she closed the gap between them.

Dak's eyes widened in surprise. He'd never seen her so angry. He didn't know what she was capable of. He'd counted on her not hurting him. He wasn't so sure about that now.

He tried to turn into smoke, but Sierra forced him back to his human form, rooting him to the spot.

The air swirled around them making it difficult for Dak to breathe. He cast spell after spell at her, but the wind carried them away.

Sierra stopped inches from him, pinning his arms to his side. "I know you're not completely responsible for your actions, but you should never have hurt my friend," she said coldly.

Without looking behind her, she made certain that Bree was okay as she sealed herself and Dak inside a bubble, the wind swirling around them.

She put everything back into its place, mending broken objects, and placing Bree gently on the sofa.

Dak struggled against his invisible bonds and tried to cast spells, but Sierra blocked them from his mind before he could complete them.

Two syringes appeared out of nowhere and plunged into Dak's right arm and left thigh, releasing the cure into Dak's system.

Dak thrashed like he was possessed, trying to fight off the cure. He concentrated, trying to expel it from his body as Sierra moved the cure through his body.

"You can't win,' she whispered coldly, stepping out of the bubble.

She opened a rip, sending Dak home to Pandora. While the rip was open, she reached out to Lazrus, asking him to take care of Dak until she returned.

As the cure flushed the disease out of his system, Dak looked at Sierra, the pain of his actions burned in his eyes. A small part of him was afraid. All of his magic had been useless against her. She was far more powerful than anyone could have imagined.

Sierra turned away from him, closing the rip, racing to Bree's side.

Bree sat up and smiled. "Where's Dak?"

"I sent him home."

Bree put her hand on Sierra's arm. "None of this is his fault," she reminded her.

"I know, but it was hard to see him that way."

"I know honey, but it wasn't him."

"I know. I still have to make sure there are no more infected, then I'll deal with Dak."

Bree nodded. "Don't wait too long. I'm sure he's more upset than you are."

"I know, and I still want you guys to move to Pandora. Please talk to your parents and let me know."

"I will. Aren't you coming back?"

"No, you're right. I need to talk to Dak, so as soon as I make sure that the infection is gone, I'm going home."

"Good. I'll talk to my parents and let you know," she said hugging Sierra. Before releasing her, she said, "Remember, it's not his fault."

"I'll remember and I really hope you'll move to Pandora."

"I'll talk to them," she promised.

Sierra waved before shutting the front door behind her. As it shut, she vanished into a cloud of white smoke and searched out for any sign of the infected. She found a couple of homeless people that weren't completely cured. A couple of clear smoke bombs took care of them, and she moved on to a group of teens in a warehouse. She filled the room with smoke and waited until the disease was eradicated.

Satisfied that the town was free of the infection, she opened a rip to Pandora.

Dak was still encased in the bubble when his mind was finally clear of the infection. He looked around frantically for Sierra, but only saw Lazrus staring at him.

"She sent me to make sure you were okay. How are you feeling?"

Dak dropped the bubble and approached Lazrus. "I feel like hell. I really messed up big guy," he said sadly. "She may never forgive me."

"Whatever it was, it was the disease, not you, my friend."

"I hope Sierra sees it that way."

"She's the smartest person I know. She knows you are not responsible for what that disease made you do."

Sierra opened a rip to Pandora near the bridge. She saw Dak and Lazrus talking. She blocked her mind, so they didn't know she was home.

She sat down and removed her black boots and stuck her feet in the cool water.

"Good evening, my lady."

"Hello Franklin, how's the musical coming?"

"Very well. Thank you for asking. You seem a little sad tonight."

"I was, but I'm better now. Thanks Franklin, enjoy your evening."

"You too my lady," Franklin said watching her pick up her boots and stroll toward the castle.

Dak and Lazrus felt her presence and turned to watch her walk toward them.

Dak watched his entire reason for being walking toward him and felt sick inside for what he'd done. He was terrified that she'd hate him, or worse, be disgusted by him.

Lazrus reached out to her, telling her to take it easy on him, before nodding to Dak and taking flight.

Sierra stopped a few feet from Dak and studied his tired handsome face. "How are you feeling?" she asked.

Dak frowned sadly. "Like a monster."

Sierra's heart broke for him, and she threw herself into his arms. "Don't ever say that again. You're not a monster."

"I acted like one," he said kissing the top of her head before resting his cheek against her soft hair.

"The disease is responsible, not you."

"I know that, but I still feel terrible. The things I did to you. How can you forgive me?"

"There's nothing to forgive. Let's go home. I'm exhausted," Taking his hand, she clasped her fingers through his and led him across the lawn as she pushed the images of her fighting against Dak from her mind.

Chapter Eight

Revenge

Mags opened her eyes and sat up looking around her throne room that looked more like a hospital.

Elanor rushed to her side. "How are you sweetheart?" She asked.

"What happened?" Why is everyone here?"

"You've all been sick."

"At the same time? How?"

"Bugs," Elanor said like that explained everything.

Sitting up and putting her legs over the side of the bed, she said, "Bugs? What kind of bugs?"

"They came out of whatever covered the castle."

Mags frowned. "Start from the beginning please?" Mags asked, rubbing her throbbing temple.

Elanor explained everything that had happened since Thomas was bitten, up until now, including that they had everything under control.

"Lorilie, it had to be Lorilie," Mags said. "Thank you for taking care of everything. How in the world did you know how to cure the bug's bite?"

"I didn't. I just knew I had to draw out the poison so you wouldn't get any worse."

Mags stood up and hugged her mother. "I'm so glad. It would have been catastrophic if you hadn't acted so quickly."

"Are you sure that Lorilie was behind this?"

"I don't know anyone else that would pull a stunt like this. How long ago did it start?"

"Yesterday morning. Why?"

"She's had plenty of time to hide. I'll help you tend to the sick. I will deal with her later."

Chapter Nine

The Trip Home

Egon concentrated and opened a rip. Iesha, Ella, Angus followed Egon through the rip.

They all stood together at the entrance to New Beginnings.

"It's just as I remembered," Ella said, tears running down her weathered cheeks.

The sun's rays cast a rainbow over the weathered valley. The wind pushing through the blue green grass carried musical notes across the lawn.

A crystal bird chirped sweetly at them, snowflakes falling from its beak.

Ben felt Egon's presence the moment he entered the realm and went to greet him along with a pregnant Eloise and Rich at the entrance to the crystal gate.

Egon's face lit up when he saw Eloise's rounded stomach. He hugged her, thrilled for her and Rich.

Angus and the others frowned at them. They hadn't forgotten what Ben, and the others had done to them and this world.

"Please come inside," Ben said warmly recognizing them as elders.

They hesitated but followed them inside.

"We need to help them," Ben whispered to Egon.

"What do you mean?" Egon whispered back.

"They are so old. I owe it to them to heal them."

Egon smiled. Ben had certainly changed. "That's a wonderful idea, and I think we should invite them to stay."

The old elders followed Rich and Eloise around their home. They clutched each other's hand as they moved from room to room, recalling the days before the war tore them all apart.

"You did a wonderful job recreating our home," Ella said, fighting back tears.

Ben gently took her hands in his. Ella felt his power enter her body. The wrinkles on her face smoothed out, and her hair went from gray to brown. Her tired eyes lit up with youthful energy.

Iesha saw what he was doing and gasped in surprise, causing the other elders to turn.

"What are you doing?" Angus demanded.

"Repaying some of the debt I owe each of you for what you've lost," Ben said.

"We don't want your power. It's what nearly destroyed us," Nela said.

"I'm not giving her power, just restoring some of her youth. I can give you some of my powers if you want."

"We gave it up years ago so our cities could survive," Angus said.

"Very little of it remains today."

"I understand, please allow me to do this for you," Ben said softly.

They looked at a young Ella and agreed. Taking hands, Ben restored their youth while causing his own hair to gray a little at the temple.

Egon had never been so proud of his son. "This is a great day for our people," he said. "There are two cities filled with our descendants and all of us are back together."

"This calls for a toast," Eloise said, and crystal glasses of champagne floated in front of everyone but her.

A fox with a bushy tail climbed from the pond fed by a cascading waterfall. It purred sweetly before racing through the wall disappearing outside.

"We hope you will make this your home," Egon said. He couldn't wait to tell Sierra that Angus was one of them.

A younger Angus took the glass and raised it, "To all my brothers and sisters. It is time to bury our terrible past and write a wonderful new chapter for our people. It is good to be home."

"But what about your families in Wyalii?" Iesha asked, concerned.

"Sierra left them a gate to Pandora. They can visit any time," Egon said.

"I will let them know and you are all welcome to visit us at any time."

Ben approached Ieshia. "I hope you will stay for a few days. We can share our history with you, the good and the bad."

"I'd like that," she said, smiling.

Ben linked her arm through his and together they walked through the wall into the library.

She was overcome by the number of books their library held, and the unique way they were displayed. She touched a crystal volume, and it lit up in front of her, the words scrolling without her having to touch it.

"This is truly amazing."

Ben enjoyed watching her as she browsed through the library.

"Your city is amazing. You should visit Wyalii. It too is amazing, but in a vastly different way."

Ben studied the lovely young woman in front of him. He was overjoyed that their people had prospered, even if it cost them their power. He suddenly realized that he very much wanted to visit their cities. "I would love to," he said. "Would you mind if I join you when you return home?"

Iesha smiled. "I would like that," she said. "What you did for your people was remarkable."

Ben frowned. "What I did to them was atrocious. It was a small token for what I cost them," he said sadly.

Iesha took his hands between hers. "They have had good lives. They might have been quite different than if you'd never had a war. But they were happy. Isn't that all any of us can hope for?"

Ben looked into her deep blue eyes and smiled. "I suppose you're right. Would you like to see the garden?"

"I'd love to," she said smiling.

Ben linked his arm through hers and together they walked through the glass library wall, the hallway, a bedroom, and a study before exiting the crystal castle into a garden like Iesha had never seen. A waterfall occupied one corner. She couldn't tell where the water came from. It fed a crystal-clear spring that ran through the garden and beneath the path that wound its way through the garden.

The path was covered in tiny crystals that glittered like diamonds and cast a multitude of rainbows across the delicate plants and flowers. She marveled at roses the size of melons; their fragrance was unlike anything she'd ever smelt. She gently touched one of the velvety, lavender petals and the most exquisite music came from the rose bush. Iesha's eyes widened with joy.

"It must like you. They don't sing for everyone."

"That is truly remarkable," she said facing the rose bush. "Thank you for sharing this amazing place with me. It is beautiful."

The rose bush changed from lavender to a deep purple and its music floated across the garden.

"It's extraordinary." Iesha said smiling.

Ben gently touched her on the elbow, guiding her down the path.

Deep blue birds flew past, singing sweetly, followed by crystal birds, singing, dropping snowflakes on them as they flew by.

Iesha reached out to catch them, smiling. This was the most magical place she'd ever seen. How could people that created such marvelous things nearly destroy themselves?

They continued to walk slowly down the path when a fox-like creature entered the path, its big blue green eyes blinked at the two humans in front of him.

Iesha bent down and the fox slowly approached her. She stuck out her hand and he sniffed it before moving closer rubbing against her leg.

Iesha gently smoothed her hand across his warm soft fur.

The fox purred loudly before darting away and racing beneath the bushes.

They reached the end of the path and could see Egon and the elders reclining on soft, lush furniture laughing and catching up.

"Why are the walls clear and why are there no doors?" She asked.

"We want to show that we have nothing to hide. If you desire privacy, the walls can turn a light blue." We never had any use for doors," he said smiling.

"I wonder if that's why our cities are all blue, to match your walls for privacy."

"It very well could be," he said.

They walked through the wall, rejoining everyone.

Did you enjoy the garden?" Eloise asked.

"It is amazing," Iesha said.

"Thank you for the tour," she said to Ben.

"It was my pleasure."

Ben and Iesha took a seat on the large soft furniture and joined in the conversation.

Iesha listened to stories of the elders from happier times, long into the night.

Chapter Ten

Destroyer

His eyes fluttered as he stirred restlessly in his sleep. Jerking awake, he opened his eyes in total darkness.

Forcing down the panic, he felt around him to try to gain his bearings. There was something above his head. Frowning, it all came back to him. He was in a cage.

Well, he had news for them, it would take more than a cage to hold him. He shattered the glass imprisoning him.

Sierra jerked awake. Something was wrong. She reached out her mind searching for something that wasn't right.

He felt her probe and couldn't block her. She was too powerful.

He broke free from the cabinet that housed his prison and discovered that he was the size of a rodent as he stood teetering on the edge of a cabinet.

He jumped to the ground, rolling to break the impact of his fall.

His pointed ears were alert to the sounds surrounding him.

He blinked his big blue eyes and frowned. She would be on him in seconds. He turned into his energy form and melted through the floor, just as Sierra and Dak entered the room.

Their eyes darted frantically around the gate room, noticing the glass on the floor. Sierra rushed to the cabinet and groaned. "Damn it. He's escaped."

Dak joined her, frowning. "He was under a sleeping spell. How did he wake up?"

"He must be stronger than we thought," she said sadly. "I won't make the mistake of underestimating him again."

Dak linked his fingers with her. "We'll find him," he promised.

"But not before he hurts innocent people," she said sadly.

The Destroyer reached out, looking for a place to go. Smiling, he located the perfect place, filled with anger and jealousy. He appeared at the base of the volcano in the Fire Realm.

He could feel the anger pouring off the creatures of this place. Concentrating, he grew to his normal size, his tail twitching in excitement.

They may have found a cure for his infection, but let's see them cure jealousy and hatred, he laughed to himself.

Dak turned to Sierra, "This isn't your fault. You did everything you could do to stop this creature."

"But it wasn't enough. He continues to hurt people. He hurt you," she said softly.

"And I hurt you," he said sadly.

Sierra turned to face him. "It wasn't your fault."

"I know, but I still hurt you."

"How do we catch something that can turn into pure energy?"

"And what do we do with him when we do catch him?"

Sierra lowered her eyes and shook her head slowly. "I don't know."

She whistled softly and several Hummingbirds appeared, waiting, while she wrote out brief notes explaining that the Destroyer was loose.

She tried to push aside the feeling that she'd failed everyone.

"We need to track him," Sierra said, waving her hand in front of her, changing into the black battle outfit from her tee shirt and shorts.

Dak changed clothes and they vanished in a black and white cloud of smoke.

She reached out searching for the Destroyer, frustrated when she couldn't find any trace of him.

They entered Opaque to meet with the council. Retaking human form, they crossed the bridge and entered the grounds.

Dak looked back over his shoulder at the trees in full bloom and the thick grass covering the forest floor. He could hear the sounds of wildlife scurry back and forth. It amazed him that the realm no longer resembled the place where he grew up.

Novrah, Avis, Vestry and Falon were the only council members in attendance.

They all sat around the council table and Sierra filled them in on the Destroyer's escape.

"I will ask my people to try and locate this creature." Novrah said shaking his smooth feathers.

"We will put together a team to look for him as well," Avis said.

Vestry put her gnarled hand on Sierra's. This is not your fault. We will put a stop to this creature's destruction."

Sierra squeezed her hand. "Thank you. Please let everyone know if you find him. Don't try to capture him alone. He's immensely powerful," she said.

Thanking them again, Sierra and Dak left to scour the realms for the Destroyer.

"What if he returned to the world, we found him in?" Dak asked.

"I will send the Wyaliians a message, warning them. But I feel him here. I just can't penpoint his location."

Crossing the bridge, she remembered how he used the ground to disable them. She knelt down and put her palms flat on the ground.

Her energy traveled through underground streams, tunnels, and crevices until she felt the Destroyer's energy as he moved through the world to surface in the Fire Realm.

A smile spread across her face as she learned from his energy trail.

Pressing her palms firmly against the soil, she blocked him from traveling beneath the realms. If he tried, he would be trapped.

"Please tell the council that he's in the Fire Realm," she said.

"How…" Dak asked. Without waiting for an answer, he turned and raced across the bridge.

Sierra whistled for the Hummingbirds, creating a missive to let everyone know that the gates were sealed until the creature was caught, except for the Hummingbirds so they could exchange messages. "We really need cell phones," she mumbled to herself.

Dak rejoined her and asked, "So I guess we're off to the Fire Realm?"

"A rip? How do I stop him from escaping by using a rip?"

Dak frowned slightly. "How did you stop him from escaping the way he did in Pandora?"

Wrinkling her brow, Sierra thought about it. Could she do it, she wondered. She wished Egon was here to help her. "Let's give it a try. I'll need your help," she said.

"I doubt that," he teased. "What are we doing?"

"I'm going to try to block his energy from entering any of the realms. He may be able to escape to another world, but he won't be able to return."

"I'm all for that."

Sierra took Dak's hand, instructing him to hold his out by his side, his palm facing away from him.

They put their palms together and Sierra stretched hers out beside her.

Concentrating on the Destroyer's energy she wove the energy around them to dispel his energy pattern if he tried to pass through and pushed it out across all the realms in a massive wave of pure energy.

She sent a message to Lazrus to let him know that the Destroyer had escaped and that he was trapped in the Fire Realm.

When she finished, they joined Vestry, Collin, Avis, Novrah, Falon and dozens of Owls, Vampires, Witches, Invisibles, and Werewolves who were waiting to enter the Fire Realm.

The Destroyer felt the energy around him change. Good, they were coming. He wasn't concerned. He reached out to all his new recruits to join him.

Before Sierra had time to close the gates, all the people across the realms, ignited by their anger, hatred or jealousy began the journey to join the Destroyer.

He smiled wickedly to himself, his tail twitching in excitement. This would be his most memorable battle yet.

The Goblins, Fire Salamanders and Imps were the first to arrive, eager and ready to serve.

The Destroyer admired their enthusiasm.

The Selkies arrived, stepping out of the water, shedding their seal-like skin for a human appearance. They appeared annoyed and confused.

To the Destroyer's delight a Phoenix joined his little team. He landed near the Salamanders, frightening them.

The Sylphs and Echo Spirits arrived together. He frowned. They were hard to control, they kept fading in and out of view.

Soon, they were joined by Invisibles, Gremlins, Griffins, Vampires, Flurries, Shifters, Nymphs, Harpies and two former Giants, Marcus and Treynor, and Lorilie, Andre, and other Water Spirits.

The Destroyer walked among his new people, smiling in delight. He'd never encountered so many species in one place. This was going to be so much fun.

Sierra opened a rip and stepped into the Fire Realm, followed by the men and women of various species, prepared to fight by her side.

The Elders felt her presence the moment she arrived. Egon and Ben went out to greet her, surprised to discover that she'd arrived with an army.

Egon frowned, "What's happened?" he asked.

"The Destroyer has escaped, and I've trapped him here. We could use your help to catch him," she said, approaching Ben and Egon with Dak at her side.

"Destroyer?" Ben asked.

"The creature that caused the infection," Dak explained.

Ben's eyes widened in surprise. "I will gather the others to help," he said, turning and entering the main house through the wall.

They could see him talking to the Elders.

Sierra caught a glimpse of Iesha and wondered why she was here.

Egon glanced over his shoulder and smiled. "I've brought the remaining Elders home," he said smiling. "Iesha is a descendent of theirs and accompanied them home."

Sierra hugged Egon, "That's wonderful. I'm so happy for you," she said.

"That's all that's left of them?"

"Yes. They gave up their magic to create their cities so they would prosper. They didn't want magic anymore after what it cost them. Unfortunately, the rest of them have died."

"That was an amazing act of selflessness," Dak said.

"We were a great people once," Egon said.

"And we will be again," Ben added rejoining them with six Elders.

"Thank you for helping us to recapture this creature," Sierra said. "He's destroyed so many and taken so much from so many."

"Lead the way, my dear. We will stop him from hurting anyone else," Egon said.

They marched from the hill to the valley below and were met by an army of Gnomes, led by Gerferlum.

Sierra smiled at the sight of the cheerful little men and women.

"We've come to join you my lady," he said.

"How did you know we were here and needed help," she asked.

"People have been gathering near the river, led by a strange fellow I've never seen. I figured they were up to no good and knew you'd be coming to help, so here we are to help too."

Sierra exchanged looks with Dak and Egon. "Thank you. How many have gathered?"

"At least one hundred, maybe more," he replied.

"That many? Thankfully, you weren't affected. Please lead the way," she said. Her impromptu army followed the Gnomes into the valley.

As they turned the corner to enter the valley, their path was blocked by Lazrus and Raziel, smiling widely.

Sierra was relieved to see them and returned their smile, climbing onto Lazrus' back as he bent down to make it easier for her. Dak climbed on Raziel. "We will put a stop to his madness Lazrus assured her."

"I know. Thanks for coming."

"My place is by your side."

She was surprised that she hadn't detected them and reached out across the realm to make sure they wouldn't encounter any surprises.

She was stunned by the sheer number of people he had infected already, then realized that they weren't infected. This was something else.

They reached the valley and could see the multitude of people waiting for them and paused to assess the situation.

The Destroyer and his recruits were waiting for them.

"What is our plan, little one?" Lazrus asked.

Sierra turned around and looked admiringly at the people fighting by her side. She reached out to them telling them that they had to capture the Destroyer any way possible, and to stay safe. She took a deep breath and relayed her plan.

Dak said to her silently. "Let's get him."

They split up as they moved forward to surround them, keeping their eyes on the Destroyer.

The Sylphs and Echo Spirits broke away from the group, as the Destroyer split them up to attack Sierra's army.

Lorilie and Andre, with the other Water Fairies, vanished into the river with the Selkies following them.

Ben tried to reach out to Lorilie, but she blocked him. He broke off from the others with four Elders accompanying him and dove into the water, gills appearing on their necks allowing them to breathe beneath the surface.

The five Elders glid smoothly through the water behind the Water Fairies and the Selkies.

Ben tried again to reach Lorilie, but she continued to block him.

As they closed the distance between them, Ben came up with a plan, communicating it to others.

They silently moved alongside them unnoticed, as they could no longer be seen.

Ben, Kate, Derrick, and Davis surrounded them. The Selkies sensed something and slowed their pace, looking out across the deep blue water.

Seeing nothing, they continued slicing through the water silently.

Matching their pace, they surround them again and together, the five of them created a bubble that surrounded them, moving with them.

The bubble rose, moving toward the surface. The Water Fairies and Selkies realized that something was happening and floated in place, looking around in confusion as they realized they were moving toward the surface.

Lorilie reached out and touched the invisible bubble. It was warm against her fingers and pulsed with life. She jerked her hand away in surprise as the bubble rose out of the water.

Everyone on the ground was momentarily distracted by its sudden appearance.

The Owls took to the skies, flying toward the Destroyer.

The Destroyer climbed on the back of a Griffin and took to the skies, hurling electrical charges at the Owls that were in pursuit.

The Owls dodged the electrical charges and continued their pursuit.

The Echo Spirits and Sylphs circled the Owls, appearing and disappearing all around them, interfering with their pursuit.

Lazrus saw this and took to the air, explaining to Sierra what he planned. Dak and Raziel were right behind them.

Ben and the Elders floated the bubble above the lake. He tried one last time to reach Lorilie.

Lorilie responded that she would kill him.

The hate and anger coming from her wasn't natural. He suddenly realized how he was controlling them.

He reached out to everyone letting them know that he was controlling them through their emotions.

Sierra and Dak thanked him for the information, as they pursued the Destroyer, avoiding his electric charges dodging them as they flew all around them.

Sierra and Dak pulled water from beneath the ground and slammed it against the Griffin and the Destroyer, tossing them through the air, tumbling out of control.

Ben raised the bubble higher as the Selkies let out a shriek that caused the bubble to vibrate. Afraid that they would tear the bubble, Ben sent a wave of energy through it, rendering them unconscious.

As their bodies relaxed, Ben pushed the anger from them. This caused the Fire Salamander, Imps, Goblins and Gremlins to go crazy with renewed anger as they rushed toward Ben and the others.

Their action ignited the Nymphs, Flurries, Shifters, Vampires, and Invisibles to join in the full-fledged battle.

An enormous Harpy swooped out of the sky with an inhuman cry.

Sierra ducked out of her way, but her talons raked across her arm, tearing into the smooth flesh, leaving a trail of blood.

"What the hell has that?" Dak yelled. Are you all right?"

Sierra healed her arm. "I'm fine."

Egon was stunned to see a Harpy and called out to Vestry for help. They rose into the air and raced toward the Harpy.

The Vampires went to the aid of the Owls, turning into smoke. They wove in between the Owls and the Echo Spirits and Sylphs. Enraged, the Sylphs constricted the air around the Vampires, making it harder for them to move through the thicker air, slowing them down.

The Owls took advantage and escaped the Sylphs and Echo Spirits, racing toward Sierra and Dak.

The Destroyer and the Griffin recovered and turned, facing Sierra and Dak, joined by Pry, an enormous Phoenix.

The Destroyer charged the air around them. It snaped and sparked all around them sending sparks of electricity dancing near them.

The Phoenix, Harpy and the Destroyer faced Dak, Sierra, Lazrus and Raziel joined by Egon, Vestry, and the Owls.

The Phoenix and Harpy let out a shrill cry that tore at their minds.

Dak covered his ears with his hands.

Sierra pushed the shrill cries back at them. The noise slammed into them with no effect.

Lazrus reached out to the Phoenix to stop this madness but was ignored.

On the ground, Ben and the Elders joined in the fight, pulling on the elements around them. They bound the Fire Salamanders, Imps, and Gremlins, wrapping them with wind and water so they were unable to move.

The Gnomes took advantage of them being unable to move and rushed them, knocking them on the head, rendering them unconscious.

Ben had to laugh as the Gnomes knocked them out, then scooped them up, stuffing them beneath their strong stubby arms, carrying them with them as they moved on to the next.

The Goblins raced around them trying to interfere, but the Elders cast a spell on them, lifting them high in the air above the battle.

They hung there, unable to cause any trouble.

The Sylphs and Echo Spirits split up. The Spirits rushed to stop the Gnomes. The husky little Gnomes ignored them, swatting at them with their clubs.

Deterred, the Sylphs joined the Destroyer, facing down Sierra and those standing with her. Their beautiful wings fluttered, reflecting the sun's rays through them. Their beauty was mesmerizing, and it was hard to believe they were facing them in battle.

Prye, the Phoenix, let out a slender stream of fire that hit the electrical currents that the Destroyer released into the air, causing a chain reaction of fire charged by electricity.

The flames hit the first electric charge and jumped to the next and the next, lighting up the sky, burning anything in its path.

It hit the ground like an explosion, slamming into Gerferlum and the Fire Salamander he was holding. It knocked Gerferlum off his feet, the Fire Salamander taking most of the hit.

Gerferlum staggered to his feet, stunned. He saw the scorched Salamander lying at his feet. He knelt down and gently picked up his limp body and stared at the Phoenix still spitting out fire.

Furious, he clutched his hammer and threw it with all of his mite. The hammer whirled through the air, end over end, knocking him out instantly as it connected with the Phoenix's head.

Pyre's wings hung limply by his side as he fell, spiraling to the ground.

While avoiding the fire charged electricity, Sierra slowed his fall as she bound him and encased him in a bubble similar to the one that held Lorilie, the Selkies and Water Fairies.

The ground battle erupted in an anger-fueled battle as the Gnomes knocked their way through the Goblins and Nymphs.

Collin led his pack into battle against the other Werewolves, overtaking them easily as they were outnumbered.

Ben and the Elders assisted Falon, Avis, Marcus and Treynor in fighting the Invisibles, Shifters, and Flurries. Ben tried to avoid looking skyward, as he was worried about his father and daughter.

Seeing Pyre fall from the sky, the Echo Spirits faded in and out attacking Egon, Vestry, Dak, and Sierra, leaving red whelps across their skin.

Sierra, Dak, Vestry and Egon lashed out with an ice spell, weighing their wings down with ice crystals, making it hard to fly and impossible to fade in and out.

The Owls swooped down on them, jerking them kicking and screaming out of the air and flew away with them.

Dak smiled as they vanished and dodged an attack from the Harpy. He hit her in the back with an itching spell.

The Harpy started to twitch and scratch, giving Dak time to hit her with a weight and binding spell.

Invisible bonds wound around her arms, pinning them to her side. She broke free of her bonds almost instantly. The weights were pulling her down, making it impossible to stay in the air. She slowly sank to the ground flinging off the remainder of her bonds while trying to scratch.

She let out an ear-piercing scream that tore through the air.

Dak and Raziel dove down after her, casting binding spell after binding spell.

She was weakening, unable to free herself as quickly.

Vestry and Egon raced after the Sylphs, casting spells in an attempt to slow them down. The Sylphs were too quick, avoiding every spell.

Alone, Sierra hurled a calming spell at the Destroyer. He continued to smile as he was joined by another Griffin.

Sierra bravely faced them comforted by Lazrus' strength and presence.

"We can take them, little one," Lazrus reassured her.

Sierra racked her brain for a way to end this.

The Destroyer leaned his head back and howled with laughter.

How could anyone be so evil and get pleasure from hurting innocent people?

The Griffins reared back and roared as they lunged at her.

Lazrus dove, avoiding their attack.

The Griffins split up, one raked its talons across Lazrus' back, digging deeply into his flesh.

Sierra winced, feeling his pain, healing him as the Griffin struck again and again, shredding his thick hide.

The other Griffin, carrying the Destroyer reached out to tear at Sierra's face. Instinctively, she put up a shield between them, trapping the Griffin's talons an inch from her cheek.

She healed Lazrus, who was having trouble dodging the repeated attacks. Smiling, she covered Lazrus in a thin, stainless-steel armor that blended with his colorful scales, and reinforced it with the same shield that was protecting her.

She threw multiple spells at the Destroyer, which he dissolved with his energy powers.

He rose from the back of the Griffin and shook off his pointy tail and ears as he turned into green glowing energy.

The Griffins pounded at them, trying to break through their shields.

Lazrus struggled to stay in the air against the constant onslaught.

Sierra glanced down at Dak struggling to keep the Harpy penned down.

She had to stop this before they were driven to the ground.

She reached out to her surroundings, calling on the elements in the air and ground.

She pulled at the energy in the air around her and the earth beneath her with all her might. She had to struggle to control it. She knew the Destroyer would counter her attack with energy and was counting on it.

The ground shook beneath her and the sky rumbled and roared, growing dark.

A geyser burst forth from the ground. Its warm spray was warm against Dak's skin. He looked up in surprise, hitting the Harpy with two new spells, one to shock her, and one to weaken her. She stopped struggling and was finally silent.

The sky opened up and lightning slashed across the sky. The lightning and water came together and slammed into the Destroyer at the same time.

He tried to block them with his electrical power.

Sierra boosted the energy from the lightning and the power from the water. They held the Destroyer suspended in midair, unable to move as the raw energy pulsed through him.

The people on the ground stopped attacking and looked around in confusion.

The two Griffins glanced at each other, then Sierra, then the Destroyer. "What is happening?" Aether asked.

"Please join the others on the ground," Lazrus said.

Sierra didn't hear them. She was concentrating on controlling the two wild forces of nature.

The Destroyer struggled against the attack and pushed out more energy in an effort to push it away. His body glowed an eerie shade of green.

He yelled and a burst of energy rushed from his body.

Sierra doubled the amount of power she was hitting him with. When the three energy sources collided, the Destroyer exploded into tiny particles.

Sierra's eyes widened in shock, and she pushed the water and lighting away, returning them to the sky and ground.

The ground stopped rumbling, and the sky grew quiet. She collapsed, exhausted against Lazrus.

Chapter Eleven

Dealing with the Aftermath

Lazrus gently landed in the soft grass. Dak rushed to his side, lifting Sierra off of his back, admiring his colorful new armor.

Cradling Sierra in his arms, he sank down with her, examining her. Finding no visible wounds, he linked his mind with hers. She was very weak. The battle with the Destroyer had taken too much out of her.

Gerferlum made his way through the crowd that gathered around. He was still carrying the dead Fire

Salamander in his arms. He laid the little creature gently in the grass and bent down next to Dak and Sierra.

Ben and Egon pushed their way through the crowd and bent down next to them.

Egon put his hand on Sierra's arm and used a healing spell on her. He was shocked when nothing happened.

He looked at Ben in desperation. Ben, Dak, and Egon, together tried to heal her, again, and nothing happened.

"She needs to heal." Egon said, more worried than he let on.

"Why aren't the healing spells working?" Dak asked, holding her closer, looking down at her pale face.

Gerferlum started to hum, deep in his throat. The other Gnomes slowly made their way closer, creating a circle around Sierra.

All the Gnomes started humming with Gerferlum and swayed gently from side to side.

The air was charged with a new kind of energy.

Gerferlum reached out and touched Sierra's forehead and hummed louder.

The air grew warm and heavy.

Gerferlum swayed softly and grew silent as he removed his hand from her brow.

The sudden silence was deafening. He touched Sierra's brow again and her eyes fluttered and opened. She blinked and looked at Dak, then at everyone and frowned as she tried to sit up.

"What's wrong? Why are you all staring at me?" she asked, pushing away from Dak so she could sit up.

"You fainted, little one," "Lazrus said.

"Really?" she said, surprised, then remembered what happened. "Oh no," she cried. "I killed him."

Dak put his arm around her, helping her to stand up. "It's over now. That's all that matters," he said.

Sierra bent down and kissed Gerferlum on the cheek. "Thank you for what you did."

"What was that you did?" Dak asked.

"It's elemental healing," he said as if that explained it. "The Gnomes have used it as long as I can remember."

"Thank you, again. Do you think I could learn it?" She asked.

Gerferlum frowned. "I don't know. You're not a Gnome."

The Harpy screamed in anger upon waking and discovering herself tied up.

Dak laughed. "We should take care of our prisoners and decide what to do with them. Do you feel up to it?" he asked Sierra.

Ben released Lorilie, the other Water Spirits and the Selkies from their bubbles. He kept them confined with the help of the Elders.

"What the hell is going on?" Lorilie demanded.

"You attacked us." Ben said. "Now we have to decide what to do with you."

"You won't be deciding what to do with us," Shaye said. "Selkies answer to no one."

"That may have been so until you started attacking others," Ben said coldly. "You will stay here and wait until we decide how to handle this. We know that you weren't entirely at fault, but you do share in the blame."

Egon, Vestry, Collin, Dak, Falon, Novrah and Sierra gathered around the Harpy.

"We will release you if you give us your word that you won't try to escape," Dak said.

The Harpy glared angrily at them, unsure if she would be allowed to leave. "I won't try to escape," Sephethe said, irritated with the weak creatures before her.

"Where are you from?" Dak asked.

"I've lived in the upper mountains for more years than you can count," she said.

Lazrus furrowed his brows in surprise. He had no idea that anything lived above him.

"Why did you join in this battle?" Dak questioned.

"I have no idea. I was angry," she said, wondering why she got involved in something that had nothing to do with her.

"He used their anger against them, and used it to fuel his attack," Egon said.

Dak frowned. "He controlled them through their anger?"

"Seems so," Egon said.

"What are you angry about?" Dak asked Sephethe, sympathetically.

"I'm a Harpy. We're not known for being particularly happy," she said, dismissively.

Egon chuckled softly to himself.

"Do you have any issue with any of us? Do you plan to try to hurt anyone here again?" Dak asked.

"I have no issue with any of you. I don't know any of you and I'd like to keep it that way. Can I go now?"

The council turned away from the Harpy and whispered softly among themselves, then turned to face Sephethe. "You are free to go." Dak said. "We'd like to invite you to visit us in the future."

She nodded slightly before taking flight and escaping to the top of the mountain. She entered a cave and was immediately surrounded by a dozen Harpies wanting to know where she'd been.

— ⚜ —   — ⚜ —   — ⚜ —

The council moved on to the next group, which was much more personal for Collin, Avis, and Dak. They stared at their friends in confusion.

"So, which one of you want to tell me why you are so angry that the Destroyer was able to use that anger against you to attack us?" Collin said walking back and forth in front of them.

Libra lowered her head. "We had no control over this," she said.

"Then tell me why?" Collin demanded.

"The pack's split up. You're in Pandora or Opaque most of the time. We need leaders. Our people are being forgotten," she cried angrily.

Collin lowered his head. "You're right. We need to put our pack back together. If we do this, do I have your word that you will not rise against the council members again?"

"We had no choice in this fight, but you asked why we were angry, so we told you," Libra said defensively.

"What about you, Ascelin?" Dak said. "Why are you angry?"

Ascelin shrugged. "I didn't know I was angry. I wish my business were doing as well as some others in town," he said, shrugging.

Dak laughed. "That's all it took for him to gain control. I'm surprised the entire clan of Vampires didn't join in the fight. I don't think we have to worry about them."

They were allowed to leave and the next group to check out were the Imps, Fire Salamanders and Goblins. Gerferlum and the Gnomes had them surrounded. They kept having to chase after the Imps and Goblins and bring them back into the circle.

"The Fire Salamanders were angry at the tricks the Imps have been playing on them. That's why they were angry. The Imps and Goblins, well, it's just their nature," he said.

"There's no point in trying to change them. It's never going to happen," Sierra said.

The stories were the same from the Invisibles, the Phoenix and the two Griffins. The Flurries were generally peaceful fairies that lived in the mountain tops at the far reaches of the Windspell.

They too, had no explanation as to why they'd been drawn into this fight.

The council approached Marcus and Treynor, who they didn't bother asking why they were angry. Egon stared at them wondering what they should do with them. "Would you two like a second chance?" he asked.

Treynor rose to his feet and frowned, studying Egon. "What do you mean?"

"I'm inviting you to join us in Opaque. If you like it, you are welcome to stay. If not, you are free to leave. If you cause any trouble, we have a jail beneath the city."

"I'm up for a fresh start," Marcus said, coming to his feet.

"Guess I've nothing to lose," Treynor added.

"Good, you can return with me when I leave."

The council approached an incredibly angry Lorilie, Water Fairies, Water Nymphs and Selkies. Their anger radiated off of them as they approached.

"Why are you keeping us prisoner here?" Lorilie demanded.

"Why were you attacking us?" Ben asked.

"I have no idea. I'm sure the others told you that we had no choice. That creature forced us."

"I know he did, but unlike the rest of the people under his spell, I think you would have joined him, had he asked."

Lorilie rolled her eyes and smiled. "Well, we'll never know, since he didn't ask."

"You think this is funny?" Ben asked.

"Not particularly. But I think it's funny that you're now helping the very people you wanted to kill."

"That was foolish of me," he said.

Asrai stepped forward. "This is nonsense. We had no control over our actions. We've done nothing to deserve this treatment. You're issue is with Lorilie, but if you don't allow us to return to our home, it will be with us as well, and the Sea Dragons will not appreciate you keeping us prisoner."

"We have no quarrel with the Sea Dragons," Egon said.

"You will, if we are not freed." Asrai said.

"There is no need to make threats," Egon said.

"You know that I never make threats," she said coldly. "Now can we leave? Then you can continue chatting with Lorilie."

Egon looked at the council members. They nodded. "You are free to go," Egon said.

"Wise decision," Asrai said, brushing past them and striding to the water and vanishing beneath the surface.

"How touching," Lorilie said sweetly.

"Now you need to set me and my people free. We had no more choice in this than anyone else."

"She's right," Ben whispered to the council.

"I'm sure she would have helped the Destroyer if he'd asked," Dak said. "But we can't punish her for what she might have done."

The council reluctantly nodded.

Ben released them from the energy that surrounded them.

Lorilie strolled slowly past the council, stopping in front of Ben. Her eyes raked over him, and she smiled.

Sierra moved next to him and said softly. "I'm sure we'll be seeing you again."

Lorilee glared at Sierra, glancing briefly at Dak. "Count on it," she said slowly walking away with Andre and the other water Spirits following her.

She delicately dove into the water with her people entering the water one by one.

"She's going to cause us trouble," Egon said.

"I want to speak to the Echo Spirits and Sylphs before we let them go," Sierra said.

Sierra slowly approached the Echo Spirits and Sylphs. She reached out to them trying to calm them and let them know that she was a friend.

She allowed them inside her mind so they might trust her. She could feel them relaxing. They had been worried and scared for a long time. They relaxed warming to her.

"I'd like to invite you to Pandora so we can all get to know one another. I think we can learn a lot from each other."

She retreated from their minds to allow them privacy.

Helairi, a beautiful girl with long, dark hair and big brown eyes approached Sierra. Her silver and blue wings rested comfortably behind her.

"The Echo Spirits are eager to learn more about you and your city."

"Thank you," Sierra said. "We are delighted to have you."

Terrane took a solid form of a young, slim man, with blond hair and piercing blue eyes. He nodded at Helairi. "We too, would like to visit your city," he said.

"I am so happy that both of you will be visiting Pandora. Let me see if our business here is finished then we can all return together.

The council stayed back, giving Sierra privacy with the two elusive beings.

Sierra smiled at Terrane and Helairi. "I will be right back," she said.

Approaching the council, Ben, and the Elders, taking a deep breath, she said, "I'm glad that is over. Thank all of you for coming so quickly when I asked for help."

"You are most welcome, my dear," Egon said fondly. "That is what the council is for."

"I'm glad we were here to help." Ben said, still wishing he could talk to her privately.

Sierra saw the Gnomes heading toward home and broke away from the council and raced toward them. She stopped in front of them and bent down and hugged Gerferlum.

"Thank you so much for what you did for me. I am forever in your debt."

"It was our pleasure, my lady." Gerferlum said, returning her hug.

"You know where to find us if you need us," he said.

Sierra proudly watched the brave proud Gnomes head for home.

Lazrus landed softly next to her.

"Are you ready to go home, little one?"

Sierra leaned into him feeling his new armor against her cheek. "Do you want me to remove the armor?" she asked.

Lazrus puffed out a cloud of smoke. "I kind of like the way it looks," he said.

"You do look even more dashing," she said. "Thank you for always being there for me."

"We are bound together, little one. I will always be here for you. Are you okay with what happened today?"

Sierra frowned. "It's not what I wanted to happen."

"I know. I'm not sure if it could have ended any other way."

She waved goodbye to the council and all the people who came to help them.

Dak and Raziel joined her. "Are you ready to go home?" Dak asked.

"Let's get our guests and go home," she said.

Chapter Twelve

Training Day

Sierra was glad to be home. The Sylphs and Echo Spirits followed the Dragons home and settled in a mountain cave. Dak went with them to make it more comfortable.

Alone, Sierra soaked in a hot bubble bath. She was haunted by the image of the Destroyer shattering into pieces.

She never wanted to hurt him, but he left her no choice. Sighing, she sank deeper into the water and closed her eyes. Would it always be like this, one disaster after another?

Too tired to towel herself dry, she used magic to dry herself and dressed herself in a grey tee shirt and pink shorts. She climbed into bed and was asleep almost instantly. She didn't stir.

Dak climbed into bed beside her an hour later.

He gently kissed her on the nose and covered her up before extinguishing the light and falling asleep.

When she awoke the next morning, Dak was already gone. She noticed a folded note on his pillow, picked it up and read that he was helping instruct the new students and if she was up to it, she should join them.

Dressed in light weight training gear, she sat down on the veranda sipping juice as she watched the new students train in magic.

She was surprised to see Slade and Rhys training. She thought they already knew magic.

Smiling when she spotted Adam and his new friends, Ellis, a young Vampire, and Skeet, a Fire Fairy training with Silver and Fin.

Several Werewolves, Vampires, Shifters, Water Fairies and Fire Fairies were training side by side, along with Jinks and Leiya.

Before long, she would have beings from every realm living in Pandora and prayed that they would continue to live in peace.

She jumped, spilling her orange juice in her lap, when a hand touched her softly on the shoulder.

Jumping to her feet, she faced a laughing Bree.

"You scared the crap out of me," she laughed.

"I can see that. What are you doing sitting here residing over your subjects?"

"Very funny. I had a rough day yesterday and I was drinking my juice watching them train until you snuck up on me. So, what brings you to Pandora?"

Smiling, Bree said, "Mom and Dad have agreed to move here if my grandparents can come too."

"Oh my gosh. Why didn't I think of that," Sierra cried.

"What?"

"I left my grandmother behind."

"That wasn't very nice." Bree teased.

"Well, Dad just needs to go and get her," she said putting her hands on her hips. Smiling, she grabbed Bree in a bear hug. "I'm so glad you'll be here. I've missed you."

"I've missed you too. Just one thing. Can I bring my car?"

"I guess that can be arranged."

"Good, then when do we move?"

"Whenever you want. Let me know when and what you want in a house, and it will be ready when you arrive."

Bree smiled. "Great. I'll let them know. Can we get a separate house for my grandparents? You know how they drive my mom crazy."

"Of course. Let me know what they want in a house too."

"One more thing. Any way we can get cable and cell phone coverage?"

Sierra frowned. "I'll have to see what I can do to allow that. I'll let you know."

"I just don't want to cut off all ties with home," Bree explained wistfully.

"Awesome. I'll let you know about the houses," she said, turning to leave. She turned back and continued, "They don't need to be next door to each other either."

"I understand," Sierra laughed.

"Great. See you later," she said as she headed toward the gate and home.

Sierra looked down at her damp pants and laughed as she waved her hand to dry them.

She watched as Dak, Mavis, Silver, Fin, and Eldrick were setting up tables with potions in the center. Sighing, she decided that it was time for her to join them.

Slowly, she walked down the marble steps and crossed the lawn.

Dak smiled at her. "I was wondering if you were going to honor us with your presence."

"I'm just a little slow getting around this morning," she said kissing him, before turning to face the students.

"Excuse me," Collin said behind them. "Do you mind if I join the students?"

Sierra smiled. "No, of course not."

"I'm curious to see if I can learn magic. If we're going to be in battles all the time, I see a great use for it."

"I hope the battles are few and far between now," Sierra replied.

"As do I, my lady." He said taking his place among the students.

Turning to Dak, she said, "I think we should split them up into groups. Some will be more adept at learning magic while others may struggle with it. I don't want it to discourage them."

"That's a good idea," he said.

"I know we can't give them the power of magic, but we can help by boosting their ability to learn it," she said.

Dak frowned. "I don't know. I don't think it's ever been done, but we can try."

Sierra took his hand to strengthen their magic and cast a spell on their students, giving them the best chance to be successful at learning magic.

She released his hand and said, "What group to you want?"

"I'll take the Vampires," he said.

Silver took the Fire Fairies, Fin the Water Fairies and Eldrick took Adam and Jinks and the Werewolves. That left Leiya with Sierra.

Sierra took Leiya inside the castle. Dak moved the Vampires across the bridge.

Fin and Silver moved to each side of the castle leaving Eldrick and his students on the front lawn.

Eldrick smiled at his students. He was excited. This was the first time he'd ever attempted to teach the art of magic.

He knew this would be a challenge because none of them knew which students would be able to master it.

The Werewolves possessed the art of transformation so it was possible they would be able to learn more.

Adam and Jinks were another story. While they were excited and eager to learn, there was a good chance magic would elude them.

"Good morning students," Eldrick said. "We are going to start with the basics." He pulled out a bag of vials that Sierra had prepared for him. "You will take turns choosing your vials or allow them to choose you. I want each of you to concentrate on the vials. Shut out everything around you. Don't worry about how long it takes. Just concentrate on the vials. When you've chosen them, I will give you the vials that you've chosen, and we will practice with them. Let's get started. Collin, you will be the first to go then the remaining Werewolves, then Jinks and Adam you will be last."

Adam frowned. He was disappointed, but he knew it was a long shot that he would be able to do magic.

Collin was nervous. He walked toward Eldrick, stepping in front of the table. He looked down at the colorful glass vials, wondering how they created magic.

"Look at the vials and shut out everything around you. Concentrate." Eldrick advised.

Collin nodded, ignoring the feeling of the other students watching him. He looked down at the vials again.

The world around him disappeared as he watched the swirling liquid move inside the glass containers.

The red one looked as if it were trying to push the sopper out. Without realizing it, Collin picked it up and Eldrick gently took it from him. The same thing happened three more times before the world around him came back into focus.

Eldrick smiled at him as he poured the potions into four new vials and put them in a small wooden box and handed it to Collin. "Well done," he said.

Collin smiled and took the box and returned to his class. He was amazed by the way he felt while choosing the vials. It was more thrilling than when he changed into a wolf. It exhausted him, yet, making him feel more alive.

Eldrick replaced the four vials in the box. They had refilled themselves and were ready for the next student.

Six Werewolves stood in front of Eldrick and were able to pick three vials each and returned proudly to the rest of the class.

Sierra's and Dak's spell appeared to be successful at increasing their ability, allowing for better results.

Jinks sauntered up to Eldrick, nervous and anxious.

Eldrick nodded for him to begin.

Nervous, he looked down at the colorful vials and swallowed the lump in his throat. He studied the delicate glass and the intricate stoppers.

The liquid inside seemed to swirl and sway. He reached out to touch one and it seemed to come alive beneath his fingers. He surprised himself by picking it up.

Eldrick took it from his shaking fingers.

Jinks noticed a second vial glowing and picked it up, and Eldrick took it as well. The world around him came back into view.

Eldrick smiled at him as he poured the contents into two vials for him, placed them in a velvet lined wooden box and handed it to him.

Jinks gasped as the two emptied vials refilled themselves. Laughing, he hurried back to the students.

Adam slowly rose to his feet, wiping his sweaty palms on his jeans. He smiled nervously at Eldrick, still in awe of the mighty Phoenix. He looked down at the vials and wanted to run away. He was terrified that nothing would happen.

He squinted and focused on the vial filled with a deep purple liquid.

"Relax," Eldrick whispered softly.

Adam nodded and looked back down at the box. It seemed like he stood there for what seemed like forever. He started to sweat. Disappointment raced through him.

He blinked and noticed a bright blue vile flowing and swirling. Relief flooded through him, as he reached out to pick it up.

Eldrick took it. Relieved that he'd finally been chosen by the vials.

Adam noticed a deep red vial swirling along with the purple one next to it. Shaking, Adam picked both of them up.

Eldrick grinned, taking both vials.

Adam relaxed and smiled up at him.

"Are you finished?"

"I think so," he replied confused.

"Good," Eldrick said, filling three vials, putting them in a velvet lined box then handing it to Adam.

Adam clutched the box to his chest. He knew his life would never be the same. He rejoined the other students, his face filled with excitement.

"Congratulations everyone. This took longer than expected. I believe we've missed lunch. Get something to eat then return here with your boxes and we will try your first spell.

They hurried to the castle, trying to ignore Fin and Silver's groups already working on casting a spell.

They hurried into the dining room and were surprised to see the other groups eating dessert.

Hurrying to an empty table, piled high with food, they quickly filled their plates, eating as they congratulated one another on their success.

Leiya and Sierra were the first to leave. Sierra glanced at Adam and was relieved when he held up three fingers and smiled.

Opening the door to an empty room, Leiya took her place behind the small table and proudly looked down at the five vials nestled safely in the velvet lined box.

"You did extremely well today, but I expected no less. As an elder descendant, your magical ability could be great," Sierra said proudly.

"This is both overwhelming and exciting," Leiya said in wonder.

Sierra led Leiya through a series of simple spells, the same way Mags did with her and Dak not so long ago but seemed like a lifetime ago.

She could see that Leiya was growing tired, and said, "That's it for today. We will resume practice tomorrow, after lunch."

Leiya carefully wrapped her vials and placed them gently in their box. "Thank you for taking the time to each me."

"You are very welcome but don't tell anyone, you're my first student."

Leiya laughed. "I won't tell, but you are a wonderful teacher."

"Thank you, but I think that's only because you are such a good student."

Leiya smiled, thanking Sierra again and hurried from the room to find Jinks. Locating him outside talking to Adam about today's training session.

Skeet and Ellis raced up just as she reached them. The two young men stopped abruptly, said a brief hello, and told Adam if he didn't hurry, they were going to be late and raced off together.

"Late for what?" Leiya asked Jinks, as she watched the three boys race off, laughing and punching each other playfully.

"A dance in Awakening," he said.

"Don't you want to go with them?"

Jinks smiled shyly. "I'd rather go with you."

Smiling up at him, she said, "Let's go then. We don't want to miss anything. I've never been to a dance before."

Smiling, they raced toward the gate to take them to Awakening.

The city was new and alive with activity. Young men and women filled the streets.

Jinks and Leiya stopped at a shop filled with customers. After waiting in line for a few minutes, they purchase succulent smelling beef pies oozing with flavor. Nibbling on the delicious treat, they purchased sweet lemonade from another vendor.

The atmosphere was fun and lively reminding Jinks of the carnivals back home.

A sweet aroma wafted across the crowded boardwalk. Jinks smiled, motioning for Leiya to follow him. He crossed the crowded polished wooden sidewalk, following the newest scent to assault his senses.

A line was already forming to purchase the sweets. When they reached the front of the line, he purchased two bowls filled with various fruits oozing out of a soft crust with a scoop of colorful ice cream on top.

Jinks handed the fruit bowl to Leiya just as she finished her pie, tossing the thin wrapper in the trash with one hand as she took the sweet treat. She brought the bowl to her nose and took a deep breath. Her eyes widened in delight.

"It smells wonderful."

They moved through the crowd making their way back outside. Finding an empty table across the street that gave them a clear view of the crowd filled shops. They took a seat and watched the crowd.

"Is it always like this?" Leiya asked.

"Three or four times a week," Jinks said.

"How exciting. I shall tell Sierra about it. Pandora needs more of a night life."

Jinks frowned slightly. "That's a great idea."

Finishing their treats, they discarded the paper bowls in the trash and strolled down the sidewalk toward the sound of music.

Entering the large two-story building, they stepped into the dimly lit building. A catchy toon was blaring from a band on center stage.

The room was crowded with people from every realm. The excitement was electrifying.

Jinks led Leiya onto the crowded dance floor, waving at Adam who was dancing with a pretty Fire Fairy.

Leiya and Jinks returned the excited wave.

The music ended and the dancers returned to the crowded tables. Jinks and Leiya joined Adam, Ellis, and Skeet, along with their dancing partners, Erica, Siris and Laris.

Skeet waved and a young female Werewolf took their drink order and returned with a sweet punch with a smooth sweet liqueur made by the Werewolves.

She set the drinks down in front of each one of them and Skeet paid her, tipping her generously.

"I like the new monetary system," Skeet said.

"It's really made a difference in the lives of my people," Ellis said. "This realm is nothing like it used to be. The transformation's been amazing, and we love it."

Skeet laughed. "That's an understatement."

"What do you mean?" Leiya asked.

"Where to start," Skeet said, punching Ellis. "It used to be dark and dreary here and barely anything survived."

Leiya looked at Ellis waiting for him to refute Skeet's description.

Ellis shrugged and laughed. "Well, it's not like that now."

"Thank goodness. You were such cranky people before, and now you know how to have fun," Skeet said laughing as he downed his drink, grabbed Siris by the hand and hurried to the dance floor as the band returned with a lively tune.

Leiya covered her mouth as she tried to hide her yawn.

Jinks smiled, and said, "We should get home. Today was a little tiring." Leiya slid off her stool and said, "Thank you for allowing us to join you. This was so much fun."

"Glad you came tonight," Erica said. "You should come back for the next one."

Leiya looked over at Jinks.

Jinks winked and smiled.

"I'd like that," Leiya said shyly.

Jinks shook hands with Adam, Skeet and Ellis before escorting Leiya from the building.

Leiya turned to face him. "Tonight was so much fun. Thank you for bringing me here," she said.

Jinks slid his arm around her waist. "It was my pleasure. We will have to come again soon."

"I'd really like that. Everything here is so different than at home," she said.

"In a good way?" he asked.

"A very good way."

They slowly walked through town; the shops were now closed up for the night.

Staying on the path they entered the dark forest. Suddenly, the trees above them lit up with tiny lightening bugs, lighting up the path for them.

Jinks linked his fingers with Leiya's, and they passed through the gate and entered Pandora. The city was dark and quiet. The lights from the castle reflected in the pond. Franklin poked his head out of the water.

"Good evening, my young friends," he said.

"Hello," Leiya said smiling down at him. This world had so many wonders.

"How are you on this beautiful night?"

"I am wonderful, thank you. I see you two are very well indeed."

Leiya blushed. "We've had an enjoyable evening."

"It is good to have fun, especially with a pretty girl."

Jinks laughed. "I better get this pretty girl back to the castle, before Sierra comes looking for her."

"Goodnight, friends."

"Goodnight." Jinks and Leiya said together.

Jinks escorted her to the castle and kissed her softly on the cheek, and turned disappearing into the night, whistling softly.

Chapter Thirteen

The Elders

Iesha hugged Egon, Eloise, and Rich. "Thank you for allowing me to visit your wonderful city." She turned to Ben, "Thank you for what you've done for the Elders," she said, kissing him gently on the cheek.

Ben smiled weakly. "I took far more from them."

Iesha took his hands in hers. "Come back with me so you can see for yourself how well things turned out."

Egon put his hand on Ben's shoulder. "Visit Wyalii son. It might help you forgive yourself."

Ben glanced over at Rich and Eloise and smiled sadly.

"It's time for all of us to put the past behind us," Egon said.

"I would love to show you my home," Iesha said.

"Very well. I would be delighted to visit your home," Ben said feeling outnumbered.

"Wonderful," Iesha said.

Egon accompanied them through the gate to Opaque and watched as they passed through the gate to Pandora, then to Wyalii.

They arrived in Iesha's office. Ben looked around and smiled. "This is where you work?" he asked.

"Yes. This is my office. Follow me and I'll show you what the Elders created when they gave up magic."

Ben followed her from her dimly lit all blue office, down ice blue stairs, through the blue tiled entrance to the outside.

He stopped in surprise when he looked out across the city with buildings more than five stories tall. The city was very modern, much like the cities on Sierra's world.

Iesha watched his reaction with pride.

Ben looked at her and smiled. "Very impressive. There is nothing like this in our realms."

"The Elders wanted us to grow and prosper, but we have also been isolated from the other cities on our world. We plan to change that."

"One question. Why is everything blue?"

"I can only guess that they wanted all of us to be similar so nothing like what happened on your world would happen here, but I think it is safe to put that practice behind us.

"I think that's a good idea. You're missing out on a world of beautiful colors," he teased.

Smiling, she led him down the nearly deserted sidewalk to her apartment building, and up three flights of stairs to her apartment, opening the door without unlocking it.

No surprise, the living room was all blue, from the floor, furniture to the walls.

Iesha frowned. "After visiting your home, it seems very drab."

"May I?" he asked.

Feeling like a child, she put her hands together and smiled. "Please do."

Ben returned her smile and changed her tile from blue to sandstone, the walls became white with a tinge of blue. The tables turned black, with a glossy shine, and the chairs white.

The blue flowers in the vase turned the colors of the rainbow, and the unlit candle in the center of the table turned three different shades of pink.

Iesha looked around in wonder. "It's beautiful. Thank you. How would you feel about transforming the entire city? After my people get to meet you, of course."

"That would be quite an undertaking," he said.

"I have one more favor to ask. Can you create a garden here, like the one at your home?"

"I can."

"I have the perfect place for it, and it's the perfect way to show my people a world of color."

"Show me where you want the garden."

"You want to do it now?" she said in surprise.

"I won't take long. Then you can treat me to a dinner that is popular in your world."

"I can do that," she said smiling, excited to be able to watch him create something so amazing. She led him out of her building, across the street to a vacant lot, two blocks long and two blocks wide.

"Is this too big?"

"No, it's perfect."

As she watched, he created solid white walls eight feet high to surround the garden, with entrances on each side.

Next, he created a shell path that wound through the empty lot.

Tall trees pushed their way out of the ground and reached for the sky, towering over them.

Iesha exhaled softly, unaware that she was holding her breath. Watching him create such beauty from nothing was amazing.

Bushes broke through the ground, blooming, red, blue, pink, purple, yellow, and white.

Birds flew from the trees, singing, snowflakes fell from their beaks. And a silver fox slowly approached Iesha.

Smiling, she bent down and let it sniff her hand before running away. "It's beautiful. Thank you. My people will be thrilled."

"My pleasure. Now about dinner?" he said smiling.

"It won't be nearly as impressive after all this," she laughed.

They exited the garden and returned to her apartment. Ben sat in her new yellow kitchen as she baked fish and a tart vegetable.

The fish smelled unusual, but delicious.

Iesha sat a plate down in front of him before sitting across from him.

Ben took a bite of the warm succulent fish and smiled. "It's wonderful."

"Thank you. I'm glad you like it."

"It's very different."

After dinner, she put a blue pudding in front of him. Smiling weekly, she apologized. "All the ingredients are blue."

Ben picked up a blue spoon and scooped up the blue confection and took a bite. It tasted like nothing he'd ever tasted. It was sweet and smooth and refreshing.

"This is wonderful."

"I thought you'd like it," she said pleased.

"You can't keep this for just your people. You must share this with my world."

"I guess that's the least I can do."

Iesha covered her mouth as she yawned.

"You're tired and we have a busy day tomorrow," Ben said.

"I'll show you to your room. Please feel free to redecorate."

Ben smiled. "Good night," he said.

Iesha entered her room and was delighted that it had been transformed to soft shades of silver and lavender.

She crawled beneath the cool lavender sheets and was soon fast asleep.

Early the next morning, Iesha rushed to her office and sent out messages all over town, to come to the new garden.

She left Ben a note next to his breakfast of her version of waffles, asking him to meet her at the garden.

A crowd was gathering as he made his way to Iesha's side.

He joined her on a raised platform.

"Good morning. Are you ready to change the world?" Iesha asked smiling.

"As ready as I'll ever be. Are you sure you want to do this?"

"Absolutely," she said confidently, and faced the crowd. "Please, everyone, if you could keep the noise down so everyone can hear me. I'd like to introduce my friend, Ben. He is a direct descendant of the very people that created our great city."

The crowd grew quiet, and all eyes were on Ben.

"He's come here at my invitation to help us make a few changes and introduce us to a part of our history that we were unaware of.

"Our ancestors were afraid of us being different because of events that happened to them, thus, why everything in our world is blue. Today we will add color to our world and show you a part of our history starting with this beautiful garden."

"As you exit the garden, let me know what colors you preferred and I can help you add them to your life," Ben said, then turned the pale blue grass to a vibrant green, dotted with yellow and green wildflowers.

The crowd gasped, collectively. Iesha stepped down from the platform. Ben followed, entering the garden, heading for one of the three exits.

"Please enjoy," she said, letting the first group enter.

They were greeted by the crystal and blue birds taking flight, raining snowflakes down on them as their musical notes filled the garden.

The Wyaliians were delighted and amazed as they walked down the glittery path. The roses sung out and changed colors greeting the newest generation of Elders.

To Ben's amazement, the Wyaliians' clothing began to change color without any help from him, giving him an idea that he was eager to discuss with Iesha.

With each change, the excitement grew. The Wyaliians were amazed and delighted with their color transformation.

Iesha proudly watched her people embrace the changes.

"This was a success," she said moving next to Ben. "They are so excited."

"I'd like to take it a step farther," he said.

"How?"

"I'd like to see if any of your people possess the traits of the Elders."

Iesha frowned. "Like magic?"

"Yes, like magic."

Iesha frowned. "I'm not sure that is a good idea. This is a decision they should make for themselves."

Ben smiled. "That's only fair."

"What good will this do if they are able to do magic?"

Ben was speechless and stared at her. "I honestly don't know. Magic has always a part of our people's lives, and it makes life easier if you have it."

"Or harder if you let it control you," she reminded him.

"Fair enough. I don't have to do anything."

"No, they have a right to know their history. All of it. Then they can decide for themselves."

Iesha kissed his cheek and walked away. She climbed up the steps to the platform and called out to the people that had already passed through the garden.

"There is more to our history than this garden and vibrant colors. Our ancestors were able to perform magic, like the magic that created this beautiful garden and our city before giving it up. There is a possibility that some of us may also be able to do magic. If you would like to find out if you too possess this ability, talk to Ben and he will discuss the steps required to find out."

Ben sat on a wooden bench, inside the garden next to one of the exits. Soon he was surrounded by those curious to learn more about magic.

He told each one a time of day to meet him at the garden. He was excited to learn if these descendants of the Elders were closely related or too far removed.

He created a spiral staircase in the far corner of the garden with a room big enough for him to live in and train. Part of him knew that he should let go of the past and leave this alone. They were happy, peaceful people. Magic could change all of that.

After the crowds thinned, Iesha found him still sitting on the bench. She glanced up at the addition to the garden. "Having second thoughts?" she asked.

"A little. Was it that obvious?"

"Yes, but it's too late now. We have to let this play out and hope for the best."

"Whatever that is," he said.

"Whatever that is," she agreed. "Now, we missed lunch and I'm starving. I know a little restaurant that I think you will love."

Rising to his feet he said, "I can't wait."

Lunch was another mysterious succulent fish with a wine sauce that was beyond amazing. "Your food is amazing. It's like nothing I've ever eaten."

"Maybe we can trade our fish for items in your world."

"That's a good idea, but your recipes need to come with it, or better yet, open a restaurant in Pandora."

"Or a restaurant and market. If we do that, we need a currency like you have in Pandora."

"I'm sure Sierra would help you get started."

"This is exciting and frightening. We are starting a new chapter in our lives."

"I hope that's a good thing. I need to meet my first group. Can I come to your place when I'm finished?"

"I would like that. I have to set things in motion for this new chapter."

Ben entered the garden and was surprised to see dozens of people waiting, lined up the stairs to his home training center.

He smiled as he moved past them and opened the door. He invited the first three to follow him.

Two young men and one woman shyly entered the room. "Do you really think we can do magic?" Reena asked.

"Were all of our ancestors able to do magic?" Cali asked.

"Yes, to both questions."

Ben escorted them to three tables with a set of colorful crystal vials in the center of each table. He instructed them to relax and concentrate on the vials. This would be their first test. After fifteen minutes he asked them to wait in the garden.

He instructed the next three to concentrate on the vials.

He met Reena, Cali, and Cam outside in the garden. "Put your palms flat on the ground and concentrate on the elements beneath your hands. Pull at it with your thoughts and bring it to the surface."

"Maybe it would help if you showed us," Reena suggested.

Ben instructed them to touch his hand as he placed it on the smooth surface and pulled a small stream of water out of the ground.

The three student's eyes widened in surprise as they felt the energy leave his hand and then the water appeared. They followed his instructions, but after ten minutes nothing happened. Their disappointment was written on their faces.

"Continue to try this at home. If you're successful, please come back. If after a week, nothing happens, come back and we will try together."

Disappointed, they left, but eager to keep trying.

Ben went through the same routine until the last three students had left. He was disappointed. He wanted magic to endure in these people.

He exited the garden and strolled down the street, smiling as he turned the pale blue city to a city of multiple colors.

He quickly climbed the stairs to Iesha's apartment and knocked on the door.

Opening the door, Iesha asked, "How did it go?"

"Nothing yet," he said.

Iesha exhaled softly. "I must admit, I'm a little relieved."

"I have mixed feelings about it myself."

They ate a light dinner of sliced meat and cheese with a side of various berries, all unfamiliar to Ben. After dinner, he bid her goodnight and returned to his temporary home and training facility.

He awoke early the next morning to dozens of young people eager to learn if they inherited the ability of magic.

He patiently led them through the beginning steps to see if there was a spark of magic, but by lunchtime he'd had no luck and broke long enough to create a bowl of potato soup and a sandwich before starting with the next group.

By nightfall he was tired and disappointed and turned in early so he would be emotionally ready for the next group.

He spent the next three days trying to pull magic out of one of them, when he decided that he was wasting everyone's time and had given these wonderful people false hope.

During the week he'd spent in the city it had come alive with a rainbow of colors. Laughing to himself. It seemed that the color blue was no longer popular.

While creating himself an omelet there was a soft knock on the door.

It was too early for the next round of students. Ben opened to a smiling young man that he vaguely recognized.

"You told me to come back if I was successful in performing magic," Cam said excitedly.

Ben's heart thumped loudly in his chest. "Yes, I did," he said calmly, not showing his inner excitement.

"If you have time to come downstairs, I can show you." Cam said, trying to hold back his own excitement.

"I did what you said and practiced for hours every day," he said as he bent down placing his open palm to the ground, and within moments, a slight stream of water eked out of the dry ground. Cam smiled up at Ben.

Ben returned the smile. It wasn't much, but it was a start. "Very well done," he said. I'd like to start training with you this evening after my last group."

"I'd like that very much sir," Cam said.

If there was one, there had to be more Ben thought excitedly.

As Ben escorted his last student to the door, he greeted an eager Cam warmly.

Cam jumped to his feet excited to find out what happened next.

"Please sit. I'm going to try to enhance your ability." He'd learned this little trick from Sierra.

"How will you do that?" he asked uncertainly.

"With magic. Don't worry, you won't feel anything."

"Were all of my ancestors really able to do magic?"

"Yes, they were."

"And they started a crazy war and some of them left and came here?"

"That they did."

"And some of the old dudes are still alive? Their magic keeps them young?"

"Something like that," Ben said, putting his hand gently against Cam's chest. He couldn't feel a faint trace of magic but tried to enhance anyway.

Taking his hand away, he said, "Hopefully that will help."

"Can I try magic again?"

"Of course. Let's go outside." Ben said.

Cam practically ran down the wooden steps, with Ben trailing behind him.

Placing his palm to the ground, he could feel the water flowing beneath the ground. His heart raced with excitement, and he pulled a stream of water out of the ground with less difficulty than before.

Ben smiled with satisfaction, as Cam jumped to his feet, jumping up and down in excitement. "Did you see that?"

"I did. That was much better. I will teach you how to feel all the elements beneath the ground."

"Awesome. I can't wait."

"Don't rush it. It will come."

"This is so exciting."

"Magic is a gift. Don't ever make the mistake your ancestors did. I'm the last person that should say this, but I'm going to say it anyway. Don't ever abuse the gift."

Cam's eyes widened in surprise. "I would never do that sir. I give you, my word."

Ben laughed. "Good to hear. Now, get some rest and come back tomorrow and be ready to go to work."

Cam woke early, ate a quick breakfast, and went outside. Looking across his back yard at the colorful buildings behind his house, he smiled. He liked the recent changes and was excited about learning magic.

He sat down in the cool grass and placed his palms on the ground out in front of him.

He ignored the grass threaded beneath his fingers and concentrated on the elements he could feel below.

He could feel the power, but it was just out of reach.

Closing out the world around him, he concentrated, putting all his energy into reaching the water buried beneath the earth.

Cam felt a sudden surge of energy as water burst out of the ground, drenching him.

Startled, he put up his hand and moved the water away from him. Smiling, he practiced controlling the stream of water before releasing it, to return beneath the surface.

Excited, he jumped up and down, pumping his fist in the air as he rushed off to his job on the farm. He used his newly discovered powers to water and feed the vegetable plants thriving beneath an enormous tent that covered the healthy plants for several blocks.

Ben tested student after student and finally discovered fifteen-year-old, Tesa, who easily passed his simple test.

Cam was surprised to see Ben and Tesa waiting for him in the garden.

The sun was setting as he joined them at the training center beneath Ben's home.

"Tesa, Ben. Ben, Tesa. You will be training together," Ben said, introducing them.

"Why us?" Tesa asked.

"I wish I knew," Ben said.

"Learning to use the elements is just one way to use your magic. Potions allow you to create spells, thus expanding your magic. Once you master the potions, new potions will be available to you if you're good enough. So, I need you to train on controlling the elements so you can try again to choose potions. Without the potions, it will be harder for your magic to grow stronger."

"So, if we get better, the potions will choose us?" Cam asked.

"Exactly. So, you will work together, devising ways to strengthen your magic, while I complete the testing. If you have any questions, please ask, and use the garden as your training ground. The magic is stronger there."

Ben excused himself to let them train, watching them from the upstairs window, as they sprayed each other with water, then blasting each other with warm air as they laughed, enjoying themselves and their newfound magic.

The weeks flew by as he added three more people to his training, disappointed that there were not more.

Senna, Ramon, and Ami joined Cam and Tesa in the garden for training.

Ben brought a table into the garden and set a box of vials in the center.

"Tesa, you're first," Ben said.

Tesa crossed the glittery path and approached the table. She took a deep breath and concentrated on the colorful vials in front of her.

Her heart was racing, pounding in her chest when she noticed the blue vial moving. She picked it up, smiling as Ben took it from her, pouring the contents into a new vial and placing it in a new box. The vial immediately refilled.

She picked a red and green vial, then smiled up at Ben, as he handed her, her very own box of vials.

Hugging it to her chest she returned to the others.

Cam was next. He picked yellow, purple, and white.

Senna chose blue and red, followed by Ramon who chose pink and yellow, and Ami chose a purple so dark it looked black and white.

Ben raised one eyebrow in concern as he handed her the box.

In the corner of the garden, beneath his temporary home, he led them through exercises to create rain, wind, fire, and snow. He taught them to mix the potions with the power of the elements to make the wind stronger.

He watched Ami closely, and constantly monitored her thoughts.

She concentrated on the tasks at hand, smiling for approval each time she was successful.

"They are doing well?" Iesha asked.

"Very," Ben said, smiling, glad that she showed up.

"Do you have a minute?"

"Of course. Please continue to practice. I will be back in a moment."

His five students nodded and continued their task.

"What are your plans for them once they master magic?" she asked.

"Plans? I don't have any plans for them." He said honestly.

"Then why teach them?"

"It's part of their birthright. I didn't want our descendants to lose this part of themselves."

Iesha studied his handsome face, believing him. "I want you to teach me. I wasn't sure at first, but I too can pull the water from the earth."

A smile spread across Ben's face and gently gripped her shoulders with his hands. "This is wonderful."

"I don't want anyone else to know," she said.

"Ok, but why?"

"I have plans for them. With their help we can prosper and repair and improve our cities at a faster pace."

"What if that's not what they want to do?" he asked.

"Why wouldn't they? It would be their job. Everyone here works, whatever else they want to do with it, as long as they don't hurt anyone, is their business."

"Ok, that sounds reasonable."

Iesha gently touched his cheek. "Not everyone wants to be in control."

Ben lowered his head sadly. "I have to keep reminding myself of that."

Chapter Fourteen

Tying up loose ends

Sierra stepped back pleased with herself. She'd successfully set up a small gate that allowed cell service and cable signals to flow into Pandora.

Bree lived in both worlds, going to nursing school during the day and helping her parents set up the new hospital in the evenings.

The schools were open and filled with students eager to learn.

Mavis was thriving in her new role at the hospital, and Enoc had proposed, so another wedding would soon be taking place.

It finally seemed as if peace had settled over the eight realms.

Sighing with contentment from her position on the balcony overlooking her home, she smiled with pride in what they had accomplished in the last year.

Three flittering Hummingbirds interrupted her thoughts. Raising one eyebrow, she wondered what took three missives to say.

To her amazement a scroll unrolled between them revealing a smiling Mags.

"Sorry if I startled you. I wanted you to be the first to see our new message system," she said excitedly.

"It's like skype," Sierra said.

Mags frowned. "So, I borrowed something from your world," she said laughing.

"Very nice," Sierra said.

"Thank you. I'll show you how it works next time I see you. Which is why I'm calling. Fin and I have set the date, and I want you to be my matron of honor."

Sierra screamed and laughed, clapping her hands. "I would be honored. When?"

"In two weeks here at the castle."

"Wow, he never said a word."

"I threatened his life if he did," Mags laughed.

"Can I help with anything?"

"Thanks, but we've got everything arranged. Just wear something dazzling."

"I can arrange that. I'm so happy for you two."

"Thank you. Invitations will go out later today with the time on it."

"Can you believe that Dak and I have almost been married a year?"

"I know. So much has happened since the day you read my spell."

"Sometimes I can't believe it. It seems like a crazy dream."

"Well, it's not a dream. It's just crazy," Mags laughed. "I will see you soon. Mom's calling me. She undoubtedly has another idea for the wedding."

"Have fun," Sierra said smiling at how normal her life was feeling.

The screen vanished and the three Hummingbirds flew away.

"Well, almost normal," she laughed to herself as she watched the delicate birds fly away.

Sierra watched the city of Pandora come to life before leaving the balcony and going inside. She quickly dressed in her training gear. Today was graduation for their first class in magic. It was a big day for the students.

They didn't know it yet, but today they would all get to ride their first Dragon as part of the celebration.

She met Dak coming out of the bathroom, his hair wet from the shower, and kissed him good morning.

"Are you ready for the big day?" he asked.

"Yes. I was thinking that we should have a proper classroom for the next class and limit the number of students so we will always have a class in training. Sort of make it a part of school for the older students."

"Sounds good to me, and we can alternate teachers so they will benefit from training with all of us," he added.

"The children seem to be enjoying school."

"It has been a good change. Thanks to you, all the realms are thriving and growing. I've never seen so many babies in my life. Before you arrived, we were barely surviving. Now, look at us, babies everywhere," he laughed.

"I'm quite sure I didn't do this alone. I think I had a little help," she teased.

"Maybe just a little," he said, twirling her around and kissing her.

Smiling, they descended the stairs together and stepped outside. The front lawn was decorated with purple and red balloons and banners congratulating the graduates.

Chairs filled the lawn for the guests, facing the stage where the graduates would sit, awaiting their diploma.

Large tables were covered with food and a fountain flowed with the butterflies' special lemonade.

Novice, Sela, and Mori were instructing six younger butterflies as they set up a beautiful spun sugar confection in the center of the table. Their special treats decorated the confection with their brilliant colors and delicate designs. It was breathtaking.

The guests were arriving. Sierra waved to Willis and his family, here to celebrate Jinks' graduation.

Dak waved to Ambro and the other Vampires as they entered Pandora. Ambro looked around in awe.

"It is a wonderful home you've made for yourself son," he said.

"Thank you. I'm glad you could join us. I hear that business is booming."

"We will have to catch up after the ceremony," he said, patting his father affectionately on the shoulder.

Sierra waved to Mags and Fin but lost them in the crowd pouring through the gate.

"We better take our seats," Dak said, escorting Sierra around the growing crowd to the stage, where they joined Eldrick who stood off to one side of the stage. Silver, Fin, Collin, Adam, Jinks, Leiya, four Fire Fairies and five Water Fairies and five Werewolves plus four Vampires took their seats facing the crowd.

As everyone took their seats, Eldrick moved to the front of the stage.

"First, I'd like to thank you all for coming. We are gathered here this afternoon to celebrate the success and accomplishments of these young men and women. They worked hard, and their hard work was rewarded with success. Since this is their day, let's get on with it," he laughed.

He called out the names of his students and handed each one a rolled-up scroll reciting their accomplishments.

Adam turned and faced the crowd, raising his diploma over his head and yelled in excitement.

Everyone laughed and applauded.

Each teacher took turns awarding their students a diploma. Sierra was last and eagerly handed Leiya her well-deserved award.

"Thank you all again for joining us in this celebration. At this time, we have a special treat for our students."

Sierra looked up and the crowds gazes followed hers. Twenty-two magnificent Dragons were circling overhead.

One landed in front of the stage. Sierra smiled at Leiya. "Go on. Take a victory lap around Pandora."

Leiya didn't have to be told twice. She jumped on the Dragon's back, using his bent leg as a step, and they took flight.

The next one landed and the students rushed to take flight, until the last Dragon and rider took flight.

Adam had never felt so alive, soaring through the air astride the powerful animal. This was the most perfect day in his young life.

They soared across Pandora. Adam realized he hadn't seen most of his new home. As they flew by the cliffs where the Dragons lived, he realized there were far more Dragons than he knew.

He hoped that someday he would be partnered with one. He looked down and saw a herd of white Pegasus playing in the river.

The ride was over way too soon and as they landed, the students rushed off to find their family.

Adam slid off the Dragon and nearly tackled Sierra in a hug.

"That was awesome," he cried. "Thanks sis. Today has been awesome."

Sierra returned the hug, kissing him on the cheek. "I'm glad you enjoyed it."

Releasing her, he turned to see Erin, James and Dak smiling at him. Erin and James hugged him tightly. Dak shook his hand and said, "Congratulations."

Before he could say anything, Jinks followed by Willis and his family joined them and introductions were made.

The two boys ran off to join the rest of their classmates. When Sierra saw Ben and Iesha making their way toward them.

Sierra looked at her mother in panic. She told Dak, inside his mind to get her parents out of here.

"I hear the butterflies made their special lemonade and their treats are to die for." Dak said, taking Erin and James by the arm leading them away just as Ben and Iesha reached Sierra.

Iesha hugged Sierra warmly. "Thank you for everything you've done for Leiya."

Ben smiled slightly at Sierra.

She returned the smile. "There isn't anything to thank me for. We've loved having her here."

Without thinking, Ben said, "Please excuse us. I need to speak with Sierra privately for a moment."

"Of course," Iesha said before turning and leaving them alone.

Sierra considered turning him into something nasty, but knew it was time to have this conversation, even if she didn't want to. She couldn't keep avoiding him.

Egon watched them from the other side of the lawn wondering if sparks were about to fly.

"I'm sorry. I really didn't plan this," Ben said.

Sierra believed him. "It's okay. Say what you came to say."

"I swear I didn't know about you."

Sierra stared at him blinking. This conversation wasn't going the way she expected.

"Slow down. Just how do you know my mother?"

"We met one night at a party."

Oh, dear lord. Her mother had a one-night stand. "Was she married?"

"Not yet. I didn't find out until later that she was engaged but was considering calling it off."

Oh good, she only cheated on Dad before they were married.

"You had a one-night stand with a woman who was engaged to another man? That's awesome."

Ben gently put his hand on her arm. "No, that's not how it was. I loved your mother, and it wasn't a one-night stand. She was the only bright spot in my life while I lived in your world. She helped me through a very dark time."

"Why didn't she stay with you then?"

"I don't really know. She told me that she made a commitment to your Dad, and she had to honor it. He was too good of a man for her to hurt him."

Sierra couldn't believe her mother would do this. She reached into Ben's mind and the truth of his words stunned her.

"I think she was confused and afraid. She probably made the right choice. I was such a mess, and she deserved better."

"I'm sorry you were hurt."

"You thought I did something terrible to your mother?" he asked sadly. "I wasn't always a monster."

Sierra felt terrible. "I didn't mean to imply that you were."

"I deserve it. But no one thing, you were conceived in love, and I wish I had known about you."

He turned to leave her alone and Sierra grabbed his arm. "Thank you for telling me the truth. And I have to admit, I'm relieved even if it is a sad story."

Ben turned back to face Sierra. A face much like her mother's with a bit of him mixed in.

"I just want to get to know you. I don't want to cause trouble for anyone. I've done enough of that to last a lifetime."

"I'd like that," she said sincerely, surprising herself.

"Please don't be mad at your mother. She did what she thought was right. And you can't keep trying to keep us apart. We have to face each other sometime."

"What will you say to her? I don't want my dad hurt."

"I promise that the secret is safe with me."

"Thank you. I can see that letting my mom go was terribly hard for you."

"I loved her and wanted her to be happy, even if it wasn't with me."

"She was happy," Sierra promised him. "So maybe you both did the right thing."

Their conversation was interrupted by Erin and James escorting Sierra's grandmother.

Erin's eyes widened in shock when she saw Ben.

Ben smiled sadly at her as he turned away.

"Excuse me," Erin said and went after him. She put her hand on his shoulder, and he turned to face her. "It is you. How? Are you from this world?"

"Yes, I am," he softly replied, his gaze raking over the face of the woman he once loved.

Erin's eyes widened in shock and understanding. "Sierra's your daughter. I always wondered, but I didn't know. I promise, I didn't know."

"It doesn't matter. That was long ago." he said seeing the distress on her face.

"You must hate me," Erin said.

"Never. Not for a minute," he assured her.

"I'm so sorry."

"There isn't any reason to be. As I told Sierra, you made the right choice."

"She knows? She must hate me."

"For being human? Our daughter is better than that."

"Our daughter," she said softly. "That explains all this," she said, looking around at the magic that was Pandora.

"I guess it does," he said proudly.

"You should get back to your family," he said. "Your secret is safe with me."

"Thank you."

"Nothing to thank me for. Just continue to be happy," he said, turning and walking away, realizing that a new chapter just opened up in his life. He had a daughter, and she didn't hate him.

Erin rejoined her family, forcing herself to smile as she tried to calm her racing heart.

"Who was that?" James asked.

"I thought I recognized him from home," she said.

Chapter Fifteen

Wedding Bells

Sierra hugged Mags tightly. "You look beautiful," she said.

Mags' hair was pulled away from her face and into an elaborate French braid. Interwoven in the pale tresses were shiny silver stars.

Her white dress was fitted to her waist and flared in folds at her slender hips.

In her ears were tiny silver stars that jingled when she walked.

"You don't look so bad yourself," Mags said smiling approvingly at the off the shoulder teal dress that hugged Sierra's slender figure.

Mavis and her mother burst into the room. Mavis's dress was the same color as Sierra's but a different style that clasped together at the base of her neck and was slit up one side, showing off her shapely legs.

Eleanor hugged Mags briefly. "Are you ready dear?"

"Absolutely," Mags said smiling.

"Take your places ladies," Eleanor said.

Mavis and Sierra stood at the threshold to the castle chapel. Dak and Quinn stood next to Fin at the altar.

The ethereal music started, and Mavis started slowly down the aisle, stopping at the bottom step. Sierra followed a few steps behind her, taking her place on the top step.

The music picked up the pace a little as Mags crossed the threshold and started down the aisle.

Fin stepped down, taking her hand, facing her at the altar.

"We are here to celebrate the joining of two lives. Marriage is a sacred covenant that is to be honored and cherished.

As family and friends, our job is to support and help guide them. Do you promise to honor and cherish one another?"

"I do," said Fin and Mags together.

"Do you promise to love and care for one another as long as you live?"

"I do," they said together.

"I pronounce you husband and wife. Please kiss your bride." The preacher said.

Fin drew Mags to him and gently kissed her.

The crowd clapped and cheered.

Mags and Fin walked down the aisle, followed by Dak and Sierra, then Mavis and Quinn.

The guests followed the bride and groom into the throne room that had been converted into a reception room.

Fin and Mags cut the cake while Quinn made a toast to the happy couple.

A toast was drunk to the happy couple.

Iera and her team had created the most beautiful and delicious cake that Sierra had ever tasted.

"We have to steal her away from Mags," Sierra whispered to Dak.

"I'm not opposed to kidnapping her," he teased.

"Do you have a butterfly net?" she giggled.

Dak reached over, taking her glass of champaign out of her hand.

"Hey. I'm not finished with that," Sierra cried.

"You are now. You have no idea how lethal that can be."

"But it's so good."

"The bride and groom are leaving, and so should we," he said. Taking Sierra's hand, he led her outside.

A dozen white doves dropped tiny silver stars on the newlyweds as they raced for their carriage drawn by two white horses.

Mags waived to her guests as she lifted her gown and climbed into the carriage.

A waiter passed by, and Sierra grabbed another glass of champaign.

Dak tried to take it away from her, but she quickly gulped it down before he could snatch it away.

"You're going to be sorry in the morning," he promised.

Dak shook his head as she pouted at him. "Come on. Mrs. Kellam, it's time to go home."

Dak opened a rip to Pandora and pulled Sierra through it. The champaign was taking effect, causing Sierra to stumble, then giggle when she tried to catch herself.

Dak caught her and set her on the bed waving a hand in front of her, he exchanged her wedding finery for a tea shirt and shorts. Pushing her backward on the bed, he caused her to giggle again and covered her with a blanket.

Sierra tried to sit up and groaned and laid back down against the pillows and giggled again before she fell asleep.

Dak extinguished the lights, shaking his head and laughed, leaving her alone in the dark, falling asleep in one of the guest rooms. He was awoken several hours later by an unholy screeching.

Jumping to his feet, he turned into smoke and raced toward the sound. Passing through the keyhole to his bedroom he retook human form with his mouth hanging open.

Sierra was sound asleep while dozens of strange birds that looked like elephants, tigers, bears, and giraffes flew around the room. He started to make them disappear when he realized they were living creatures, and he relocated them to the far side of the city.

He cast a spell over Sierra so she wouldn't dream and returned to the guest room to get some sleep. He couldn't help laughing as he pulled the covers up to his shoulder and closed his eyes.

Sierra awoke early the next morning as the sun's rays shined through the windows. She groaned when she opened her eyes. The room spun and dipped as she tried to sit up.

She slowly laid down and closed her eyes. She tried to put together a spell to rid herself of her hangover, but she couldn't concentrate.

Dak entered the room and softly closed the door behind him.

"Can you make this go away?" she whispered.

"Nope. Spells don't work against it."

She groaned. "You have to be kidding?"

Dak handed her a smoking green drink.

She opened one eye and frowned. "It smells terrible."

"It will help. I promise," he said slipping his hand behind her shoulders, helping her to sit up.

Holding the glass to her lips, he helped her drink it laughing as she choked it down, coughing.

"It's terrible."

"Drink it."

"I hate you."

"I love you too. I tried to tell you not to drink anymore."

"I'll never drink it again," she promised.

"I don't blame you. Now get some sleep. It will help."

"Whatever you say."

"Remember that when you feel better."

Sierra didn't hear him. She was already asleep.

Dak kissed her gently on the forehead and quietly left the room.

Sierra woke again around lunch and Dak encouraged her to drink more of the disgusting smoking green slush.

She tried begging him to leave, but not until she'd finished half of the drink.

She finally felt like she could get out of bed, just as the sun went down. She located Dak outside on the balcony.

"Glad to see you've survived." He teased.

"That's not funny."

"I think it is, but not nearly as funny as the animals you created."

Sierra frowned. "What are you talking about?"

Dak sat forward. "Well, while you were under the influence, you created several new breeds of birds. We now have flying miniature elephants, giraffes, tigers, bears, and a combination of a few of them. I've contained them for the moment near the gate to Pandora Two."

Sierra covered her face with her hands and groaned. "I thought I dreamed that."

"Oh, you did. You dreamed them into reality."

"Did I do anything else?"

"No, I stopped you from dreaming after that."

"Thanks."

"Anytime," he said laughing. "They are really cute."

"Shut up."

Dak roared with laughter.

Chapter Sixteen

Things Come Together

Marcus and Treynor hesitantly approached Opaque, grateful for a second chance.

Egon warmly greeted them at the bridge leading to Opaque. "Welcome to Opaque," he said.

"Thank you," said Treynor. "We sort of found ourselves without a place to call home. We are grateful for the chance to start over."

"Come inside. This is the perfect place to start over." Egon pointed them to the living quarters. "Pick out your rooms and join me in the garden."

They nodded and hurried off in the direction of the housing area, choosing two suites. On their way across the courtyard to meet up with Egon, two Harpies flew over the wall and landed in front of Egon.

Sephethe spread her wings in front of Egon as she was joined by Morus.

Egon stepped back ready for a confrontation. Sephethe glared down at him, still stinging from their last meeting.

"What brings you to my humble city?" Egon asked politely.

Sephethe shifted from one bird like foot to the other. "Now that our existence has been discovered, we see no reason to remain hidden and would like to negotiate a trade agreement with you."

Egon was surprised and smiled. "I would love to discuss that with you." Egon turned to a stunned Marcus and Treynor as he waved to Avis to join them.

Avis raced over, avoiding Sephethe and Morus, stopping next to Egon.

"Can you please get Marcus and Treynor settled while I speak with our guests?"

"Of course. Please follow me," Avis said. "There are many jobs that need to be done to keep Opaque running. I'm sure you will find something that will interest you. We train together and work together."

"Sounds good," Marcus said, looking around at the growing, thriving city.

"Wonderful. Let me show you around," he said as he escorted them around the walled city.

Egon escorted the Harpies inside the meeting room. They struggled to make themselves comfortable on the floor.

"Thank you for seeing us. I realize that we met under unfortunate circumstances, but we are not a hostile people."

"I'm aware that you are not responsible for what the creature made you do."

"Thank you. That was most unfortunate," Sephethe said.

"How can we help you?"

"We are aware that the realms have started trading and growing their communities. We would like to be a part of that growth."

"That's wonderful," Egon said, excitedly. "We would love to open trade with your people. We will help you any way we can."

"Thank you for your generosity. I am grateful that you don't hold the unfortunate incident against us."

"If you need help getting started, I would be glad to help."

Sephethe and Morus exchanged uncomfortable looks. They are uncertain about anyone visiting their city.

"Is there something wrong?"

"No. It's just that we've never had visitors before."

"Then I would be honored to be the first."

"We are the ones that would be honored," Sephethe said, pushing aside her nervousness.

"Shall we go now?" Egon asked.

"That would be wonderful," Morus said excitedly.

"Lead the way," Egon said excited to see the home of the Harpies. He followed them in a white mist through

Opaque to the gate to the Fire Realm. They flew over the Elders' city to the mountains of the Dragons, past the Dragon City to the top of a cloud covered mountain. They landed in a lovely colorful city decorated with unusual plants and trees.

Egon landed on a smooth cobblestone street in the middle of a clean colorful town with Harpies of all different heights and colors.

The Harpies stared at the stranger in their city, smiled and moved on.

Egon looked around the Harpy City with the clouds hovering above them. He couldn't resist, and reached out touching one, smiling.

"Your city is beautiful," he said.

Sephethe smiled, "Thank you. We are very proud of it, but we have room to improve. We already have many shops but would like to add more and start a trade with all the realms," she said excitedly.

"I will make a list of the items you have to sell and let the realms know what you have to offer. We can discuss what they have to offer, but I would suggest that you visit each realm to see for yourself and get to know the people."

Sephethe lowered her head and frowned. "I'm sure that would be for the best, but we are a shy reclusive people."

"There is no time like the present to change that," Egon said, covering her taloned hand with his.

"I know you are right," she said, leading him inside a quaint shop that sold the most unusual candles. Their scent was intoxicating. The young Harpy behind the counter was quick to overcome her surprise at seeing a stranger in her shop. She offered him a sample of the sweets also sold in the shop.

Egon eagerly took the sweet from her small, clawed hand. The chocolate melted on his tongue. It was nothing like he'd ever tasted. It would give the butterflies' tarts a run for the money.

"It is truly amazing," he told the young Harpy. Her features were more human than Sephethe's.

The young girl blushed and said, "Thank you."

Please give him a sample to take home," Sephethe said.

She carefully placed the treats in a bright pink box and handed it to Egon.

"Thank you," he said politely bowing his head as Sephethe ushered him outside. She took him to furniture shops, markets, a pottery store, an art gallery, and a delicate glass shop.

Egon was overly impressed by everything he saw and a little ashamed to admit that he had thought they would be primitive.

Sephethe noticed that it was getting late and said, "Thank you for visiting us, but I'm sure you're ready to return home."

"No, not at all. I thought I'd spend the night here and discuss doing business with Opaque in the morning."

Sephethe looked panicked. "Stay the night," she stammered, fighting down panic.

"Is there something wrong?"

"Well …."

"Please tell me what is troubling you. You can trust me."

Sephethe took a deep breath forcing back tears. "If we are to be friends, we must trust one another. So, you will learn the secret of the Harpies and why we stay hidden. Come with me."

Confused, Egon followed her to a small yet crowded outdoor café. She ordered them both a spiced chocolate drink that was warm and refreshing.

The other Harpies were uncomfortable with his presence. Some quickly left the café. As the sun sank behind the mountain Sephethe began to change. Her facial features softened, and she slowly became a beautiful young woman losing all her birdlike features.

Her claw hands softened into fingers as she turned human.

Egon stared in amazement as he looked around at the attractive young people watching him to see his reaction.

"This is your secret?" he asked sadly. "I don't understand."

"I came to you as Harpy because that is how you know me. We never let anyone see us as Harpies. We have visited your cities in the past as humans, but during the day we look like the monster you saw."

Egon squeezed her hand between his. "Do not ever call yourself a monster."

"Thank you for saying that, but we know what we look like, that is why we've kept to ourselves. We are completely human until our eighteenth birthday, then we begin to change when the sunrises and change back at sunset."

"How extraordinary," he exclaimed. "I might be able to help you," he said, having an idea.

"You can make us human all the time?" she asked excitedly.

"Better than that. Being both human and Harpy makes you the wonderfully talented people you are. I would hate to change that."

Her face fell with disappointment.

"But what if I can give you the ability to change whenever you choose? Being a Harpy allows you the strength to defend yourself. You don't want to lose that."

Her blue eyes widened with excitement. "You can do that?"

"I believe so."

"I can't speak for everyone, but I certainly would love that."

"Find out how the rest of them feel about this and I will try to make it happen."

"Wait here. Please don't move," she said touching his hand affectionately. Sephethe raced to the nearby table and told them what Egon was offering to do for them. The three young attractive women glanced briefly at Egon in excitement then back at Sephethe. "Pass the word," she said.

Nodding, they jumped to their feet, and each approached a table while Sephethe went to another table. They too glanced at Egon in surprise.

Egon waved with his fingertips and smiled genuinely happy that he could help them.

Within a few minutes the café was empty, and Egon waited alone, sipping his chocolate drink, waiting patiently.

He didn't have to wait long. Sephethe returned with dozens of people following her. With more to come.

"There are more coming. How can we thank you for doing this for us?"

"More chocolate," he said holding up the empty pink box, smiling.

Laughing, Sephethe said. "I'll give you a lifetime of chocolates," she promised. "What do I need to do?"

"Are you ready?" he asked.

"I'm ready," she said struggling to contain her excitement.

Egon rose to his feet, put his hands on her shoulders and whispered a simple spell and released her.

"That's it?" she asked, afraid that he couldn't help her.

"That's it. All you must do is concentrate on changing to a Harpy to change and the same to change to a human. Try it."

"What if I don't change back?" she asked nervously.

"Don't be afraid. It will work," he promised.

Sephethe closed her eyes and concentrated on her Harpy form and in the blink of an eye she changed, but she no longer looked as terrifying. Her features were more like her human self, but with talons, wings, and a tail.

The crowd waiting for their turn gasped in awe.

Sephethe turned and caught a glimpse of her reflection in the glass window of a flower shop next to the café. She blinked back tears. "I don't know how I can ever repay you. If you ever need us for anything. All you have to do is ask," she said returning to her human form.

Egon smiled, pleased that he could help his new friends. He spent the next several hours changing the Harpies and when he was finally finished, they celebrated by honoring him with a feast. There was roast pork in a sweet sauce, caramelized potatoes, a strange but tasty green vegetable and more of the candy that he had developed an addiction to.

While Egon was enjoying the party with his new friends, Sierra and Dak received a visit from the Echo Spirits she had invited to Pandora.

"We have decided to accept your invitation," Elvia said, fading in and out of view.

"Welcome to Pandora," Sierra said, offering her and her friend a seat on the balcony.

They appeared to have the substance of a spirit as they stood in front of them fading in and out. They eased themselves down slowly on the plush wicker furniture and their forms solidified.

"My friend Jalinda and myself are excited to see your kingdom. We are no longer happy in our home since that creature infected our minds."

"The creature is gone," Dak reminded them.

"But our association with the creature has tainted us," Elvia said.

"I'm sorry to hear that," Sierra said. "You are welcome in Pandora."

"Thank you," said Jalinda. "There is a dozen of us that wish to relocate."

"I'm embarrassed to ask, but we are used to our home environment...." Elvia trailed off.

"If you tell me what you require, I can create it for you."

"Thank you. We promise not to cause you any trouble. We are a peaceful people. I don't know what that creature did to us."

"You are not responsible for what he did," Dak said.

"Thank you for saying that, but our people feel we share in the blame," Jalinda said.

"I have the perfect place for you behind the Dragon's mountain. It is secluded and the perfect new home for you."

"You are too kind. You won't regret this," Elvia said.

Sierra kissed Dak. "I'll be back in a bit." Turning to the Echo Spirits she said, "Follow me."

She turned into a white mist and raced across Pandora to the Dragon's mountain. She circled around the left side of the mountain where the river wound its way around the mountain.

Elvia and Jalinda landed in the tall green grass and admired their new home. A waterfall cascaded down the side of the mountain emptying in a crystal-clear lake that connected to the rivers throughout Pandora.

Low hanging clouds hung just beyond the treetops.

"It's beautiful here," Jalinda said.

"I've invited Wind Spirits, Sylphs, Tree Nymphs, Mist Elves, Nymphs, and Flower Fairies to make their home here as well.

The two Echo Spirits glanced briefly at each other, unsure of living with all these different people. "Elvia said, "Your realm is home to many of these species already?"

"Is there a problem?" Sierra asked.

"No. We're just not used to living with so many people," Elvia said.

"You are all very private, so I doubt you will run into each other, but at the same time, you can learn from each other," Sierra said.

Jalinda put her spectral hand on Elvia's arm. "It will be good for us to make new friends. We need to learn how to interact better with others. The creature may not have been able to affect us so easily if we hadn't been so alone."

"You're not alone anymore," Sierra reminded them. "Everyone in Pandora is family. Welcome to the family."

"We've never been part of a family," Elvia said. "We won't disappoint you."

"If you need anything, you know where to find me," Sierra said before turning into a white mist and vanishing.

"Are you okay with this?" Jalina asked. "I meant what I said. I believe this will be good for us. We've kept to ourselves for too long."

"I agree. I'm excited about our future. Something I've never thought about before."

"Wonderful. Let's bring our people home."

When they returned to Pandora, their new home was teaming with life. The Nymphs, Spirits, Fairies, Elves, and Sylphs were settling into different areas. The Flower

Fairies looked like delicate flowers with tiny faces spread out across the meadow, laughing as they took root in their new home. With their eyes closed, they resembled ordinary flowers.

The Sylphs and Wind Spirits went off together, floating above the clouds, the sun's rays casting a kaleidoscope of colors on the ground as it reflected off of their iridescent wings.

Some of the Nymphs went off to the waterfall with the Mist Elves, blending in with the blue water, and finding a labyrinth of caves behind and beneath the waterfall.

The remaining Nymphs faded into the forest with the Tree Nymphs, finding homes inside hollowed out, living trees.

The Echo Spirits faded out to explore their new home.

Chapter Seventeen

Unlikely Friends

Sierra's head jerked around in surprise, listening. Something was suddenly different in Pandora.

"What is it?" Dak asked, looking out over the city, shifting the shopping bags to his left hand.

"Someone or something just entered Pandora," she said.

"Where?"

Sierra listened as she reached out across Pandora. Her eyes widened in surprise and concern. The bags she and Dak were carrying from their shopping trip vanished, appearing in their bedroom.

"We have visitors near the underwater kingdom of Yarnish and Kellam's people."

"Let's go," Dak said turning to black smoke. Sierra followed in her white mist form. They raced across Pandora to the Eastern most point of Pandora.

She felt them the moment she landed. "They're in the water," she said just before she dove in.

Dak dove in seconds behind her, surprised when he could breathe beneath the water. As they swam deeper, they encountered the most beautiful and fierce looking Sea Dragon and Selkies working together to build something.

"Excuse me," Sierra said inside their minds. "What are you doing?"

Startled, they stopped and stared at Sierra and Dak in surprise.

"We were told that we would be welcome here," the turquoise and blue Sea Dragon replied, blinking its big blue eyes.

"Do you mind coming to the surface so we can talk for a minute?"

They nodded in agreement, following Sierra and Dak to the surface. The Sea Dragon burst from the water and landed with a thud on the soft grass.

The Selkie climbed from the water, transforming from a creature that resembled a sea lion into a beautiful woman.

"Did we do something wrong?" asked the Sea Dragon, Fallon."

"No," Sierra assured him. "We didn't know you were coming. How did you get to Pandora?"

"Through the gate," said Ashleon.

"What gate?" asked Dak.

"Kallam said you wouldn't mind," Fallon said.

"Mind what exactly?" Dak asked.

"I created a gate between Pandora two and Pandora," Fallon said proudly.

Sierra hid her surprise. "You can create gates?"

"Only copy them. I'm sorry if I shouldn't have. We needed more room since we decided to relocate from Kallam's kingdom."

"We're glad to have you. Is Kallam okay with you leaving?" Sierra asked.

"We didn't all leave. We have been secluded in her kingdom most of our lives. We'd like to visit more of our world and yours and reconnect with our brothers, the Dragons."

"I hope you don't mind that a few of my people have joined them. We haven't seen Sea Dragons in years," Ashleon said.

"We don't mind. There are other beings living in this section of Pandora. I hope you get to meet them. If there is anything we can do to help you, please let us know," Sierra said smiling.

"Thank you," they said in unison.

"Sorry to disturb you. We will let you get back to work."

Sierra and Dak vanished, leaving them alone to dive back beneath the surface and return to building their home.

Sierra reached out to Lazrus and told him of their encounter. He was excited that the Sea Dragons had surfaced. He was afraid that they hadn't survived the infection.

He promised to pay them a visit and let her know how it went.

Sierra and Dak took human form on the steps of the castle.

"Lazrus is going to check on our new inhabitants. I don't like the way they just showed up here," Sierra said. It made her feel vulnerable.

"Me either. I don't trust Selkies either."

"Well, I'll make sure the Selkies stay put," she said, casting a spell that prevented them from leaving the Eastern edge of Pandora.

"What about the Sea Dragons?" Dak asked.

"Lazrus will know if they can be trusted."

Lazrus and Raziel entered the Eastern edge of Pandora and dove into the crystal-clear blue water. It didn't take long to find several Sea Dragons and Selkies working together to build a home.

"Would you like some help?" Lazrus offered.

"That is most kind of you," Fallon replied, happy to see his Dragon brothers.

Using their magic together, Raziel and Lazrus created an open sided building with sleeping quarters for the Sea Dragons. On the left side of the building were smaller open areas for the Selkies.

"Thank you, brothers," Fallon said.

"You are most welcome," Lazrus said.

"What happened to your kind back in our world? We haven't seen you in many years," Lazrus asked.

"We got trapped in Kallam and Yarnish's underwater kingdom and had to hibernate in order to survive."

"I'm so sorry," Raziel said. "You will be happy in Pandora."

"We are excited to have a fresh start and I'm eager to visit your home."

"We are on the other side of Pandora on the top of the mountains. Please visit at any time."

"I hope we didn't do anything wrong coming here," Fallon said. "Sierra didn't seem very happy."

"You were just unexpected, that's all."

While Lazrus kept him talking Raziel reached out and searched his mind to make certain he was telling the truth. Satisfied, he then visited the Selkie, discovering that she was from the same world and wasn't hiding anything.

"Please visit us soon," Raziel said.

"We must go. We can't stay in the water too long," Lazrus said.

"Thank you," Fallon said. "We shall visit soon."

"Wonderful, and welcome to Pandora." Lazrus and Raziel broke free from the water and flew across Pandora, back to their mountain home. On the way, he let Sierra know that they could be trusted and that the Selkies weren't from the Eight Realms and posed no threat.

Chapter Eighteen

The Gate from Devon Shade

Dak joined Sierra outside on the balcony. He was juggling a plate piled high with eggs and bacon.

Sitting down beside her, he frowned when she stole a piece of his bacon, chewing on it slowly, lost in thought.

Dak moved his plate out of reach as she absently reached for another slice of bacon.

Confused when her hand encountered the table, she looked at the empty space, glanced at his plate, frowning at him.

"Would you like me to get you a plate?" he asked.

"No, I'm fine," she said absently.

"I'm sure you are. What has you so lost in thought?"

"What? Sorry, I didn't hear you."

"Obviously. What's up?"

She laid a miniature gate on the table. "I've been thinking, it's time for us to explore the gate we found in Devon Shade."

"I agree, so what's the problem?"

"This may be the home of the Destroyer, or more people he infected."

"And?"

"And I'm trying to decide who we should take to explore."

"You, me, Lazrus, Raziel and Gerferlum."

"Gerferlum in case we get infected?"

"Yes. If this world is the home of the Destroyer, I don't want to risk a large group on our first trip in."

"I think Eldrik and Egon should be on your list."

"Okay. Then that's our team. We need to be prepared for anything. Take your potions and the cure. This time I'm taking a few tricks from my world."

"Tricks?"

"Hopefully, you won't have to ever find out what they are. I'll send them a missive to let them know our plans. I'd like to go as soon as everyone can be ready."

"Yes ma'am," he said teasingly.

Sierra frowned, glaring at him as she reached for another slice of bacon from his plate.

"Is that one of your tricks?" he asked, laughing.

Within minutes of the missives being delivered, Gerferlum, Eldrik, Lazrus, Raziel, Egon and Mags were in Pandora.

"I don't remember you being on my list," Sierra told Mags teasingly.

Mags put her hands on her slender hips. "You talked me into staying behind the last time. Not this time," she said. "And before you say anything, Mavis, Ben and the council can send a rescue party if we are not back in time, and I've already sent all of them a missive."

"Well, since you've thought of everything, welcome to the team," she laughed, hugging her friend.

Sierra called out to Tharos to see if he would carry Mags on their mission. Egon declined the use of a Dragon. He would travel in mist form.

Within minutes you could hear Tharos' mighty wings cutting through the air. He landed with a thud, thanking Sierra for inviting him to join them.

Sierra stood in front of her exploration party on the lawn, dressed in her signature black pants, boots and dark tee shirt.

"Thank you all for coming on such short notice. We're going through the gate we discovered in Devon Shade. This could be the home of the Destroyer or another world he's destroyed."

"So, we're just going to take a quick look around?" Gerferlum asked.

"Yes, but we have tried to be prepared for anything. You will carry the cure with you in case we get infected. We will have potions with us in case we need them for anything unexpected."

"The plan is to fly across the world and see what state it's in and then decide what our next move is," Dak added.

Sierra loaded her packs on Lazrus as the others did the same. Egon handed his to Eldrik to carry for him. Sierra called out to Collin, Fin, and Silver to guard the gate in their absence.

Fin, astride Shalon was the first to arrive, landing softly next to Mags, taking her hand, and squeezing it gently.

Sierra laid the gate on the ground and enlarged it. The surface of the gate shimmered a dark green, menacingly daring them to enter.

Sierra assisted Gerferlum onto Lazrus. He clung to the saddle horn, holding on tightly. Sierra climbed up behind him, securing him safely in front of her.

Dak led the way on Raziel, followed by Mags and Tharos, then Egon, Eldrik then Sierra. As they passed through the gate, they each felt something strange.

On the other side, they immediately took to the air, Egon in a pale grey smoke form flew between Eldrik and Mags. Sierra was overcome by a sense of strangeness.

They flew over the lush green land reaching out for any signs of the infected. They were delighted when they couldn't detect any sickness. They could sense the inhabitants, but it was weak, not giving them a very clear picture.

They flew above the clouds to remain undetected. Sierra noticed a light being reflected off something on the ground. Egon flew closer to see what it was and was startled to discover that it was another gate.

Egon flew around the open meadow and discovered three more gates. He spread out his search, assuring Sierra that he would catch up with them soon.

His search took him to seven more gates, and he hadn't encountered a living creature. He rejoined the team as they continued their flight across the unknown world. Thirty minutes into their flight, they flew over a large city laid out like a military base back on Sierra's home.

They reached out to try and learn something about them, but they were unable to discern much. They flew past the city and were surprised when they didn't see any farms or farm animals.

They continued their flight for another fifteen minutes before they turned around and headed back to the city.

"We need to get a closer look at the city," Dak said.

Agreeing, they decided to land outside the city. Mags, Egon and Gerferlum would enter the city. Sierra and Dak would remain behind in case they needed rescuing.

Mags slid off Tharos and smoothed her knee length white skirt that reached the top of her white riding boots.

Egon draped his cape around his shoulders, looking more like the Egon she'd first met. Gerferlum put his tiny hammer inside the thick vest he wore, and they headed toward the city walking down a worn dusty road.

As they drew closer, they could hear voices coming from inside.

"At least it isn't deserted like the rest of this place," Gerferlum said.

Before Egon or Mags could reply, two guards stepped out in front of them.

"Where do you think you're going?" one of the tall brutish men asked, looking at Gerferlum strangely.

"To the city," Egon said, trying to sound frail.

"Did commander Slade request your presence?"

Mags, Egon and Gerferlum exchanged glances. Before they could respond the men realized that Gerferlum wasn't a child. He was something they hadn't seen before.

The guards backed up, raising their guns that resembled muskets from long ago on Sierra's world.

"What is that thing?" they demanded, pointing at Gerferlum.

"I'm a Gnome, not a thing," Gerferlum answered proudly.

"Where are you from?" they demanded.

"The commander will want to see them," said the older guard.

"They aren't from the feeders. They must be from the sick gate," the older guard said in alarm.

The younger guard raised his weapon. "If you try to run, we will shoot you. Now move," he commanded.

As they continued toward the city, Mags said inside their heads to do as they said.

They nodded in understanding as they passed through a steal gate.

Mags let Dak and Sierra know what was taking place.

"What do you want to do?" Dak asked Sierra.

"We wait until they see the commander," she said to Dak and Mags.

The heavy gate closed behind them, giving them a glimpse of the city, and trapping them inside the cold grey city that was walled off to keep everyone inside.

Mags, Egon and Gerferlum were led down the main street toward a dark two-story building that was three times the size of the remaining buildings.

They were instructed to ascend the grey concrete steps and ushered inside the cool, dimly lit building. The room was lit by gas lamps hanging on the blank walls.

A third guard stopped them, whispering to the other two guards. He looked at the three strangers and hurried off through the door.

Egon shrugged at Mags and Gerferlum. The door reopened and the guard motioned for them to move forward. As they passed the threshold the third guard stepped in front of the older guard, blocking his way.

"Back to your post," he ordered before closing the door in his face.

The older guard frowned and hurried from the room followed by the younger guard and returned to their post outside the city.

Egon, Mags and Gerferlum were ushered down a dark carpet. They could make out very little on each side of them. The room was too dark.

The only light was at the end of the room from a gas lamp sitting on a battered wooden desk. A man in his mid-thirties sat behind the desk. He waved them forward.

"Thank you, Charles," he said in a soft melodic voice. "You came through the gate from the sick world?" Commander Slade asked.

"We escaped from there," Egon lied.

Slade leaned forward on his tanned arms. "Now why don't I believe you? No one has come through since the sickness. And you don't look sick to me."

"He's telling the truth," Mags said trying to sound sincere.

He studied Gerferlum closely but refrained from saying anything to him.

"We came here for help," Mags said innocently.

Slade laughed. "I'm afraid you came to the wrong place. Put them in a cell Charles until I decide what to do with them, or they decide to tell the truth. I do know that you don't come from the feeders, and you may have managed to fight the sickness, but I doubt it. So, where did you come from? Don't tell me. It will be fun making you confess the truth," Slade said to their backs as Charles led them through a side door and into a cell, locking them inside.

Mags gripped the bars with both hands. "What is wrong with you people? We came here for help, and you lock us up."

"As the commander said, there is no help here. You," he said, pointing at Egon, "can serve in the army, but you two are no good to us," he added, turning, and leaving them alone.

Mags reached out to Dak and Sierra telling them what had just happened. "Did you hear that?"

"Every word. We are going to collect the gates to their feeder cities, then we will come help you," Sierra said.

"Try not to cause any more trouble," Dak teased.

Climbing on Lazrus and Raziel, they raced to the first three gates Egon found. Sierra slid off Lazrus' back and tried to shrink the gates, but nothing happened.

Lazrus tried with the same results. "There is no magic here, little one," Lazrus said.

But Egon turned to smoke," she said in confusion.

"That is different than magic, it's part of who he is," Dak said.

So, Egon and Mags can escape on their own, but Gerferlum is stuck there until we go and get him, great," Sierra said, frustrated.

Removing the potions from her bag, Sierra squatted in front of one of the gates and stirred up a potion to shrink the gates. It took longer than normal, but the potions did their job, and the gates shrunk.

Dak raised one eyebrow, impressed.

Sierra smiled as she picked up the three gates and placed them in the bag next to the potions and returned it to Lazrus' back before climbing on. They raced to the other seven gates where she repeated the process and after ten minutes the gates shrunk and were added to her pack. The only gate remaining was the one to Pandora, which she would have to leave.

"Let's go get our friends," she said ready to leave this world.

"Should we be interfering with them when we have no knowledge of their culture?" Egon said.

"They shouldn't have locked you up for no reason," she said as they neared the city. "Egon, Mags, leave now please. We will come and get Gerferlum."

Tharos, Eldrik, Lazrus and Raziel would circle above the city waiting for them. Egon and Mags started to protest, but Sierra said, "I have a plan, and you have to leave."

Reluctantly, Mags and Egon agreed since their magic didn't work. Turning to smoke they passed through the bars and under the closed door. They stayed to the shadows in the dark room where Slade sat at his desk.

Safely outside, they hurried to locate the others as Lazrus swept close depositing Sierra on the roof where Dak joined her.

They silently made their way down the stairs. Thanks to Mags description of the building, they knew the general direction of the cell.

Sierra shifted the bag slung over her shoulder as she waited in the stairwell for Dak to see if the coast was clear.

For the first time in a long time, she was scared. She had depended on her magic to protect her for so long that it was scary to be without it.

Dak returned, "Follow me," he said. He led the way inside the prison from the opposite side that Charles led them in.

Nearly half of the cells were occupied, and the men jumped to their feet. "Let us out," they cried.

"Shh," Sierra hissed. "If I let you out you have to promise to be quiet."

"Please they are going to execute us," a tall man said.

"Why?" Sierra asked in alarm.

"We tried to leave the army and return home to our families."

"That's horrible. Where are your families?"

"Through the gates," he said.

Crap, she thought to herself. "The gates are gone. There is one West of the city. It won't be open long so hurry."

"How are they gone? What about our families?"

"They are safe. Go to the gate and wait for us. It won't take you to your families, but I will explain everything," she promised.

"Okay. We will make it."

Sierra put a drop of potion on the lock, dissolving it and setting them free. "Go out the back way. It's clear, but hurry."

The twenty or so men raced out the door running for their lives. As soon as they made it outside, they ran to the East end of the city to a small hidden door and ran through it and ran as fast as they could toward a Western gate, praying that it was there, and she hadn't lied to them.

Sierra and Dak pushed open the door to see an annoyed Gerferlum glaring at a large man threatening to shoot him.

Dak turned to smoke and appeared a moment before reaching the man, plowing into him, knocking him away. His gun went off just as Dak hit him. The shot barely missed Gerferlum.

Sierra melted the lock and called out to Lazrus to come get them fast.

Dak jumped to his feet racing behind Sierra and Gerferlum, then turned to smoke to be ready to clear the path for them if he needed to.

Hearing the shot, Slade jumped up and raced across the room to the cell that housed Gerferlum just in time to see him escaping with two strangers.

He yelled for his men as he ran after them. He paused when he entered the prison, then ran after them again. He fired a shot, but it went wide, hitting the wall.

Sierra pushed Gerferlum ahead of her, turned while pulling something out of her pack, pulling the pin out with her teeth as if she'd done it a hundred times and threw it behind her.

The flash grenade went off with a loud bang and a blinding light swept over Slade. The light pierced his eyes, stopping his mad flight after them.

Sierra caught up to Gerferlum and they raced up the stairs to the roof, where Lazrus, Raziel, Eldrik, Egon, Mags and Tharos were waiting.

Dak appeared on Raziel as Sierra practically tossed Gerferlum on Lazrus and with one foot on Lazrus' bent leg, she leapt on his back. They took flight just as Slade and his men reached the roof.

"Burn it down," Sierra said.

"What, little one?" Lazrus asked, thinking he'd heard her incorrectly.

"You heard me. Give them room to escape but burn it down."

"As you wish," he said turning back releasing a stream of fire, setting the building on fire.

Slade and his men dove for cover, some jumped off the roof while others raced for the stairs.

Anger boiled inside of Slade. He vowed to make them pay.

"That was a terrible place. It needed to be destroyed," Sierra said as they flew toward the gate.

As they neared the gate, they saw two dozen men racing in its direction. Sierra and her team landed in front of the gate. "Hurry. I will wait for them," Sierra said.

"I'll wait with you," Dak said.

Sierra nodded. "Tell them to be ready for more refugees."

Eldrik didn't say anything but waited near Sierra as the men reached the gate.

They stopped, afraid of the Dragons and Phoenix.

"It's okay. They are our friends, hurry, they are right behind us."

They hesitated but stepped through the gate into Pandora. Dak and the others followed them through.

Sierra turned to shrink the gate and became alarmed when nothing happened. Terrified she'd lost her magic she called out to the elements, relieved when she felt them respond.

Turning to Lazrus, Eldrik and Raziel, she asked, "Can you carry it away from the city? For some reason I can't shrink it."

"We will take it to the top of the mountain. We can guard it more easily there," Lazrus said.

"Are you sure? We don't know what these people may do." she said.

"But we know what they are capable of, and trust me, they are no match for us," Lazrus promised with a chuckle.

Sierra kissed his scaley nose. "I'd die if anything happened to you," she whispered to him.

Lazrus hugged her with his mighty wing. "Nothing is going to happen to me, little one. Take care of your terrified guest. We will take care of the gate," he promised. Gripping the gate in his huge talons he and Eldrik carried it safely to the top of the mountain placing it on a rocky shelf.

Raziel and Tharos followed closely in case they needed help.

Sierra exhaled sharply and turned to the men she'd freed from the prison.

"Welcome to Pandora," she said with a weak smile.

Chapter Nineteen

The Prisoners

The two dozen men looked around in awe. Avery, the tall thin man, approached Sierra warily. "What are you going to do with us?"

"We'd like to talk to you while we serve you a nice meal," Sierra said. "Please follow me."

Sierra led the way through Pandora and across the great lawn to her castle home. Once inside they followed her out onto the patio, having sent a message to the butterflies to prepare food for their unexpected guest.

Before they reached the patio, she added additional tables and chairs in the corner, removing the large vases filled with plants to provide additional seating.

The butterflies had just finished setting the tables and filling them with food, flying away as they entered the patio.

"Please, help yourselves," Sierra said, taking a seat near the patio door next to Dak, Mags, Egon and Gerferlum.

The men were frightened of the strange beings. They hesitated, having never seen so much food at one time and hesitantly filled plates with fruit, eggs, bacon, sausage, and potatoes.

Sierra stood, taking a crystal pitcher and refilled their glasses with water, juice, or milk. As they ate their fill, Sierra pulled her chair next to Avery and said, "I need to know about your people."

"The people in the city are not my people."

"What can you tell me about the people in the city?"

"They invade other worlds making the inhabitants slaves to feed their army. If you're young they force you to serve in the army. We tried to escape and return home to our families. We were caught and would have been executed if you hadn't released us."

"Where are your people?"

"Through one of the gates in the field, guarded by Slade's army. They conquer other worlds to feed and serve them. They will try to do the same to you."

"Let him try," Sierra said.

"What will happen to our families? They could kill them because we escaped."

"No, they won't. I have the gates."

"How?" Avery asked in disbelief. "How did you remove the twelve gates?" Avery asked in awe.

The men murmured among themselves, and Avery said, "If you speak the truth, when can we see our families?"

"How many gates are there?"

"Twelve," Avery answered between bites.

"Twelve?" Sierra asked. "We only saw ten."

"There are two beyond the city. We know very little about the people from there."

Sierra turned to Dak and the others. "It looks like we will have to go back."

"Are you sure you want to?" Egon said.

"Of course. He is forcing people to serve in his army with the threat of death. We have to help them."

"We will have to enter each world and capture Slade's men so they can't threaten them anymore. Since they are cut off from their home world, they won't know what to do when they can't leave." Dak said.

Sierra created a three-story home beyond the Muricks' neighborhood for the men, thinking that they'd feel safer together. She stocked it with everything she could think of that they might need.

"Thank you for saving us," Avery said, again. "Commander Slade won't ever forget it. He won't be happy until he controls your world like he does the others. We will do whatever we can to help."

"Mr. Slade would be wise to forget he ever met us," Dak said, smiling.

"Do you know if the creature that made the other world sick came from one of your worlds?" Egon asked.

The men looked back and forth at each other, shaking their heads.

"We don't know. We've been told to never pass through the gate because the sickness will eat away your insides," Avery said.

"I've set up a temporary home for you. If you need anything, just ask anyone in town. You are welcome to come to the castle if you'd like or need anything," Sierra said.

"You are most generous," Avery said.

"Our world is very different than yours. We have many different beings living here," she said.

"Like him?" Avery said pointing at Gerferlum.

"Yes. Please don't be alarmed. Everyone here would defend you with their life. Our technology may be different from what you are used to. I hope it doesn't cause you any problems. I have vehicles outside to take you home. I've stocked the house with food and clothing and anything you may need. Please make yourselves at home and we will talk again tomorrow."

"Can we see our families tomorrow?" Avery asked.

"We will talk again tomorrow," Sierra said. "Get some rest."

The newly graduated students were waiting outside in golf carts to drive the refugees to their temporary home. Once they reached their destination, they showed them how the shower worked, where to find food and how to load the dishwasher.

Tired, overwhelmed, amazed and grateful, they were glad to finally be alone.

"This is amazing," Jay said looking around the elegant furnishings.

"So, what do you think about our rescuers?" Bradford asked. "They are no match for Slade's army."

"I don't know about that. You saw the huge creatures," Carl said.

"At least our families are out of Slade's reach," Will said.

"How can, we be sure? How did they move the gates? We didn't see them. They could be lying," Bradford said.

"Why would they lie to us?" Avery said. "They could have left us in our cell, but they didn't. I say we trust them for now."

"I trust that I'm going to get to sleep in a real bed," Jay teased.

Avery laughed. "Tonight, we feast and rest. Tomorrow, we will find out about our families," he said, looking around at the luxurious room.

Slade, Charles, and the other men barely made it out of the building before Lazrus burned it to the ground.

The fire roared and crackled in front of them as they stared at the burning building in anger.

"What do you want us to do sir?" Charles asked.

"Search the other worlds until you find them."

"They said they were from the sick world," Charles reminded him.

"They only said that to throw us off," Slade said. "There hasn't been anyone in the sick world for years."

"Yes, sir. We will search the other worlds. If they are there, we will find them." Charles marched over to a large round gold disk. He picked up a mallet and slammed it into the disk, making a noise that sounded like a thousand symbols crashing together.

The noise reverberated down the gravel streets and within minutes, soldiers were piling out of the buildings, combat ready.

As they lined up, Slade stood in front of them, admiring the army he'd amassed. "Find the people responsible for this destruction and bring them back along with the escaped prisoners."

The army led by Slade's top four general headed to the stables to retrieve their horses and rode out of the city, leaving behind a cloud of dust.

Hundreds of young men on horseback raced across the countryside. They split up into two groups. The larger group headed in the direction of the seven gates, while the smaller group headed toward the three gates.

Arriving at their destination they looked around in confusion at the nearly empty field. Only one gate remained. They assumed it was the gate to the sickness. General Martock examined the ground where the gates once stood and looked at his men with a mixture of fear and confusion.

With no recourse, he climbed astride his coal black stallion and led his men back to base, meeting up with the other team.

"The gates are gone," General Williams said in awe. "What could have done this?"

"I don't know. The commander will figure it out."

Slade frowned when he saw a cloud of dirt heading his direction so soon. He stepped out of the rubble and waited. They couldn't have located them so quickly.

The army entered the city with the gates closing behind them with a resounding metal grinding against metal.

The four generals dismounted and nervously approached Slade, who looked around for the prisoners. "Well?" he asked.

Gulping back his fear, Martock said, "The gates are gone, only the sickness remains."

"Impossible," Slade said, looking at his generals he most trusted.

"He's telling the truth sir," Williams said. "Not a trace of them anywhere."

"Check the gates to the West of the city," Slade ordered.

They quickly remounted their horses, racing through the city to the far exit. They hurried across the green meadow, oblivious to the lush green grass that was trampled beneath the powerful hooves of the horses.

The sparkling brook teaming with fish, held no interest for them. They slowed as they entered the dark forest, scaring away a family of deer.

Two gates stood in a clearing, the sun breaking through the trees, shining down on their glittery blue surface.

Relieved that the gates were still there, General Martock ordered his men to stay and guard them while he returned to report to Slade.

He retraced the previous route as he made his way back. He found Slade overseeing the cleanup from the fire, watching his men remove the rubble.

General Martock slid off his horse and said, "The gates in the forest are untouched. I left my men to guard them."

"Well done General," Slade said. "I want two hundred men guarding them at all times. Also, send fifty men through the gate to guard the other side and to increase production. They will have to make up for the shortages until we find how the gates have been hidden. We are fortunate that the harvest was completed, or we would be facing food shortages. He was so tired of always being afraid of there not being enough food to feed his people.

"Yes sir, but...."

"I'm aware that these two worlds can be difficult, but I trust your men to follow orders. We should also clear land to plant crops here for the next harvest. Get a team on that as well."

"Yes sir," he said, but didn't attempt to leave.

"You have something to say?" Slade said coldly, disliking anyone to question his orders.

"I was wondering sir, if we were going after the ones that did this."

Slade smiled, proud of Murdock for echoing his own thoughts. "As soon as we have things back under control here, we will hunt them down and they will pay dearly for this."

General Murdock smiled, delighted. "Very well sir," he said, mounting his horse to carry out his duties.

Slade put two fingers in his mouth and whistled sharply.

Charles rushed to his side instantly. "Yes sir?" he asked.

"Bring me Sam and Lutack," he ordered.

Charles tried to hide his surprise as he raced away. He walked quickly past the burnt-out building, down a side street and entered one of the bunk houses.

Four men were sitting at a scarred and battered table playing cards. They glanced up when he entered, then returned to their game, ignoring him.

Charles watched them nervously and said, "Commander Slade sent me to get Sam and Lutack."

The two men laid down their cards and glared at Charles. They enjoyed how nervous he was around them.

"He's waiting for you next to the burnt-out building," he added, when they showed no sign of moving.

"You told us, now go," Lutack said, irritated.

Charles hesitated, then hurried from the room. He heard them laughing as the door shut behind him. He wished he had the courage to face them, but he knew he wasn't any match for them.

Frustrated, he hurried back to continue overseeing the cleanup. He heard the door slam behind him moments later and picked up his pace.

Sam and Lutack arrived a few seconds behind him, ignoring him as they nodded to Slade.

"I have a special assignment for you," he said eagerly. "Let's go to my temporary office to discuss," he added leading them to a building across the street from the ruins.

Inside the three-room building a long table with a dozen chairs had been set up. Slade slid into one as the two men sat across from him.

"As you are aware, we had strangers in the city, and they helped our prisoners escape. They said they came through the gate with the sickness."

Sam and Lutack frowned. This didn't sound good at all.

"I need you to see what's on the other side of that gate. Try not to be seen. Take a look around and report back."

"And if we get sick?" Lutack questioned.

"I think you know the answer to that."

"You're the boss," Lutack said sarcastically.

Slade ignored him as Lutack and Sam rose to their feet and left the room.

Outside, Lutack ordered one of the cleaning crew to fetch their horses. The young man covered in soot raced away to return within ten minutes leading two solid black horses.

Lutack took one of the reins and mounted his horse in one smooth move.

"Thanks," Sam said, taking the reins from his outstretched hand before mounting his horse.

They galloped out of the village, turning right and racing across the meadow in silence. The sun beat down on them, their dark clothing absorbing the heat, holding it in, causing them to perspire.

They reached the gate standing alone in the empty meadow. Its green surface rippled as they dismounted.

Sam slowly approached the gate and turned and looked back at Lutack. "Have you ever been through this gate?"

"No one has as far as I know. There was a sickness that destroyed all the inhabitance, or that's what I heard."

"Guess we were lucky none of them ever came through."

"It is weird that they didn't after all these years. I'll go first. Enter right behind me."

Sam nodded as Lutack stepped through the gate and onto the top of a mountain in Pandora. The cool air cooled his damp skin as he looked around at the snow-covered mountain top.

Sam stepped through behind him, pausing to look around. Looking down at the lights of the city far in the distance he frowned.

Lazrus watched them from behind a bolder, hidden in the shadow of the mountain. He wanted them to move farther away from the gate so they couldn't escape through it before he could capture them.

"Looks like a city down there," Sam said.

"No way they are mindlessly sick if they can build a city," Lutack said.

"It's too far down for us to go take a look."

"We've seen enough. Let's go," Lutack said, turning back toward the gate.

Lazrus quietly stepped out of the shadows. Sam's eyes widened in surprise as the enormous Dragon loomed over them.

Lutack looked over his shoulder and shoved Sam through the gate backwards as Lazrus picked him up in his talons and took flight toward the castle.

Lutack was smart enough not to struggle. He didn't want the monster to drop him. He had to wait for an opportunity to escape. He realized that they were heading toward the city. His first thought was the monster was taking him somewhere to eat him. Now he was curious as to where it was taking him.

To his surprise, the monster landed on the balcony of an enormous building. A beautiful woman dressed in black entered the balcony, followed by a brooding looking man.

The monster dropped him in front of them. "The other one got away," Lazrus said.

Lutack is shocked that Lazrus can speak.

"Why are you here?" Sierra asked him.

"Why did you burn down one of our buildings and help prisoners escape?"

"Maybe you shouldn't try to lock up people just because they visit your city."

"We don't like visitors."

"I noticed."

"This isn't getting us anywhere," Dak said. "Lock him up for the night and see if he feels like talking tomorrow."

"He doesn't seem like the talkative type," Sierra said, shrugging her shoulders. "Let me guess, you came here to scout out our world because you like to destroy other worlds and kidnap their people forcing them to serve in your army."

Lutack shrugged. "Lucky guess."

"So, what world did you come from?" Dak asked, "And why do you serve this guy? If you worked together, you could overthrow him and return to your home."

"What makes you think Callis isn't my home?"

"Even more reason for you to protect it and your people," Sierra said.

"What makes you think we need protection?"

"The fact that he was going to kill over two dozen men because they wanted to go home to their families." Sierra answered.

"They broke our laws. But thanks to you, they will never get home to their families."

"Why is that?" Sierra asked.

"You destroyed the doorway to their homes, and yet you criticize us for invading them. Cutting them off from their families forever is cruel."

"You weren't going to let them return home," Sierra reminded him.

"I have no control over that," he said.

"Yet here you are doing his dirty work," Dak said. "What's his hold over you?"

Sierra moved within inches of Lutack. "He holds your families against you."

Lutack returned her even stare. "I don't have a family."

"So, you just like destroying people's lives? How sad for you," Sierra said.

"Put him in a cell for the night," Sierra said, turning and walking away.

Dak took him by the arm. Lutack turned twisting his arm around jerking free. He took one step and Lazrus said, "Going somewhere?"

"Doesn't look that way, does it?"

"No, it doesn't."

Dak took his arm again, led him inside and down the back stairs, putting him in a cell. As he closed the door behind him, he asked, "Wouldn't you like a better way of life? Don't you want to be free?"

Lutack sat down on the cot in the corner. "What makes you think I'm not free? I like my job, and I'm good at it. We will take over your pretty little world, just like we have all the others. We will make you regret destroying the doorways."

"At least the people are free of you," Dak said.

"Yes, but you locked them in with some very angry soldiers."

"That are outnumbered by some very angry farmers," Dak added, laughing as he turned, leaving Lutack alone.

Alone in his cell, Lutack stood next to the bars to get a closer look at his surroundings. He tried unsuccessfully to pick the lock, then sat back on the cot. There was no use trying to escape. He couldn't reach the gate, so he was stuck here unless they sent him home.

Home. He lied when he told them Callis was his home, but at least the doorway to his home was still intact, and someday he might be able to return.

Sadly, he barely remembered his home. He'd been taken from it as a small child and hadn't been allowed to return.

Exhaling softly, he buried his face in his hands. What was the matter with him? Why would he want to return? Anything was better than the life he was living. Slade had them all so well trained that he was too stupid to tell them what they needed to know.

After giving it some thought, there was no way Slade could pull off a full assault on this world. The location of the gate made it impossible. Maybe, just maybe he had found a world where he was safe from Slade.

For the first time that he remembered, he relaxed and fell asleep without being afraid.

Chapter Twenty

Sam

Sam raced to his horse and his foot barely touched the stirrup as he vaulted on his back and raced toward the city. His heart was racing in his chest from the image of the monster coming out of the shadows toward Lutack.

He dismounted in front of Slade's temporary office and raced inside.

Slade rose to his feet as Sam entered the room. He waited for Lutack to follow.

"What happened?"

"After we went through the gate, a giant monster attacked and Lutack pushed me through the gate just as it grabbed him."

"You're kidding?" he asked in disbelief.

"No sir. The gate is on the top of a mountain and a giant monster is guarding it."

Slade turned his back to Sam and said, "How is that even possible? How did they get past the monster to come here?"

"I don't know sir."

"Something isn't right. Are you certain of what you saw?"

"Yes sir. I know what I saw. What do you want me to do now?"

"Nothing for now. There is more happening here than we know. We need more information before we can do anything. We have enough to deal with to ensure the well-being of our people. We will deal with these intruders at a later date."

"Yes sir," Sam said, turning and leaving. He grabbed his horse's reins and walked him back to the stable, handing the reins to the stableboy. "Please retrieve Lutack's horse from the Eastern gate."

"Yes sir," the boy said.

Sam walked down the gravel street, past his barracks to the edge of town. He quietly exited through the gate and walked into the forest. Finding a secluded spot, he sat down on a hollowed-out log.

He slowed his breathing and tried to relax. He was worried about Lutack. He was tired of living the way they were forced to live, and with the other gates destroyed, he'd never get to return home, but the others would be safe now. Slade couldn't get to them. He knew it wasn't all Slade's fault. He'd inherited the problem. No matter what they did, there was never enough food.

Before he could change his mind, he rose to his feet and walked around the walled city, back to the gate. He should have returned immediately and not left Lutack alone.

He slowly approached the gate, took a deep breath, and stepped through.

Raziel smiled down at him and said. "I thought you might return."

Sam swallowed the lump in his throat and stared at the massive creature looming over him. "You can talk," was all he managed to say.

Raziel laughed. "That I can. Would you like a ride down or shall I carry you?"

"A ride would be nice."

"Very well," Raziel said, bending his leg so Sam could climb on his back. "Hold on," Raziel said taking flight and soaring to the castle.

Sam looked around in awe and surprise at the city below.

"Amazing, isn't it?" Raziel said.

"Yes, it is," he replied.

Raziel landed on the lawn after reaching out to Dak and Sierra, who met him on the lawn.

Sam slid off Raziel and smiled at them. "Thank you for the ride," he said.

"You are most welcome."

"Why did you return?" Dak asked.

"I was worried about my friend. I shouldn't have left him alone."

Sierra frowned. "So, you came back to help him?"

"I came back to help you stop Slade."

Dak raised one eyebrow, "And we're just supposed to take your word on that?"

"No, I don't suppose you should," Sam said. "His policies have hurt people on multiple worlds and it's time someone put a stop to it."

"With all the men at your disposal, why haven't you or someone put an end to this?" Dak asked.

"He pits us against each other. We have no friends. We can't trust anyone. If we tried anything, he'd find out and kill us or worse," he said sadly.

"Worse than death," Sierra repeated. This situation sickened her. "No wonder they don't rise up against him. He controls them by fear. Just like Hitler," she whispered.

"Who?" Dak asked.

"The worst man in history on my world."

"You called Lutack your friend. Do you trust him?" Dak questioned.

Sam lowered his head. "No, I don't. He'd probably kill me if he knew I was here talking to you. He's the closest thing to a friend I've ever had."

"Let's go inside. I'm sure you could use some refreshments," Sierra said, leading the way inside, up the stairs and out onto the balcony, giving Sam a clear view of Pandora City in the distance.

"I've never seen anything like this. It's beautiful."

"So, what can you tell us that we can use against Slade?" Sierra asked.

"How do we know he didn't send you?" Dak added.

"You don't, but I hope I can earn your trust. His army is huge. Every available man in all the worlds serve in the army. He has four generals that relay Slade's orders. They are loyal to him. You caught him off guard by destroying the doorways to the other lands. You cut off his food supply and future recruits. But you also made many in his army angry. You destroyed any chance they had of ever going home."

"We didn't destroy the gates," Sierra said honestly. "We moved them."

Despair washed over Sam. "Then he can find them. I hoped they'd finally be free of him."

"He won't find them," Sierra promised.

"If that's true, he will be more determined to conquer your world."

"He's welcome to try," Dak said.

"He will send many innocent men to their death to conquer you."

"We won't kill his army," Sierra said.

"Then he's won already," Sam said sadly, lowering his head.

Sierra touched his hand gently. "Do we look worried? You want us to trust you, well trust me when I tell you, he will never conquer this world."

"How can you be so sure?"

"Trust me. I am."

"Then he will reign terror on the two remaining worlds. Can you do anything to help them? Lutack is from one of them. He may know something that can help."

"He's not very talkative," Dak said.

"I'm not surprised."

Sierra asked Gerferlum to bring the refreshments out instead of the butterflies. She didn't want him to see magic if they could help it.

He entered the patio carrying a tray of sliced beef, cheese, fruit, and a pitcher of lemonade along with the butterfly treats.

Sam was surprised by the sudden appearance of the Gnome but tried to hide it.

Gerferlum raised the tray above his head and slid it across the table.

Sam's mouth watered at the sight of the food. Food was so limited in their world.

"Thank you Gerferlum," Sierra said.

"No problem, my lady," he replied.

"Please, help yourself," Sierra said.

Sam had to resist the impulse to wolf down the food. He forced himself to eat slowly, savoring the succulent food. "Thank you," he said between bites.

"Can you tell me where the two remaining gates are located?" Sierra asked.

"They are in the woods, West of the city. They are being heavily guarded. The city can't survive without its feeder cities. There is always a shortage of food."

Sierra and Dak exchanged glances. They knew he was telling the truth.

"Thank you for the information," Dak said.

"We'd like to put you in the cell next to Lutack and see if he has any information that you don't," Sierra said.

"I'll try anything to help if it will free the men of Callis," he said.

"Callis is the name of your city?" Sierra asked.

"It's the name of Slade's city," he corrected. "My home was Lenora Ralis. It was a thriving happy place until Slade invaded us."

"I'm sorry you have suffered because of him. I have one last question. Where are the women in Callis?"

"There are none. They stay in the feeder cities. They bare future soldiers and do all the farming."

Sierra's eyes widened in disgust. "That's horrible. I can't believe no one has tried to stop him."

"They have and paid for it with their lives. That's why I came here to warn you and hope you might be able to help us."

"We will see what we can do," Sierra said. "In the meantime, see if you can learn anything from Lutack."

"I will try."

"Please follow me," Dak said.

Sam slowly followed him down the back stairs to the jail.

Sierra followed behind them with a tray of food.

Dak unlocked the cell door and pushed Sam inside.

Sam looked over at Lutack and smiled weakly.

Sierra slid the tray of food inside the cell and left the room, followed by Dak.

Alone, the two men looked at each other. "I'm quite sure I pushed you through the gate. Why did you come back?" Lutack asked.

"I came back to help you, didn't quite work out the way I planned," Sam said.

Lutack gripped the bars between them. "So, how do we get out of here," he asked.

"And go where? Do What?" Sam asked. "We can't get to the top of the mountain."

"We should try."

"Why? What do you have to go back to?"

"A hope that I can someday go home," Lutack said wistfully.

"You know that wasn't ever going to happen," Sam said sadly.

"It never will now, unless I can get back."

"Or unless we stop Slade from invading these people."

"I'm listening," Lutack said.

"I'll never get back to my home, but the only way you have a chance, is for Slade to lose."

"He never loses."

"Then it's time he does."

"What do we have to lose," Lutack said.

Sierra sat next to Dak in the conference room where they had been watching Sam and Lutack through the wall. "What do you think?" Sierra asked.

"I think they don't have anything to lose, and that makes them dangerous," Dak replied.

"I agree. That's why I think we should move them to Pandora Two. They won't be able to find the gate no matter how hard they try, and from there, we make plans to steal the other two gates."

"I expected you would want to do that, then what?"

"I don't know. I haven't gotten that far."

"We can't let them starve," Dak reminded her.

"I know that. I bet half of his army would run if they thought they could get away."

"I agree, so how do we get them to run away?"

"Give them a new gate to run to," she said.

"Slade's loyal soldiers would run to it too."

"I haven't worked all of this out yet," she said shrugging. "Let's get them moved. We need to relocate our war party to Pandora Two until after we take the other two gates."

"I'll send out missives. We can use more Vampires and Shifters since your magic doesn't work there."

"Sounds like a plan. I have technology that will take the place of my magic," she said reaching over and kissing him softly. "I'll see you and everyone in Pandora Two. Please ask Eldrik and Lazrus to bring the gate with them. I will put up a barrier that will stop anyone from leaving Pandora Two."

Dak kissed her again. "We will see you soon. He won't be expecting us to return so soon, or at all, so we will have the element of surprise."

Sierra waved her hand, opening a rip and vanished, reappearing in Pandora Two. She changed their home to resemble the original and put up a protective barrier around the entire lands of Pandora Two.

She reached out to the Dragons, Shifters, and sea people, letting them know what was happening. The Dragons offered to help and awaited the relocation of the gate.

Dak sent out missives across the realms informing them of the situation. Sierra's army was ready to enter Pandora Two.

Adam, Jinks and Leiya asked to join them. Dak had to tell them that they were not ready yet, but they could help Pandora while they were gone.

Sierra's army had grown to over three hundred. Dragons, Fire and Water Fairies, Vampires, Shifters, Invisibles, Owls, Witches, and Sorcerers were the bulk of the army.

She watched proudly as they streamed through the gate ready for battle. Mags, Egon and Gerferlum were the last to pass through.

Dak entered Pandora Two followed by his father and his army, Aswaa, Elon, Shari and ten other giants, and an army of Gnomes.

Eldrik, Raziel, Lazrus and fifty more Dragons entered Pandora Two carrying the gate and flying it to the top of the Dragon's mountain until they were ready to use it.

Sierra reached out to all of them at once, "Thank you for coming. My plan is for us to go fast and high. I will distract the soldiers with weapons from my world. When the soldiers scatter, keep them away from the gates so I can shrink them. Once I have the gates, get out as fast as you can."

"What is step two?" Mags asked.

"We wait a few days for them to worry about what will happen now that we've taken their food source."

"Desperate people are more dangerous," Egon reminded her.

"We are at a disadvantage if we attack them in their world. We are outnumbered, and they aim to kill. If we can drive them here, fewer people will get hurt," Sierra said.

"How about we drive some of them here immediately after we attack?" Dak suggested.

"How?" Sierra asked.

"Force them through the gate as we encounter them and secure them once they are through."

"It's worth a try," she agreed.

"As they come through the gate, they will have to get them under control and put them in the jail beneath the castle. I've added a door on the outside and added more rooms. Hopefully, it will be enough to hold them," Sierra said.

"Sounds like a plan," Dak said.

Chapter Twenty-One

Battle Ready

Slade readied his army. He added another hundred men to guard to the two gates and moved three hundred to guard the gate to the other world.

He reminded his men that the loss of the other gates threatened their survival. He relocated most of the women and children to the city and immediately started planting fields.

Construction started on new buildings outside of the city on housing for the women and their children, along with pens, barns, and coops for the animals they'd relocated.

They were preparing to be able to sustain themselves in case they lost the other two feeder cities. All guards inside the feeder cities were relocated to help construct new homes and facilities they needed to be self-sufficient.

He pushed them, forcing them to understand his sense of urgency that they prepare for an invasion.

Battle ready, they prepared to be invaded. They were used to being the invaders. Their adrenaline was pumping, and the excitement was so thick you could feel it.

They planned, watched, and waited. Slade and his generals moved through the city getting their people ready.

Teenaged boys sat in the weapon's room cleaning and oiling guns. Another group of boys groomed and fed the horses, making certain they were ready at a moment's notice.

Early the next morning, Dak led the first team through the gate. The Vampires flowed through the gate, appearing like smoke from a billowing fire.

The guards stepped back, unsure what to do, wondering if they planned to burn them away from the gate.

They waved the smoke away, watching it appear to dissipate as the Vampires moved away from the gate.

The second wave through the gate were a pack of fluffy black dogs with large feet and fluffy tails.

"What the hell?" said one of the soldiers. "What kind of trick is this?"

Another guard watched the dogs' race away as the third wave of mixed breed dogs came through the gate, splitting up as soon as they were through.

The next wave drove Slade's army to the ground as Sierra's army flew through the gate on Dragons, giant Owls, Griffins, Pegasus, and a Phoenix.

They were above the trees in seconds, more than one hundred of them.

Recovering from the surprise, they quickly sounded the alarm and fired off several shots at the retreating army.

Wave four was led by Mags, followed by Egon and the Giants.

Slade's army fired at the Giants as they raced to get away from them. The bullets stung but did minor damage to them.

The Shifters were growling and snapping at the soldiers protecting the two gates. The soldiers fired at them, wounding several, who ran back through the gate to be healed.

The Giants arrived behind the shifters, driving the army away from the gates. Sierra dove down and the giants backed away as she dropped flash grenades, blinding the soldiers. She dropped the potion on each gate, shrinking them, grabbing them as Lazrus scooped her up and flew back toward the gate. She had spent time perfecting the potions to shrink the gates quickly.

The army raced toward the gate, intercepted by clouds of smoke. The packs raced around the soldier's legs as they passed through the gate, followed by the Vampires.

A handful of soldiers passed through the gate while defending their home. They were immediately captured and placed in a cell.

As the last three teams reached the gate, which were protected by hundreds of armed soldiers.

Sierra and her army circled above the gate as the Dragon rained down streams of fire next to the soldiers. As they jumped out of the way, Mag's team rushed through the gate, taking several soldiers with them.

The Giants picked up soldier after soldier tossing them at each other, knocking several of them through the gate.

The army scattered away from the Giants, firing at them as they ran. The bullets dug into their skin, then burned into their flesh, nearly crippling them as they tore through their ankles.

They dove through the gate, forcing the soldiers to move back.

Sierra dropped a dozen flash grenades as the Dragons swept the area with fire, unfortunately several soldiers were singed by the flames.

The Dragons hit the gate at an accelerated speed, as Sierra dropped a dozen more flash grenades, blinding them, causing them to stumble through the gate.

As the Dragons cleared the gate, Eldrik grabbed it in his talons with the aid of Barthos. As they carried it to the mountain top, two men came through the gate.

Cade and Nermous darted out of the gate, tumbling through the air. The Dragons caught them and deposited them on the ground between Sierra and Dak.

Fin and Silver grabbed them and escorted them to a cell. Mags and Egon quickly healed the Giants, while Collin, Sierra and Dak healed the Shifters.

Sierra looked around shaking her head. The battle hadn't gone as planned, but at least everyone was all right, and they had accomplished their task. As much as she wanted to help these people, maybe they couldn't be helped without too many on each side getting hurt.

They may have to learn to help themselves, she thought sadly.

Slade wasn't happy that they managed to destroy the other two gates, but he wasn't surprised. His men did well against the odds they faced.

They were not normal people. He didn't know how to fight against giants and flying monsters.

He doubled the guards at the gate in case they returned. He looked up at the night sky as he rode among his men congratulating them for a job well done. He ignored their haggard, scared expressions and pretended not to notice when one would decide to step through the gate in hopes that things would be better on the other side.

Slade rode up and down the gravel streets and realized that things had changed, and he was powerless to stop it. He was glad he'd had the foresight to move most of the women and children out of the feeder cities. Ever since taking over command he'd worried about feeding so many with so little.

He would have to use some of the men to help with farming and ranching until they made it through the next harvest.

When he returned to his office, he was surprised to see dozens of his people waiting for him. Andre bravely stepped forward to address him.

"Sir, as you know, many of us have been reunited with our families and we want to be together as a family."

Slade watched him and the others closely as he took his seat. "Go on," he said.

"Things have to change sir," he said, looking back at the others for confirmation.

"In what way?" Slade asked, truly interested in what he had to offer. He certainly didn't have any answers at this point.

"Not all of us are cut out to be soldiers. Some of us were farmers back home. We raised crops, had children and were happy. I know you can have us killed, but we chose to speak with you instead of running away."

"I appreciate your candor," Slade said, aware of the numbers that chose to run.

"Our world prospered. This one can too. You just need to find a balance. We need families. There is more to life than preparing for war," he finished, relieved that he'd been given the chance to say his piece.

Slade sat back, linking his fingers together. He had to admit it, Andre was correct. Cut off from the other worlds, except one, one that could destroy them, he had to refocus his people.

"You're right about everything. We must be able to protect ourselves and have to refocus our energy. We need to get our farms plowed and expand them. We need to breed our animals and build a new family friendly town and bury that gate so we can live in peace," he concluded.

The men stared at him in shock and surprise. They never dreamed that he'd agree with them.

"Since you are the spokesman, Andre, you're in charge of getting the farms up and running. Don, you are in charge of constructing a new city for our families. We will start first thing in the morning. We no longer have to fear the sickness, so we can concentrate on taking care of our people. Now if that's all, let's bury the gate."

Slade's only regret was losing the feeder cities. He'd hoped to ramp up farming there soon. Little did the invaders know, they had taken trouble off his back. It was getting harder and harder to control all the worlds they'd conquered.

Throughout the night, Dragons brought hundreds of men from Callis to occupy the cells beneath the castle.

By the time the sun rose over the mountain, it had been hours since the last arrival. Dak turned to smoke and rose up the side of the mountain. His plan was to pass through the gate and take a look around so they could decide what their next step would be.

He was careful not to disturb the sleeping, Dragons. They had worked late into the night carrying fleeing men from Callis.

Barthos opened one blue green eye as he sensed Dak's presence. Dak took his human form and waved before turning back into smoke.

He attempted to pass through the gate but couldn't. Something was blocking it. Retaking human form, he put his hand through the gate and pulled it out with a handful of dirt.

He turned to Barthos. "They buried the gate," he said.

"We will continue to guard it in case it is a trick," Barthos said.

"Good idea," Dak said. "I need to let the others know." Dak returned to Pandora Two. Sierra, Mags, Fin, Egon, Raziel, Lazrus, Silver and the Giants were waiting for him.

"They buried the gate," he said.

"Well, didn't see that coming," Egon said.

"What can we do?" Sierra asked.

"Nothing we can do," Egon said. "We can hope things change for them."

"All that's left is to decide what to do with their refugees," Mags added.

"And decide what to do with the worlds we brought back with us," Sierra said.

"Well, we don't have to do that today," Egon said.

"If it is okay with you, we will return home," Aswaa said.

"Thank you for your help," Sierra said.

"Call on us anytime, my lady," he said, nodding respectively before joining his people to return home.

Ambro and his army were the next to leave. Ambro invited them to come for a visit before he vanished in a cloud of smoke.

Chapter Twenty-Two

Refugees and the Twelve Gates

As the sun rose over the castle in Pandora Two, Sierra climbed out of bed not quite ready to face the day.

Dak stirred from the other side of the bed but remained sleeping.

Sierra passed her hand in front of her exchanging her tee shirt and shorts for her signature black pants and tee shirt. Pushing open the French doors, she stepped out onto the balcony, shutting the door softly behind her.

She sat down looking out over the empty lands, missing Pandora city. Exhaling softly, she hated having to make decisions that affected other people's lives. Some days her life was too much, and she longed for a simpler life. At the same time, she wouldn't trade this life for anything.

She dreaded telling the men in the cells beneath the castle that they couldn't return home. At the same time, she could tell them that feeder worlds were safe, and they could return to one of them if they desired.

And what was she to do with twelve new worlds? She needed more information about these worlds before she could decide. She needed to talk to Sam to see what he knew about each world; then she'd have to visit each one.

Satisfied that she had a plan, she opened a rip and entered the castle in front of Sam's cell.

Feeling her presence, he opened his eyes and saw her standing in front of his cell with a small glowing orb. He sat up in alarm. "Is there something wrong?"

"No. I want to speak with you."

"Okay," he said, concerned.

Sierra opened the door to his cell and said, "Follow me please."

Sam followed her past the cells of the sleeping Callis' citizens, wondering how many were here.

She led him up the stairs to the conference room where breakfast was waiting for them. "Please help yourself," she said, pouring herself a glass of orange juice before sitting down next to him. "What can you tell me about the other worlds? The ones you called the feeder worlds."

"Slade invaded them, leaving the women and children behind to work the farms and ranches, taking the men to serve in the army. He also left behind a small army to keep them under control."

"What are the worlds like?"

"I don't know firsthand. Most of us weren't allowed to visit them. From what I heard peaceful until they met Slade. One of the worlds had the sickness, so no one ever went there. The last two, near the forest, put up a fight against Slade's army. They never accepted him trying to control them. Sorry, that's all I know."

"You've been very helpful. Thank you."

"What happens to all of us?"

"I'd like you to return to the worlds you originally came from. If you didn't come from any of them, then maybe you can pick a new place to call home."

"Can we choose to stay here?"

"If that's what you'd like." Sierra said.

"Thank you. It's been so long since I've been home. I never thought I'd see it again," he said sadly.

"My people will make sure that it is safe for you to return, then you can rebuild your lives," she said encouragingly.

Sam covered her hand with his. "You've given us the opportunity to try. Thank you."

"I hope the others feel the same way," she said hopefully.

"If it will help, I'll talk to them," he offered.

Sierra thought for a moment. "It can't hurt. If you're finished with breakfast, now is as good a time as any."

"Of course," he said, pushing his chair away from the table as the sun rose above the mountains in the distance.

Sierra led the way beneath the castle and stood aside to let him enter the first room that had ten cells with ten sleeping men.

She created a glowing orb that cast a warm glow across the room. Sam looked at the orb in wonder, curious as to where the light came from.

As the men pushed away the remnants of sleep, Sierra reached out to her army to let them know that they were visiting some of the gates today and to please get ready.

The drowsy men threw back the cover and climbed out of bed and approached the bars of their cells.

"Good morning," Sam said nervously. "Lady Sierra has graciously offered to return us to the home we lived in before Slade forced us into his army."

"How can that be?" Rurick asked. "The doorways were destroyed."

"No, they weren't. I took them so he couldn't hurt your people anymore," Sierra said.

Rurick's eyes widened in wonder. "Is this true?"

"Yes, it's true."

Tears filled Rurick's eyes. "I don't know what to say. Thank you, isn't enough."

"We will try to return you as quickly as possible. Try to be patient," she said, turning, taking Sam with her.

The men in the other cells chatted excitedly with Rurick the moment they were alone.

Outside, Sierra's army was waiting. She asked Dak to get Sam acquainted with Sven, the horse he would be riding, to join them in visiting the first world.

While Sam was distracted, Sierra created supplies to take with them that included grain, food and building materials. They could send more later if it was needed. She removed the gate from her pocket, enlarging it.

Sam asked, "Are you certain you don't mind if I ride you?"

The black stallion laughed a deep, hearty laugh. "It is my pleasure sir," Sven said cheerfully.

Wide eyed, Sam looked at Sierra and Lazrus, who moved up next to him. "I've never seen a talking horse before," Sam said.

"It is amazing," she said, leading the way through the gate, followed closely by Dak on Raziel and Fin on Shalon, with Eldrik bringing up the rear.

They entered a vast farm that had recently been harvested. A small village was at the end of a dusty road.

As everyone cleared the gate, Silver and Collin stayed behind to ensure that no one tried to leave. The rest moved past the empty fields. Sam broke the silence.

"This used to be my home," he said softly to no one in particular.

As they rode closer to the city a group of soldiers stepped out in the middle of the road, blocking their way.

They looked confused and afraid. A young man with long dark hair stepped out in front of the other men.

"We don't want any trouble," he said more bravely than he felt, looking at the strange creatures he was facing.

"What is your name," Dak asked, stepping forward.

"Sly. My friends call me Sly. Can you tell us what's happening?"

"Commander Slade is no longer in control of the gate to your world," Dak said.

Sly turned and looked back at the other six men and turned back to face Dak. "What happens to us?"

"That depends on you."

"I don't understand sir."

"We don't want to hurt you. We are here to help you take control of this world," he explained.

Sly looked confused. "We don't want trouble. We were just following orders."

"Can you follow new orders?" Dak asked.

Sly looked at the frightening creatures they had with them and said, "Yes."

"Good. I need you and your men to go to the gate and retrieve the supplies we brought to help you rebuild."

"Yes sir," Sly said, his men followed him, careful to give Lazrus, Eldrik and Raziel a wide berth.

Sierra laughed and said, "You scared them to death."

"We have to be tough. It's what they're used to," he explained, leading the way into town.

A small boy saw them and raced away ringing a bell near the center of town.

Slowly, the town's people gathered near the town square, looking at Sierra and her army in terror, exchanging worried glances among themselves.

Sam saw his mother and father in the crowd and jumped off his horse and raced to them. He stared at them for a moment, noting how they had aged, before hugging each one briefly.

"I didn't think I'd ever see you again," cried his mother, Mara.

Squeezing her hand, he said, "These people are here to help us."

"Help us, how?" his father, Bert asked.

"Help us rebuild. Slade won't ever bother us again."

The crowd looked at him in shock. "Are you serious?" asked a young boy. "I won't have to serve in his army?"

"Never again, my lad. We are free." he said excitedly.

"What about them?" Mara asked softly.

"They freed us and look," he said, pointing to the carts full of supplies. "They are helping us rebuild."

The crowd of people cheered and raced to embrace Sierra and the others.

After the supplies were unloaded and stored away, they all sat around a cozy fire near the center of town, drinking a cool ale and chatting about rebuilding and men finally being able to return home.

The young people started dancing, as a group of older men played a lively tune, and a celebration began that lasted longer than Sierra and her army stayed.

"The gate will remain open for now. If you need anything, just let us know. Once we visit the other worlds, we will decide the best way to proceed," Sierra said as they said their goodbyes.

"Thank you again for what you've done for us," Sam said, bidding them farewell.

Sierra and her army returned home. "That went well," Dak said.

"Much better than expected," Fin added.

Sierra smiled, pulled the next gate from her pocket, and placed it on the ground, enlarging it. She created more supplies as an offer of friendship, and they stepped through the gate. Sven bowed and left them as they entered the gate.

This world was almost exactly like the last. They didn't encounter any guards as they made their way down the narrow-overgrown road to the small town.

As before, the fields had been harvested and everything was quiet. As they entered the dilapidated town, a weary soldier raced up to them looking at Lazrus, Raziel and Eldrik in fear.

"I don't want trouble," he said, laying his weapon on the ground.

Sierra looked at his worn uniform and dark rimmed eyes and frowned. He was malnourished and afraid.

"We are here to help," Dak said, picking up his weapon and handing it back to him. "Please get the villagers. We've brought food and supplies."

His eyes filled with tears of gratitude as he raced off to get the town's people.

It broke Sierra's heart to see how thin and tired they were. She drew some of the women to the baskets of food and their eyes widened in shock as they helped set out plates of beef, bread, cheese, fruit, and deserts for the starving townspeople.

As they ate, they relaxed and began to talk. "Our crops didn't yield enough this year. So, there was little left for us," Brian, the mayor of the town said. "This food has saved our lives."

"We will send more when we return home," Sierra promised, watching the women admire the bolts of cloth she'd added.

"Are we really free from Slade robbing us blind? What about our men that he forced to serve in his army?"

"I honestly don't know," Dak said. "We have several men that left Slade's army, and they will be returning soon."

"That is good to know," Brian said.

"What do you know of the other cities?" Sierra asked.

Brian speared a red grape from his plate and popped it into his mouth. "Legend has it, that we were all one world, but a great magic split us up and created the gates. But that's just a story."

"Or is it?" Sierra wondered.

"Thank you for allowing us to visit," Sierra said. "We will send another load of provisions. If you need anything, please let us know."

"Milk for the children, blankets, food, and oil for the lamps," Brian asked shyly.

"We will send that and more," she promised, covering his worn thin hand with hers.

Brian, standing in front of his town's people, watched them leave with a new hope for a better tomorrow.

As soon as they were through the gate, Sierra created all the things they'd asked for, including toys for the children, battery operated lights, coats, dresses, pants, and shirts.

"Fin, will you deliver these to them and show them how the lights work?"

"It will be my pleasure," he said attaching the wagon to two horses and leading them back through the gate astride Shalon.

"I know what you're thinking," Dak said.

Sierra's brows drew together, and she stuck out her tongue at him. "You think you're so smart," she teased. "Why can't we put their world back together? Someone separated them. Then they could help each other rebuild."

"I think it's a great idea. We need to see how many of the worlds go together. Like a giant puzzle," he teased.

"So far, they look similar. I bet the others do as well. My guess is, the two in the forest don't belong with them from what Sam said."

"We should split up and check out the remaining eight. Then we can visit them once we put them back together," Dak said.

"Good idea," she agreed.

They each picked a gate after Sierra returned them to normal size. Sierra, on Lazrus took one gate, Dak and Raziel another, Silver another. Fin, having delivered the supplies, another. Eldrik, Collin, Winter and Egon took the remaining.

The rest of the army remained behind, ready to assist if they were needed.

Sierra entered a lush green world. She knew instantly that this world was different than the others and much larger.

"I don't believe this one is part of the others," Lazrus said.

"Neither do I," she agreed. "We can return later to explore."

Lazrus made a wide turn in the air and flew back through the gate.

Underground, something stirred in the darkness, unseen and undetected by Sierra or Lazrus as they left.

Sierra slid off Lazrus, shrunk the gate and slipped it in her back pocket with the other two gates.

After the others returned, certain that nine of the gates made up one world, they joined hands to increase the strength of their magic and Sierra dissolved the gates, pushing each world inside of one.

Let's send our prisoners home, then I have another idea," she said.

"What's that?" Dak asked intrigued.

"We need to have a chat with Slade."

"How?"

"I can open a rip, then we can use a gate back here and I can use a potion that will dissolve it once we leave."

"And why do we want to chat with him?"

"These people need to be reunited with their loved ones. They are trapped in his town, which I think is part of the worlds."

"He's not going to like that."

"I don't really care," she said smiling.

"I'd like to know who split them up in the first place," Dak said.

Sierra, Dak, and Fin took flight on Lazrus, Raziel and Shalon with Eldrik taking the lead.

Chapter Twenty-Three

Making Peace

Sierra and Dak stood together at the opening of the temporary jail, and opened all of the cells, releasing the Callisians, leading them up the stairs into Pandora Two and the gate leading to their collective homes.

"I apologize for locking you up. We had to make preparations to send you home," Sierra said.

"How is that possible?" Lutack asked.

"If you are from the gates in the meadow, you can return there. They will not be as you remember. They are one world now, as they were meant to be," she said.

The men murmured among themselves, afraid. "How?" Lutack asked again.

"That's not important. Getting you home is all that is important. If you are from one of the two gates in the forest, you can wait here until we return, then we will visit with them."

"I'm from there," Lutack said.

"You can wait here, or you are welcome to go with us to the new world."

"I would love to see the new world," Lutack said excitedly.

Dak and Raziel led the way, followed by wagons loaded with food and supplies. Cows, sheep, chickens, and goats were herded through by Siera, Fin, and Silver along with Eldrik and Lazrus made sure the livestock didn't run away.

The air was fresher, the sky bluer and birds filled the air. The world just felt right, no longer broken.

Dak and Raziel took to the air, visiting each village, informing them of the change in their circumstances and inviting them to come fill their coffers and meet their new neighbors.

They set up a celebration waiting for the villagers to show up. They weren't disappointed. Soon the meadow was filled with people from all the villages.

Sam eagerly led the way toward them, followed by his family and friends.

Brian led his people eager to meet the people from the neighboring villages.

The remaining seven villages slowly moved toward the others shaking hands and welcoming each other warmly.

Sierra invited them to help themselves to the food they'd brought to honor the occasion.

Soon, thousands of people were laughing, drinking, eating, and swapping stories. The men were reunited with their families and wept with joy to be with them again.

Sierra moved next to Dak and smiled. This had been a good day. "It's time to pay Slade a visit, but we have to tell them," she said.

"Let me do it," Dak said.

"My hero," she said smiling.

Dak moved to the center of the crowd and whistled loudly.

The crowd quietened and looked at him expectantly. "We would like to bring all of your family members home. For us to do that, we have to bring Slade's village here."

Cries of "No," filled the air.

Dak raised his hands and said, "Here me out. It won't be like it was before. Only men and women that want to join the army will join. Those that wish to leave will be free to leave. We will leave the gate to Pandora open in case there is any trouble."

"We plan to assist you in any way you need to make sure each village is rebuilt strong and secure," Sierra said.

Sam moved forward. "Can you guarantee us that Slade won't try to take control again?"

"Yes, I can. If he tries, he won't be allowed in your world."

The crowd cheered. They liked the idea of no Slade.

"Do we have a choice?" Sam asked.

"Not if you want to be reunited with your families."

"Look what they've done for us already. We can trust them," Alice, a middle-aged woman said as she pushed through the crowd. "I want my son home."

"Yes," cried several women. "Bring our sons and husbands home."

"Please continue with the celebration. We will return soon." Dak said, rejoining Sierra and the others. "Let's do this," he said.

"Silver, stay here with them please. Try to keep them calm when Slade's city shows up."

"I'll do my best," she said intrigued to see what happened when they were rejoined.

Sierra, Dak, and Fin took flight on Lazrus, Raziel and Shalon with Eldrik taking the lead.

As soon as they passed through the gate to Pandora Two, Sierra opened a rip to Callis that swallowed up the gate as they passed through with it.

They took a flight and headed toward Callis. They passed over the city and landed in the street in front of Slade's temporary office.

Slade rushed out of his office hearing Dak, Sierra and Fin calling his name.

He cautiously approached them as his troops moved between him and the intruders.

"How did you get here? We buried the gate." he asked in shock.

"That's not important. We just want to talk to you," Sierra said.

"So, talk."

"Your city is part of a world that includes all the cities beyond the gates. The people deserve to be with their families," she said.

"You can have an army, but not by force," Dak added.

"I agree," Slade said surprising everyone. "When the sickness destroyed the world through the gate and split our world apart, our ancestors formed an army to keep us safe. It was my job to continue this practice."

"We want to put your world back together. We need your word that you and your army won't hurt anyone and that they are free to leave the army if they choose," she said.

"You have my word," he said.

"Please bring their gate next to ours. I need it moved to Pandora so we can rejoin it with the others."

"I'll get it," Eldrik said, flying away. He landed next to the mound of dirt that covered the gate. His sharp talons ripped through the soft dirt until he hit the gate and pulled it out of the ground, took flight with it and carried it through the gate into Pandora Two.

"We will join you and the others once we rejoin your worlds," Sierra said.

Slade and his army watched them fly away, anxious about what was about to happen and excited and worried about the future.

Once they were through the gate and in Pandora Two, Sierra called out to Egon to come help them.

Egon turned into mist and flew out of the castle and joined them on the lawn, retaking his human form.

Taking hands with Sierra, he squeezed her hand fondly. Sierra linked hands with Dak, and Raziel put his massive claw on Dak's hand, covering Lazrus' with his and Lazrus and Eldrik awkwardly touched claws. Sierra pulled energy from the ground, feeling a brief encounter with something foreign, yet familiar.

The gate to Callis shimmered then was sucked into the other gate. Sierra and the others hurried through the gate, eager to see the changes.

Callis stood one-hundred yards from the gate. It stood proud, ready to defend its people.

Slade and his army stood where they left them, unaware that anything had changed.

"Come join the celebration," Dak said, waving them toward the others. The other villagers stopped and glared as Slade and his army approached them. Men split from the army to be reunited with their families, eagerly hugging them in excitement.

Slade moved in and out of the people apologizing for the way he had mishandled things.

Dak whistled again to gain their attention. "Just so you understand, Slade followed the rules established by your ancestors in an attempt to keep you safe from the sickness."

"This is a new beginning for all of you. I trust you to make the most of it. The gate to Pandora will remain open and you are all welcome to visit," Sierra said.

Several villagers hugged Sierra and Dak before they waved goodbye, leaving them to their celebration.

Once they passed through the gate, Sierra put a spell to block anyone except themselves and the people of the new world from passing through.

She reinforced the spell, blocking Pandora Two from the other realms. Life was getting more complicated.

Lutack passed through the gate moments later, smiling. "Will you be putting my world back together next?" he asked. Many of my people were forced to serve in the army as well."

Sierra sighed, pulling out the two similar gates and placed them on the ground, enlarging them. With the help of the others, she rejoined them. She then sent the gate into the other world, searching for whatever she'd felt before, but didn't find it.

"Please go and gather your people. We have one more celebration," she said, not wanting him to see her create supplies out of nothing.

Lutack rushed through the gate to the celebration. He saw Slade laughing and smiling with some villagers and was amazed. He quickly rounded up the people from his village and returned to Sierra with them following closely.

Lutack led the way through the gate and was immediately surrounded by men pointing weapons at him.

He smiled at his brother, Ramos. "Put that away," he said, hugging him tightly. "Today we celebrate."

The men stood back as Sierra and her people passed through. They eyed the food and animals greedily as they stared at Raziel, Lazrus and Eldrik in fear.

They set up a table to celebrate their freedom and reunification, but they didn't get a warm feeling from Lutack's people. They were more primitive than the people from Slade's world and while grateful for the supplies, they were eager for them to leave.

Sierra pulled Lutack aside and said, "If your people entertain the idea of attacking Slade's world, we will intervene on their behalf. Please tell them to put this behind them and move forward. If you need anything from us, please ask."

"I will do my best to keep them calm and to move past this. We fought a long and hard battle against Slade to keep him away from our people."

"You are free again. Make the most of it," Sierra said, bidding him goodbye, glad to put this mess behind them. They just had one more gate to deal with before they could return to Pandora.

Chapter Twenty-Four

The Final Gate

Having sensed no sign of life on her first trip through the gate, they decided to take a small party on the second trip. Only Sierra, Dak, Fin and Eldrik, including their mounts would be going.

Egon stayed with Silver and Collin to lead Pandora's army if they didn't return in a few hours as agreed.

Fin and Shalon let the way with the others following closely behind them. The air was crisp and cool.

Everything beneath them played out in a splash of color as they soared above the land.

They followed a twinkling stream, hoping it would lead them to any signs of life, but after following it for miles, they saw nothing but snowcapped mountains, streams teaming with life, plants, and trees with a scattering of birds.

"How odd," Sierra said to the others. "This place is beautiful. Why didn't anyone live here?"

"I guess they were afraid to after the sickness," Dak said.

Out of the fluffy white clouds hanging above them a flock of large birds suddenly swooped down on them.

"What the heck is wrong with them?" Lazrus said, ready to fry them. He did love fried bird.

Sierra laughed reading his thoughts. "Let's see where they go," she said.

As they drew closer to them, they could see that they were small, sturdy Dragon-like creatures with tiny pale green, slender people the size of a ten-year-old astride them.

"Let's see what they want," Sierra said. "Don't use magic until we get a chance to speak to them," she added, wondering why she didn't sense them before she saw them.

There was a dozen or more of them and they surrounded Sierra and her party and without a word tried to force them into following them.

"Go with them," Sierra said. "Let's see what they want."

Silently, they followed them down the side of a mountain and inside an enormous cavern. They passed over thousands of eggs of two different sizes.

They were forced to land in the center of the cavern, where an elf-like woman with long dark hair braided down her back stood among the eggs. She wore a green skirt and jacket with dark green leggings and boots. She circled around them, studying them silently.

To their surprise, she erected a large metal cage around them. "Where do you come from?" she demanded in a melodic voice.

"We came through the gate," Sierra said.

"Do you think I'm stupid? How else would you get here?" she said rudely.

"I meant no disrespect," Sierra said, pushing down her anger. What was with the people in these worlds? Lock you up and demand answers.

"I'm sure you didn't," she said smugly. "I haven't seen creatures like you before, but we have been asleep for a long time, while the sickness died out and our land healed."

"The Destroyer infected your land?" Sierra asked.

"I have no knowledge of a Destroyer, just a terrible little man that brought an illness to our world."

Sierra could feel the eggs stirring. They were all about to hatch. They had to get out of here before that happened.

"I guess the world beyond the gate has changed while we were resting. As soon as the others awake, we'll pay it a visit," she laughed, sounding like glass tinkling.

Dak frowned at her, tired of her game.

"We meant no harm, we were just exploring your lovely land," Sierra said.

"Of course you didn't. You were scouting us, and you will say anything to save yourselves, but it won't do you any good. I don't buy your sweet little act, and once the others awake, I'll destroy you and take your world," she said nodding to one of the Dragons, who let out a thin shrill cry that cut through their brains.

Sierra reacted instantly, blocking the sound, but not before they got a taste of the searing pain and inability to think.

Dropping to the ground, she covered her ears pretending to be in pain. The others followed suit.

Sierra took the opportunity to let the others know what she was about to do.

While the elf woman laughed, Sierra opened a rip, and they vanished while she had her back to them.

They reappeared in the center of the eggs where Sierra opened another rip taking hundreds of the eggs with them and reappeared on the other side of the gate in Pandora Two.

She immediately shrunk the gate and turned to the others shaking her head in frustration.

"Well, that was fun," Dak said. "Why in the world did you bring these nasty creatures back with us?"

"I don't know. I felt like I had to. I have a bad feeling about this, and I think we will need them to fight their own kind."

"You shrunk the gate. They can't follow," Fin said.

"I don't think that will stop them."

Egon hurried to her side, looking at the eggs all around them. "What's this?" he asked.

"We have to program them to be good," Sierra said excitedly. "We will need them."

Dak shrugged. "She's had a vision or something," he said.

"What happened?" Egon asked.

"It's what's going to happen, that we have to prepare for," Sierra said, trying to fight back her growing panic.

"How do you know this?" Egon pressed.

"I don't know," she said in frustration. "These people are like no one we've met. They are more like the

Destroyer, and we have to prepare. We can't let them come here."

"You think the Destroyer came from this world?" Dak asked in alarm.

"Yes. We have to return the gate to the world we found it in, cutting off any access to our world," she said.

"Those people don't stand a chance against them," Dak reminded her sadly.

"We can help prepare them," Egon said. Maybe their magic won't work in Callis either."

"But we don't know that for sure," Sierra stated, so we prepare them and build a fortress against them near the gate on their world. If they pass through the gate and don't see the world they are expecting, it will raise more problems."

"Aren't we rushing into this?" Egon asked.

"We have to hurry," Fin said. "When those eggs hatch, they will attack Callis. She said as much. We have to help them."

"Fin, send missives to all the realms. We are going to need help. Let them know we are dealing with the

Destroyer's people without the illness. Egon, we need those eggs to be friendly and on our side. They emit a sound that renders you unable to function as a pain tears through your brain. They possess magic, so we have to assume they can counter our magic."

"Very well my dear. I will make sure they are loyal to you," Egon promised.

Fin quickly summoned the Hummingbirds to deliver the messages as Egon and the eggs vanished and reappeared beneath Opaque, and he began the task of reprogramming the Dragons and riders.

"Are you okay?" Dak asked Sierra.

"I will be once we are ready," she said.

"This has really shaken you up," he added, worried about her.

"I can't battle another Destroyer," she said fearfully. I'm going to take the gate to Callis and warn them. I'll take supplies to prepare them for a war they can't begin to imagine," she said sadly. "Hopefully their magic won't work in Callis, so they will be disadvantaged," she added.

"Do you want me to come with you?"

"No. I'll be fine. Really. Please be ready to go to their world to build a fortress. We need all the sorcerers and Elders to put protection spells to combat their magic."

"We'll be ready. Don't worry. We will protect the people of Callis. I won't let anyone hurt you."

Sierra smiled and leaned into Dak's shoulder. "I know you will do everything in your power to keep me safe, but we saw how powerful the Destroyer was. What can we do against an army of them? We can't let these Dragon people find our world. We have to protect them," she cried.

"We won't let them find us," he assured her.

Sierra created wagons loaded with firearms, grenades, and flash grenades, as well as body armor, helmets, and headsets to block out the Dragon's screech and opened a rip to Callis, closing it behind her and Lazrus. She placed the shrunken gate on the ground before continuing on to the city.

Sliding off Lazrus, she crossed the gravel street to Slade's office building and entered the dimly lit room.

Slade rose from his creaky chair surprised to see her again so soon. "What's happened?" he asked, knowing instantly that something was wrong by the solemn expression on her face.

Sierra felt sick. Guilt washed over her. She hated doing this to them, but protecting her people came first. Taking a deep breath, she said, "Dragons and riders from the last gate threatened to invade your world."

Slade frowned in confusion. "There's nothing in that world. We've explored it several times."

"They were sleeping, waiting for them and the land to heal from the sickness."

"My army is half the size it was," he said worriedly. "If they are no longer sick, what exactly are we facing?"

"I'm not exactly sure. They use magic and since magic doesn't work here, we will have to wait and see. We will be here to help, and I've brought you better weapons," she said.

Slade smiled intrigued, "Better how?"

"Come outside and I'll show you," she said, having a tough time wrapping her mind about going to war with these people. She prayed they'd be able to stop them from entering Callis.

Slade's eyes widened at the body armor. He'd never imagined anything like it. He felt that their chances against the Dragon's and riders just got better.

He rang the gong for his army to assemble and get familiar with the new weapons and gear.

"I'll inform the villages of the situation," he said. "Thank you for the warning, weapons and assistance," he said. "I'm sorry about how things started out with us. We are still struggling to restructure our communities. This is going to put an added strain on it."

"Let's all stay alive so we can make up for it," she said shaking his hand before climbing on Lazrus and flying away. Using the vials to grow the temporary gate, she returned to Pandora.

Dak and half of the people from each realm were crowded together waiting for her. Sierra smiled, choking back tears of gratitude and fear. This was all her fault and some of these wonderful people could pay for it with their lives.

Reading her unprotected thoughts, Lazrus said, "Stop blaming yourself. We went through the gate trying to help. It's the Dragons and riders who are at fault. We did nothing wrong."

Seeing the pain that briefly crossed her lovely face, Egon pushed through the crowd and hugged her. "Don't you dare try and take the blame for this," he scolded her gently.

Lazrus snorted. "That's what I told her, but does she listen? Nope, not at all."

"Thanks guys," she said, smiling, knowing they were trying to make her feel better. "I don't want to ever see a new gate again."

Lazrus spoke to her alone. "You've helped so many people. Without you, so many would have died. Trust yourself as we trust you to do the right thing."

Sierra smiled and took a deep breath as she turned to the crowd assembled and reached out to them with her mind. "Thank you all for coming. There are no words to express my gratitude. These Dragons and their riders are like nothing we've encountered before. They kill for the sport of it," she said, while casting a protection spell on all of them and a healing spell.

"As far as we know, this is the home of the Destroyer, so we have to take every precaution to protect ourselves. We will go in two groups, one to build a fortress in Callis and an underground shelter for them. The other to build a fortress in the Dragon's land and protect it and our fighters. Don't forget that magic doesn't work in Callis."

"Any questions?" Dak asked, smiling weakly.

No one said anything, so he said, "Ready when you are my dear."

Sierra opened a rip right outside Callis. The army had gathered and put on their new gear, ready and waiting for an attack.

It took five minutes for everyone to pass through the rip, and the giants quickly went to work building a fortress and digging out a shelter. They did in minutes what would take them days.

Horses pulled the supply wagons up to the giants and were quickly emptied and sent to gather people from the villages.

Satisfied that they had everything under control. The people with magical abilities moved toward the gate.

Ambro approached Sierra and Dak. "Be careful. My people will stay and fight here."

Dak and Sierra hugged him. Sierra fought back tears. "Be careful Dad," Dak said.

The moment they entered the Dragon world Sierra was overcome by the flood of anger that slammed into her from the inhabitance. Using magic, they quickly built a fortress in white stone, casting multiple spells on it to protect and defend against magic as well as physical assaults.

The witches worked with Mavis and Mags to create spells to attack with, while Ben, Egon and the other Elders examined the natural elements of the world in order to use them against the Dragons and riders.

Ben slipped away and approached Sierra as she set traps all around the fortress. He hugged her and said, "You are the bravest most unselfish person I've ever known."

Sierra stared at him in surprise. "I don't feel brave or unselfish. I feel responsible. If I weren't always trying to fix everything, this wouldn't have happened."

Ben gently touched her cheek. "That's what makes you so extraordinary my dear. Most people would have turned their back on the Calliasians, but you take the fight head on and make everyone's lives better that you touch."

"You don't think we should be here?" she asked in surprise.

"That's not what I'm saying. The fact that we're here is because you have such a loving heart."

"Thank you," she said feeling awkward.

Ben smiled at her and cast a linking spell on her, so he'd know if she was in danger. "I know that I have no right to be, but I'm so proud of you and grateful that I've gotten to know you."

"You make it sound like one of us isn't going to survive this and that's not happening," she said, glancing at Gerferlum and his people, ready to perform their magic should someone get gravely wounded.

Sierra hugged him, kissing him on the cheek. "I want us to get to really know each other, so stay safe."

Chapter Twenty-Five

Dragons and Riders Battle

Rialda stood on a ledge protruding out of the side of the cave overlooking the sea of eggs below. Soon they would hatch, and they would rebuild their cities. The disease had forced those that survived into hibernation, and the next generation of Dragons and riders were ready to hatch.

The mothers of the next generation that she'd created would replenish their population in no time, then they would rid their world of intruders and conquer their world.

She glanced at the two large pink misshapen masses pushing out egg after egg with the amplified sound of giant snails moving across the slick ground of the cave. She hoped this new breed would be healthy since they were magically created.

A glistening, glittery egg swallowed by the mass of eggs cracked. Rialda immediately sensed its presence and smiled. Soon she would have enough to scout for intruders.

A ripple of cracks appeared in hundreds of eggs, and within moments, tiny Dragons and riders pushed their way out of their pearlescent eggs.

The riders sensed their Dragons and climbed over the broken shells and emerging Dragons or riders to team up with each other.

Once they'd paired up, Dragon and rider grew until they reached their full size. Soon the cavern had over two hundred fully grown Dragons and riders. It was time to locate the intruders and teach them a lesson they wouldn't soon forget.

Making a shrill noise from deep inside her throat, Rialda signaled for her people to prepare for battle.

A small, muscled man, just a few inches taller than Rialda approached her and looked out at their new army.

"Are you sure they are ready?" Chase asked uncertainly, staring at her intently with his dark eyes.

Chase frowned. He didn't understand the rush to create magical duplicates of themselves or to start a war with beings they knew nothing about.

He would prefer to slowly rebuild their cities and their empire, rather than to rush to regain what they'd lost by unholy means.

"We will take the newborn on a trial run against these invaders to see how they perform as we gauge the enemy. I won't put our people at risk, only the newborn," Rialda said.

Chase nodded, relieved that she was being a little cautious.

"In the meantime, we need to rebuild our city."

Chase smiled. "I will gladly get a team working on that," he said bowing slightly, turning, and slowly walked away.

He could feel Rialda's dark eyes watching him. Her mistrust of everyone made her a good leader, while her bloodlust made her a dangerous leader that almost drove them to extinction. He refused to let that happen again.

He silently entered a smaller cavern. His soft soled boots allowed him to move unheard into the cave.

Risha, a small blond Elfin girl, dressed in a lime green skirt and yellow tunic and green leggings that disappeared in soft leather green boots, very similar to what all their people wore, except Alexi.

Risha glanced over at Alexi. She was slightly taller than the rest of them. She came from a long line of strong and noble Elfin. She wondered what her thoughts were on the newborn. But she was afraid to ask. It might get her killed.

Chase approached Risha and motioned for the other Elfin to join them. The Elfin gathered around Chase waiting for instructions. Alexi stood apart from the group listening.

"We are charged with rebuilding our city while Rialda and the others take the newborns out for a trial run," he said.

"What is this trial run?" Alexi asked, surprising the others.

"To scout the intruder's home."

"Exactly why are they doing that when we have just awakened?"

"I don't question our leader, and you shouldn't either," Chase scolded.

Alexi frowned but held her tongue. Calling to her Dragon, Alton, a grey-blue Dragon that matched the color of her tunic and leggings, making it hard to tell where she ended, and the Dragon begin when she was astride him.

The other Elfin did the same and they raced from the cavern, into the large cavern, out the mouth of the cave and across the forest to the edge of the massive crystal blue river that divided their land in half.

Alton reached out to Alexi and asked, "Are you going to let her continue to lead our people?"

"What can I do that won't end with getting both of us killed? I can't overthrow her by myself."

"If you kill her, by rights you will replace her," he reminded her.

"I'm aware of our laws, but I will still end up getting us killed," she said wearily.

"Just watch for a chance," he said.

"I will continue to do so," she said, shielding her thoughts from him.

Alexi and Alton landed next to the river. She pictured, in her mind, the city she grew up in. Raising her arms out in front of her, she brought her mind's image to life without waiting for the others to assist her.

She built a massive structure that straddled the river and fanned out across it, reaching up six stories into the sky and out across the valley with a wingspan of twelve stories across, resembling the Dragons that they partnered with.

Each living quarter had a large balcony entrance. Inside, were living quarters for an Elfin and one for their Dragon.

Beneath the structure were Dragon boats used to train maneuverability by hitting the boat at full speed, then the rider, using magic and the Dragon's wingspan to move down the curving river at enormous speeds, a talent that Alexi excelled at.

Chase and the others landed near her in awe at the magic she possessed to create a replica of their city.

Chase frowned worried that Rialda would be displeased.

"You should make two more buildings at the bends in the river," Alexi suggested innocently, knowing that their limited abilities wouldn't allow them to create anything as grand as her building.

Before they could ask for her assistance, she said, "I'm going to make the finishing touches to the interior and pick out my home."

Chase didn't have a chance to argue as she took flight, leaving him alone with his team.

Alexi's friends, Cain, Jax, Kari, Wynn, Carin, Joel, Masso, Ralli, Missi, Braka and her boyfriend Dimitri followed her to the top of the massive building, entering a large apartment divided into multiple rooms.

Alton and the other Dragon left to inspect their new living quarters.

"Let me show you the bathing quarters," Alexi said, leading her friends into the lush, tiled room, shutting the door behind them.

"Can they hear us?" Dimitri asked.

"No. I've blocked them from being able to hear us," Alexi said.

"It's not safe for you to taunt Rialda," Jax said in concern.

"I know. I couldn't help it," she said shrugging.

Dimitri slipped his arm around Alexi's waist and said, "It is a wonderful tribute to our people."

"Of course, it is," Braka said smiling, showing off his perfectly white pointed teeth. "But we can't afford trouble. There are so few of us left."

"I will behave," Alexi promised. "But just in case I've upset her, I have a protection spell that will stop any attempt she makes on any of us."

She slowly raised her hands, swirling the air around them, enacting a spell over her friends.

Jax smiled. "Thank you. I'd really hate for her to eliminate us so soon after waking up." Looking around the luxurious bath with a large square marble tub in the center of the room to the marble sink with water slowly cascading out of a silver wide faucet, she asked, "Do all our quarters look like this?"

"Of course," Alexi said smiling. "Nothing but the best for my friends. You should claim your quarters before the others arrive," she said.

"They will be a while," Joel said, shifting from one foot to another. They are going on a trial run with the newborns to scout the intruder's world."

Alexi frowned, shaking her head. It was too soon after awakening.

Dimitri briefly glanced at Alexi, then the others. "I'm going to pick my quarters," he said, opening the door and calling to Baliss, his red and golden Dragon.

Dimitri sprinted to the balcony, jumped as Baliss swooped beneath him and turned sharply to the right, landing on the balcony next to Alexi's, entering the spacious room.

Baliss trotted to his room admiring the massive bed in the corner of the room, with a shear canopy to draw around the bed to block out the world should he desire.

Next, he checked out his bathroom, eyeing the massive, tiled tub with the wide mouth faucet. Just like he remembered from before.

Rialda stood on the shelf protruding above the newborn. She cast an energy spell over them and linked their minds to hers so they would know what to do.

With six of her people by her side, she led her newborn Dragons and riders out of the cavern, up and out over the forest toward the gate's location. Instead of the gate, she found an armed fortress. She ordered half her team to enter the gate while she led the other half toward the fortress.

She had to admit that she was impressed by how quickly they had prepared for an attack.

Sierra and her people watched, waiting to see what the Dragons and riders would do.

The Dragons and riders burst through the gate and swept across Callis, seeing the newly erected fortress.

They tried to reach out with their minds, but their magic was useless. Confused, they swept across the world, taking note of four villages with the people in hiding.

They headed back to the gate to find that it was blocked by four giants. Changing course, they split into two groups and flew around the gate toward Callis, intercepting Slade, flanked by his army.

Slade held up his hand, ordering them to hold fire.

Fortis and his army hovered a few feet in front of Slade's army, sizing up the situation. Without magic they were at a disadvantage, but they couldn't show weakness.

"What do you want here?" Slade yelled.

Fortis flew forward, looking around at the army opposing them.

"We have been asleep for a long time due to an illness that nearly destroyed us."

"I'm sorry about your situation, but that doesn't explain why you are here," he said calmly.

"We were taken by surprise when your people entered our world," Fortis said.

"Is that why you imprisoned them?"

Fortis frowned. This wasn't going the way he planned. "We were simply making certain that we are safe."

"Right," Slade said tired of his game.

Fortis smirked, "Now, if you don't want to get hurt, get those monsters away from that gate so we can go home," he said coldly.

"I suggest you stop hovering like an overgrown bug if you don't want to get hurt. You invaded my town, and I don't like invaders," Slade said smugly.

Fortis glared at him and turned back toward his troops giving instructions to them.

Slade motioned for his army to be ready. Ambro and his vampire army took position in front of Slade's army, along with fifty or more Werewolves in human form.

When Fortis turned around, he estimated that he outnumbered them two to one. This should be over quickly.

Without the benefit of magic, they flew toward Slade and the vampire army then quickly rose above them, preparing to dive down, but the Vampires, taking their smokey form, flew up, taking shape long enough to grab the newborn Elfin off their Dragon, letting them fall to the ground as they vanished into smoke again.

The stunned Elfin was captured by Slade's men and escorted to the new jail.

From below, it looked like the Elfin were falling off their Dragons as they were engulfed in smoke.

Seeing what was happening, Fortis sent the riderless Dragons after the fallen riders, snatching some of them away before Slade's men could reach them, raining streams of fire at the retreating men.

The fire was useless against the Vampires as they continued to appear and disappear, unseating the Elfin.

Slade's army fired high-powered rounds at the Elfin, wounding several of them and the Dragons.

Bleeding and frustrated they continued to rain fire down on the armies below them as they pushed their way toward the gate.

The Dragons let out their shrill cry, but it had no effect with the headgear the army wore. It was cut short as bullets rained down on them striking their thick hides.

The riderless Dragons moved closer clawing and burning their way toward Slade's troops.

Slade released several flash grenades, blinding them, giving his men a chance to fall back to the fortress.

Once they were inside, he sent rounds after rounds of bullets at the Dragons and riders while the Vampires continued to pluck the Elfin out of the sky.

As they moved nearer the gate the giants moved forward, swatting the Elfin away like flies.

Fortis ordered only his troops to make for the gate between the Giants while ordering the newborn to distract them, then make for the gate.

With hundreds of Dragons swirling around them, Fortis and his team made it safely through the gate. Seeing that they were safe, the newborn rushed the gate. Many of them were stopped by the Giants, Werewolves, Vampires, and Slade's army. They surrounded the wounded Elfin and

Dragons, muzzling the Dragons so they couldn't rain fire on them and put them in separate jails.

Ambro's army took their human form to assist, frightening the Elfin they'd unseated from their Dragons.

Ambro smiled. "That went better than I expected."

They gathered up their wounded and started treating their burns and scratches, feeling victorious.

The moment Fortis and his team vanished through the gate, Rialda focused her attention on the newly constructed fortress.

Sierra and her people waited to see what they'd do. Sierra felt the odd disturbing presence again but ignored it. She didn't have time to bother being concerned with it now.

Rialda cast a spell showering the fortress with an acid rain. Sierra threw up a shield, but a few drops managed to get through, burning through the floor of the fortress, and stinging the back of Ben's hand.

Irritated, Ben sent a wave of chilling air in the face of Rialda and her newborns, blowing them back. Several newborns tumbled through the air, end over end, before struggling to stop their wild descent.

Before they fully recovered, Sierra and Mags hit them with an onslaught of burning insects and a swarm of poisonous flies. The burning bugs left small burns on the Elfin's skin, and the Dragon's hide, while the poisonous flies left burning, inching welts across their flesh.

The Dragons let out their shrill cry with no effect. Sierra's spell protected them.

Rialda and her Elfin kin launched multiple assaults against the fortress, using hot oil, a cascade of arrows, a swarm of fat multicolored bugs the size of birds that dropped colorful ooze that paralyzed everything it touched. Rialda didn't care if she killed Sierra's army, while Sierra's army fought to disarm them, not kill them.

Dozens of Mags' army were no longer able to lift their arms. One of the witches couldn't move, being covered in several colors of the colorful ooze.

Sierra made a mental note to learn that trick. It was quite effective.

Egon cast a binding spell on the Dragons, causing them to plunge from the sky, their wings lying useless pinned to their side. They became frantic, crying out, emitting a new sound that shook everything around them.

Mavis rushed from affected to affected to heal their wounds and cure the paralysis. She brushed her hair out of her eyes and smiled as Minerva joined her, quickly healing the burns on Mavis' arm.

"Thank you," Mavis said.

"My pleasure. We need to teach these annoying Dragon flies a lesson," she cackled, winking at Mavis.

Mavis smiled in understanding and stood next to Minerva, smiling. Together, they sent a blue green cloud from their fingertips out across the walls of the fortress and up in the air. It surrounded the Elfin and Dragons turning them into blue-green Dragon flies.

Confused and bewildered, the tiny creatures flew away from the fortress. Minerva and Mavis doubled over with laughter.

Sierra smiled in appreciation. She grabbed Egon's hand and turned both of them into small drab birds that flew from the fortress, across the valley to the cavern with the endless piles of eggs.

Retaking human form, they looked out at the mountain of eggs. "If these hatch, we won't be able to defeat them. There are too many. I want you to take as many as you can to Pandora Two to train them to fight for us." Sierra said.

"You need me here," Egon said.

"I need you to do this more."

Exhaling softly, he nodded in agreement as Sierra opened a rip and sent thousands of eggs through to Pandora Two. Egon sent thousands before stepping through the rip, leaving Sierra alone with the remaining eggs.

She noticed the two pink abominations spitting out egg after egg and sent a chilling spell deep inside them, freezing them, ending the outpouring of eggs. The pink ooze seemed to melt since it was no longer producing eggs. She then cast a calming spell, sprinkling the eggs with a fine powder that soaked into each egg and into the Elfin and Dragons inside. She prayed that it would change them, making them less angry.

Worried that she'd be discovered, she turned back into a small brown bird and retraced her flight pattern back to the fortress. She flew through the blue-green Dragonflies and noticed a large Dragon leg pop out on one, sending it spiraling toward the ground.

Before it hit the ground it turned back into a Dragon and Elfin rider. Soon, she was surrounded by Dragons and riders.

She dove down into the fortress, taking human form as she hit the ground. "It's time to end this she yelled inside everyone's head."

Lazrus flew to her side, and Sierra climbed on his back. In moments, Dak, Fin, Ben, Mags, and Minerva were astride Dragons and took to the air.

They flew in the middle of the much smaller Dragons, knocking them out of the air with their massive talons.

Eldrik joined in the fight, pushing his way through the smaller creatures, ripping through their tough hides like it was butter.

The smaller Dragons clawed at the larger Dragons and soon the air tasted and smelled like blood, mostly from the smaller Dragons.

Rialda sent out messages to her people and they cast multiple spells only to have them deflected. She called out to the true born to join them. Alexi and her friends heard the call and climbed on their Dragons and raced to the fight.

Sierra could feel them coming and knew they couldn't keep up this fight much longer.

The sky turned dark, and the sounds of flapping wings filled the air.

"We can't win this today, little one," Lazrus said.

Sierra knew he was right. It was time to leave.

Alexi and her friends were the first to arrive. Instead of attacking, Alexi jumped from her Dragon knelt on the blood-soaked ground, placing her forehead on the ground.

Startled by her actions, but trusting their friends, Dimitri, Cain, Jax, Kari, Wynn, Carin, and Joel did the same. Enraged, their Dragons didn't know what to do, but finally followed their rider's lead and placed their snouts to the ground.

Stunned, Sierra watched them, reaching out to them and asked, "What are you doing?"

"Seeking asylum," Alexi replied. "Take us with you."

Before Sierra could react or Rialda could respond, the sky grew a deep blue, and tiny pinpoints of bright light came out of every tree, flower, and plant. They shined and shimmered between the two opposing sides, blinding them, and forcing them back.

The lights continued to come together, growing bigger and brighter. The air around them was filled with tiny bright lights.

After several minutes of the lights swirling around them, they began to take shape.

Everyone, including Alexi and her friends rose to watch the strange lights. The lights swirled and moved taking the shape of something a little smaller than the Elfin.

A few more moments passed as the lights moved from one form to another, making certain they were in the right place.

"They're people," Sierra whispered softly. She was correct. Soon there were hundreds of small men and women standing all around them. They resembled the Elfin, only shorter and had larger pointed ears.

They looked around in surprise seeing the Elfin and Dragons above them and Sierra and the larger Dragons on the other side of them.

A chill swept through Sierra. She felt this presence before, from the Destroyer. She looked at the small people around them. They didn't resemble the Destroyer. She had to be wrong.

Rialda looked at the tiny creatures in horror. "This can't be," she screamed.

"Let's get out of here," Sierra said, opening a rip. Her people raced toward it.

Fortis and his people passed through the gate just as Sierra opened the rip, pausing to try to make sense of what was happening.

Sierra called out to Alexi and her friends to follow them. Alexi hit Dimitri's arm, and he followed her through the rip, followed by the others.

The rip closed behind them as the last of them stepped into Pandora Two.

Rialda stared at the Elfin that nearly destroyed them, before ordering her people to retreat.

The Destroyer looked down at his body, examining his small hands. He was home, and so were his people.

He quickly ushered his people to leave the area, returning them to the other side of the world where they'd lived before Rialda tried to eliminate them.

Alexi approached Sierra and Dak, who were whispering together.

"Thank you for taking us with you," she said.

"What happened back there?" Mavis asked.

Alexi turned to Mavis and said, "Nothing good."

Chapter Twenty-Six

Answers

Sierra turned to Alexi and the other Elfin and said, "Tell me everything you know about them."

"They nearly destroyed my people and themselves," Alexi said.

"I don't mean to be rude," Sierra said, "but they tried to destroy us too."

"While you deal with this, I want to check on everyone in Callis," Dak said.

"I'm sorry. Please, follow me," Sierra said, leading the Elfin to the castle, followed by Mags. "My friends, thank you for everything you did today. Please eat and get some rest. I'm afraid that this isn't over."

Fin kissed Mags briefly before heading off toward the side entrance to the castle.

The Dragons and Eldrik took flight toward the mountain, not far behind Dak's smoke form. Mavis and the others followed Fin to the gate to Pandora, hidden in a secret room on the side of the castle.

Sierra and Mags led the Elfin up the marble steps. The Dragons hesitated and Sierra stopped and turned around to face them. She felt their anger and distrust, but also their loyalty to their riders.

"Please join us," she said sweetly.

They looked at each other uncertainly. Alexi reached out to Alton. "I'm sorry. I know this isn't what you want, but let's see where this goes and if you're not happy, you can return."

"Without you?" Alton silently asked.

"I'll never return," Alexi said softly.

Alton sighed and slowly moved up the steps, followed by the others. Inside the great foyer, Sierra reached out to the Butterflies to please bring refreshment for their guest.

Sierra offered them chairs and the Dragons big fluffy cushions. "I have so many questions that I don't know where to start," Sierra said.

Mags sat next to Sierra facing the Elfin. "Why don't you tell us why you asked to come with us?" Mags said.

Alexi looked around at her friends. "Not all of us are like Rialda," she started. "We were a peaceful people that started using technology to improve our lives."

"We were one of five cities," Dimitri added. "Our city prospered and advanced while the others clung to the old ways and actually started to regress."

"Rialda started an expedition into other parts of our world and discovered a new race of Elfin, like the ones that came from the light," Alexi said.

"She exploited them using them for the unique craftmanship they had to offer," Jax added. "Later she tried to wipe them all out and take their land."

"They fought back," Alexi continued. "Their magic is different than ours but extraordinarily strong. To rid themselves of Rialda and those threatening them, they created a sickness, but it didn't just make you sick as intended, it killed and spread quickly."

Rialda tried to counter the sickness with a spell and a spell to rid her of the other Elfin. Their village exploded in a million lights and the disease spread more quickly. To survive, we went into a type of hibernation that lasted until a couple of days ago," Dimitri said.

"Not a very happy awakening," Sierra said sadly. "I'm sorry how everything played out for you."

"Thank you for allowing us to come with you," Alexi said.

"Yes, thank you," Dimitri said.

"We want a fresh start without trying to destroy each other. Thank you for giving us that chance," Alexi said.

"You are most welcome," Sierra said. "We can use your help."

Alexi and the others exchanged curious looks. "How can we help?"

Sierra took a deep breath before continuing. "We brought several unhatched eggs back with us. We need someone to train them and guide them."

Alexi glanced at Dimitri nervously. "You brought the newborn here? They are like Rialda. They will be dangerous."

"I hope that doesn't turn out to be true. We have made some positive enhancements to them to give them a more positive outlook."

Alexi smiled excitedly. "That would be wonderful. Have any of them hatched?"

"Not yet."

"I would like to be there when they do, if that is all right."

"More than all right. I want you to feel at home here and give the newborn Dragons and riders a chance for a good life."

"Dragoneers, the riders are called Dragoneers. We are paired with our Dragons at an early age. We train and learn with them. We live with them our entire lives," Alexi said.

"That sounds wonderful," Mags said.

The newborn that hatched, growth was accelerated by Rialda. If you want these to be kinder Dragoneers and Dragons, they need the chance to be children and to grow and learn together," Alexi said nervously. She didn't feel she had the right to ask for so much from people she had just met, but she had to try.

Sierra reached over and covered Alexi's hand with hers. "Everyone deserves a happy carefree childhood. We will do whatever we can to see that they get it," she promised.

Alexi wiped away the tears that threatened to spill over and said, "Thank you. I will do my best for the newborn."

"Why do you call them newborn?" Mags asked.

"They are born out of magic, not from traditional parents. Rialda created them to be expendable. I'd rather the ones you rescued never feel that way," Alexi said.

"I see no reason that they know the details of their birth," Mags agreed.

"Neither do I," Sierra added. "May I suggest that we create a warm, welcoming environment for them to grow up in. I can recreate your home if you would like."

"Thank you, but if you don't mind, I can do it. If you will give me a small parcel of land to call home." Alexi said, surprising Sierra and Mags.

"I can do better than a small parcel," Sierra said, smiling warmly. "If you will please follow me."

The Dragoneers looked around at their new home for the first time. The land was lush and fertile with a wide river running through it fed by the snow-covered mountains in the distance.

To her left, she felt a magical barrier blocking off part of the world.

Sierra caught a glimpse of Alexi's home from her thoughts and said, "Please build a home like the one you grew up in."

Alexi's eyes widened in surprise, and she smiled excitedly. "Are you sure?"

"This is your home now. I want all Dragons and Dragoneers to feel at home here. It is part of your history and should be part of their history growing up."

Surprising them both, Alexi threw herself at Sierra and hugged her tightly. The Elfin's head barely reached beneath Sierra's chin.

Sierra returned the hug and said, "As soon as you build your home, we will relocate the eggs and wait for them to hatch."

"Thank you," Alexi said. "What are you going to do about Rialda? She will never stop looking for us, or you."

"She will have a hard time finding us, and I'm sure her hands are full for the time being."

Alexi giggled softly. "That's an understatement."

Sierra and Mags watched in amazement as Alexi created her family home. For the second time in one day a four-story building arose from nothing and spread out across the river. It resembled the Dragons they shared their lives with.

Like before, small sleek boats rested beneath the structure, ready for the games that the newborn would learn and play.

It's beautiful," Sierra said in awe. "Where do you want the eggs?"

"Twenty in each room, except for the top floor if that's okay."

"There's a little problem with that," Sierra said. There are more eggs than you have rooms."

Alexi blinked several times as her words sunk in. "I guess I need another building. Then divide them up and we will work it out as they hatch. Rialda is going to be so mad," she said laughing. "This is going to be awesome."

Jax laughed. "We're going to be parents to thousands of Dragoneers and Dragons. I can't wait."

Sierra reached out, asking Egon to join them as she and Mags relocated the eggs to their new home.

Each room contained fifty eggs, twenty-five Dragoneers and twenty-five Dragons. Each were nestled in a soft velvet bed, totaling twenty-five hundred Dragons and Dragoneers.

Alexi and the others could feel them the moment they were in place.

Egon's smoke form dissolved into his human form in front of the smaller Elfin. He bowed respectively at them and said, "About three hundred of them are about to hatch. We didn't have time to slow the growth process. Come with me, this is a momentous occasion."

Egon, Sierra, and Mags took their smoke form and the Dragoneers climbed on their Dragons, nearly appearing as one and followed Egon's dark flowing form across the castle grounds to the river and up onto the balcony holding the first fifty new lives about to enter the world.

As each Elfin hatched, they took turns comforting them and holding them. They were so tiny, about the size of a newborn kitten. They had big blue eyes and soft pale blue-green skin.

Alexi studied them with interest. "They are different," she said comparing her soft green skin to theirs. "Their eyes are so pretty," she said comparing them to her dark eyes.

"It must be because of the spell we cast on them," Egon said.

"What spell?" she asked in alarm.

"For peace, health and happiness," he said. "We hoped it would make them less thirsty for war."

"My people were not warriors like Rialda. We were philosophers, builders, teachers, and artists. I hope the new breed will bring a new beginning for my people. It is good that they look different because they are different."

A large cracking noise echoed in the room. Jax turned to see a small blue nose poke through the blueish-white egg.

Alexi bent down and picked up the egg, cradling it in her arms. The tiny blue-green Dragon poked its head through the soft shell, scaring it, making him retreat into the shell.

Hearing everyone laugh, he stuck his head out and blinked his big blue cat-like eyes and looked around at everyone and hiccupped loudly.

When everyone laughed louder, he squinted his eyes together, arched his back and growled.

Sierra covered her mouth, but her giggle escaped, and the tiny Dragon leaped from his shell, and flew using his tiny blue-green wings for the first time and flew to Sierra and hovered in front of her growling softly.

His blue-green eyes met hers and he studied her intently, then did a leap and landed on her shoulder and licked her on the cheek.

Sierra laughed, gently patted him on the head and scratched him beneath the chin, making him purr like a kitten.

"He's so cute. I think I'm in love," Sierra said.

The remaining eggs began to crack, and their tiny heads poked out of the shells.

Within seconds, there were twenty-five blue-green Dragons racing around the room, climbing on the furniture, and diving in the bathtub.

The Dragon on Sierra's shoulder jumped down and raced after a tiny blond-haired girl, tackling her, licking her on her face, bonding with her.

Soon the Dragons and future Dragoneers were pairing off, connecting with each other, bonding.

The tiny blue-green Elfin climbed over the tiny Dragons, playing with them, laughing and giggling.

"They are so happy," Mason said, cuddling a newly bonded Dragon and Dragoneer. I don't remember us being this carefree."

"Neither do I," Dimitri said, plucking a Dragon off his head. "So, we're going to take care of all them?" he added.

"Yes, we are," Alexi said with more confidence than she felt.

"Don't look so worried," Sierra teased. "I think you will have an endless supply of volunteers to help you."

"Thank you," Jax said as he was tackled by a feisty Dragon. "I don't think we can handle them on our own."

"When will the next ones hatch?" Braka asked while balancing a couple of Elfin on his shoulder.

"In about a week," Egon said. "I've slowed down the maturation rate as much as I can. These should mature before the next babies hatch. I also slowed down their growth rate, so they won't be adults in an hour, but they will be preteens by the time the next batch arrives."

"Good, then they will be able to help with them when they hatch," Mason said.

"We can take care of these guys for a week, then we can take turns training and nurturing." Alexi said.

"We will leave you then," Sierra said, patting the little Dragon on the head before she, Mags and Egon turned to smoke leaving them alone with their new family.

"So, we're really doing this?" Joel said, brushing back his long dark hair. "This is crazy. We wake up, a war starts, we defect and now we're parents and that's just the first week.

One of the Elfin climbed in his lap and tugged on his hair. Joel thumped him gently on his pointed ears, causing the little guy to sneeze.

"Yes, we are," said Kari. "They may not be true born, but they are a new beginning for our race."

"We have a lot of work to do to train them. We have no way of knowing what level of magic they will have," Alexi said.

"By the way, thanks for bringing us here," Kari said. "That was very brave of you."

"I didn't feel brave. I couldn't stay and watch Rialda destroy us."

"I hope she never finds us," said Missi, her blond hair tangled in a Dragon wing.

Chapter Twenty-Seven

Confrontation

The Destroyer and his people ran as fast as their short stubby legs could carry them. His mind raced as he tried to put the pieces together as to what had happened since his battle with Rialda which resulted in nearly annihilating both of their races.

He ran through the lush forest trampling down vibrant red and blue flowers as they made a path through the forest.

He could hear the forest creatures scurry away in fright as they pushed their way through the overgrown foliage.

Suddenly, he made a sharp left, taking them away from the area of their former home.

"Atmos," cried a middle-aged Elfin named Glory. "You're going the wrong way."

"I know," said Atmos, the Destroyer. "We have to settle in a new place."

Without arguing, they continued to follow Atmos deep into the forest. They finally stopped at the base of a giant tree that barely allowed a trickle of sunlight to break through, casting a pleasant glow on the forest floor.

Tiny flowers floated and danced in the sun's rays before settling on the carpet of green covering the forest.

Breathing heavily, the four hundred or more Elfin gathered around Atmos, waiting for instructions.

"Why don't we go home papa?" Muriel, his daughter asked.

Atmos smoothed her blond hair away from her soft cheek. His fingers lingering just a moment to appreciate that she was here and had survived the war.

"There is nothing left of our home," he explained.

"What do you mean?" asked Eldin. "What happened to it?"

Atmos looked out at his people in surprise. They didn't remember. Maybe it was for the best. Only time would tell. But he had to tell them something, so he exhaled softly and began.

"I don't understand why none of you remember the terrible battle with Rialda, but it nearly destroyed us and her people."

"That's crazy," Cletus, a battle scared Elfin said. "How could we all, except you, forget something like that?"

"I wish I knew. But if you don't believe me. Go to our home. There is nothing there."

"I believe you papa. Why would he lie to us?" she asked the others.

"Where are the rest of us?" Cletus asked.

"I wish I knew," Atmos said sadly.

"Were they lost in the battle?" asked Glory.

"Many on both sides were lost. We escaped by a spell that turned us into pure energy. We've only just been returned to our natural selves."

"You do know how crazy that sounds," Cletus asked.

"I do, but it is the truth. We have to find a place to call home while hiding from Rialda."

"How can we hide from her? Her riders will find us no matter where we go," Glory said fearfully. "Why won't she leave us in peace?"

"She would have if we'd let her make slaves out of us," Atmos said.

"I remember that." Cletus said. "She kept asking for us to make something for her, until we had no more to give. She kidnapped our children," he said horrified.

Relief flooded over Atmos that he had remembered.

"That's right," Leland added. "We snuck into her castle and took them back. I don't remember what happened after that."

"She attacked the village with her riders. They burned it to the ground. We were expecting the attack, so no one was in the village. We had created a spell to make them sick, but something went wrong, and it nearly killed them and turned us into energy," Atmos finished.

"Can't say I feel too bad about it killing them," Cletus said. "But we're all that's left. It's a sad day for our people."

"But at least we survived to rebuild our proud race," Glory added.

"True, true," Cletus agreed. "But how do we stop her from finishing what she started?"

"I know a spell that will hide us from her," Atmos said.

"Are you sure it's safe?" Cletus asked.

"I'm sure," Atmos promised. "If this place agrees with everyone, we can settle here. A small vein of the river is just a few feet away, but small enough that she won't think to look here. The trees won't allow the riders to see us, and the spell will render us invisible."

After murmuring among themselves, they agreed to settle. Working together, they transformed the thick forest into a lovely village with quaint colorful cottages with mushroom shaped roofs.

Tiny colorful paths appeared leading the way to each home and shop. Shops sprung up where beautifully crafted furniture would take shape; culinary delights would be created and much more.

The light of their magic floated through the newly created village casting a soft warm glow around them.

Past the village, plots of land were cleared and planted. A water well took shape in the center of town to provide water for all.

Miniature animals appeared in a fenced area. They resembled cows, pigs, and sheep, only much smaller. Tiny colorful chickens appeared in their new house and began to lay colorful eggs that would need to be collected.

Atmos redirected the lush tree branches to keep everything shaded from view, then cast two spells over their new home to keep it hidden and protected.

One to make it look like a thorny patch with sharp poisonous thorns. He created four actual thorn bushes to make it appear a natural phenomenon.

The second spell would make anyone sleepy if they wandered too close to them. After a second thought, he created a thorny patch around them with a small hidden path to allow them access to the forest.

"You did good dear," Glory said, putting her arm around her husband.

"I hope so, but you know Rialda. She won't give up."

Rialda and her riders retreated back to the cavern. She tried to shake off the fear that threatened to overcome her when she saw Atmos and his people. She'd thought he had been destroyed. Now he'd returned at the worst possible moment.

She collected herself in the cavern. Her people and the newborn were right behind her. She slid off Enid and turned to face her people. Her mind was racing for the correct words to say to them.

The other true born Slavern, Mertz, Danver, Cromas, Skylar and Martoon hurried off their Dragons and raced to her side.

They too, were stunned by the unfortunate turn of events. They had to remain calm. They couldn't make the same mistakes they did the last time they had dealt with the smaller Elfin creatures. None of them would survive another battle, surely, everyone realized that.

"How is it possible that they survived? We saw them explode," asked Skylar, a very pretty girl with dark blue-black hair and big dark eyes. Her pale skin was flushed with concern.

"Somehow the explosion didn't kill them, it scattered them, and now they have returned," Slavern said wearily, shaking his head, his long dark hair obscuring the scar that ran down the right side of his otherwise handsome face.

Fortis finally caught up with them and jumped from his Dragon to join them. "Tell me I'm seeing things," Fortis said. "This can't be happening. I refuse to believe it."

"We have to face this, my friends, before we tell the others. We have to decide how to handle this setback," Rialda said more calmly than she felt.

"They can't have been too happy to see us either," Skylar said. "None of us can survive another battle. If we leave them alone maybe they will leave us alone," she suggested.

"That's not our way," Rialda said softly.

"It better start being our way," Mertz said, annoyed that they were unwilling to accept that you can't win every battle. "We have to make a truce with them."

"Are you out of your mind?" Rialda yelled, spinning around to face him.

"No, but the rest of you are if you can't see that this is our only hope for survival. We've just awakened and already gone into battle. Now our biggest defeat has returned and if we don't play this smart, this could be it for us. Is that truly what you want?"

"Of course it isn't. But there has to be a way to defeat them," Rialda said.

"If they use the spell again, it could kill all of us this time," Skylar said sadly.

"We have to find a way to counter the spell," Rialda said.

"And until we do, they are off limits," Mertz said.

"That is the wisest choice until we can defeat them," Rialda agreed. Turning to Fortis, she asked, "How did your battle go?"

"Not well. I'm afraid our magic doesn't work in that world, which caused us a bit of a difficulty."

"Was it a spell that stopped your magic?" Skylar asked.

"I don't believe so."

"But you can't be certain?" Skylar asked.

"I guess not."

"We will have to assume that we can't use magic until we discover otherwise. But Mertz is correct. We've just awakened and must regroup and assess our situation. This was a trial run to see how the newborn performed, and they did very well."

"What was that with Alexi and the others?" Cromas asked.

Rialda frowned. "I've no idea but we will take care of them at a later date. We need to train the newborn the way we were trained, finish rebuilding our city and when we are ready, we will face our enemies," she said confidently, while hating to wait, but realized the wisdom of waiting.

Chase raced into the cavern breathlessly. "Something has happened to the mothers," he said.

Rialda's head jerked around as she raced to the birthing room. She slowly walked around the two misshapen creatures. Her brows drawing together in wonder, frowning as she waved her hand, making them vanish.

She turned and looked out across the massive cavern filled with eggs. She turned as the others entered the cavern. She waved her hand across the future of her people removing the acceleration spell.

"Move them to the city. They will grow and train the way we did. Keep them separate from the grown newborn. Skylar, you are in charge of getting a training team together. Mertz, the grown newborn are yours to train and educate."

Mertz frowned. He wasn't thrilled about the accelerated newborn, but he reminded himself that this wasn't their fault. "I will do my best for them," he said.

"I'd expect nothing less," Rialda said, smiling sweetly at him.

"Will you replace the mothers?" Martoon asked.

"Not until these have hatched and we see how they progress. We don't want our entire race to be populated by newborns," she said smiling.

"So, get busy having babies," Slaven teased.

"Something like that," Rialda said, "And keep the trueborn children separated from the newborn. We need to study and compare them."

"Very well," said Skylar. "I will get them relocated before the first ones hatch."

Turning to Chase, Rialda said, "Please prepare more buildings to house us and the eggs."

"Yes ma'am," he said racing from the room.

While Skylar and her team relocated the eggs to the new buildings, Chase was struggling to build housing faster than she filled them. Rialda and the trueborn moved into the luxurious building that Alexi had created.

Rialda and Enid moved into the room Alexi had chosen for herself. She crossed the spacious room and stood at the balcony and watched their new city take shape.

Off to the left, she created a massive white marble structure with wide columns and a statue of a Dragon and rider in the center of the square in front of the new council building. Next to it she made a school. The children would be educated there.

Next, she created an art gallery and a museum. Other buildings would be added later as needed. She recognized that not all her people were meant to be warriors. She would encourage their craftmanship. This was a new beginning, and she had to accept that things had changed.

Chapter Twenty-Eight

Aftermath

Dak flew through the gate, entering Callis. He was relieved to see that the city was still standing. He smiled in admiration at the fortress the giants had built.

He scaled the fortress wall and took shape at the same moment his father, leading his troops, rounded the corner on the top wall, startling them.

Ambro jumped back in surprise, then grabbed Dak, hugging him tightly. "How goes the battle?" he asked. "They ran from us," he laughed.

Dak laughed, returning the hug, stepping back to acknowledge the vampire army. "So, I'm guessing their magic didn't work?"

"Nope. I think it freaked them out a little. You should have seen us. I can't remember the last time I had so much fun."

"Fun? Only you would think fighting is fun."

"It was pretty fun to watch," Collin said joining them, giving Dak a brief hug.

Dak frowned. "What did you do?"

"We played catch and release," Ambro said smugly.

"You used a kid's game against them?" he asked in confusion.

"Well, a tweaked version of it," he said with a grin.

"Explain please."

"We took form and tackled them in the air and tossed them off their Dragons before turning back to smoke."

Dak grinned, nodding his head in approval. "Bet that did look funny."

"They were so surprised they couldn't even get out one of their weird cries," Collin said.

"They were at a loss without magic, but my guess is, they will be better prepared the next time, so we're all staying around for a while. The giants are rebuilding all the cities while we wait," Ambro said.

"Sounds like you have it all worked out. Send for us if they come back. We're preparing a surprise for them when they do."

"How did it go in their world?" Collin asked.

"We were a bit outnumbered. When the remaining eggs hatch, we could have a bit of a problem. We won't be taking the fight to them. Sounds like we'd stand a better chance here," Dak said.

"It's hard to be prepared for a battle against a foe you don't know. We captured a few of them. We will see what we can learn from them," Ambro said.

"Let me know if you learn anything useful, like why they attacked in the first place," he joked.

Ambro hugged Dak again. "Take care son. These Elves are ruthless. Life doesn't seem precious to them."

"Same to you Dad. I'll check back soon," he said before turning into smoke and sailed over the fortress wall, past Callis to the gate to Pandora Two. He passed through and Raziel greeted him telepathically, relieved to hear that the other's battle went well.

Dak floated across the land very much like their home, concerned for the beings living here. They had to warn them of the pending danger.

He saw the enormous structure in the distance and altered his course to check it out, landing on the balcony where Sierra and the others were playing with tiny Dragons and Elfin children.

They all saw him at once and raced to him, jumping, and climbing up his legs, crawling up his back to perch on his shoulders.

Dak frowned and asked, "And how many of them did you bring back with you?"

Sierra and the others burst out laughing. "You have to admit they are cute," Sierra said.

Dak turned his head and looked deep into the big blue eyes of a blond Elfin girl who had been pulling on his ear and said, "Nope, don't have to admit anything. You guys have fun here. I'll see you at home."

Smiling, he plucked the Dragons and Elfin children off his shoulders, back and legs and handed them to Sierra.

Sierra quickly handed them to Alexi and Jax. "How did things go in Callis?" she asked.

"Very good, but we have to prepare for the next time when they are better prepared to attack without magic."

Dak looked past Sierra at Alexi and the others. "Is there anything you can tell us that will help us defend against your people?"

Alexi frowned and said, "I can teach you spells to counter the spells they use in battle."

Dak nodded in appreciation. "That would be helpful."

"Is there any way to talk to them and make peace?" Sierra asked.

"As far as I know, Rialda's clan never made peace with anyone. You can issue a challenge of Omnis Khan, but you will die if you lose."

"What is Omnis Khan?" Sierra asked.

"It is a battle between two people for the clan leadership."

"And the loser dies?" Dak asked.

"Yes."

"You're not doing that," Dak said, glaring at Sierra.

Sierra's eyes widened as she glared at him. "You're not, so stop glaring at me," he continued.

"We will help you anyway we can," Alexi promised. "Even though you slowed down their growth, the Dragons and Dragoneers will be old enough to fight in two months if we train hard."

"That's not much of a childhood," Sierra said sadly. "I will try to slow down their growth more. They deserve to be children."

Alexi hid her shock that Sierra cared more about the Dragons and Dragoneers' lives than for their ability to fight. She choked back tears and softly said, "Thank you." She wished her magic could help them and bravely asked, "Can you teach me how to slow the aging?"

"I will try. I can't promise you that it will work."

Sierra summoned her vials and sat them on a table that she created as she was setting them down. She created a white marble bowl and poured a teal liquid and a blue liquid along with a white glittery liquid. "The liquid makes the spell stronger. All I do to make the spell is think about what I want it to do. In this case, I concentrate on the children and slow their aging."

"I can see it," Alexi said excitedly.

"Now touch my arm and see if you can feel the power of the liquid."

The colorful liquid was swirling in the bowl ready to be released.

Mags smiled. Her student was now an amazing teacher.

"I feel something powerful," Alexi said excitedly.

Sierra released the liquid, and it grew and spread over the hatched children and the ones still encased in their eggs. She could feel it working as it soaked into their skin and through their shells.

"I think it worked. That should give the children at least nine months. The eggs will hatch in a week or so and they will grow slower than the children."

"Don't you need them to fight Rialda?" Alexi asked.

"When they are ready, and only if that's what they want to do. We have other ways to deal with Rialda."

Overcome, Alexi grabbed Sierra and hugged her, "I'm so glad you came to our world."

Sierra smiled. "I hope we all feel that way after Rialda comes looking for you."

Chapter Twenty-Nine

Unnecessary Agreement

For six months, Rialda patiently watched thousands of newborns hatched and move into the new housing created by Chase and Alexi, before she turned traitor.

The children had grown into young adults and would soon be ready.

Rialda dismissed the people in the non-magic realm. They were not worth the time or energy. They just had to get past them to get to the gate that led to where Alexi escaped to.

She wasn't really surprised that Alexi took the first opportunity to defect to a new world. She came from an old, prestigious family that believed in a unique way of governing their people.

She always had a propensity for causing trouble. Maybe she should leave her alone and be glad she was gone.

Shaking her head, she laughed out loud. No, she wouldn't do that. She would teach her and the strangers a lesson. But first, she had to take care of the forest Elfin and make sure they didn't pose a problem to them anymore.

Calling out to Enid, he sauntered in from the other room. She climbed on his back and seemed to melt into him. She flew off the balcony of the majestic room that Alexi created and soared into the sky.

She could see hundreds of young Dragons and Dragoneers racing about beneath her. She turned away from them and headed toward the forest. As she entered the darkest part of the forest, she landed in a small clearing beneath a canopy of trees.

She reached out, searching for any sign of the Forest Elfin, and failed. They had done too good a job hiding themselves.

Atmos felt her presence the moment she entered the forest. He knew eventually she'd come looking for them.

Coming alone, surprised him, wondering what she was up to, he reached out and asked her why she was in his forest.

Rialda turned around in a circle. The voice inside her head appeared to be coming from every direction at once.

She replied that she needed to talk to him. That she wasn't here to fight, just talk.

Atmos appeared next to her. "What do you want to talk about?" he said, startling her.

Enid snarled at the smaller Elfin. Rialda put her hand on his scaled head to calm him. "Thank you for coming. I'm here to make a truce and ask you for something," she said wasting no time getting to the point.

"You want a truce? Sorry if I'm having trouble believing you," Atmos said.

"I expected you to have trouble believing me," she said with a slight laugh. "So, I'm prepared to offer you a blood truce."

Atmos' grey brows drew together in surprise. He never expected this. "What do you want so badly that you'd end your fight with me and my people?"

"The truce is only as good as long as I'm the leader of my people. My predecessor can change relations between our people if he or she chooses," she reminded him.

"I don't see you stepping down anytime soon," he said.

"I don't plan to," she said, honestly.

"So, what is it you want more than you want us?" he asked again.

"The people that invaded our world," she said.

Atmos studied her with interest, giving nothing away. He recalled seeing Sierra and her people when he materialized in the meadow. He knew they were not there to invade their world. They found the gate and were seeing what lied beyond it.

Even though he had done terrible things to them, he owed it to his people to accept the truce.

"The blood truce first. Then I will help you," he said, pushing aside any feelings of guilt.

"I expected nothing less," she said. Using her blood red fingernail, she magically cut a narrow cut in the palm of her hand and murmured a soft spell and held out her hand to Atmos.

Atmos opened a small cut in the palm of his hand, murmured a spell of his own and roughly clasped his hand to hers.

The air seemed to explode around them. The sky grew dark, and lightening flashed across the sky. The ground beneath their feet shook violently, then everything was quiet. The sky lightened as the sun broke through the trees to shine brightly on Atmos and Rialda.

Rialda looked up, the sun shining on her face as she relaxed her hand, withdrawing from Atmos. "That was extraordinary," she said softly.

"I've never seen anything like that," Atmos said. "A blood bond is a serious bond."

"More powerful than I realized," Rialda said.

"When do you want my help?" Atmos asked.

"I will let you know. Until then, please let your people know that we will cause them no harm and we would love to resume trade with you."

"I will tell them. This is what's best for our people."

"I agree. I will speak to you soon," Rialda said as she climbed on Enid. She nodded to Atmos as she flew off.

She glanced down at the clearing and felt a sense of relief at her agreement with Atmos, which wasn't a feeling she was accustomed to.

She landed in front of her building and reached out to her people informing them of the truce. She could feel that they were surprised yet pleased that they no longer had to fear another war with the smaller Elfin.

The idea of being able to trade with them again was pleasing as they were great craftsmen. She looked across the newly planted green fields and felt that they were on the right track to rebuilding.

All that was left was to wait for the army to mature and grow, she thought with a smile.

Sierra watched the first of her Dragons and Dragoneers grow and train. She sat in the newly created stands next to Dak and Ben, along with Mags, Egon and most of her newly formed army waiting for the training games to begin. She felt like she was at a football game and smiled.

Off in the distance a low sounding horn blew and the Dragons and Dragoneers swooped out of the top of the training tower, diving low, picking up speed.

The first four hit their boats, landing low in them so all you could see was the top of their heads and the Dragon's wings.

The boats took off down the river steered by the rider and the Dragon's wings. The other twelve teams hit their boats moments after the first four in hot pursuit.

They dodged cones while picking up flags with their colors and rounded the curve fading out of sight.

Within a few minutes, after racing down the river, they took flight, turning in midair to fly through hoops and avoid obstacles being shot at them, while picking off their flags.

Anissa and her Dragon, Twinkle, were the first to land in front of the spectators, to a round of applause. She was quickly joined by the other teams. The top four teams would advance to the finals.

The flags were counted, and the top four teams waved to the crowd and moved closer to the spectators to watch the next competition.

The games lasted until late afternoon and the finalists took their place at the top of the tower and the horn sounded. Anisse and Twinkle were instantly ahead of the pack and hit their boat a full four seconds ahead of everyone.

She raced through the obstacle course with no trouble picking off all of her flags and took to the air nearly finishing before the others joined her.

Landing with pride she smiled for the audience as she handed over her flags to be counted. She'd missed only one and was confident that she'd be named the winner.

She looked over at Steph and winked at him. She stuck her tongue out at him and smiled as her name was called as the winner.

Steph came in second and Armond was third.

Alexi hung ribbons around their necks with heavy crystals at the end of them depicting their winning rank.

"She's fast," Dak said.

"Very. They are all so good and in such a short time," Sierra said.

"Let's join the celebration," Egon said. "The butterflies made special treats."

They all laughed and quickly followed Egon off the bleachers and across the yard to the celebration.

Ben managed to catch up with Sierra and touched her gently on the arm. She turned, smiling at him.

"I informed the other realms of the danger they were facing. I put a protection spell on all of them. I think the Willow Wisp hope we lose," he said.

"I'm not surprised," she said.

"None of them will be much help against Rialda's army. We have to stop them here."

"I know, but what if we can't?" she asked worriedly.

"You have the power of your ancestors. Don't be afraid to use it," he reminded her. "I know you don't want to hurt them, but this is war. Your kindness is a weakness she will use against you."

"I know. I will do what I have to do to protect this world," she promised.

"You have a strong army, and we will drive her home, and make her think twice about messing with us."

"I hope you're right. She seems to thrive on battles. We must make it very distasteful for her."

"Now, all we need to do is figure out how to do that," he said smiling.

"I have an idea, but it would be a horrible thing to do," she said, looking around to make sure no one could overhear them. "You can't tell anyone, even Dak."

"You have my word," Ben said, honored that she was trusting him with her secret.

"I've been working on the infection the Destroyer inflicted on everyone and I found a way to alter it."

"Alter it how?" he asked curiously.

"If I infect them, it will make them sick, not like the disease the Destroyer used, but vomiting, dizziness, flu-like symptoms that will continue until they return home."

"That's not horrible. It's genius. Why don't you want anyone to know?"

"If I can figure out how to alter it, so can someone else and they could use it against us."

"I see your point. How will you infect them without anyone knowing?"

"You and I will carry the disease without getting sick. All we have to do is get near them and they will catch it."

"How will we stop from getting it?"

"Only the Elfin will get it, and I will vaccinate. our Elfin against it."

"Seems like you've thought of everything."

"There's just one catch. Since we don't know when she will attack, we need to inject ourselves with the disease the moment she shows up."

"So, we need to carry it with us at all times without anyone knowing," he said.

"Yes."

"I can do that. Your plan guarantees their defeat, and the safety of the realms."

"I'm sure that makes you very happy now that you've made it your home," Sierra teased.

Ben took Sierra's hand between his, choaking back tears. "I've asked Iesha to marry me."

Sierra threw her arms around his neck, hugging him tightly. "That's wonderful," she said.

Ben eagerly returned her hug before releasing her. "Thank you. I want to help them any way they will allow me too. I feel like I owe them."

"You're different now. You need to put that behind you," she said.

"I'm trying. Iesha helps a lot."

"She's a good person. Much better than Lorelie," she teased.

"I wasn't interested in Lorelie."

"Sure, you weren't," she said laughing.

"We should join the celebration," he said changing the subject.

"Whatever you say," she said, laughing, following him to where the Dragons and Dragoneers were celebrating with Dak and the others.

⁕ ⁕ ⁕

Lorelie, Birch and Leon led the way through the underwater gate beneath the crystal-blue water of Pandora Two. They were followed by a hundred of Lorelie's faithful followers.

They moved unseen, as small ripples through the water, past the city where Kallam's dwelled. Lorelie briefly admired the city, pausing to remit it to memory before moving on.

They rose unnoticed out of the water as a cool mist, a trick she'd learned from the Mist Elves. As they climbed higher toward the mountain, they appeared as nothing more than a cloud of vapor.

The Dragons guarding the gate yawned sleepily as the cloud grew closer, thanks to a sleeping spell, allowing them to pass through the gate without raising any alarms.

To their surprise, they couldn't hold on to their mist form once they passed through the gate near Callis.

"What's this place?" Birch asked, alarmed to discover their magic no longer worked.

"Relax. This isn't our destination," Lorelie purred. "There's another gate."

They quickly made their way across the blue green grass and encountered Slade and his army as they approached the gate.

Lorelie seductively approached Slade. Her smile lit up her beautiful face.

Slade was instantly mesmerized by her beauty. "What brings you here?" he managed to squeak out.

"We are on a peacekeeping mission," she said sweetly.

"I can't allow you to go in there. You will be killed," he replied in alarm, looking at her fragile, beautiful people.

"We are stronger than we appear. We have no quarrel with the Elfin. We wish to broker peace with them. Please allow us to pass?" she asked sweetly.

Slade frowned. He had no right to stop them. If they got themselves killed, he'd warned them, and if they were successful, so much the better.

"Step aside men. Let them pass," he ordered.

"Thank you," Lorelie said, smiling.

"Good luck," Slade replied.

Lorelie smiled as she took in the breathtaking view on the other side of the gate.

They immediately took their mist form and traveled over the lush green valley. In the distance they could see the Dragons and Dragoneer's city and turned away from it, continuing until they reached the vast ocean miles away.

Retaking their form, Lorelie stood on the sandy beach and pulled at the land beneath the sea. An island rose out of the ocean's depths to rest off the coast of the smooth turquoise water.

Enormous trees and mountains rose up out of the island. A crystal-clear waterfall cascaded off the top of the mountain emptying into a large lagoon.

"Our new home," she whispered, excited how flawless her plan had worked. The moment she heard about the new world, she knew it was time to relocate her people.

She couldn't remain in hiding forever, and she'd die before Mags or Sierra told her how to rule her people. This place was perfect. The inhabitants hated them almost as much as she did. Now all she had to do was end up at war with them herself.

Turning to her people, she said, "Come, let's go home."

Lorelie waded out into the water and dove beneath the surface and glided through the water toward their island home. Her people followed. She floated in the water as she created an underwater city, very much like the one beneath Pandora Two.

Strange looking blue fish that glowed blue and green swam close to the city to inspect the castle that had just appeared.

The door to the city was open, welcoming anyone who wished to take a look. The garden surrounding the castle was filled with colorful flowers that flowed back and forth in the current.

Tiny seahorses raced in and out of the open windows playfully. Lorelie smiled as she reached out and petted the glowing fish, causing it to turn a bright red.

She floated through the door, followed by her new pet that had turned back to a soft blue green.

She added a canopy of beds, held by underwater trees, and sighed in contentment.

She swam toward the surface, promising her pet that she'd return soon. Before she rose out of the water to inspect their surface home, Anil, a young Water Fairy hurried to catch up to Lorelie and said. "It's beautiful. Thank you for bringing us here."

"You are most welcome, my dear. Our people are going to thrive here," she promised.

Turning to face her people, she said, "Make this place our home. Explore this new world, but be careful, some of the inhabitants are not so friendly, yet. I will inform them of our arrival soon, but first, we celebrate and see what this world has to offer."

The Water Fairies cheered. Some dove back into the water, while others found a place among the trees and green thick vines to hide themselves from others.

Lorelie created a table filled with treats, another thing she'd learned while in hiding, and they feasted and celebrated their new beginning.

They drank Fairy wine and danced until the sun rose above the smooth blue water, casting a warm golden glow across the island.

Turning to mist, they explored the Western side of the world, careful to stay far away from the city of Dragons and riders.

Excited, they discovered a tiny village of Flower Fairies and invited them to visit. They met a warrior race of butterflies that threatened them if they didn't move on. Feigning fright, they left them in peace.

Nearing the end of their exploration, near the edge of a small pond, they discovered a very different race of Water Fairies standing on the beach.

They looked remarkably similar except for the gills in the side of their necks, and their razor-sharp teeth. No more than twenty of them gathered around Lorelie and the others as they took their human form.

"I'm Lorelie and these are my friends," she said. "We are new to this world."

An attractive dark-haired young man eyed them with uncertainty, asked, "What do you mean, new to this world?"

"We come from a place far from here," she said.

Ranok looked at her in confusion. He had no idea what she was talking about.

"Your name is?" she asked.

"Ranok," he answered, watching her closely.

"Are there more of you?" she asked excitedly.

"Why do you ask?" he asked uneasily.

Lorelie put her hands on her hips in frustration. "You're not very friendly, are you?" she asked rudely.

"Not when strangers pop out of nowhere and start asking silly questions," he replied, staring down at her.

Lorelie laughed. "Well, at least I got a reaction out of you. Sorry if my questions seemed silly. We are just excited to meet others like us."

"We are not like you," he said, coolly. "We can't turn into vapor."

"Maybe I can teach you," she offered sweetly.

"We are Ocean Fairies. We spend most of our time in the ocean."

"We too are Fairies of the water," she said.

Ranok's eyes widened in surprise. "How can that be? Where are your gills? You would surely drown."

"I assure you; we won't drown."

"Then follow us to our home beneath the surface."

They quietly dove into the water and could swim amazingly fast.

Lorelie and her people had trouble keeping up, but managed to arrive at their enormous city, nestled between two underground mountains and framed by a colorful bed of coral.

There had to be thousands of them swimming and working around the city. She even spotted youngsters playing some sort of sport with a ball and a net.

It was amazing. Ranok escorted them into the city and inside a large white building that was large enough for all of them to enter comfortably.

At the end of the room sat an attractive blond-haired man. His hair was pulled back into a ponytail that hung down to the middle of his back.

He turned at the sound of their entrance and stared at Ranok.

"Sir Drake," Ranok said, surprising Lorelie and the others. They couldn't speak aloud underwater. "I discovered these strangers while I was on patrol."

Drake swam slowly toward them. "Welcome to Altas."

Lorelie tried to reply inside his mind but was unable, so she smiled.

Frowning at her inability to speak, he raised his hands, closing all the doors and windows leading to the room and drained the water.

It happened so fast that Lorelie stumbled to stay on her feet.

Drake reached out and took her arm to steady her. "I apologize. I forget that it can be a little unnerving if you're not used to it."

"It is definitely different," she said, smoothing back her dry hair.

Drake frowned touching her hair, then the sleeve of her dry dress. "How is it possible that you are dry?"

"It's just part of being a Water Fairy," she said simply.

"Outstanding," he said, smiling. "Yet you don't have gills?" he asked, touching her smooth neck.

"And they can become vapor," Ranok added.

Drake looked at Lorelie in wonder. "Astonishing," he said. "Please, come. Make yourselves comfortable," he added pointing to the colorful chairs that lined the wall and scattered around the room. "Where are you from? Why haven't we encountered you before?"

"We've just arrived from another realm."

"Realm," he said confused. "What is this?"

"Another world," she explained.

"How is that possible?"

"There is a gate on the surface that is a doorway to another world."

"Is this doorway always open?"

"Yes."

"Why have we never seen it?" he asked no one in particular.

"Do you travel inland or visit the other side of this world?"

"That must be it. We tend to stay near the waterways. We may need to change that. Seems there is more out there than we knew."

"Watch out for the Dragons and riders. I hear they are not too friendly."

"We haven't seen them in many a year," he said.

"Well, they are back."

"Interesting. Ranok, please order refreshments for our guests. We shall celebrate your arrival."

"Please, you don't need to go to the trouble."

"No trouble. You are welcome to stay here."

"Thank you, but we have a home. It's on an island, not too far from here. You are welcome to visit anytime."

"I don't recall an island," he said puzzled.

"It's new," she said, smiling.

"You created an island? That is amazing. I would love to visit and learn more about you."

Two dozen young girls and boys entered the room carrying trays filled with drinks and refreshments.

Lorelie accepted the fruity drink and a small disk-shaped treat. The punch was sweet and like nothing she'd tasted before. The treat grew inside her mouth and was some sort of sponge cake, equally as good as the punch.

"You like?" Drake asked.

"Very much," thank you."

"You can't find anything like them anywhere else," he said.

"Are there other people or cities near here?"

"Not in a long time, but there used to be. If the Dragons have returned, maybe the Elfin have returned as well. I know of no other cities, but as you reminded me, we don't travel far from home."

"I do hope you will visit us soon. I too have delicacies that I'd like to share with you," she said sweetly.

Drake returned her smile. "I will let my people know of your warm invitation. Thank you."

"You are most welcome," she said, placing the empty glass carved from a seashell on serving tray as the young girl passed by. She smiled at the young girl before she could race away.

Drake raised his hands, and the double doors opened but held back the water.

Lorelie was impressed by his control over the water. She and her people passed through the door and into the cool water and quickly rose to the surface. They turned into mist to continue exploring.

To her surprise, they found a large settlement of Gnomes. The Gnomes were equally surprised to see the Fairies.

A gnarled old Gnome named Simetain cautiously approached the strangers, looking up at them warily. He nodded at them and extended his hand. "I'm Simetain, but you can call me Simmy, everyone does." he said.

Something about the warmth and trust warmed Lorelie's heart. She bent down and took his hand and truthfully said, "It is very nice to meet you, Simmy. We are new here and are out to meet our neighbors and to invite you for a visit."

"I don't remember having neighbors before, except, well, you know, the people in my village," he said, smiling.

Lorelie laughed. "Well, you do now. We are not too far. We live on an island not too far from the shore."

"How would I get there? I can't swim," he said sadly. "Arms and legs are too short for swimming. I sink like a stone."

"There will be a boat at the dock just for you," she said.

Simmy's cheeks flushed a bright pink. "Come see our village. Well, you can't all come at once. There's too many of you and you're too big. You just won't fit."

"Birch, why don't you join me? The rest of you can wait here or look around. We won't be gone very long."

Birch and Lorelie followed Simmy down a narrow path between two large boulders that opened up into a tiny quaint village with Gnomes rushing back and forth between stalls selling goods to a number of Gnomes.

"It's market day. Gnomes from other villages come here to sell or trade their goods."

"How many villages are there?" she asked.

"Now let me think," he said giggling. "Of course, you'll let me think. Around twenty. I believe. Not all of them are as grand as Graberdin," he said proudly.

The other Gnomes stopped to meet the strangers and offered them a taste of jams, jellies, and a variety of berries.

Birch bravely tried their stout ale and turned white, then red. His eyes watered as he held out his mug for another shot.

The Gnomes laughed, patting him on the back and watched expectantly as he downed a second cup. His face flushed and his eyes watered to the delight of the Gnomes, and they laughed when he declined the third.

Lorelie thanked them for their hospitality and handed them a map she created, with directions to her island, while they were busy watching Birch.

Simmy escorted them from the village, leaving them alone on the path.

"That was fun," Birch said, surprising Lorelie.

"Yes, it was," she agreed. "I don't remember the last time we really had fun."

"Neither do I," he said sadly. "My throat my never be the same."

Lorelie laughed, something she realized she'd done a lot today. "How would you feel if we didn't get in the middle of the Dragons fight with Sierra?" she asked, surprising herself.

Birch stopped and faced Lorelie in surprise. "It's all you've thought about."

"I know. But everyone here has been so nice. I'd forgotten what it felt like to be accepted and not hated, and I like how it feels," she said honestly.

Birch frowned gripping her shoulder with both hands. "I liked it too," he said.

"What do you think the others will say?"

"I think they'd be happy to settle down peacefully instead of fighting."

"It does make sense when you put it that way."

"I guess we should tell the others that the war is off," he teased.

"But we do have to prepare for a confrontation with the Dragons and riders. We might very well end up at war with them.

Chapter Thirty

Face to Face with the Destroyer

The Water Fairies were delighted to hear that they wouldn't be entering the war with the Dragons and riders.

They had battled against the Eight Realms, and it was time for peace. Traveling past the gate, they avoided the Dragon city and entered the forest.

Spotting a small Elfin village hidden deep in the forest, Lorelie and the others took form near the river.

"The rest of you wait here. Birch and I will approach the village."

Pushing their way through the dense forest they finally reached the quaint little village nestled in a clearing with rays of sunshine casting a warm glow across the bustling village.

When the Elfin noticed Lorelie and Birch had entered the town, everyone seemed to freeze. They didn't even blink. As if by not moving it made them invisible.

Unsettled by their reaction, Lorelie smiled and said, "I'm sorry if we startled you. We are new here."

An older Elfin shook off his surprise at the sudden appearance of two strangers and slowly approached them.

Behind him, the Elfin seemed to return to life. They watched Lorelie and Birch warily.

Atmos came out of his shop, catching Lorelie's attention. She looked at him and frowned, her brows drew together in concentration, then she gasped, clutching her hand to her chest as she slowly approached him.

She glared down at him with a mixture of shock and disgust. "It is you. I will never forget those eyes," she whispered.

Atmos didn't remember her, but he knew that he must have infected her or someone she cared about. "I sincerely apologize for anything I did to you while I was infected," he said sincerely.

Lorelie glared at him, resisting the urge to turn him into some foul-smelling swamp creature. She recalled the horrible infection creeping into her mind, while it ravaged her body and shuddered with disgust. She didn't know what to say.

The other Elfin gently touched her hand, startling her.

"He couldn't control what happened to him. We are all deeply sorry by whatever happened to you."

"How? How did this happen?" she finally asked after staring at him what felt like forever.

"Please, sit down and we will tell you," Cletus said.

Lorelie and Birch followed the Elfin inside a small Pub, ducking so they wouldn't hit their heads on the door frame.

They sat around a small table, their knees pressed against their chest as they sipped the potent ale.

"We used to live in harmony with the Dragoneers," Cletus began.

"Dragoneers?" Birch asked.

"The Dragon riders," Atmos explained.

"They loved the furniture we make, the jams, treats, you name it, they liked it. Too much in fact. We couldn't keep up with their demands for more. This made them angry and for some reason they kidnapped some of our people so they could create for them."

"Of course, we rescued them and brought them home." Atmos added.

"This enraged Rialda and she declared war on us."

"We had no defense against them and retreated in the underground caves. While we were hiding out, we created a weapon, hoping to stop the attacks on us. Once the weapon was released, it engulfed everything in its path, changing us, and nearly killing most of us and the Dragoneers." Atmos said.

"How horrible," Lorelie said.

"Since our return, we negotiated a truce with them, but we know that at any moment they will do as they wish, so we hid here in the forest.

"Is the disease gone?" Lorelie asked.

"Yes. It was a terrible thing we created and I'm terribly sorry."

Lorelie surprised herself by reaching across the table and covered his hand with hers. "I'm sorry that happened to you and glad to hear the disease is gone."

Atmos smiled in gratitude.

"Thank you for your hospitality and feel free to visit us. I'd rather you not tell the Dragoneers that we are here. I'd like to do that myself," she said rising to her feet.

"We won't say a word. You should be careful when you approach them. I doubt they will be glad to see you," Atmos said.

"I hope to make them feel differently," Lorelie said.

"I wish you well and hope to see you again," Atmos said.

"You and your people are welcome to visit," she said, bidding them goodbye.

Rejoining the others, she sent them home instructing them to prepare in case the Dragon riders are not happy with them relocating to their world.

Lorelie and Birch continued to the Dragon city as a thin mist, retaking their human form just before entering.

Within moments, they were surrounded by half a dozen Dragons and riders.

Lorelie frowned at Birch and said, "Not a good start."

Birch shrugged. "Maybe they are the welcoming committee."

"I doubt that," she whispered.

"Who are you?" Skylar demanded.

"I'm Lorelie, this is my friend Birch.

Skylar looked at her suspiciously. "Why have we never seen you before?"

"Have you met all the Water Fairies?" she asked.

Skylar looked at her and frowned. "I suppose we haven't," she said. "Why are you here?"

"We want to meet our neighbors."

Rialda made her way through the gathering crowd surrounding the two strangers, studying them as she approached.

"So, where are you from?" she asked.

"An island off the coast. You are welcome to visit," she said.

"I'm curious why we haven't seen you or your people before."

"This is our first time to travel so far from home. Have you traveled to the other side?"

Rialda frowned. "No. We are not explorers."

"You should visit us. It is quite beautiful."

Rialda studied the two strangers before her and didn't trust them. "So, what brings you to our fair city now?"

"We too are not explorers but decided to get acquainted with our neighbors and have enjoyed our visit to each city."

Rialda's eyes widened in surprise. There were other cities besides the Elfin. "You have met the Elfin in the forest?" she asked.

"Yes. They told us about your great city."

"I'm sure they did," she said wondering what they had told the strangers. "I apologize for all the questions. We are not used to visitors."

"No apology necessary. I'd like to extend an invitation to visit us and maybe you will meet some of your other neighbors."

So, there are others, she thought. "I will consider your invitation."

"We've taken enough of your time, and we still have a little more exploring to do before we return home," she said sweetly.

Rialda didn't want to let them leave, but she needed more information about them before she started anything. One battle at a time, she reminded herself. "Very well," she said. "I'm sure we will see each other again."

Turning to her people, she added, "Please escort our visitors out of the city."

"Thank you," Lorelie said resisting the urge to turn her into a toad. She was certain that when they did meet again, it wouldn't be pleasant.

The Dragoneers slowly escorted Birch and Lorelie through the city and watched them walk away until they faded in the distance.

"Something tells me she doesn't like us very much," Birch said.

"I can't imagine what it was," she replied laughing. Believing they were far enough away from the city and wouldn't be seen, they turned into mist and headed for home.

They didn't discover any other villages or see any people on the return trip home. Lorelie considered their trip a success. The Dragons and riders were going to be a problem, she was certain of it, but the other people they met would be an asset, especially the other Water Fairies.

Lorelie cast several spells to warn them if anyone came too close to the island. She was delighted to see that several Flower Fairies had decided to make the island their home.

To her delight, she discovered the Flower Fairies would deliver her invitations to her celebration to the other villages.

Using a large leaf and red dye for ink, she wrote out invitations for a celebration a week from today. She included a map to their location and handed them to the tiny Flower Fairies with soft petals framing their tiny faces.

The Fairies took the large leaves and vanished from sight, reappearing at each location to deliver the invitations.

Rialda jerked it from the startled Flower Fairy's hand, startling the young girl who vanished immediately reappearing safely on the island and planting her tiny feet beneath the soil to relax and soak up nutrients.

The Gnomes, Water Fairies, Flower Fairies, and the Elfin living in the woods readily accepted Lorelie's invitation.

Excited about the upcoming celebration, Lorelie busied herself and her people into preparing for the event. It didn't take long to realize that she needed to enlarge the island and underwater buildings to accommodate all of the Water Fairies.

Her concentrated preparations to relocate came in handy as she enlarged the island. She was struck by inspiration and opened a large pool in the center of the island connecting the island city with the water city.

A spiral mountain rose majestically from the water and dripping with water as she formed colorful buildings and paths around the edges.

Large trees with thick vines covered the mountain giving it an exotic appearance. A breathtaking waterfall cascaded down one side of it, emptying into the pool.

Across from the island she created a large dock with a dozen boats to ferry her land limited guests across the water in comfort.

Satisfied that she had enough room she entered her quaint cottage decorated with flowering vines and earthen furnishings. She sat down on a white chair with a plush red cushion and began to plan her menu and festivities.

⚜ ⚜ ⚜

Rialda stared at the leafy invitation in her hand, resisting the urge to crumple it. She called out to her trusted riders to come assist her.

They arrived in minutes, astride their sleek Dragons. She showed them the invitation, which to her surprise, they were excited to attend.

"I'd like to check this place out before accepting the invitation," she said warily, not at all happy that they didn't find their sudden appearance disconcerting.

"We can scout it out to see if anything is amiss," Mertz said.

"I'd like to meet the other people she mentioned. All this time, we thought it was just us and the Elfin here," Skylar said.

"There's no time like the present. If things look okay, we can stop in and accept the invitation," Rialda said, not at all pleased with their excitement over attending a celebration.

Taking flight, Rialda, Mertz, Skylar, Danver, Slaven, Cromas and Martoon, flew past their city, entering the endless sea of green for the first time.

They crossed the smooth flat land until they reached the vast blue-green ocean. Viewing it for the first time was awe inspiring.

"It's beautiful," Skylar whispered.

They followed the coastline until they saw the island in the distance and crossed the water to reach the island. They had never seen anything like it as they circled the island to get a clear look at the marvel that had emerged from the sea.

Seeing nothing suspicious, they landed on the white sandy beach.

Anil and Leon had just come out of the water as they landed on the beach. Anil smiled warmly at them and said, "Hello."

"We've come to accept your invitation to the celebration," Rialda said.

"That's wonderful," Anil said. "Would you like to tell Lorelie, or shall I let her know for you?" she asked.

"You can let her know. Thank you," Rialda said.

"She will be pleased," Leon said.

"We are looking forward to the celebration," Skylar said.

"We look forward to getting to know our neighbors," Anil said glancing at the sleek Dragons in admiration as they shifted uncomfortable in the warm sand. "They're beautiful," she added.

"Thank you," Rialda said, climbing back onto Enid's back. "We shall see you again in a week."

Enid rose into the air and the others quickly followed. They took the same path home and when they arrived, Skylar couldn't contain her excitement. Rialda knew she would have to do something to keep her people focused and away from the newcomers.

Chapter Thirty-One

Lorelei's Celebration

Lorelei was dressed in a magical creation that looked like a waterfall with sparkling shells and crystals woven through it. It shimmered and sparkled with every step.

The underwater city sparkled with glowing sea urchins and the island city was lit up by tiny fireflies inside pastel paper lanterns.

The grand ballroom's ceilings were a starlite night, something she borrowed from Mags. Tables with white linens lined the walls with decadent desserts, pastries, seafood delights, fruits, breads, and cheese. In the center of each table was a cascading fountain of a special passion fruit punch.

Satisfied that everything was in place she joined her people to wait for their guests. For a brief moment, panic hit her that no one would show up. She wasn't the same hated person. She was doing things differently this time. They didn't know the old Lorelie.

Hearing a soft sound behind her, she saw Drake and a few other Ocean Fairies climb out of the pool connecting the underwater city.

"Your home is amazing," he said. "The others are looking around your city and will join us soon," he added while waving his hand in front of his wet clothing to dry them.

"Thank you. Please help yourself to refreshments and later I can give you a tour."

"I would like that," he said, nodding to her before he strolled over to the refreshment tables, followed by his people.

Soon, the Gnomes arrived in a whirl of excitement. Simmy raced across the white marble floor to say hello to Lorelie.

She bent down and hugged him tightly. "I'm so glad you could come," she said. Surprised that she actually meant it.

"I couldn't miss my new friend's party," he said proudly. "I hope you don't mind, Gnomes from the other villages tagged along."

I don't mind at all. Please help yourselves to refreshments," she said, spotting the Destroyer and the Forest Elfin entering the room.

Atmos slowly approached her, looking Simmy up and down.

"Welcome. I'm so glad you made it,' she said. "Atmos, this is my friend Simmy. He likes to make beautiful things too."

Atmos smiled. "Wonderful. What do you make?" he asked as the two of them walked off together with Atmos' family trailing behind them laughing.

The room filled up as more Gnomes, Fairies and Elfin arrived.

Lorelie's Fairy band started playing soft music from the corner of the room. They used reeds as flutes, shells as horns with soft covered empty turtle shells as drums.

Tiny bubbles floated out of the pool, twinkling in the starlight above.

Dozens of couples filled the dance floor and Rialda's people still hadn't arrived. Sighing softly, she turned to join her guests when Drake put his hand on her arm, startling her.

"May I have this dance?" he asked.

Putting her hand in his, she walked out onto the dance floor and felt like a fairy princess. Never in her wildest of dreams did she ever think she'd be in a place like this, smiling and dancing.

This was a dream come true. As Drake twirled her around the dance floor, she spotted three or four dozen Dragon riders entering the ballroom.

They hadn't dressed for the occasion, but she assumed they had no idea how to dress for a party.

Skylar's pretty face lit up as she looked around the room at the elegantly dressed men and women. She looked up at the ceiling and smiled. Everything was so pretty.

"Excuse me," Lorelie said to Drake. "New guests have arrived. Would you like to meet them?"

"I would love to," Drake said.

Lorelie and Drake seemed to glide across the floor, stopping in front of Rialda and the other riders. "I'm so glad you made it. I'd like to introduce you to Sir Drake, King of the Ocean Fairies," she said. "This is Rialda and forgive me for not remembering all of your names. Rialda is the leader of the Dragons and riders."

Drake held out his hand to Rialda. "Please call me Drake. I am pleased to meet you."

"I'm Skylar," she said taking his hand, when Rialda didn't. "We're called Dragoneers."

"Why is that?" he asked.

"We bond for life with our Dragon," she said excitedly.

Drake's eyes widened in wonder. "You have a Dragon?"

"We all do. Would you like to see them? They are on the beach. And thank you for providing them with refreshments."

"You are most welcome," Lorelie said.

"I would love to see your Dragons, if they won't mind."

"They won't mind," she said, leading Drake outside.

"Thank you all for coming," Lorelie said. "There are refreshments on all the tables and a performance will start in a few minutes. Please mingle and meet some of the other guests."

Rialda wanted to cage them all but forced a smile on her face and headed toward the refreshment table. Her eyes scanned the room as she sipped her punch.

The other Dragoneers split up and after getting refreshments, introduced themselves to the other guests.

Lorelie led Drake down to the beach. He was in awe at the sight of the small Dragons.

"They are amazing," he said softly.

"Yes, they are," she agreed.

The Dragon, Hawk, took an interest in Drake, studying him.

"His kind are familiar," he said inside Lorelie's mind.

"How's that possible?" she asked.

"Because we used to have Dragons," Drake replied, having also heard the exchange.

"What happened to them?" she asked.

"That's a story for another time. It's a party. No sad stories tonight," he replied, taking her arm through his and escorting her back to the party.

She eagerly accepted his offer to dance, enjoying the music and laughter. It all ended too soon, when a group of Water Fairies put on a funny play at the other end of the room.

They had everyone laughing until they cried at the end of the play.

The play was followed by more dancing and drinking, and the night ended with fireworks that lit up the sky and the city beneath the water.

The party had been perfect and Lorelie hated to see it end.

Skylar hugged her and Drake goodbye before joining Rialda, who had already left.

The Ocean Fairies made their exit beneath the island as the Gnomes and Elfin traveled back to shore together, already fast friends.

Lorelie's people bid them goodnight before returning to their homes, leaving Lorelie and Drake alone.

"It was a wonderful party," he said.

"Yes, it was, but something's been bothering you," she said.

"You read me way too well. But it can keep," he said. "I don't want a dark cloud on tonight."

"Please. Tell me what is troubling you."

"It's the Dragons," he said reluctantly.

"What about them?" she asked puzzled.

"They used to belong to my people until they were all killed or stolen."

454

Chapter Thirty-Two

The Dragons

"That's terrible," Lorelie said, her eyes widening in horror.

"The story is, that when my great grandfather was a boy, our people lived on the land and trained and sold Dragons. When a trainer wouldn't sell to a man known to be cruel, he came back with dozens of men and killed many of the Dragons, stealing the rest."

"That's awful."

"That's when my people shut out the rest of the world and retreated to the ocean's depths to a kinder, gentler world."

"Are these Dragons the offspring of your Dragons?"

"I believe so. I'm thrilled to see that they survived and weren't wiped out. But sad that my people and I don't get to experience the joy of connecting and riding with them."

"I can guarantee you that Rialda won't let you near her Dragons."

Touching her arm gently, he said, "I'm sorry. I didn't mean to make you sad."

Lorelie smiled mischievously. "I'm not sad. I'm thinking that we should steal some of their Dragon eggs so your people can raise them again."

"You're serious, aren't you?" Drake said in surprise.

"Absolutely."

"You could be caught and I'm afraid she'd kill you."

"I'm tough to kill and I think we can pull this off without her having any idea who did it. Besides, she is planning a war. She won't have time to worry about a few missing eggs."

"A war? With whom?"

"Someone from my home, but that is a very long story. I will get my people, and we will do this now. She won't be expecting anything. Go prepare a place for them beneath the ocean so she can't find them."

His hands gently gripped her arms, and he stared down into her lovely face. "Are you sure you want to do this? I don't want you to get hurt."

"Yes. Don't worry. I will see you soon," she said kissing him briefly before she raced from his side. It felt good to be doing something right.

She called Birch, Leon, Leesa, Amoi, Deni, and Maude. They quickly joined her still dressed in their party clothes. She quickly told them what they were going to do. They were excited to help the Ocean Fairies and turned to mist and drifted off into the night.

They traveled across the land and into the Dragon city. They located the unhatched. They picked up two tiny eggs each and placed them beneath their clothing and became transparent.

They snuck out of the city and began the long journey home, using the wind to propel them faster. They traveled through the night carrying the precious eggs.

Once they were closer to home, Lorelie called out to her people for assistance. They arrived on winged Griffins and retrieved them of their cargo.

Lorelie safely stored the two extra eggs she'd picked up in a large pocket of air in her underwater city. There's no reason, she thought, that we can't have Dragons too.

Once they were safe, she put the remaining eggs in a silk lined bag made of a strong vine, interwoven together. She climbed onto Celos, her Griffin, and hurried on into the night toward Drake's city.

Leaving Celos on the beach, she walked into the water, carrying the heavy bag. Once she submerged, she swam down toward Drake's city.

She stepped through the watery doorway into the dry room.

Drake quickly crossed the room, excited to see her and the large bag she carried. "You really, did it?" he said, fighting back tears.

"That I did," she said. "You must keep them hidden unless you want a war with Rialda."

"I will keep them hidden for now. Eventually, they will seek the sunlight."

"I see trouble in your future then," she said, smiling.

"I would imagine that you are correct," he said, shrugging one shoulder. "It's a good thing they can't breathe beneath the water."

Lorelie laughed, knowing that a fight with Rialda was inevitable.

⁕ ⁕ ⁕

Rialda was furious after they arrived home from Lorelie's celebration. Her people were losing focus. She returned to her room after the celebration and spent the night formulating a plan that would bring her people back in line and exact revenge on the invaders at the same time.

In the wee hours of the morning, she went to visit all of the newborn. They were created for battle, and battle is what they were about to do. She put an enhancement spell on them, making them stronger and faster.

When the sun rose, she would call her people to war. If they hesitated, the newborn would imprison them in a specially prepared prison. She wasn't taking any chances.

She called out to Atmos, receiving a reply that he'd be there soon. She had done the right thing making peace with him.

She looked out at the sea of newborns and was pleased to see that they were anxious for battle.

Atmos arrived just as the sun rose and she put out a war cry. She was happy to see all the Dragoneers arrive within minutes of the alarm being sounded.

"Good morning my fellow Dragoneers," she said. "After last night's celebration, I realized that we need to finish our battle with the intruders so we can put it behind us and concentrate on rebuilding our city and getting to know our new neighbors."

No one said anything. They simply waited for instructions.

"Atmos is here to help us. He will open a doorway to their world right before we enter through the gate, allowing us to outflank them. The moment you arrive, sound the Dragon cry, and don't stop. We outnumber them and it should be quick and painless.

"Take their leader and Alexi and return home. Our battle is only with Sierra. She is their leader and gave the order to attack us while we were sleeping. Let's ride."

Nearly one thousand Dragoneers rose to the sky headed for the gate. The moment they passed through, Slade raised the alarm. The Dragoneers didn't attack, they headed for the gate to Pandora Two.

Slade tried to sound an alarm but was knocked unconscious by the swarm of Dragoneers. They hit the gate so fast it rocked back and forth as they poured into Pandora Two.

Atmos frowned and opened a rip to Pandora. He had no idea there was another Pandora, so he sent them to the wrong place by accident.

All of a sudden, three hundred newborns appeared out of nowhere in Pandora. It was a busy shopping day, and the city was filled with shoppers.

Adam saw the strange swarm first and called out to everyone in Pandora to ready for battle.

The Dragons dove down the mountain, racing toward the city to intercept the intruders. Three of them stopped long enough to pick up Adam, Jinks and Leiya.

Narvon, Sali and Moree, spread their giant white wings and followed the Owls into battle. The visiting Vampires turned to smoke and followed the Owls.

The giant Phoenix left their resting place atop the mountain to assist in defending their new home. Fire Fairies, Water Fairies and Nymphs changed into their battle gear and joined the fight.

Vestry cursed beneath her breath and called to Cali to give her a ride into battle. The great white Owl swooped down and picked her up, placing her on his back.

Werewolves and Shifters brought up the rear, until Gerferlum and several other Gnomes came out of a shop and saw what was happening.

The tiny Gnome whistled and Gorreth, a giant blue and gold Dragon, swung back around and picked up Gerferlum and tossed him on his back.

Fallon, the mighty Sea Dragon, raised his head from the sea and rose majestically from the water, followed by two dozen Sea Dragons, and joined the others racing to intercept the invaders.

The three hundred Dragoneers were surprised by an army of one thousand. They let out their Dragon cry just as Adam, Jinks and Leiya cast a spell to block the cry.

They were just a couple of seconds late and a partial cry reached the ears of the approaching army.

The Dragons and Sea Dragons laughed at the puny noise, but Adam, Jinks and Leiya covered their ears in pain.

Vestry swatted away the annoying sound and flew in the middle of the Dragoneers, casting a spell over the Dragons making it hard for them to stay in the air.

They let out another cry, just as the Vampires turned solid, throwing them off their mounts and turned into smoke again.

The Werewolves and Shifters stopped whimpering as the noise ripped through their brains.

The Dragon's blew streams of smoke at the oncoming Dragoneers setting them ablaze and spiraling toward the ground.

The Sea Dragons ripped them out of the air, tearing them apart and tossing them aside.

The Werewolves started howling to combat the Dragon cry. It helped, but it slowed them down.

The Phoenix knocked the small Dragons from the sky. The shifters and Werewolves secured them once they hit the ground.

A swarm of Dragoneers headed straight for Gorreth and Gerferlum, screaming in unison. Gerferlum raised his tiny hammer and screamed a returning battle cry.

The Dragoneers and Dragons heard it and stopped, dropping from the sky, spiraling out of control toward the ground. The terrified Dragoneers jumped off and floated safely to the ground, where Jinks, Adam and Leiya cast a binding spell on them, making them unable to move.

"What did you do?" Gorreth asked Gerferlum.

"I screamed the Gnomes battle cry," he said simply.

"I'm going to fly all around them, and you scream your battle cry until we knock all of them from the sky," he instructed, excited at the sudden weapon on his back.

Gorreth flew around and between the small Dragons as Gerferlum whooped and yelled threatening them with his mighty hammer.

The Vampire's smokey forms paused briefly to watch the Dragons fall from the sky. They were terrified with nowhere to retreat to. The Dragon's yelled and valiantly fought on, wondering where Rialda was with the remaining army.

Adam, Jinks and Leiya helped the Werewolves and Shifters contain the prisoners as they crashed to the ground, healing the wounds as they bound them. Gorreth looked down at the grisly battlefield. Dozens of the small Dragons had been killed or ripped apart during the brief battle.

Thankfully, only a few Dragoneers had been fatally wounded.

"Thanks to you, thousands of lives were saved today, Gorreth said.

"Who knew my battle yell could do that?" he said smiling mischievously.

"Thank heaven it did."

Rialda and her riders poured through the gate into Pandora Two, unaware of the battle raging in Pandora.

Lazrus called out to everyone letting them know they were under attack, as he and the other Dragons flew through them, blasting them with Dragon fire.

Sierra reached out to Alexi that it was time. Alexi climbed on Alton. They melded together and it was hard to see where she stopped, and he began.

Dimitr and Baliss landed on her balcony. "It's time to see if all the enhancements you and Sierra made to the Dragons and Dragoneers will be enough to beat Rialda's army," he said.

"We are not fighting her alone," she reminded him, instructing Alton to hurry.

They caught up with the Dragoneers and she and Dimitri took their places in the front of their army.

Lazrus and the other Dragons picked up their riders.

To Sierra's surprise a wave of black was moving across the ground. One by one, the black fluffy dogs leapt into the air, snatching the riders off their Dragons.

They placed their huge heavy paws on their chest, baring their white sharp teeth.

A few Dragoneers tried to fight them off and were mauled for their trouble.

Their Dragons came to their aid, blowing fire at the packs, which moved, using the Dragoneers as shields. The confused Dragons rejoined the army.

The dogs licked the burned Dragoneers soothing and healing their burns. The newborns hadn't been trained in magic and were helpless against the mighty creatures.

Rialda and the others were shocked to see hundreds of Dragons and Dragoneers racing toward them. For a brief moment she thought it was her army, but their coloring was very different than theirs.

Gone were the blues and greens. These Dragons were blue and purple and the Dragoneers wore matching colors.

The Dragons on both sides let out a piercing cry, but Rialda's Dragon's cry did nothing.

Alexi's Dragon's cry was painful to the other Dragon's and Dragoneers.

Rialda quickly cast a spell to render the cry harmless.

Sierra reached down deep into the earth locating a pool of hot water. She reduced the temperature, still not wanting to seriously hurt anyone and pulled it out of the ground like a geyser, hitting Rialda's army with the hot water, sending them tumbling backward through the air.

Rialda quickly righted them, and they were on their way again.

Mertz spotted Alexi at the front of her army and cast a spell to get her to switch sides.

Alexi batted it away and sent him a message to go home. This wasn't a fight he could win, and it wasn't worth dying over. He was on the wrong side in this war. Her forcefulness surprised him, and he briefly wondered if she was right.

Lazrus and Sierra followed by Dak, Mags, Mavis, Ben, and Egon tore their way through the Dragoneers.

Sierra's virus that she and Ben were carrying slowly infected Rialda's Dragons and Dragoneers. Sierra frowned as she watched the wounded Dragons and Dragoneers fall from the sky.

She cushioned their fall, hoping to keep them alive.

Rialda was angry when her backup army failed to arrive and sent a team back to get reinforcements.

Thinking that they were retreating, Sierra allowed them to leave.

Spells clashed between Rialda's army and Sierra's, lighting up the sky above them like fireworks.

Collin and his team on the ground cast binding spells on the Dragoneers that the black dogs were holding prisoner. The dogs leapt in the air again, capturing a new group of prisoners.

Rialda sent a combination fire spell and lightening spell at them.

Collin stepped between them, trying to ward it off. The spell hit him in the chest, knocking him to the ground, burnt and scorched.

A large black dog leapt at Rialda. She turned just in time, but his powerful paw swiped across her face, leaving deep scratches on her face.

Several of the black dogs licked at Collin trying to heal the burning flesh on his chest.

The dog that maimed Rialda took the shape of a man, cut his wrist, and forced the blood between Collin's pale lifeless lips.

He tilted his head back and let out an ear-piercing cry that could be heard throughout Pandora Two.

Sierra and the others looked down at Collin's lifeless body and sent healing spells to him, unable to stop to help him.

Dodging and clawing their way through Rialda's army, Sierra waved her hand to clear the blood from her black fighting gear.

She was so disappointed that her disease didn't work. She looked up in dismay to see more Dragons and riders coming through the gate.

On the ground, Collin gasped and tried to sit up. He touched his scorched chest in wonder. He should be dead. The man who saved his life, picked him up like he was a child and carried him beneath the trees.

"Rest. You should be safe here," he said before turning back into a dog and raced back into the fight. Collin sat on the soft ground trying to regain his breath, wondering what had happened.

Skylar looked down at all the dead newborns beneath them and felt sick. She reached out to Slaven, telling him that there was no way they were going to capture Alexi and Sierra.

Gorreth and Gerferlum appeared through a rip, distracting everyone mid-battle. Gerferlum let out his war cry and several of Rialda's retreating troops fell from the sky.

Slavern agreed but told her to keep fighting. The first wave of nausea hit Skylar, nearly causing her to fall from Hawk. Hawk groaned, letting her know that he was sick as well. The sickness swept through Rialda's army quickly.

Feeling the first pangs of the illness, Rialda called out to her people to retreat. As much as she wanted revenge, she didn't want her people to die needlessly. Something in this world was making them sick. And with the appearance of the screaming Gnome knocking their people from the sky, it was time to retreat.

Her incoming troops hit Alexi's army hard, tumbling through the air in hand-to-hand battle. They were stronger and faster than the first group.

They jumped from their Dragons to throw the Dragoneers off, sending them tumbling to the ground.

Sierra and the large Dragons along with Eldrik sliced their way through them.

Rialda's first wave made it through the gate and the sickness vanished. Confused, they turned around and went back through the gate to assist their reinforcements, and the pain ripped through them.

Rialda was furious. Somehow entering their world made her people sick. Leading the way, she took her people home, furious by their defeat.

The new wave was unaffected by the sickness.

Furious that Rialda was getting away, Alexi took her army after them, encountering them in Callis. Rialda called to her reinforcements to retreat.

Following the retreating army, Sierra, and the Dragons passed through the gate.

"Rialda," Alexi yelled.

Rialda turned, glaring at the young woman.

"Are you happy with yourself? Many died today because of you."

The Giants, Vampires and Slade's army surrounded the angry Dragoneers waiting to see if they would continue fighting.

Rialda turned, instructing her people to return home.

Skylar glanced at Alexi then Rialda, sending them both a message that this was wrong as she turned and flew through the gate.

Skylar was right. This was wrong. Sierra and Lazrus flew next to Alexi. "Go home. If you return, you will get sick. We're not trying to invade your home. We were exploring. This ends here or the sickness will destroy you the next time."

Rialda glared at the two women with hatred. As her reinforcements caught up to her, she led them home. It wasn't over yet, no matter what Sierra said.

Rialda instructed her new troops to gather all the remaining eggs and join her in the mountains. Her people would rebel after this debacle, so she would save them the trouble and rebuild her army without them.

As she passed through the gate, she called out to any newborn that wished to join her and was delighted to see half of them take flight and head to the mountains.

"What's happening?" Skylar asked.

"She's leaving us," Cromas said, "Why is she leaving us?" he asked, taking flight to join her. Danver and Martoon quickly followed them leaving the others to watch in confusion.

"Looks like we need a new leader," Mertz said smiling. "What in the hell just happened?"

Skylar faced her friend with her hand on her hips and said, "No idea. Looks like we are on our own now. We must do things differently. One person making all the rules is just silly. We have to stop treating the newborn as if they are disposable."

"She's right," Slaven said. "They will be our army for when Rialda returns. If you think she won't you're crazy."

"Why would Rialda come after us? She's the one that left us. This makes zero sense."

"Maybe she won't. Who knows, but we have to take care of the newborn and move on. She's left us little choice," Slaven said.

The four-remaining legacy Dragoneers assembled the Dragoneers and newborn. The newborn would start training in magic and flying combat.

It was decided that the four leaders would work together toward a new future for their people.

Alexi glared at the shimmering gate in disgust.

Sierra put her hand on her arm. "It's not worth it," she said.

Alexi frowned. "I know. Let's go home," she said sadly.

Sierra turned to face the army that had been protecting Callis and said, "It's time to return home. Hopefully we have seen the last of her," she said.

"How can, you be sure?" Slade asked.

"She can't use magic here and if she does return, your army can defend you. I don't think she will return. Not anytime soon."

Dak moved next to Sierra. "I'd like to know how you're so certain she won't be back," he said, raising one eyebrow in question. "Sure, is funny how they all got sick."

"It sure was," she replied. "Time to go home and take care of the dead and wounded."

Rialda, Danver, Cromas and Martoon sat around a black shiny table in their new hall of leadership that Rialda created in the center of their mountain hideaway.

"I know we're disappointed in the outcome of today's battle," Rialda said. "But we learned many important lessons from it.

"There is magic in this world far greater than ours. We have got to increase our skills in magic."

"How will we do this?" Cromas asked.

"We will train harder. I will enlist the aid of the Elfin to teach us as well. I have enhanced many of their abilities, so they will be stronger and faster," Rialda said.

"What about the rest of our people? Are we going to abandon them?" Danver asked.

"For now. I'm afraid the long sleep made them weak. Let's see how they do on their own. Then we will decide their fate."

Cromas looked out the window at the new city built in the side of the mountain. Their new home was inside the mountain with only the balconies protruding from the edge of the rocky surface.

A large fountain in the center of the square reflected the sun's rays in the clean crisp mountain air.

He could see the enhanced newborn hurrying to class in the silver and grey building whose walls were made entirely of glass.

Farther in the distance, he could almost make out the training field. He saw several Dragoneers swoop down from the sky and fade from view.

This is what they should have done before they took on Sierra and Alexi. He was glad they were now moving in the right direction.

He was uncertain if they were correct in abandoning the others, but they could have come with them, and chose not to.

Time would tell if they had made the right choice in leaving them behind. The mountains served as a good fortress. You could only approach the city from one side, so any attack would be visible immediately.

Since many of the buildings were built directly into the mountain, you would have to bring down the mountain to destroy them.

The only thing susceptible to attack were the fields and orchards built farther down the mountain. To make certain their food sources couldn't be cut off during a prolong battle, there were hydroponic gardens inside the mountain along with shelters in case Atmos ever released his disease again.

It seemed like they had thought of everything.

"All I ask is for everyone to help the newborn. They are our people now and we have no contact with those we left behind," Rialda said interrupting his thoughts.

"What if they want to join us?" Martoon asked.

"They had their chance. My concern is, they would be here to spy on us."

Martoon could see the wisdom in this. Fortis and Chase entered the room, taking their place at the table.

"How are the newborn?"

"Training is going better than expected. I have a suggestion," Fortis said.

"Go on," Rialda said.

"Okay. We need to stop calling them newborn, so they don't feel separated from us," he said.

"That is a wise suggestion. Thank you for pointing it out."

Fortis nodded. "Each of us possess various levels and skills in magic. We need to all train the students as well as working to enhance our own magical skills. Since we are at peace with the forest Elfin, I suggest they train with them as well.

Rialda sat forward. "I will seek out Atmos and make a deal with him to train our children. They are, after all, descendants of our people."

"Wonderful. Let me know when you have it arranged," Fortis said.

"How are the gardens?" she asked Chase.

"No problems to report. Everything is going smoothly," he said.

"Wonderful. Then no one has anything to add. I will speak with Atmos." Enid met her outside and together they took flight.

She looked down at the new city and smiled. It felt right. For the first time since coming out of their long sleep, things felt right.

She entered the forest, landing in the same clearing as before and reached out to Atmos.

Atmos felt her calling to him, put down his hammer on his workbench and left his craft shop next to his house to hurry down the trail to the clearing. He found Rialda standing in the clearing looking up as the sunlight broke through the trees, shining on her lovely face, the scarred side turned away from him.

"You called for me?" he said.

Rialda opened her eyes and turned to look at the smaller Elfin. She really looked at him for the first time and smiled. He was from a mixture of her people and a race that vanished a long time ago. She had been taught that they were inferior, but she no longer believed that to be true.

"Thank you for coming so quickly. Please sit. I have much to tell you," she said excitedly.

She sat on a moss-covered log. Atmos hesitantly sat a few feet away from her.

Rialda took note of his distrust of her and vowed to fix it. He would learn to trust her.

"I gather the battle went well?" he asked.

"It didn't go as expected," she said honestly.

Atmos tried to hide his fear. Blood truce or not he was terrified of her. She was capable of killing them both to enact her revenge.

"Are you here to kill me?" he stammered.

Rialda reached out and covered his hand with hers. "No, my friend. I am here to ask for your help. Besides, the blood truce prevents me from hurting you without causing my own death," she reminded him.

"But I'm not sure if the truce is valid anymore. I've split from most of my people to start over."

Atmos was shaking so hard he struggled to stay seated on the log.

Rialda felt sorry for him and squeezed his hand reassuringly. "I overreacted when I awoke and found intruders in our home. I'm taking a step back to rebuild our kingdom the right way."

Atmos relaxed a little. "Why split with your people then?"

"They may take their lives in a different direction. It isn't right for me to try and force them to conform to my ways. I wish them the best, which is what I want for my people."

"What do you want from me?"

"I want you to train our children in your ways, which will include magic."

Atmos was stunned. He never expected this.

"Your children are welcome to attend our school and can even have a Dragon of their own if they show they possess the ability to train with them."

"Why are you doing this?" he whispered in shock.

"We share a common ancestor. We should work together for the betterment of our people. We nearly killed ourselves off over nothing. It's time we come together as the family we should have been."

"I don't know what to say," he said honestly.

"Say you will think about it," she said.

"I definitely will," he said. All his people ever wanted was to be treated as equals and Rialda was offering that to him willingly.

"These strangers we encountered have very strong magic. I want our people to be able to survive any future encounter with them," she said honestly.

"I will speak with my people and let you know," he said.

"I don't mean to rush you, but if you could speak to them now, we could get started now. Your children could return with me and begin school, and I can send students to you until you move."

"So soon?" he asked. "Move?"

"I don't see a reason to wait, Besides, do you want to continue hiding in the forest?" she replied sweetly.

He knew many of their children would love the chance to train with the Dragons. It was a dream come true. "Wait here. I will be back as quickly as I can."

"Thank you," she said.

Atmos hurried over the overgrown forest floor. His mind was racing. Was this a trick to steal their children again? Would the blood truce do anything if she hurt them? If she were telling the truth, this would finally bring their races together as he always thought they should be. They would be stronger and better, and no longer hiding in the forest.

He didn't think Sierra would seek them out to do them harm, but it wouldn't hurt to be ready, just in case.

He entered his village at a run yelling at the top of his lungs.

His people raced to him, terrified that he'd been hurt.

"What is wrong Atmos?" his wife Glory asked.

"We have a decision to make, and we have to make it now," he said breathlessly.

He quickly told them what Rialda had offered. They listened in stunned silence. When he finished, he asked, "Well?"

"It's what we always wanted," Cletus said. "And she's just giving it to us? Why now?"

"She admitted that she's been wrong and wants to make it right."

"And we can visit her new city?" Eldin asked.

"Yes. We will not be treated any differently by them."

"I can't believe this," Glory said. "And they're going to let us move into their new fancy city?"

"She said something about moving, but honestly, I was too stunned to ask what she meant. It would make sense if we did. If we are going to be teachers and our children students, it would be easier if we lived in the same city."

"Do we really want to do that?" Leland asked.

"We should consider it," Atmos said.

"This will change all of our lives. No more hiding. Our children get to be Dragoneers."

"What about the other Dragoneers she left behind?" Glory asked.

"She said they've chosen another path. I'm not sure what that path is, but I liked what Rialda has planned out and I think it will be good for all of us."

"Then tell her yes," Cletus said, "If we get to move to her city."

"Are we in agreement?" Atmos asked excitedly.

They looked around at each other and one by one, slowly nodded their heads.

"I will tell her and be back," Atmos said as he turned and raced down the path again.

He found Rialda still sitting on the moss-covered stump. She rose to her feet when he entered the clearing.

His expression gave nothing away. She was worried that his people told him to tell her to go to the devil, and she couldn't blame them.

"We want to live and work in your new city. To really become one people."

Rialda blinked as his words sunk in. "That's wonderful," she said smiling. "It would help our two cultures merge and better influence one another."

"We will gather our belongings and join you," he said.

"I do have a question. Would you like me to create more modern housing for you? You can alter it to suit you once you move in."

"That would be nice. We will need land for our animals and to farm."

"There is a perfect area a little higher up the mountain that would be perfect for those who wish to farm and ranch. You can set up your businesses in town and live in town if you prefer."

"I think we will have to decide once we arrive."

"Very well. I will make arrangements. We will see you soon," she said, turning to leave, then turned back again. "I am terribly sorry for what I caused all of us. We let something foolish get out of hand. I promise to control my temper and try to be wiser. I expect you to teach me how to be understanding."

Atmos was shocked by her apology and smiled, "That's a tall order, but I'll do my best," he said.

Rialda smiled. "I've learned a lot since we woke up and I hope to do much better from now on."

"I will do my part to hold you to that," he promised.

"I'll hold you to that," she teased, and it felt good. She decided that relaxing and not being so angry and in control felt pretty good.

Smiling, she climbed on Enid and hurried home to make preparations for their arrival.

She called her people together to give them the news. At first, they were stunned, then excited at the prospect of learning stronger magic, mostly, they were surprised by the sudden change in Rialda. The recent battle had changed her. Never before in her lifetime had she fought a battle that she knew she couldn't win, and it terrified her.

Chapter Thirty-Three

The Aftermath

Jinks, Adam, Leiya, and Minerva moved among the wounded, healing them as quickly as they could and moved to the next.

They made the dead and body parts vanish.

There would be no burials for the Dragons and Dragoneers.

The Dragons transported the smaller Dragons and Dragoneers to separate dungeons. A binding spell was placed on them so they couldn't practice magic and escape.

Adam looked out over the meadow still covered in blood. The Dragons had ripped so many of the smaller Dragons apart.

A thrill of pride and sadness washed over him. He'd done well in his first battle, but so many had died and for what.

Leiya came up beside him and asked, "Are you okay?"

Adam turned and smiled at her and said, "I'm fine. We fought well today."

"Yes, we did. Any idea why we were attacked?"

"Sierra pissed off their leader by entering their world," he said shrugging. "Some people get bent out of shape over the smallest things."

Leiya laughed. "Minerva had me send Sierra a message to let her know what happened here."

"Good. She'll know what to do with our prisoners," he said.

Speaking of Minerva, she joined them on the small mound of grass and set about erasing all signs of the battle.

She removed the blood from the grass and returned everything to the way it was before the attack.

"It's like it never happened," Leiya whispered softly.

⁂

Lazrus landed in the soft grass and Sierra jumped from his back and raced across the grass and knelt next to Collin.

Collin groaned and tried to sit up. His shirt was ripped and covered in his blood.

Sierra ran her hands over him, trying to find his wounds. Not finding any, she sat back and looked at him. "Are you okay?"

Collin rubbed his fingers through his hair and said, "I think so."

She sat back on her heels, relieved, looking out across Pandora Two. Blood and carnage were everywhere. The screams and the cries of the wounded echoed in her head.

Reminding herself that it could have been worse. She wanted to scream at the uselessness and waste.

Dak bent down next to her and pulled her into his arms, cradling her head against his shoulder.

"This is too much," she said sadly.

Dak kissed the top of her head, holding her close to comfort her while he erased all traces of the battle.

He moved the bodies of the Dragons and Dragoneers to a new building where they could honor them at a later time.

Sierra was right. This was too much. They were too young to have died for nothing.

He helped Sierra to her feet just as Alexi caught up with them.

"We should go after them," Alexi said.

Dak frowned. "There's been enough death for one day," he said.

Alexie looked back and forth between Dak and Sierra and nodded, leaving them alone.

"I need to talk to Gerferlum and find out how he knew we were under attack," she said.

"I want to learn that yell of his," Dak said.

Sierra managed to smile. "He's definitely full of surprises."

They located Gerferlum and Gareth telling Mags, Mavis, Ben, Fin, and Egon about the battle in Pandora.

They were taken by surprise that they'd reached Pandora.

"The Destroyer must have opened a rip," Sierra said. "He must be helping Rialda."

"Seems that way," Mags said.

"What was this illness that suddenly overcame them?" Mavis asked.

"I gave them the flu," Sierra said.

Dak raised one eyebrow and frowned.

"The flu?"

Dak burst out laughing.

"I'm glad you find it amusing." Sierra said.

"They certainly didn't look very well when they left." Ben said, smiling at Sierra.

"They will regroup and come back," Alexi said. "That's why we should go after them."

"They were beaten badly today." Dak said. "There's a good chance they've realized that it is useless to return."

"You don't know Rialda," Alexi said. "She never gives up."

"We will bury our dead, then decide what our next step will be," Sierra said.

Alexi grabbed Demitri by the arm, pulling him away with her. "You know I'm right. We should go after her and finish this."

Dimitri stared at her in surprise.

"Why are you looking at me like that?"

"You sound just like her," he said.

"Like whom?" Alexi asked frowning.

"Rialda," he said softly.

Alexi stared at him in surprise. "I just want this to be over. I don't want to have to worry about her for the rest of my life."

"Her newborns took a beating today. I don't think she will return any time soon, and when she does, we'll send her home again."

Alexi smiled. "I hope you're right," she said, knowing in her heart they were making a mistake.

As the custom of the Dragoneers, a huge funeral pyre was erected, and the scented wrapped bodies were placed side by side.

Prayers for the dead were said by Alexi and Dimitri and the fire was lit as Demitri's voice trailed off.

The remaining Dragoneers paraded by, one by one repaying their respects to their fallen friends.

Alexi lit the pyre with a torch, and they stood back, softly humming.

As the fire engulfed the dead, the Dragons and Dragoneers moved away from the blaze.

Dak put his arm around Sierra's waist. "This isn't your fault." He reminded her.

"I feel like we brought them here, just to die, defending us," she said sadly.

"That's not exactly the way it was," he said.

"I know, but it is still terrible. When is the violence going to stop?"

Dak kissed the top of her head. "I don't know sweetheart. Has it stopped in your world?"

Sierra groaned. "No, and it never will. I guess it's just a part of life, and I have to accept it."

"I refuse to accept it. Pandora is peaceful and thanks to you, so are the other realms."

Sierra smiled. "I'm going to break the spell protecting that gate. Then I can shrink it and put it away so they can't return."

"That would solve our problem."

Sierra kissed him and turned to mist and raced across Pandora. She sped up the stairs and into her spell room and retook form. She pulled out her crystals and concentrated over them, mixing and casting spells.

— ∙ — ∙ — ∙ —

Alexi and Dimitri returned to Alexi's home. The Dragons went off to Alton's room, while Alexi and Dimitri relaxed on her plush sofa.

Alexi sat forward, still seething with anger. "I know you don't agree, but we have to go after Rialda."

"We won this round today. Why isn't that enough?"

"I'm tired of her getting away with destroying lives and walking away undamaged. She destroyed my city and my family, and we must adjust. I can't adjust anymore."

"Please don't do this. You brought us here to start over."

"And she followed us here."

Alton sauntered into the room glaring at Dimitri.

"We tried to walk away, and it didn't work. Alexi is right. We should return home and put an end to Rialda." Alton said.

Alexi smiled in gratitude at him.

Dimitri shook his head sadly "If you return, I won't be going with you," he said, sadly.

Alexi's eyes widened in disbelief.

"You can't be serious. You would break us up?"

"You're breaking us up for revenge, and I won't have any part of it."

"You want to stay here alone? You can't be serious."

"I don't think I'll be alone," he said. Calling out to Bayliss, he climbed on his back and dove off Alexi's balcony and flew above the funeral pyre that was starting to burn out.

"She's angry. She could change her mind," Bayliss said.

"She won't change her mind," he said sadly.

"What will you do? You love her. You can't let her go without you."

"That's exactly what I'll do. Her thirst for revenge would come between us anyway."

"So, we stay here?"

"You can go home, if that's what you want. This is my home now."

"You know I won't leave you."

"Even if you think I'm making a mistake?"

"I didn't say it was a mistake. I just said that you love her."

"I do love her, but it must end somewhere. I can't live with her desire for revenge. Either way, I lose her."

Alexi put her arms around Alton's neck "You don't think he will really stay here if I return?"

Alton nuzzled her head with his. "Yes, I do."

"What do I do?"

"Follow your heart."

"If I do that, I stay with Dimitri."

"Your heart can tell you more than one thing," he said.

"I have to face Rialda. She can't keep getting away with destroying lives. What if I can't stop her, and I throw away my life for nothing?"

"Only you can make that choice," he reminded her. "Doing what you think is right is never easy," he added.

Chapter Thirty-Four

Finding your way

Skylar, Slaven, Mertz and Narla sat around a glossy wooden table looking back and forth at each other.

"We have to get organized," Mertz said. "The newborn are looking to us for directions."

"We have to pull it together," Narla said. "Rialda is gone, but she could return, and we have to be ready for when that happens."

"Where do we start?" Skylar asked. "This is new for all of us."

"We better figure it out fast."

"The newborn need training. I will get started on that," Slaven said.

"They are confused about the others leaving."

"We need to elect someone to lead us," Mertz said.

"I think the four of us should lead together," Narla said. "We need to break with the way Rialda did things."

"I agree," Skylar said.

"Ok, then can we all agree we have to train and guide the newborn. We need to establish a relationship with the other cities and get our farms back into production." Mertz said.

"We're going to need friends and allies."

"I'll visit Lorelie and inform her of Rialda's departure," Skylar said. "I think she could be helpful to us."

"That's a good idea. Rialda didn't like her, so she will be an asset to us." Mertz said. "The rest of us will put things back together here."

Skylar had Hawk meet her outside and climbed on her back and headed toward Lorelie's city.

Mertz, Slavan, and Narla called for all the Dragoneers to meet them in the center of the city.

They looked across the bricked square at the nearly two thousand confused faces, looking to them for guidance.

They split them up into three groups. Mertz took his group to the training field where they reunited with their Dragons. They practiced flying through the courses that Alexi had created.

Narla and Slaven took their groups to the field near the training grounds and walked them through a series of simple magic spells.

The newborns were eager to learn and excited to have a sense of direction.

They took to the training absorbing it like a sponge.

Narla and Slaven learned that they were good teachers.

"Why did Rialda leave?" Narla asked while they were watching the newborn run through their exercises.

"She thinks we are weak because we don't agree with every decision she made." Slaven answered.

"That's not fair. She should have cared what we thought."

"Well, she didn't. No sense dwelling on it. There used to be six cities of our people. Now there are two. We will show Rialda that we are anything but weak."

Narla nodded. She was glad they'd talked. She felt much more confident.

Skylar and Hawk landed on Lorelie's island.

Curious, Lorelie went down to the beach to greet them. Skylar looked upset but was trying to hide it.

Lorelie smiled and said, "I didn't expect to see you again so soon. Please come inside and have some refreshments."

Skylar nodded. "Thank you," she said.

Lorelie served her a glass of nectar tea on a small flower shaped crystal cup and served her tiny leaf shaped pastries that melted on her tongue.

Skylar relaxed after her second cup of nectar and said, "Thank you. It's been a trying day. I've come here to inform you that Rialda has left us and built a new city in the mountains. We would like to form an allegiance with you and your people."

Lorelie sat back in thought. She was surprised by the sudden turn of events. She'd expected trouble from Rialda, but not this.

"So, you want a peace accord between our people in case Rialda returns to cause you trouble?"

Skylar frowned. "It sounds terrible when you put it like that."

"My apologies. I want to make certain I know what you're asking for."

"We had such a wonderful time at your celebration. We want the fun and joy that you have." Lorelie felt sorry for Skylar. "You haven't had much of either in your young life?"

"No, my people haven't known much joy or fun. We've known war and death and training for more war and death. We want to change that, but still be ready in case Rialda returns to retake the city."

"I think it would be in our best interest to join our people together, along with the Gnomes and Ocean Fairies," Lorelie said.

"Thank you. I will let my people know."

"I will prepare a celebration where we will all join our people together."

"Thank you again," Skylar said, feeling much better now that they were allies.

"We will open trades and training between our people. This will be good for all of us."

"I believe you are right," Skylar said.

"I will let you know when we will meet," Lorelie said.

Skylar nodded. "I will see you again soon."

"I'm looking forward to it."

Skylar relaxed as she strolled down the flower strewn path to the beach, she admired the beautiful flowers that lined the path and inhaled their soft fragrance. She liked it here and wished that their home could be more like it.

She smiled when the path opened up onto the beach and she saw Hawk rolling around on the warm sand.

Hawk grinned sheepishly as she rose to her feet, shaking off the sand. "What?" she said. "You should try it. It feels wonderful."

"I'll take your word for it," she said, climbing on her back.

Hawk took flight, soaring before diving down into the water and flying out, shaking the water off of them.

Skylar laughed and Hawk dove into the water again.

Skylar shook her wet hair and laughed as Hawk soared and picked up speed to dry them.

⁓ ༻✦༺ ⁓   ⁓ ༻✦༺ ⁓   ⁓ ༻✦༺ ⁓

Three days later, they all gathered at Lorelie's. The Dragoneers took their place next to Lorelie and greeted Drake and the other Ocean Fairies.

Simmy led the other Gnomes toward Lorelie. He introduced King Aubrey and Queen Orla.

The two Gnomes bowed in respect before taking their place beside them.

Lorelie brought out a large parchment that spelled out the terms of their agreement. To attack one, was to attack all. They would work together for the betterment of all their people.

Lorelie signed for her people, Drake for his, Aubrey for his and Skylar for hers.

With the last signature in place, the parchment glowed, sending out a warm glow that cast a binding spell on all of them.

If they were in trouble, the others would know immediately so they could come to their aid.

Crystal flutes filled with honey rose nectar were passed around and a toast was drunk to celebrate the union.

At the final toast, the crowd cheered, and the dancing and celebrations began. The party lasted until the sun rose the next morning.

Excited about their future, the four allies bid each other goodbye, already preparing to meet at the annual Gnome's fair.

With a light heart, Skylar, Mertz, Slaven and Narla headed for home.

For thirty days, Alexi tried to push aside her desire to go after Rialda, but the desire only grew stronger.

She hated that Dimitri was avoiding her. She wanted them to do this together, but he refused to listen. Exhaling softly, she decided that she had already waited too long, and it was time to return home.

Alton was at her side without her having to call him.

"This is for the best," he assured her.

"I hope so. It's killing me to leave without Dimitri. I feel bad leaving after they welcomed us here."

"You are doing what's best for our people," Alton reminded her.

"I know. Let's do it before I change my mind."

Alexi climbed on Alton, and they circled around their homes, calling out to their people.

Dimitri and Sierra heard her call and Dimitri called Bayliss and raced outside, ignoring Alexi as he too called out to their people.

Sierra turned to mist and retook her human form, standing in the courtyard looking up at the four-story buildings that housed the Dragons and Dragoneers.

Dimitri landed next to her.

"What's happening?" Sierra asked.

"Alexi is going after Rialda," he said sadly.

"Are you going with her?"

"No, not all of my people have her taste for revenge."

"You can't talk her out of it?"

"I tried. She feels she has to do this."

Sierra nodded in understanding.

"As soon as I figure out a way to break the spell on the gate, I will seal it. She won't be able to return."

Dimitri took a deep breath, pushing aside the painful idea of never seeing her again and said, "I will see that she knows."

Soon the courtyard was filled with Dragons and Dragoneers.

Steph and Armond pushed their way through the crowd and approached Dimitri. "Can't you stop her?" Steph said.

"You know I can't," he said.

"This is wrong. She knows it's wrong," she cried.

Dimitri hugged her gently. "She believes that it's the right thing for her."

Steph approached Sierra. "Can't you stop her?"

"I will try to talk to her," she promised.

Alexi landed near Sierra and Dimitri, forcing the crowd to move back, to make room for her.

She slowly approached Sierra, avoiding looking at Dimitri.

"I want to thank you for taking us in and giving us a home," she said.

"I hoped it would be a permanent home," Sierra said.

"Please don't leave," Steph said.

Alexi looked at her in confusion, then jerked her head up to look at Dimitri. "What have you done?" she asked.

Dimitri looked at her with such pain on his face, Sierra had to look away. "Not everyone feels the way you do. This is the only home they know."

Alexi blinked back tears and looked at Steph. "You can always come for a visit," she said softly.

"That may not be possible for long," Sierra said.

"Why not?" Alexi asked in alarm. She didn't want to be cut off from them.

"As soon as I can break the spell cast on the gate, I will seal it."

"But why?"

"Too many have died because of the need for revenge. Rialda showed little thought to the lives lost, and we don't want that to become a normal part of our life."

Alexi pushed down a sob and looked at Dimitri. She thought she'd always be able to come back and convince him to join her. The thought of never seeing him again was tearing her apart. "Knowing this, you still won't come with me?" she asked.

"And knowing this, you still want to leave?" he asked, looking at her beautiful face for one last time.

Alexi didn't know what to say. This wasn't how she wanted things to end. She nodded her head slightly. "Please let me know before you seal the gate," she asked.

"I will, and please know that you always have a home here."

"Everyone that is with me, let's ride," she said with one last look at Dimitri.

About five hundred of the youngest Dragoneers took flight, following her toward the mountain and through the gate.

They nodded to Slade, the Vampires, and the Dragons as they went by before entering the gate toward home.

Sierra followed them, stopping to talk to Slade, the Vampires, and the Giants.

"I'm going to shrink their gate, but with their magic, they can enlarge it at any time. I am working on a spell to break the spell on the gate leading to my world. Once I do, I will seal it from my side."

"Why can't you seal their gate?" Slade asked.

"I would have to do it from their side, and they could just undo the spell. They can't undo it from this side" She explained.

"Because we don't have magic?" he asked.

"Yes."

"So, we will have to deal with them alone?"

"I'm sorry. You are welcome to relocate to our world."

"No, thank you. This is our home. We will defend it if we have to."

"Then it's time to return home," Ambro said.

"Thank you all for helping us," Slade said.

"It was our pleasure," Ambro said shaking his hand. "Good luck my friend."

"I wish the same for you," Slade said.

Sierra watched as they all filed through the gate to return home.

"Are you certain you want to remain here?"

"Yes. This is our home and without their magic, they aren't too scary," he said laughing.

"I will check in on you from time to time to make sure you are okay," she promised.

"Thank you," he said, squeezing her hand affectionately.

Sierra kissed him on the cheek before turning and stepping through the gate and racing back to her lab to try to break the spell.

She was surprised a few moments later by Ben and Egon, offering their help to break what had to be an elder spell.

***

Alexi returned home, saddened that she was doing it without Dimitri or her friends.

She warned her people to watch out for an attack from Rialda's troops, but all was quiet.

They reached the Dragon city without any incident, and landed in the center of town and were surprised that only Mertz, Skylar, Slaven and Narla came out to meet them.

Mertz frowned slightly seeing Alexi accompanied by her small army.

"Have you come to attack us?" Skylar asked.

"Where's Rialda?" Alexi asked.

Skylar pointed to the mountain, "She left the same day we returned from the battle with you."

Alexi frowned. "Left. Why did she leave? Why didn't you go with her?"

"You sure ask a lot of questions for someone who ran away and abandoned us," Mertz said.

Alexi frowned. "Well, I'm back now," she said.

"To settle the score with Rialda?" Narla asked.

"Don't you want the same thing since she abandoned you?"

"Like you did?" Slaven said.

Alexi frowned. This wasn't going anything like she expected.

"There's nothing here for you. Things have changed while you've been gone," Mertz said.

Alexi glanced sadly at Skylar, who quickly looked away.

Alexi took flight, taking her new people with her. She rode across the thick forest to the coast, the opposite coast from Lorelie and the Ocean Fairies.

They landed in tall soft grass. The young Dragoneers were confused by what had transpired since their return, but they waited patiently to see what she'd do next.

For the third time, Alexi recreated the city she grew up in. She erected five two story buildings with a third floor connecting all of the buildings. This would be where she and Alton lived and trained the Dragoneers in magic.

She tried not to think about how alone she felt as she created the training ground, and as a final thought, she put up a wall surrounding Dragon's Pride, the name of her new city, and cast a spell, protecting it from outsiders.

Then to her horror, she created a new building that would house the newborn and Dragon mothers. She had to increase the size of her army, or Rialda would destroy them in minutes.

She was surprised that Rialda had deserted some of her people and would love to have a peek inside her new city, but that would have to wait.

Alton reminded her to create fields so she could feed her people. He promised the Dragons would learn how to fish, and he'd conduct the training until the students could become the teachers.

She wished Dimitri were here to help her, but she could count on Alton, and soon the others would be able to help.

She allowed them to get settled, and early the next morning she continued the magic classes they'd started in Pandora Two.

Alton ran them through the races, impressed with their abilities.

His gaze kept wandering to the mountain far off in the distance.

He pushed thoughts of Rialda from his mind and concentrated on the young Dragons and Dragoneers in front of him.

He was pushing them through their routine. They had just hit the boats when an alarm rang out. Someone was outside the gate.

Six Dragons and Dragoneers opened the gate ready to attack the intruders, but it was only Skylar smiling warmly at them.

"I came to see Alexi," she said sweetly.

Alexi instructed them to escort her to the training room.

Skylar looked around the city that looked very much like hers. She felt bad that they hadn't invited her to rejoin them.

Looking around her training studio, Skylar was impressed. She smiled and waved slightly at Alexi.

Alexi gave the students a break while she went to see what Skylar wanted. Part of her was glad to see her, but she couldn't afford to let those feelings rise to the surface.

"What brings you to Dragon's Pride?" Alexi asked.

"Dragon's Pride. I like the name," Skylar said sincerely.

"I'm glad you approve." Alexi said, wishing she'd get to the point.

"I wanted to make sure you were all right. We weren't very nice to you yesterday, and I'm sorry. We were friends once. I'd like to be friends again."

"I'd like that too," Alexi said, knowing she could get information out of Skylar. "How will the others feel about it?"

"They won't care, and if they do, well, it's too bad. I don't have to follow anyone's orders anymore."

"Why did Rialda leave you?" Alexi asked.

"Honestly, I think she was afraid we weren't going to continue to go along with her plan, so she cut and ran."

"That's not like her. I'm sure she's planning something. You know her. She never gives up."

"I know, but we're preparing for that."

"How? I could use some pointers." Alexi said sweetly.

"Oh, my goodness. You don't know. There are other races here."

Alexi leaned forward with interest and said. "What? Where?"

"There's a race of Ocean Fairies. They have a city beneath the ocean. Then there are Water Fairies. They are different than the Ocean Fairies, but not by much. Then there are the Gnomes. They are so funny."

"Wow. How did you meet them?"

"We attended a celebration on the Water Fairy's island. Rialda wasn't happy and left us that day."

"So, Rialda doesn't like these strangers?"

"They're not strangers. They are our friends."

"That's wonderful, but how can you trust that they are truly your friend?"

"We've signed an agreement with them. If Rialda comes after us, they will come to our aide."

Alexi laughed. "Rialda won't like that."

"Too bad. You will like these people. They are fun and happy. I want to be happy and have fun."

Alexi reached over and covered Skylar's hand with hers and squeezed it gently.

"I know you do. With Rialda out of your life, maybe you will find happiness and have fun."

Skylar smiled. "I hope so. What are your plans for Rialda? Maybe she's retreated to the mountain and won't ever return."

"You know her better than that. I will train my people and be ready for her when she does return."

"That's pretty much what we're doing. You should meet the others and join us."

"I would like to meet the others, but I don't think I'm in any shape to join anyone but thank you for inviting me."

"Don't be a stranger. Visit us sometime."

"I will, and please come back. I really enjoyed our visit."

Skylar rose and kissed Alexi on the cheek. "I'll see you soon. You must attend the Gnome festival. I'll bring you the details. That will give you a chance to meet everyone."

"That sounds wonderful. I'd love to attend."

"Great. I'll see you soon."

Alexi's guards escorted her back through town to the gate and watched as she mounted Hawk and flew away.

As soon as she returned, she reported her visit to the others, satisfied that for now, she was training her army for Rialda's return.

Chapter Thirty-Five

Rialda

With the help of Atmos and the other Elfin, Rialda was discovering that there could be joy in life.

The Elfin and Dragoneers were thriving together in ways they'd never accomplished alone. The Dragoneers magic was different and more of a challenge to learn, but the Dragoneers were mastering it, along with Rialda.

The Elfin children took to the Dragons with a natural grace and excelled at the games forcing the Dragoneers to step up their game.

The city was often filled with laughter as the Dragoneers and Elfin played tricks on one another.

She looked out at her people from her balcony and realized that they were happy.

She couldn't keep up with how many weddings they'd had, and how many expecting mothers there were. She eagerly awaited the next generation who had no knowledge of the sickness.

Enid came up beside her and asked, "What's troubling you?"

"Nothing, and it feels good, but very strange."

"Are you still seeking revenge?"

"I'm finding that life here in the mountain agrees with me and for now I have no desire to leave."

"That is wise. Our people are happy. I think we all deserve happiness."

"I agree. Now go. I have dinner plans with Cromas."

"I'm going. Crotus and I will continue our game of cards. I'm one set ahead and he's not too happy."

"You two have fun, but you need to see Navi again."

Enid snorted. "Don't play matchmaker."

Rialda threw up her hands. "Fine. I won't say another word."

Cromas and Crotus landed on her balcony and Crotus hurried off with Enid, eager to continue their game.

Cromas smiled and handed Rialda a small bottle of wine the Elfin had made.

She smiled and said, "Thank you. I'll be right back."

She returned a few moments later with two crystal glasses, pouring them a generous amount of the Elfin wine.

Clinking their glasses together, they said, "To us."

Rialda crossed the room, standing at the balcony looking out over the city. She'd never imagined that things could go so well. She could see the Dragoneers racing across the sky in some sort of game.

Cromas eased in next to her.

"Our lives are quite different now. How do you feel about that?" she asked, turning to face him.

Cromas looked back over the city then looked at Rialda again. "I like it. I feel, for the first time ever, that we're actually living.

"Before the sickness, we were at war with our own people over how we should rule. Then we were at war with the Elfin."

"And now?"

"We prepare for a war, I hope never comes," he said honestly.

"Maybe it's the mountain air, but I'd like for the peace to continue."

Cromas looked at her in surprise.

Rialda laughed. "You never thought you'd hear me say that?"

"Honestly, no. What about Skylar and the others? Why did you leave them?"

"They were not with us, which is fine, but we didn't need to be fighting among ourselves if we are to truly start over."

"They will be fine. I think they will look to their new friends for help."

"That could be good for them."

He raised his glass in a toast and said. "Here's to them, not looking for trouble."

Rialda raised her glass against his. "And here's to being ready for trouble."

Cromas laughed and drained his glass.

⸻   ⸻   ⸻

Alexi stood over the unhatched egg and cast a spell on two dozen of them, shrinking them to the size of sparrow eggs.

Then, she accelerated their growth and watched while the tiny eggs hatched. She cast a spell flooding their minds with information.

The tiny Dragoneers climbed on the equally small Dragons and flew away.

Splitting them up, some flew to Rialda's new city. Others were sent to Skylar's, Lorelei's, and the Gnomes. Their mission was to watch and learn.

Rialda felt something was off the moment the tiny Dragoneers entered the city. She stood alone at her balcony looking out over the city. Using magic, she scanned the entire city for anything unusual and didn't detect anything out of the ordinary, but yet, something was off.

She called out to Enid and the two of them flew across the city, watching and looking for anything unusual.

The tiny Dragoneers moved out of sight as she flew by, watching her as she flew around the city.

One of them followed Rialda back home and circled around her building.

Rialda sensed her presence and was puzzled when she couldn't see anything. She knew something was out there. How did she find what she couldn't see?

She cast a spell across the city to alert her if anything or anyone tried to enter the city. Unfortunately, the Dragoneers didn't register since they were so small and already inside the city.

The tiny spies watched each city for several days before returning to report to Alexi.

In their absence, Alexi had doubled the size of her army.

Her thirst for revenge intensified with each passing day.

She was surprised to learn that Rialda had teamed up with the Elfin, and wished her spies could get closer to learn what they were teaching her Dragoneers.

Confident that her magic was greater than Rialda's, she didn't see the Elfin as much of a threat as long as they didn't bring back the sickness.

Using her magic, she turned all of her new Dragons black and silver, and her Dragoneers wore the same colors, to distinguish them from the other Dragons and Dragoneers.

She trained them tirelessly, day after day. Still hoping that Dimitri would reconsider and join her.

She thought he had reconsidered when he showed up one day outside her walls.

Racing to the gate to let him in, she threw herself into his arms.

Dimitri clung to her briefly before releasing her.

"I'm so glad to see you," Alexi said.

"You've created quite a place here." He responded as his gaze swept across her home and training grounds.

"I can give you a tour," she said proudly.

Dimitri frowned sadly, "This is still what you want to do?"

"Yes," she said excitedly. "I'm rebuilding my father's legacy."

"Your father wouldn't want you to do whatever it is you're planning on doing," he reminded her, recalling the kind, caring man.

"You're wrong. Rialda destroyed our city. I will destroy her. I'm guessing that you didn't come here to join me, so why are you here?"

"To let you know that Sierra broke the spell on the gate, and she will be sealing it."

Alexi's eyes widened in shock. So soon? She'd thought she would have more time.

"I see," she said softly.

Dimitri took her hands between his and looked into her eyes pleadingly.

"Come back with me. Abandon your revenge and make a new life with me."

Tears threatened to spill from her eyes as she said, "I can't. Will I be able to reach you once this is over?" she asked sadly.

"Sierra will check on the people of Callis from time to time. You can leave a message with them."

She nodded her head slightly in understanding. She wished she could convince him to stay but softly said, "I love you."

Dimitri groaned and crushed her to him, kissing her before releasing her saying, "But not enough to give up this foolishness."

He strode away from her, climbed on Bayliss, and flew away.

Dimitri flew over the Alexi's home before turning toward the gate.

The giants had moved the gates closer together and he quickly passed through the second one that was now next door to the castle in Pandora Two.

He nodded to Sierra as he flew out of the gate.

Sierra felt sorry for him. She could feel his pain and sadness.

She quickly sealed the gate and shrunk it. Picking it up from the ground, she wished that she didn't have to abandon the people of Callis, but the Dragoneers were too unstable and too much of a threat. Her fingers closed over the tiny gate as she opened a rip to her vault in Pandora and put the gate away for safe keeping.

She was ready to return home, and as soon as Ben's wedding was over, she was going home. She was tired and needed home to sooth her.

Alexi called to Alton and flew recklessly toward the gate. She couldn't accept that Dimitri would let Sierra cut him off from her.

When she entered Callis, she was both surprised and excited to see the other gate still standing.

She climbed off of Alton and slowly approached the shimmering gate and touched its smooth surface. It rippled beneath her fingers.

When she tried to put her hand through it, nothing happened.

She stood there staring at the glittering surface. A single tear rolled down her smooth cheek.

She climbed back on Alton and flew back through the gate, toward home.

Chapter Thirty-Six

Ben and Iesha

Iesha sat at an ornate dressing table combing her long blond hair. She studied her reflection in the mirror and smiled. Today was her wedding day.

She expertly braided her hair, leaving tendrils hanging down to frame her face.

Leiya entered the room, wearing a long fuchsia dress. "Are you ready to get dressed?"

"Yes. Thank you again for helping me," she said.

"I'm so glad you asked," she said, lifting the voluminous dress up and over Iesha's head.

The ivory dress clung tightly to her slender waist, with a heart shaped neckline, interwoven with tiny seed pearls.

The skirt hung in folds, interwoven with more pearls.

Iesha turned in a circle to get the full view in the floor length mirror.

"You look beautiful," Leiya said.

"Thank you. I feel like a princess."

"Well, your prince grows impatient. I think he's terrified that you will change your mind."

Iesha shook her head, slightly rolling her eyes. "Silly man," she said.

"The music is starting. It's time to go."

Taking a deep breath, she picked up her bouquet and led the way out of the room.

Stopping at the threshold to the chapel, she smiled at Ben, who was grinning from ear to ear. Next to him stood Dak, as his best man, looking very handsome in his black tux.

Across from him stood Sierra, wearing a strapless, burgundy gown, with burgundy shoes peeking out at the hem.

Egon stood facing her, ready to officiate the wedding, and the room was filled to capacity with her people and the Elders.

She smiled. Her marriage to Ben was bringing his journey full circle. He was finally ready to allow himself to be happy.

Leiya tugged on her arm to get her moving, as she escorted her down the aisle, handing her off to Ben before taking a seat.

"This is a glorious day," Egon began. "I have the pleasure of joining my son and his lovely bride in marriage. This is a wonderous time for them and our people."

He gently led them through their vows, to love, honor and respect each other, before pronouncing them husband and wife.

The entire city showed up in support of Ben and Iesha's wedding.

Sierra couldn't believe the changes since her last visit. The city was filled with vibrant colors, gone was the pale blue.

She watched Ben and Iesha dance, smiling at how normal today was.

Dak came up next to her, taking her hand, leading her onto the dance floor.

"Whatever you're thinking about, stop it and relax and have fun."

"Yes sir," she said, smiling up at him as he led her across the dance floor.

"Have I told you how beautiful you look?" he asked.

"Just a few times," she teased.

"I should dress up more often," she said.

The evening goes by in a blur as they cut the cake and toast to a long happy life.

Collin is about to make a toast when he clutched his chest, his eyes widen in a mixture of shock and pain.

He dropped his glass as he went down on his knees.

Dak and Egon rushed to his side, holding him up.

Sierra put her hands on him, performing a healing spell, but it didn't help.

Collin cried out. His cry was more of a howl than a human cry.

Egon and Dak can't hold him as he dropped to the ground, his body twisting and jerking.

"He's trying to turn into a wolf, but something's wrong." Egon said, trying to help him.

Collin's body tensed, then relaxed just as the man who had cured him during the attack, entered the room.

"I apologize for the interruption," he said. "I felt that he was in trouble. I'm here to help. Pardon me for being rude," he said pointing to his chest. "My name is Armond. I'm from the clan Mori."

Egon stepped in front of him, blocking his path to Collin. "How can you help him?"

"When I found him on the battlefield, he was mortally wounded. My people's blood has healing powers, and I used it to heal him. He's trying to change, but he could be different now.

"Different how?" Sierra asked.

"Let me help him and we shall see," he said.

Egon looked at Collin thrashing on the floor and stepped aside.

Armond bent down next to Collin, putting his hand on his chest, calming him.

He put his other hand on his forehead and Collin shifted into a fluffy black dog. Gone was his slick grey wolf form.

Collin rose to his feet and shook himself. He looked down at his massive black paws and threw his head back and howled a long mournful howl, then retook his human form.

He realized that everyone was staring at him and frowned, asking, "What happened?"

He noticed Armond and said, "You saved my life. Thank you."

"My pleasure," Armond said.

Sierra stepped toward Armond.

"Please thank your people for coming to our aide. We might not have survived without you."

"It's our home too. We will always defend our home," he said.

He turned to Collin and said, "I'm sorry that you have been affected."

"So, did I really turn into a big black dog?"

"Yes. It is a result of the transfer of my blood that saved your life."

"Will I do it again?"

"More than likely."

"Will I be able to do crazy tall leaps and knock Dragons out of the sky?"

Armond shook his head and laughed. "It's a possibility. You have to learn how to shift into one of us, so you don't get caught in between change."

"And you can teach me this?"

"Yes, I will teach you."

"Thank you and thanks again for saving my life."

"My pleasure. You are welcome to visit us at any time. I apologize for interrupting your celebration," he said, bowing, and leaving the room.

Collin shrugged and said, "I think I was about to give a toast to the happy couple, so let's raise our glasses," he said pretending to raise a glass, "and toast the happy couple."

They raised their glasses and cheered for Ben and Iesha.

Ben and Iesha raised their glasses in a toast and swallowed down the sweet nectar then tossed the glasses behind them and kissed.

Sierra and Dak whistled and cheered, clapping their hands.

Hand in hand, Ben and Iesha approached the smaller table with a white cake with small yellow and lavender flowers on it and together, cut a small piece and fed it to each other, before the cake was cut and served to the guests.

Together, Ben and Iesha bid their guests goodbye and climbed into a white carriage pulled by two white Pegasus and flew off to a replica of the island where Sierra and Dak spent their honeymoon.

Sierra leaned her head onto Dak's shoulder and sighed. "This was nice, other than Collin turning into a cute dog," she teased.

"Don't let him hear you call him a cute dog."

"He was cute, and you know it."

"Yeah," he laughed.

Ben and Iesha landed on the beach of the island, admiring the romantic getaway that Sierra created for them. Ben pulled Iesha into his arms and kissed her.

"I can't believe we're married," he said.

"Regrets already?" she teased.

"Never. I've never been happier and it's all because of you."

Iesha kissed him softly. "I'm glad. Are you certain you want to remain here? You won't miss your home?"

"My home is with you," he said kissing her softly.

Iesha slipped her arms around his, returning the kiss.

Chapter Thirty-Seven

Tying up Loose Ends

Sierra and Dak returned to Pandora Two to check on Dimitri and the other Dragoneers.

They were worried about them being able to move forward after Alexi's sudden departure.

They appeared together on Dimitri's balcony. Dimitri greeted them, hugging Sierra briefly.

"How was the wedding?" he asked.

"It went well. Thank you for asking. How are you?"

"I'm fine. I said goodbye to her," he said sadly.

"I'm so sorry. I know that couldn't have been easy."

"She made her choice. I have to respect that."

"She can always change her mind," she reminded him.

"She won't," he said sadly, shaking his head. "Where do the Dragoneers go from here?" he asked.

"Nothing's changed. You are in charge of them now. You have a wonderful team to help you continuing training."

"Then what?"

"It's time you meet the other inhabitants of this world and together, you all decide your place in the world."

"What is our place in this world?"

"Protectors."

"Protectors from what?"

"From whatever."

"From Alexi?" he asked.

"Possibly. She's angry and smart. She will figure out a way to come back to you."

Dimitri exhaled sharply. "It terrifies me that you may be right. How do I fight the woman I love?"

"I don't know. I hope it never happens, but this world has no one to really protect it. It needs you."

"It has you," he reminded her.

"It's time for us to go home," she said, linking her fingers with Dak's.

Dimitri looked at them in surprise.

"You won't desert us?"

"Never," she promised. "But we can't be here all of the time."

"Will I have access to you? I'd like to visit your home."

"Of course."

"I would like to meet the others then."

"You should set up a council like they have in the Opaque. It should be made up of all the members of this world, and together you decide what is best for all your people.

"That sounds fair. How soon can we meet?"

"I will arrange it and let you know. It shouldn't take long."

Sierra and Dak sent out a missive to all the leaders in the realms, even interrupting the newlyweds who'd just arrived at their island paradise.

She created a room next to her castle for them to hold the meeting.

The room was octagon shaped with large bay windows on each wall.

The center of the room was filled with a large shiny wooden table. The same shape as the room.

Seating occupied one section of the room for anyone interested in hearing council proceedings.

Within a few hours, Armond arrived with four of his people. Willis was the next to arrive. Armond, accompanied by two men and two women.

Iesha and Ben arrived, representing Iesha's people.

The Willow Wisp ignored the invitation.

The Dragons Mylanth and Briam represented the Dragons. One of the walls opened up to allow them to stick their heads in to attend the meeting.

Crastid and Blargi came representing the underwater kingdom.

Dimitri and Jax represented the Dragoneers.

Sierra and Dak could only assume that the other races weren't interested in serving on the council.

Together, they greeted everyone and asked them to choose one person to represent their people and take their seat at the council table.

The groups huddled together as Willis, Iesha and Dimitri took their seats.

They were soon joined by Armond, Briam and Crastid.

Iesha turned to Sierra and Dak and said, "There is one seat left. Sierra, you should join us."

"Thank you, but this is your council."

"None of us would be here without you."

"She's right," Willis said. "The council will not be complete without you."

Sierra reluctantly took her seat, and they all joined hands and Dragon claws.

Sierra said a spell, binding them all together for the betterment of their people.

It was agreed that only two gates to Pandora would remain. One with Iesha and at the bottom of the sea in the water kingdom.

Willis agreed to increase trade with the other cities as did Iesha, in return they would be protected by the Dragons, Dragoneers and the Weredogs.

The water kingdom would also increase trade but felt confident that they could protect themselves; but in case of another attack, they would help defend.

An agreement was signed, and Sierra promised that she would always help defend this realm.

A white light circled the table, drawing energy from each member sitting at the table and cast a bright light blue light in the center of the ceiling.

Each member of the council could feel a slight tug, binding them all together.

Willis stood to address the council members. "I ask that everyone increase food production in their cities. This could quickly become a problem for all of us. If you need assistance, I will be happy to help."

"Pandora Two absolutely needs to increase our production and we welcome your help," Sierra said. "We would like to extend an invitation to the Dragoneers to expand into our world to better protect this realm. Having all our fighters in Pandora Two isn't good strategically." Iesha said.

"Can you reroute the rivers, so we have access by water to the other cities?" Crastid asked. "We can better help with defense that way."

"I will take care of that," Sierra promised. "Then Dak and I will return to Pandora so we can continue building our city."

"Plus, it will give you a chance to work together without interference from us," Dak teased.

The meeting broke up and Sierra went outside and quickly rerouted the rivers, so they all flowed into each other. Then she met with Willis, hugging him warmly.

"It's good to see you," she said.

"Very good to see you again my dear. You look well," he said, kissing her on the cheek.

"I appreciate your taking the time to help me set up our farms in the most productive manner."

"Why do you grow food when you can create all you need?"

"It doesn't feel right. The food should be natural whenever possible."

They walked through the farms and orchards. Willis pointed out suggestions to get better crop yields and better irrigation techniques before heading back toward the castle.

The Dragoneers were on their way to Iesha's city to build a second location.

Jax agreed to head the new location, and to get it up and running.

Dimitri was impressed with his first glimpse of the modern city. It gave him hope for a better tomorrow.

Iesha gave him land to build outside the city. With Jax's assistance they created a new city. Its design was vastly different than their other cities.

All the buildings were single story and built around the training facility. The buildings were larger and round, with open balconies all the way around.

The river ran through the center of the city and giant trees draped the city in shade. Their sweet blossoms filled the air with their unique fragrance.

"It's lovely," Jax said.

"Yes, it is," Dimitri agreed.

"Are you certain you don't want to relocate here?" Jax asked. "I think it would be good for you."

Dimitri looked out across the city then turned to look at Iesha's city behind them. "If you don't mind, I think I will. You're right; it will be good for me."

Jax took his hand between hers and squeezed it affectionately. "We can always switch if you change your mind," she said.

"Thank you for being such a good friend."

"Aren't that what friends are for?" she teased, wishing she could take away his pain.

"It's lovely," Iesha said. "Do you require anything before we continue our honeymoon?"

"No, please go enjoy yourself." Dimitri said.

"We will see you when we return then," Ben added, before they turned to a white mist and hurried back to the island.

"I'd like to learn how they do that," Dimitri said.

"I'm sure it comes in handy." Jax teased.

Chapter Thirty-Eight

Lorelie

Lorelie sat in a vine woven swing in the center of a garden watching the two tiny blue and green Dragons chase each other like kittens.

She heard an odd noise, and quickly scanned the trees trying to locate where the sound was coming from.

Always paranoid, she cast a spell to shield her from prying eyes and to stop any unwelcome creatures from spoiling her moment with the Dragons.

Ari and Grace darted between the trees and around in circles as Ari tried to catch Grace.

But Grace was too quick for him and when he went straight instead of turning, he plowed right into Lorelie's leg.

Shaking her head in amusement, she picked Ari up and settled him in her lap as she stroked his soft, but scaley back.

He almost purred like a cat as he curled up into a ball and fell asleep.

Grace continued to race around the garden, tugging on his tail every time she passed by him, trying to wake him up.

Lorelie smiled. They were so cute. She wished she'd taken more eggs for herself and was about to attempt to remedy that mistake.

On Grace's next round, she scooped her up, holding her squirming body out in front of her.

Grace's eyes drooped, giving Lorelie a sad face. Lorelie glared at her, and Grace stopped squirming allowing Lorelie to hold her closer, kissing the top of her head.

She opened a hidden door in the ground and stepped down the cool stone steps, depositing them on the soft grass.

Ari curled up and went back to sleep. Grace sniffed at him, exhaled in frustration, and curled up next to him. With one last irritated look at Lorelie, she closed her big green eyes and went to sleep.

Lorelie smiled at the two sleeping Dragons and looked around the room littered with toys and objects. Holes near the ceiling allowed them to climb to the top of the room where there were small cave-like rooms for them to hide.

The sun streamed in through the ceiling, undetectable from the outside.

She wanted to keep them a secret as long as she could for their safety.

She strolled down the garden path to a small pond and stepped down beneath the island.

She gracefully swam beneath the surface toward Drake's underwater home.

She slowly approached the magnificent white columned structure. She passed through the opened doorway into the dry grand meeting room.

She was almost knocked over by a blue and silver Dragon, racing past her, being pursued by a green and blue Dragon.

"Excuse me," Suri said inside Lorelie's head.

Lorelie smiled and wove her way through the rambunctious Dragons to Drake, who had risen to greet her.

"I'm sorry. They are outgrowing this room."

"They have gotten quite big," she said, glad that she had slowed the growth of her own Dragons.

"They will be full grown in a few weeks, and I could use your help creating their own wing. I'd also like you to give them gills so they can move freely between here and the surface."

"I will be glad to help you and ask for a favor in return."

"Of course. Anything."

"I would like one of the first sets of eggs from your Dragons," she said, watching him closely to gauge his reaction.

Drake smiled warmly. "Of course. I wouldn't have them if it weren't for you. I knew you wouldn't be able to resist their rambunctious charm."

Lorelie relaxed and smiled. "Thank you. They are something else." She was overcome by his kindness and generosity. She liked this world more and more each day.

Drake took her hands between his and kissed her gently on the cheek. "I would like to speak with you about uniting our two kingdoms."

"Oh," she said interested in hearing his proposal.

"Please, let's leave the Dragons to their play and discuss my proposition," he said leading her to a comfortable room filled with soft plush furniture with floor to ceiling walls, giving them a complete view of the city and ocean around them.

Lorelie stood at one of the windows admiring the city before joining Drake on the velvety red sofa.

Drake turned to face her, taking her hands between his. "You have to know how I feel about you?" he asked clumsily.

Lorelie smiled, waiting for him to continue.

"I would be honored if you would become my wife and queen."

Lorelie was overwhelmed. Her pulse was racing. She forced down the fear that threatened to overcome her. She'd never felt about anyone the way she felt about Drake, and it terrified her.

Drake frowned. "I'm sorry if I made a mistake. I thought you felt the same."

"I do." She said, squeezing his hands.

"Then what is troubling you?"

"I think you deserve someone much better than me."

Drake looked at her stunned. "How can you say that. You are the kindest, sweetest, most generous person I know."

"You wouldn't say that if you really knew me," she said tearfully.

"I do know you, and I don't care about your past."

"The past is part of who I am."

"It's part of who you were. I know who you are, and that is all that matters."

"Are you sure?" she said softly. "I don't ever want to hurt you."

"You won't hurt me, unless you say no."

"Yes. Yes, I'll marry you," she said tearfully.

"This is supposed to be a good thing," he said.

"These are happy tears," she said kissing him.

Drake cupped her face in his hands and kissed her again, then released her. "I would like the marriage to take place as quickly as possible."

"How do we unite our kingdoms?"

"I'm not sure, but I'm sure we can decide the best way to join them."

"I'd like to continue to govern my people and let them choose how we come together."

"That's probably a good idea. We shouldn't rush our people."

"So, shouldn't we get started on the new Dragon wing before they destroy your meeting hall?"

Drake smiled. "Your magic is much stronger than mine, but I think together, we can build it."

Together they built a new addition in the shape of a large Dragon. It was white and stood nearly as tall as the meeting hall. Its bright blue eyes watched the sea around them.

They both sat back exhausted.

"I've never created anything like that before," Lorelie said, looking at the building in wonder.

"Nor have I. It takes hundreds of us working together for hours to create anything. You know what this means don't you?" he asked.

"No. What?"

"We're meant to do great things together."

Lorelie laughed. "I'm sure that's what it meant."

"Shall we give the Dragons gills, show them their new rooms, and then the world above."

"Sounds like fun, but aren't you worried about the Dragoneers seeing them?"

"They will eventually. I will explain that they were stolen from my people, and we simply took some of them back," he said innocently.

"I'm not sure they will see it your way. Please prepare yourself for them to be angry. This could end our truce with them."

"I hope that doesn't happen, but we will deal with it."

"It might go better if we let them know we took them from Rialda, and they will see them in the skies soon."

Drake smiled, "That's probably a better idea."

"I will do it, since I took them."

"I won't let you take the blame for this."

"I will send a message to them through the Flower Fairies. They can get away quickly if they get angry."

Drake laughed and kissed her briefly, then kissed her longer, pulling her into his arms. "I'm sorry that my asking you to take them caused this," he said.

Lorelie stroked his face with her fingers. "We will deal with it," she promised. "Let's take the Dragons on a tour of their new home and show them my home, then you can start planning a wedding while I try to keep the peace." She laughed to herself.

Her, a peacekeeper. My how her life had changed.

Using a combined spell, the Dragons were given gills and taken through the water for the first look at their rooms.

They were delighted with the design and the open wall to the ocean beyond. After a brief argument, they each chose their new room and were eager to fly to Lorelie's kingdom.

Drake astride the back of a Dragon was exhilarating. They circled the island before landing, then took off alone for several minutes before returning for Drake.

Drake kissed her goodbye and returned home, excited to tell his people of the upcoming wedding.

Lorelie went out into her garden to talk to the Flower Fairies. She knelt down next to them and asked them if they would take a message to Skylar.

The fairies frowned but agreed to deliver the message.

Lorelie handed them a neatly written note, which Peony slipped in her stem before they hurried away.

The Flower Fairies vanished beneath the ground in Lorelie's garden and reappeared minutes later inside the Dragoneer city.

They looked around for Skylar and spotted her walking across the courtyard.

Hurrying across the courtyard on their tiny root feet, they intercepted her, blocking her path.

Skylar stopped and stared down at the colorful flowers standing determinately at her feet. She bent down and said, "Hello What can I do for you?"

Peony slipped the note out of her stem and handed it to her.

Skylar unfolded it and quickly read the note. At first, she was angry and upset. Then she was sad that the Ocean Fairies had lost their Dragons. This happened long before Rialda. Who could have done this to them and why? She looked at Peony and said, "I will respond in person. Thank you."

Peony nodded and disappeared beneath the ground, quickly followed by the other four fairies.

Skylar called out to Hawk, jumping onto his back before he completely landed. They raced across the sky toward Lorelie's island.

Minutes later, she landed on the beach. Lorelie felt her presence and braced herself for a fight.

Lorelie strolled down to the beach, dressed in a cool breezy yellow and green dress that swirled around her as she walked.

Skylar met her on the path. She felt ashamed of her people again. When would it stop? "I received your message," she said sadly.

"I didn't expect you to respond in person," Lorelie said closing the distance between them.

"I felt I had to. Please let Drake know how sorry I am that my ancestors stole the Dragons from his people. I honestly had no idea."

"You're not upset that I took them."

"No. I'm glad you did. I just wanted to apologize in person."

"Thank you. That's really kind of you."

"We consider you friends and don't want anything to come between our relationship."

"You can let your people know that this has been resolved and no hard feelings," Lorelie said. "I have a favor to ask of you."

"Whatever you need."

"I need a friend. Someone to stand next to me at my wedding."

Skylar gasped and grabbed Lorelie in a hug. "That's so exciting. I'd love to stand up with you. When is the big day?"

"Soon. I'll let you know as soon as we decide."

"That's wonderful. I can't wait."

Drake stood at the altar that was decorated in soft delicate flowers. Their scent filled the chapel on Lorelie's island.

He couldn't believe how quickly everything came together for the wedding.

He frowned at the Flower Fairies. They couldn't seem to stand still. Peony pinched Rose and hissed for her to be still.

The garden path was strewn with colorful flower petals.

A soft glow filled the chapel as candles floated about their heads.

Drake shifted from one foot to the other. Warren, his best man, cautioned him to be patient.

The soft music from a harp floated in on a warm breeze and Skylar slowly made her way down the aisle. Her lovely face was alight with happiness.

Lorelie stepped on the threshold and the crowd of fairies, Dragoneers and Gnomes rose to their feet.

She was dressed in a soft ivory gown, interwoven with tiny flowers. The same flowers were woven through her hair.

The dress seemed to float around her as she made her way to the altar.

Drake took her arm in his, smiling down at her.

Drake's family priest welcomed all the guests and praised them for signing an accord, binding them together in peace.

He blessed them for the return of the Dragons and nodded at Skylar.

To Lorelie's and Drake's surprise, Skylar stepped forward. "My people would like to celebrate this wonderous occasion with a special gift."

Six Dragoneers made their way to the altar, each carrying a shiny blue green Dragon egg.

"May you be blessed with a long, happy life." Skylar said, taking her place on the other side of Lorelie.

The Dragoneers carried the eggs back down the aisle and placed them carefully at the back of the chapel.

The priest said a prayer for the happy couple and all their guest then asked Lorelie and Drake to pledge their love and devotion to each other before pronouncing them husband and wife.

Drake gently kissed Lorelie then let out a loud yell, raising his fist in the air.

The crowd laughed and clapped in appreciation, as arm in arm the newlyweds made their way out of the chapel to the garden where refreshments were set up.

The happy couple stood with their heads together smiling beneath a purple wisteria. Lorelie didn't know anyone could be this happy.

They were soon surrounded by friends and family hugging and congratulating them.

"Happy, sweetheart?" Drake asked.

"More than you can imagine," she whispered.

They cut the three-tiered wedding cake together, each taking a small bite in celebration.

The Water Fairies band played soft music, encouraging the happy couple to dance.

Drake took Lorelie in his arms and led her around the dance floor as other smiling couples joined them.

The Gnomes played a happy, faster tune and Lorelie stopped dancing to watch her small friend dance a lively jig.

She clapped her hands in encouragement.

Simmy took Lorelie by the hand and tried to teach her the jig.

After a few minutes of laughing, an out of breath Lorelie put her hands up in defeat.

A tiny female Gnome took her place and easily danced the jig.

Lorelie shrugged and rejoined Drake and watched them easily dance the feisty dance.

The party raged on throughout the night until the sun started to peak over the smooth ocean.

Exhausted, Lorelie and Drake bid their guests goodbye.

They stepped into the water and entered a carriage pulled by giant seahorses that took them to a small romantic room secluded from their celebration.

As the sun rose, they celebrated their first morning as a married couple with a sumptuous breakfast of fresh fruit and wild nectar, and tiny boiled eggs. A gift from the Gnomes.

As they ate, they looked out to the brilliant blue ocean and saw a school of fish light up, spelling congratulations, before swimming away.

Chapter Thirty-Nine

Pandora

Sierra fell back on the bed delighted to be home. It felt like she had been gone forever.

As much as she wanted to crawl between the cool sheets and sleep for days, she had a meeting with the council and if she didn't see her family, she was certain her mother was going to kill her.

Forcing herself off the bed, she allowed herself time for a real shower. The warm water was the most wonderous thing she'd felt in weeks.

Wrapping a fluffy bath sheet around her, she stepped out of the shower and realizing the time, waved her hand in front of her, exchanging the towel for a pair of jeans and a pink tee shirt.

She had grown tired of black. She wanted color and peace in her life.

All she wanted to experience in the immediate future was ribbon cutting for new businesses opening up.

Taking the stairs two at a time, she joined the council members.

Taking a seat she said, "Sorry I'm late."

"No problem, my dear," Egon said.

"Thanks to you, we've no urgent business to discuss."

"And thanks to me, I've drug all of you through one disaster after another."

"I..."

"Stop blaming yourself." Dak said sharply. "Our world is at peace for the first time ever. We have restored the Elders to this world and have many friends in other realms. Did it all come easy, or without a price? No.

Nothing ever does."

Sierra lowered her eyes, not knowing what to say.

"The Invisibles still need help. They haven't started construction on a city, and they need assistance in farming methods," Falon said.

"The giants are a little behind due to the time spent in Callis, but they should be back on track soon," Novrah said.

The Opaque is expanding its borders to make room for more of the Muricks. They have grown quite fond of our realm.

Our town isn't growing as quickly as I'd like," Mags said.

"My people are having trouble embracing change. I've asked Ambro to help and he's agreed."

Sierra couldn't help it. The more everyone talked, the more she wanted to laugh, until she couldn't hold it back any longer and burst out laughing.

"I'm sorry. It's just that for nearly three years, we've been in one battle after another and now we're sitting here discusses growth and futures like a corporation and it seems really weird to me."

"None of them know what a corporation is." Egon said, which caused Sierra to start laughing again.

Dak leaned closer to her and whispered, "Why is this so funny?"

Sierra looked at his earnest expression and laughed even harder.

"Would you prefer us to always be at war?" he whispered.

"No, of course not. I'm sorry," she repeated. "I don't know what's wrong with me. Please continue without me. I think I'll go lie down."

Before anyone could say anything, she pushed away from the table and hurried out of the room.

Instead of going up to her room, she went outside and headed toward the city. The change was amazing.

The town was thriving. People were everywhere. Many of them she didn't know, which made her both happy and sad.

Outside a coffee shop, she ran into Bree, who hugged her so tight, she thought she'd broken a rib.

"It's so good to see you. You've been gone forever."

"I know. I'm sorry. How's school and the real world?"

"School is good. I graduate after this semester."

"So soon. I feel like I've missed so much."

Bree led her inside the coffee shop and ordered them both milk shakes.

"This feels like old times," Sierra said wistfully.

"Ok, spill. What the hell is the matter with you?"

"I'm not sure, but I don't know what to do now. We ran the bad guys off. Pandora is thriving. What am I supposed to do now?"

Bree sat back chewing on her lip. "What did you want to do after college?"

"You already know the answer."

"Do you still want that?"

"I don't know, but here? Wouldn't it be weird?"

"Hell no. You could always do it in both worlds. I am."

"It will be easy here, but a challenge back home," she said liking the idea more and more.

"I think that's your problem. With your powers, nothing is challenging anymore."

Sierra blushed, ashamed. Bree was right. As long as they had battles to fight, she had a purpose. Now she felt lost. "You're right. If I try to get my work published back home, it will be hard and challenge me."

Bree crossed her arms in satisfaction. "Of course, I'm right. Going back and forth between the two worlds keeps me grounded. It's easy to get lost in this place. I do have a suggestion now that all the fighting is over. To keep your troops in fighting mode, you should have some world-wide competition, like the Olympics."

Sierra smiled. "You are not only beautiful, but you're also brilliant."

It won't hurt to introduce this place to some modern ideas." Bree said.

"What? The games are a good idea, but I need to be challenged. I'm going to enroll in college."

"That will challenge you?"

"Yes. I can feel normal again. We can do normal things. It's worked for you, going between the two worlds."

"But I'm not the queen," she said softly.

Sierra frowned. "I'm not a queen."

"Well, you run the damn place." She said, crossing her arms over her chest.

"Whatever," Sierra said rolling her eyes.

"Are you having second thoughts about living here?"

"Not really. I just need something normal in my life."

"What will Dak say?"

"He'll want me to do what makes me happy."

"But it will bother him?"

"Probably, but he will get over it."

"So, come with me tomorrow and enroll."

"I think I'll do just that," she said laughing.

Sierra kissed Dak goodbye and grabbed a small, cinched bag off the bed.

Dressed in worn jeans and a tee shirt she was excited to re-enter her world as a normal girl.

"Have fun at school," Dak teased.

Sierra created a small snowball and turned, throwing it at him, hitting him in the face, catching him off guard.

Dak wiped the wet mess off his face, glaring at her. "You act that way and you'll be staying after school."

"You are so funny." Sierra said kissing him briefly on the lips.

He pulled her onto his lap, kissing her while asking, "So, going to school's going to make you happy?"

"Yes. It will also help with my magic."

"I didn't know you needed help with your magic."

"You never know," she teased, "But I'm going to be late if I don't leave now."

"Be careful," he said, letting her go.

She blew him a kiss, and rushed out of their bedroom, raced down the curved stairs, her face lit up with excitement.

She opened a rip at the bottom of the stairs and appeared next to Bree's car, sitting in the driveway of her old family home.

"You scared me," Bree said.

"Sorry," she said shrugging slightly.

Climbing in her car, she unlocked Sierra's side. "Is Dak cool with this?"

"Sure, but he doesn't understand it."

"Did he ever go to school?"

Sierra laughed, "Not really."

Standing in line to register for class was exciting. Watching all the students rush around getting ready for school felt so good, and normal.

After registration they went to a movie and lunch.

"This was fun," Sierra said.

"Just like old times," she teased. "Before you became the queen of Pandora."

Sierra broke off a piece of bread and threw it at Bree. "I'm not a queen."

"Whatever," Bree said.

Sierra popped a piece of the buttered bread into her mouth, glaring at her.

"Were you able to get all the classes you wanted?"

"Yes, I think chemistry will help my magic."

"That's an interesting idea."

"That's what I thought. It can't hurt."

Sierra shivered. She had the strangest feeling all of a sudden. She looked out through the window of the restaurant. She didn't see anything unusual, but she could feel it. Something just didn't feel right.

"Are you okay?"

Sierra frowned. "I don't know. Something feels strange."

"Strange how?" Bree asked looking around.

"I don't know how to explain it."

"Maybe it's just weird being away from Pandora."

"I've been away from Pandora lots of times and never felt this way."

"Maybe it's being home."

"Maybe?" she said trying to shrug it off.

After lunch, they went to pick up supplies for class, then Bree drove them home.

Sierra hugged Bree goodbye and opened a rip and stepped through to her old bedroom.

Instantly, she felt like someone had been inside her room.

Sitting down on her bed, she picked up her stuffed rabbit, hugging it to her chest. She looked around the room and smiled. So much had changed.

Sighing, she stood up and opened a rip back to Pandora.

A week later, Sierra was sitting in class surrounded by twenty other students, when she felt like someone was watching her. She slowly glanced around the room and didn't see anything out of the ordinary.

She looked back at the professor and tried to concentrate on what he was saying.

She couldn't shake the feeling she was being watched but pushed it aside so she could enjoy her first day of class.

When class ended, she closed her book and picked up her purse, following the rest of the students out into the hallway.

The feeling grew stronger, and she jerked around trying to see anyone that looked out of place. She frowned, confused when no one seemed to be looking her way.

The moment she stepped outside, on her way to meet up with Bree, a young man with wild blond hair stepped up beside her and linked his arm through hers.

Sierra tried to jerk away, but his words made her freeze.

"I've been looking for you for a long time," he whispered, speaking with an odd accent.

"Why? Who are you?"

"Who I am doesn't matter. You're upsetting everything?"

"And just how am I doing that?"

"You've interfered in things that don't concern you."

Sierra pulled away from him, turning to face him.

"Just what do you think I'm interfering in? I'm just a student who was minding my own business until you accosted me for no reason."

Mace grabbed her wrist and pulled her toward him. Face to face, he hissed. "We both know that you are more than a student. Others are watching you. We shouldn't stay in one place too long," he said pulling her along.

Sierra didn't resist. She wanted to know who was watching her and why.

Her sudden lack of resistance didn't go unnoticed by Mace as he led her down the steps, and behind the building.

He looked around to make sure no one was watching.

"You've made people unhappy."

"Stop being so cryptic and tell me who and how I've made 'people' unhappy."

"By interfering in the lives of other beings," he said.

"What do you mean?"

Mace glared at her, "You know exactly what I mean. You've traveled to other worlds and interfered in lives you shouldn't have. I have no idea how you managed to do this since you don't have the sight."

"Sight?"

"Come with me," he said.

Sierra moved away.

"I won't hurt you," he said, staring at her. "I promise."

Reluctantly, Sierra followed him back to the front of the building, across the courtyard to a closed in walkway between two buildings and pulled her down on a wooden bench.

"There are things of this world that you can't see," he explained.

"I have no idea what you're talking about," she said, wondering if he was mentally ill. "Are these unseen things watching me?"

"Some of them are."

"Why can't I see them?"

"You haven't looked close enough," he said.

"Show me how to look closer," she said humoring him.

"You may not like what you see," he whispered softly.

"Explain to me how you think I'm interfering," she said.

"I told you already. By traveling to other worlds and messing in their lives."

Sierra stared at him in shock. How could he know this?

"I just don't know how you did it, when you can't see the lines."

"What lines."

"Ley lines."

"What on earth are you talking about?"

Taking a deep breath, Mace stared at her with his deep blue eyes. "Let me start over. You've upset the assembly by interfering in the lives of other worlds, and they are looking for you. I came to warn you."

"What is the assembly? I helped these people. They could have died if I didn't," she said sadly.

"The assembly governs travel between worlds, and they don't care about saving lives. They care about the balance."

"Can you help me get the sight so I can see them?"

Mace stared at her, studying her.

"They won't like it," he said.

"Why warn me, if you won't help me?"

"Will you tell me how you travel without it?"

"Yes."

He touched the side of her head gently with one finger. She felt a slight tingle and a flash of light behind her eyes.

"It will look weird at first, but you can control how much you see."

Sierra blinked a few times, and the lights disappeared.

"I traveled through gates."

"Gates?" he questioned.

"You pass through it from one world to another," she said trying to explain.

"Like the portals?" he asked.

"I guess, since I don't know what a portal is."

"There are portals all along the ley lines if you can see them. Some are very dark, and you want to stay away from those. The bright ones are safer, but you still have to be careful."

"Tell me about the assembly."

"They create our laws and govern the ley lines and the worlds along them."

"How many worlds?"

"How many? Who knows? Too many to count."

Sierra's eyes widened in surprise.

"Are you serious?"

"Of course, I am."

"Why are you telling me all this?"

"To warn you. The assembly has a bounty on you for travel crimes. I don't think they are being fair, so here I am to warn you."

"Thank you."

"You are most welcome. Humans are not usually travelers."

"Humans? Aren't you human?"

Mace laughed, "I look human, but I'm not like you."

"Is it because I'm human that your assembly doesn't like me traveling?"

Mace tilted his head to the side and said, "It could be, but they don't like you changing things."

"How do they know I changed things? How do they know about me?"

"They saw creatures here from another world. They'd never seen anything like them, so they assumed you traveled to one of the dark worlds. They followed you here, captured some of them and took them back."

They didn't know about the Eight Realms, she thought, and relaxed a little.

"Why do they want me?"

"To punish you."

"And how will they punish me?"

"I don't know, but it will be bad, really bad. That's why I had to warn you."

"Will they hurt you if they find out you warned me?"

"It's a possibility," he said.

"Then you need to go. They can't see us together."

Mace touched her hand gently and said, "They will catch you."

"They might, but I'll be okay," she said.

"No, no you won't. They can be bad."

"Then I need you to be safe so you can tell my friend Bree if they catch me. Can you do that for me?"

"Yes, but how will that help you?"

"It will help me," she said.

"I will tell your friend," He promised.

"Thank you. Now please go. I don't want you hurt because you helped me."

"I will keep an eye on you. Be careful," he said and vanished, startling her.

Sierra took a deep breath, trying to digest everything Mace had just told her. Most of it didn't make any sense, but the thought that someone was out there watching her was unnerving.

Who were these people who weren't human, and how long have they been looking for her?

She considered opening a rip and returning to Pandora and forgetting the strange encounter with Mace, but she'd be looking over her shoulder every time she returned if she walked away now.

And a part of her wanted to see what this sight was that Mace gave her, so she stepped out of the closed walkway and into a world she'd never imagined existed.

Moving among the humans, unseen, were more people like Mace. They were brighter and more vibrant than the humans.

There were fairies and Gnomes, and cute furry animals she'd never seen before. One of them looked like a bunny with a kitten face.

There were even trees and houses that didn't exist in the human world, and she could tell that many of these beings were watching her.

She ignored them and pretended she couldn't see them. She even walked right through a couple talking.

It felt very strange, making her wonder if she'd be able to do that again, now that she could see them.

How was this even possible, she wondered, noticing faint lines along the ground. These must be the Ley lines Mace was telling her about.

She turned and followed them for a couple of blocks and saw the entrances he'd told her about. So, all of these were different worlds? She had no desire to visit any of them. But how was she going to get this assembly to leave her alone?

The farther she got away from the school the fewer 'other worlders' she saw. Some were dressed from centuries passed, but she couldn't get a good look at them without revealing the fact that she could see them.

She was amazed at how many dark doorways there were compared to light ones, and she could only guess that the assembly did nothing to interfere with whatever happened to them to turn them dark.

She turned away from them and headed back toward the school wishing she couldn't see the other worlders. How creepy to know they were here all the time and humans couldn't see them.

Again, she felt someone seize her by the arm. Thinking that it was Mace again, she turned to face him.

It wasn't Mace this time. It was an elderly gentleman dressed in a top hat and long coat. He had long grey hair pulled back in a ponytail. His eyes were a piercing grey that instantly unnerved her.

A long scar ran down one side of his face, disappearing in his long grey beard.

"Excuse me," Sierra said, trying to free her arm.

His grip tightened and he hissed, "Don't try to escape. You are coming with me."

Sierra pretended to try to get free from him and he squeezed her arm until it hurt. "Where are you taking me?" she demanded.

He glared at her in disgust and silence, before saying, "You will find out in a few minutes."

The other worlders looked at him in fright and hurried out of the way. Many of them looked at her in pity.

She spotted Mace among them. His eyes met hers and he fell into step behind them.

"Why are you following us?" scar man asked.

"You found her. I want to know what the assembly plans to do with her."

"It's not your concern since you failed to locate her."

"Whatever you say, overlord," Mace said and turned away.

"The assembly will want to speak with you after they sentence her." He reminded him.

"I'm sure they will," he responded as he hurried off to locate Sierra's friend, Bree, knowing there was nothing she could do for her, but at least they would know what happened to her.

He located Bree as she was exiting a coffee shop, appearing right in front of her.

Bree stepped back, startled.

"Your friend, Sierra sent me to give you a message," he said.

"Oh, okay," she said.

"She's being taken to the assembly to be judged for interfering in other worlds."

"Whoa, what? What's the assembly?"

Mace frowned sadly. "There's nothing you can do to help her. I will try to help her, but I must go," he said disappearing in front of her.

"No, wait, please come back," she cried as he raced away unseen.

Sierra and the overlord reached a bright doorway and stepped through it, but not before Sierra put up a marker that Dak would be able to see.

There was a flash of bright light, then a thick green forest took shape before them. Sierra turned back and could see the gate behind her. She put up an invisible beacon to guide her back to it, thankful that her magic worked. Chastising herself for not thinking that it couldn't, and she'd be trapped here.

The overlord located a path releasing her arm since he believed she had no choice except to follow him.

She didn't know if she was supposed to be able to see the things around her, so she remained quiet as she looked around at the strange world as it unfolded before her.

In the distance she saw a tall blue and silver spiraling building, reaching up toward blue fluffy clouds.

The trees literally moved out of their way as they passed them, staring down at her with interest. This world was a walking fairy tale, or a nightmare.

The path opened up into a colorful town. The windows on each house had flower boxes filled with flowers.

The short plump people stopped and stared at them as they passed.

"They've never seen a human before," he said.

"Well, I've never seen them before either," she said sarcastically, which was lost on him.

They passed through the quaint village and were intercepted by a small grey fox with a long neck and fluffy ears like a bunny.

It wagged its fluffy tail before running off.

They passed through a tall iron gate that closed behind them with a loud bang.

The sky turned darker as they continued down the path toward the dark grey and green building with a dark green wooden door and no windows.

Sierra shuddered; the building looked foreboding. She stopped on the first step.

The overlord gripped her arm tightly and pushed her forward. Sierra considered changing him into a skunk but resisted the urge. She had to find out what the assembly was and try to reason with them.

The dark wood door appeared to open by itself, and Sierra entered a dark room with a long dark hallway. Floating lights moved quickly down the tunnel toward her, stopping a few feet in front of her to light the way.

The room was completely quiet. She had to force herself not to reach out and read their thoughts.

She needed them to believe that she was a helpless human.

After about ten minutes, the hall opened into a large dark room with more floating lights.

She could see about twenty people sitting in chairs lined up like a movie theater.

She couldn't tell what they looked like, since they were hidden in the shadows.

The overlord stopped her in the middle of the room where a chair appeared out of the floor, and he shoved her into it.

He was definitely going to pay for being so rough with her. A skunk was too good for him. He was going to spend some time as the cockroach he was.

Four floating lights hovered above her like a spotlight. She sat patiently to see what would happen next.

After a few minutes, a booming voice said, "The assembly is now in order. Do you know why you are here?" he asked.

"No," Sierra replied.

"No one told her. That is unacceptable. I will explain then. You were seen with creatures from a dark world. It is forbidden to enter or interfere with the other worlds."

"I didn't know the dark worlds existed until today," she responded.

"You lie."

"I assure you, I do not."

"Then where did these creatures come from?"

"They had a terrible disease that made them the way you saw them."

She could hear the assembly whispering.

"Why are you spying on humans? Aren't you interfering with my people by bringing me here?"

Chapter Forty

Assembly

"Your insolence won't help your cause." the voice said.

"So, it's okay if you break the very rule, you're accusing me of breaking?"

"Silence," the voice boomed, echoing around the room.

Sierra pierced the darkness so she could see her accusers. Most of them looked human, with long hair and pale skin. Some resembled fairies with finer features. None of them looked happy.

"What did you do with the creatures from the dark world?"

"The creatures, as you called them, were cured of the illness and returned home."

"Why would they choose to reenter the dark world?"

"Why do you choose not to listen? They are not from a dark world."

"You are not helping your case, human," he said spitting out the word human, like it was a curse.

"If you dislike humans so much, why are you spying on us? Would you like it if humans came to your world, spied on you, then decided they had the right to judge you for something they didn't understand?"

"Lock her up. See if that will jog her memory?"

"Whatever you people are, your laws don't apply to my people. You need to think long and hard before you make enemies of us."

The assembly laughed. "You can't even see us. We visit your land; some even live there, and you aren't aware of it."

"We are now," she said coldly.

"You won't be leaving here to tell anyone," They threatened.

Sierra rolled her eyes but remained silent. She wanted to tell them not to be so sure about that.

The overlord jerked her up and shoved her through a door into an eight-by-eight-foot room.

Sierra sat down on the floor to wait to see what happened next.

Within five minutes, Mace appeared in the room with her. "You made them mad," he said sadly.

"Did you tell my friend where I am?" she asked.

"Yes, but she can't help you. They will send you to a work camp," Mace said sadly.

"Your people are very screwed up," Sierra said.

"Screwed up?" he questioned.

"Messed up," she said. "How did you get in here without anyone seeing you?"

"I'm a shiner," he said.

"What is a shiner?"

"We can bend the area around us to move wherever we want to go," he explained.

A rip, Sierra thought. Did the Destroyer visit here? Was he responsible for the dark worlds? "That must come in handy. Can you take someone with you?"

"If I help you escape, they will hunt me down and kill me," he said suddenly scared. "I should go. They can't find me here. I just wanted you to know that I admire you for helping others."

"Please don't go yet. I won't ask you to risk your life to help me. I just want to know more about your world and the ley lines."

"This isn't my world. My world is a much happier place or used to be."

"Do you work for the assembly?"

"Sometimes. I did this time so I could warn you. Can I ask you something?"

"Of course."

"How have you been able to hide from the assembly for all this time? Where have you been?"

"I moved away," she said evasively. She wasn't telling them anything about the Eight Realms.

"We looked all over your world for you. You are exceptionally good at hiding."

"Does the assembly govern your world?" she asked.

"They are pushing to control more worlds along the lines. Many of the worlds are resisting their control, while just as many don't care."

"But you care?"

"I don't think they should try to control worlds they know nothing about."

"Doesn't make sense for them to think they know best for people they don't even know. Why do they prohibit helping other worlds?"

"Most of the dark worlds are warrior worlds. They want them out of the way so letting them destroy themselves solves a problem for the council," he explained.

"That's terrible and heartless."

"That describes the assembly."

"Does anyone openly oppose the assembly?"

"No. They are too afraid."

"The council makes people disappear. I'm sorry I can't help you," he said sadly.

"My friend will help me," she said.

"How? She can't see our world."

"She's resourceful," she said, smiling.

Mace frowned. "You don't seem afraid. Why?"

"Kidnapping a human will only bring trouble to your world. I don't think the assembly wants trouble from my world."

"How can your world fight what it can't see?"

"We always find a way," she said smiling.

"I will come back if I can," he said before vanishing, leaving her alone.

⁂

Bree raced home, accessed the gate to Pandora and raced through the city. She raced down the path, out of the city, toward the castle.

Racing up the steps she rushed inside the castle calling for Dak. She met him halfway up the stairs.

"Sierra's been kidnapped," she said breathlessly, bent over to catch her breath.

"That's worse than being kept after school," he teased. Seeing the look on her face, he said, "You're serious?"

"Yes. Some guy told me then vanished in front of me."

"Take me to the school. Sierra would have left something for me to locate her with if she allowed someone to take her."

"You think she went with whoever it was willingly?"

"She had to. No one could force her if she didn't want to go with them."

Dak tried to remain patient as he walked back toward the gate with Bree. They passed through the gate and into her bedroom closet. Dak hesitated getting into Bree's red mustang. He remembered Sierra teasing her about her driving.

Bree noticed his hesitation and put her hands on her hips. "I promise, I won't kill you."

Dak smiled and climbed inside. "I didn't say you would."

"You didn't have to," she said glaring at him before backing out of the driveway and heading to the college.

She pulled into a student parking lot and Dak climbed out, looking around and listening. He didn't feel Sierra anywhere, but he picked up something.

"This way," he said walking toward one of the buildings. He retraced the steps Sierra took with the overlord and stopped where she left a beacon for him.

Puzzled, Dak stared at the empty space around him. He reached out his mind searching for Sierra. He could feel a faint trace of her far in the distance.

He frowned slightly looking at the empty field in front of him. He cast a simple open spell, and a door appeared in front of him.

"What in the hell is that?" Bree asked.

"I don't know, but Sierra's in there, and I'm going to go get her," Dak said.

"I'm going with you," Bree said.

Dak looked at her in surprise. "Are you sure?"

"I'm not letting you go in there alone."

"If you're sure, let's go?" he said opening the doorway.

Bree grabbed the tail of his black shirt and followed him inside.

Dak immediately saw Sierra's beacon and closed the door behind them. Reaching out, he located her and told her they were on their way.

"Who is we?" she asked.

"Bree insisted on coming," he responded. "Are you okay?"

"I'm fine. Stay out of sight until I learn why they took me," she said.

"She's fine," Dak explained to Bree. "She said for us to stay out of sight for a bit, so we will wait here."

"Okay, but where is here? How can there be a doorway to another world? How many more are there?"

"I can't answer that. This is weird, even for me."

Bree sat down on the thick green grass and looked around.

Dak plopped down next to her, when they both noticed that the trees had eyes and were staring at them.

Bree looked at Dak in surprise. Dak shrugged and said, "Hello."

The tree tilted its massive head and said, "Good day sir, madam."

"Where are we?" Dak asked.

"Molovice," the tree said.

"You have a very nice forest," Dak said.

"Thank you. Why aren't you going to the city?"

"We're waiting for a friend," Dak said.

"If you want to stay out of sight you should move deeper into the forest. Anyone coming through the door will see you," the tree said.

"Oh, thank you," Bree said, coming to her feet.

Dak and Bree followed the tree deeper into the forest to a stone bench beside a river. The tree stood next to them offering them shade.

"You're not from around here?" the tree asked.

"That obvious?" Dak said.

The tree laughed. "I'm afraid so. You are friends of the young lady the overlord escorted to the city?"

"Yes, we are," Dak said.

"I'm sorry. She won't be meeting you. He took her to the assembly. No one returns from the assembly."

The door to Sierra's cell opened and floating lights escorted her back to her chair in front of the assembly. She sat down and waited for round two.

"Are you ready to answer our questions honestly?" A woman's voice rang out in a calm caring manner.

"I have been honest," Sierra said.

"I realized this is unusual for you. As a human you've not experienced anything like this, but we are the peacekeepers of the worlds along the ley lines. If you stumbled on a dark world and allowed the inhabitance to escape, you can't be blamed for an accident."

"Escape? I thought they were free to leave. Do you understand your own laws or are the laws for everyone except the assembly?" she questioned sweetly.

"Enough," yelled one of the male members. "She is not going to tell us. She should be executed for her crime."

"Executed? For charges you've made up. I've done nothing. Not that it matters to any of you."

To Dak she said, "I think you should head my way."

Dak jumped to his feet and helped Bree up. "Come on, let's go get our girl."

"You can't go," the tree said. It's not safe," he called as they raced down the path, not slowing until they reached the city, where everyone stopped and stared.

Bree looked at the colorful city in wonder, as she stayed close to Dak as they moved through the crowded streets.

"Oh, you've done plenty," an elderly white-haired man said. "Your actions could bring on a war and we need to stop it before it starts."

"This is the first time I've been in one of your worlds and the last," she yelled back.

"If you refuse to help us, we will have to make an example out of you to hopefully put the rebellion to rest."

"You people are crazy. So that's it? You've decided that I'm guilty of something so, you kill me?"

"If you tell us how you discovered our world, we will make your death quick and painless," a woman said.

"Let me tell you something. If you attempt to hurt me, my people will rain down on you like nothing you can imagine."

The assembly laughed. "They can't see us. How can they fight what they can't see?"

"I thought you said I can see you. What makes you think you can't be seen?"

Their laughter abruptly ended. They looked as Sierra with a mixture of disgust and fright. "Do you really want us to take on your world? I don't think humans will fare very well."

"You take on 'my' world and your world will never be the same," she promised.

Dak and Bree entered the long hall and jogged to Sierra's location, entering the arena, surprising the assembly.

"Making friends, I see," Dak teased.

Bree linked her fingers through Sierras, glad that she hadn't been hurt.

"What is the meaning of this," cried a younger assemblyman.

The overlord rushed in and before he could reach Dak, Dak froze him in place as he kissed Sierra on the cheek. "Honey, why don't you introduce me to your new friends."

"You're not human. What are you?" demanded the elder assemblyman.

"Guess you're feeling pretty foolish about now. See, you don't know everything. You're right. I'm not human and I'm not from your worlds. That means my wife was telling you the truth."

"You lie, the same as she does, and can die with her," he said, clicking a button.

Several shiners entered the room, including Mace. His eyes met hers and he frowned sadly.

Sierra reached inside his mind and asked him to come with them.

Mace nodded his head at Sierra as his people raised their hands to trap Sierra, Dak, and Bree.

Dak knocked away their spell as Sierra told him that she didn't want them to know she could do magic.

Mingling with the humans is forbidden," a woman yelled. "Is she worth the exile of your people?"

"Lady, you don't know who my people are?" Dak said shaking his head. "I don't like your new friends."

The shiners recovered from their surprise at Dak deflecting their spell as they set to strike again, Sierra pulled Mace to her side, Bree took Dak's hand as a rip opened and the four of them vanished.

"Where did you send them?" The council demanded.

"We didn't do that," Doni replied.

"Why did they take Mace with them?"

"To interrogate him. Find them. Find that creature's home world and bring them back."

"Yes sir," Doni said, and the shiners vanished leaving the assembly alone.

"Teach the human a lesson. Attack her city."

Chapter Forty-One

Mace

They entered Pandora through the council room.

Mace looked around in surprise and asked, "How did you do that?"

"We have a few tricks up our sleeves," Sierra said.

"They will never stop looking for us," he said worriedly, sitting down in one of the plush chairs. "If they think I came willingly with you they will punish my people.

"I'm sorry you got involved in this," Sierra said.

"It's my fault. I wanted to meet the person that cared enough to help other worlds."

Bree sat down next to him and said, "They will look for you at home."

"I know. This is crazy. Who knew all these worlds existed in our backyard? How long have they been watching us?" Sierra said.

"Wait, what? They are watching us. Now that's weird and very wrong," Bree said.

"For a long time, your people were helpless against them," he said sadly. "This is my fault. I should have taken you and hidden you somewhere."

"This isn't your fault," Dak said, "but please explain why they are so mad."

"They believe Sierra went into the dark worlds and tried to help them."

Dak looked confused. "Why is that so bad?"

"Most of the dark world are people that opposed the assembly, and they want them to die out. They don't want anyone helping them to restart the rebellion."

"Then that's exactly what we're going to do," Sierra said.

"How did I know you were going to say that?" Bree said shaking her head.

"We have to make sure they leave our home alone first," Sierra said, whistling softly.

Within a few seconds, two Hummingbirds appeared. Sierra filled out two missives requesting assistance, sending the birds on their way.

"What was that?" Mace asked.

"They deliver messages," Sierra explained.

"We're not on your world, are we?" Mace asked.

"Not the world you know," Sierra said.

"That's why they can't find you," he laughed.

"Tell me what we're up against when we go against the assembly? Do all the worlds agree with their way of governing?"

"I don't know, there are so many worlds. Many are too far for the assembly to reach. Some hate what they've done, but don't fight back. My people, to my knowledge have the most power."

The door opened and Ben and the Elders entered the room. Sierra stood up and hugged Ben, then Egon.

"Thank you for coming so quickly."

She quickly filled them in on what she encountered, then had Mace show her how to give them the sight.

"So, these beings spy on people? Now, that's just creepy," Egon said.

"We'll send them home in no time," Ben promised. "What's the plan?"

"Dak and I...."

"And me," Mace interrupted.

"And Mace are going to visit these dark worlds and see if we can find out what has been going on."

"Didn't you start school today? How did this happen?" Egon asked, confused.

"It wasn't how I wanted my first day of class to end. Bree, please tell my professors that I've a family emergency to tend to."

"I will. I want the sight so I can see these voyeurs." Bree said. "It gives me the creeps to know they could be anywhere watching us."

"Only if you're sure," Sierra said, placing her hand over Bree's eyes. "Be careful. The Elders will keep an eye on you as long as you are home."

"Let's go," Sierra said.

Egon opened a rip, and the Elders stepped through. They were taken by surprise by the sheer numbers of the other worlders milling about.

They didn't waste any time in going after them, forcing them to flee in fright, unused to being seen.

Within a matter of minutes, they had rid the area of them and waited outside their doorway waiting for others to arrive. They didn't have long to wait.

The other worlders were stunned to be intercepted and threatened to never return.

The shiners showed up right behind the Elders and tried to subdue them, but the Elders pushed them back, casting spell after spell, overwhelming them easily.

"Tell your assembly that this world is off limits and that we're coming for them. You touch my daughter again and I'll destroy all of you," Ben hissed to one of them.

The shiners vanished and returned to relay Ben's threat to the assembly.

"Who are these people?" The elder assemblyman asked.

"I'm afraid we are going to find out," Doni said nervously.

"Send for our best warriors. We will show these humans."

"They're not human," Doni whispered.

⁕ ⁕ ⁕

Sierra, Dak, and Mace stood in front of the first dark world and slowly stepped through the door. True to its name, the world was very dark, but you could feel life in the distance. Sierra cast a spell to dispel the darkness, and the world grew brighter.

The tall grass was dry and brittle covering a long unused path. They pushed their way forward, looking for any signs of life.

After twenty minutes of walking, they heard the sound of someone, or something coming toward them and stopped to wait.

They were confronted by a group of scared, beaten down men and women, ready to defend themselves.

They were surprised to see three strangers standing before them smiling.

"Who are you?" asked Marni, a middle-aged woman.

"We've come to help you," Sierra said.

The crowd laughed. How did these three people think they could help? "How can you help us?"

"We got rid of the Darkness," Dak said, smiling.

"If you did that, you just assured that the assembly will attack us again," she said sadly. "There isn't anything we can do against them. They will destroy us this time."

They were so broken that Sierra's heart went out to them. The assembly destroyed these worlds for power. Anyone that opposed them was destroyed.

"You should go back where you came from before they return and save yourselves," she said, turning away in defeat.

"Come with us," Sierra said, surprising them.

"If we step through that door, they will kill us and anyone who lets us through their door. They don't see us as a threat and were leaving us alone."

"To die. They left you here to die. You all deserve better. Trust us and I promise, it will get better."

"You have a shiner with you. He works for them. Is this a trick to get us to leave so you can kill us now?"

"I don't work for them anymore. I joined them to offer my help."

"What can we do to prove to you that we are here to help you?" Sierra asked.

"If we follow you, will you take my daughter to a healer? She's been sick for a long time?"

"Show me to your daughter?"

"She's back in our village."

"Take me to her?"

"You're a healer?"

"Among other things," Sierra said as they followed them to their village that looked like a bomb had gone off in the center of it.

Marni pushed open the door to Carrie's bedroom, revealing a young woman lying on a threadbare bed. Her eyes were sunken in, and she was far too thin.

Sierra sat next to her on the bed, taking her thin hand in hers. Her pulse was so weak she could barely feel it. The poor girl didn't have long to live.

Sierra flooded her body with healing energy forcing out the illness that threatened her life. The color returned to her cheeks and her face filled out. She opened her eyes for the first time in days.

"Mother," Carrie cried, her voice no longer weak. "What happened?"

Marni looked at Sierra through tears of gratitude and hugged her before hugging Carrie, crying on her shoulder.

"We will go with you," Marni said. "Can you give us time to pack our few belongings?"

"Yes. I will do everything I can to protect you," Sierra promised.

The people returned to their village one last time to pack whatever meant something to them. They were once a proud race of thousands that were wiped out during the war with the assembly.

With their heads held high, they passed through the door as Sierra extinguished the light to their world.

Sierra and Dak could feel the battle raging with the other worlders, but Ben assured them that they were handling it.

They led the refugees to the next dark door, reaching out to see what was beyond the door. The violence and hunger that they felt propelled them to the next door.

"Evidentially, not all dark worlds are the same. This is so weird that this was here all this time, and no one could see it." Dak said.

"I know," Sierra agreed as they approached another door and felt that it was safe to enter. "Stay with them," she said. "I'll be right back."

Sierra vanished and appeared in the assembly room. There were only a couple of assemblymen present. She grabbed them both by the wrist and vanished, taking them with her and reappeared in front of Mags and Fin, startling them.

"It's a long story, but I need you to keep these two here and teach them that it's not nice to destroy worlds."

"Wait. What?" Mags stammered. "What worlds did they destroy?"

"Seems there are doorways all over the human world. There are hundreds, if not thousands of other worlds and these two are part of a group that have been destroying them for who knows how long."

"I'll be glad to help," Mags said looking at her two guests in disgust.

"Thousands of worlds?" Fin said softly. "Please tell me you're not going to war with all of them."

Sierra frowned, blew them a kiss, and said, "of course not," before she vanished and reappeared next to Dak and Mace.

Fin and Mags stared at the two strangers and smiled.

The sky was dark and overcast, Sierra didn't lighten it this time, deciding on a less subtle approach. They walked across an open field looking for signs of life.

Ben and the Elders continued to patrol along the ley lines. When a door to a dark world slowly opened and a dark black cloud rolled out like fog. It rose in the air, hovering over them before moving away.

Egon cast a spell to slow it down. The fear and hate emanating from the cloud was overwhelming. Ben blocked the emotions from affecting the Elders then cast another spell to block it from the humans. He spread the spell across the world.

Egon redirected the cloud to pass through the first gate, pushing it toward the assembly. The cloud fed off their fear, growing bigger and bigger. The assembly ran from the cloud but couldn't escape it.

The shiners popped in, seizing the cloud with a spell and sent it back to its world. The assembly members stumbled to their feet in shock and surprise. Things were getting out of hand quickly. They sent out a call to other worlds for assistance.

"It's time to show them who they are dealing with," Ben said.

"What do you have in mind?" Egon asked, smiling.

They sent in a swarm of bees carrying an illness that would spread, causing confusion and chaos. Following the bees was another dark cloud containing a powerful storm that was unleashed as it passed through the door.

"Let's see how they like that," Egon chuckled.

"That should keep them busy for a while," Ben said, smiling.

A timid, slender man hesitantly approached Egon and Ben. He kept looking nervously around him. As he moved closer, they realized he had floppy ears like a dog hidden beneath his hat. He was an otherworlder.

"Excuse me kind sirs," he said nervously. "My name is Anton, and I've lived here for some time. I'd like to go home."

Ben looked at him and said, "Your people attacked this world."

He raised his hands up in surrender. "Not my people. The assembly's people."

"And how do I know the difference?" Ben asked.

"The assembly's people don't live outside their worlds."

"Good to know. If we let you return, will you help us?" Egon asked.

"How can I help you?"

"To contact the other worlders that oppose the assembly," Ben said.

Anton's eyes widened in horror. "If I did that, they would kill me."

"How would they know?"

Anton pursed his lips together. "I don't know," he said. "I can pass the message on, what do you want me to say?"

"Let them know that the assembly has declared war on the humans, and we're fighting back."

"I can do that, but they don't care about the humans."

"Make them care," Egon said.

Alton nodded nervously. "Then I can go home?"

"Yes."

"Good. I'll get a message going. I'll be back," he said racing away.

"Think it will do any good?" Egon asked.

"Not really, but it was worth a try. I'm going to crash at Sierra's for a while. If you need me, let me know," Ben said.

"Get some rest. It may be quiet for a while."

Ben patted him affectionately on the shoulder then vanished.

⸻⸻

Sierra, Mace and Dak let the other worlders closer to a dark city, reaching out to the inhabitants, relieved to feel hundreds of people.

As they reached the city gate, several men and women came out to meet them. They looked at all the other worlders in surprise.

"Why are you here?" asked Wesley.

"We've come to help you," Dak said.

Wesley smiled. "And how do you plan on helping us? You look like you're about to drop where you stand."

"Our friends are tired and need a place to stay," Sierra said.

"Are you crazy? No one is allowed to travel to the dark worlds, and we can't leave."

"Those rules don't apply anymore," Sierra said.

Wesley's friends gathered closer. "When did that happen and how?"

"Since the assembly attacked humans."

"Why would they do that? We've never interacted with humans. Why would they hurt them?"

"They thought I interfered with the dark worlds."

Wesley smiled, "Well, aren't you?"

"I am now," she said, smiling.

"Be careful. Some of the dark worlds are scary places."

"We will avoid the scary ones. We need your help to fight against the assembly."

"You can't fight them. They destroyed our cities, killing hundreds of thousands.

"Why?" Sierra asked, sickened by their brutality.

They wanted control of the ley lines in this region. We didn't want to be controlled so we fought against them. The shiners helped them gain control of the dark ones and they nearly destroyed us.

Mace lowered his head sadly.

"What are the dark ones?" Dak asked.

"They live in some of the dark worlds," Mace said. "They destroy everything they encounter."

Wesley looked at Mace in horror. "You're a shiner?"

"I had nothing to do with that. I'm here to help."

"He saved me from the assembly," Sierra said.

"You can't expect us to trust him."

"I hope you will give him a chance to earn your trust," Sierra said.

"How can the three of you do what thousands couldn't?"

"I don't know, but we can't let the assembly kill humans and force to you to stay here waiting to die."

"She's right, Wesley," said Alena, a young woman in her twenties. "We deserve to have the freedom to travel to the other cities along the lines. We are prisoners here, waiting to die."

"What is your plan?"

"First, I want to bring all the people from the dark worlds together," Sierra said.

"That will take some time," Alena said. "Please, where are our manners? Come inside where we can sit and talk."

The other worlders followed her through the crooked gate, putting down their meager belongings and sat down to hear Sierra's plan.

"It won't take as long if I go to each world and send them here," Mace said.

"That would speed things up. Be careful. Can you trust any of your people to help us?"

"I don't know. They will be afraid, but I will talk to them."

"Be careful. We will stay here to protect them."

"I'll check back after I visit the dark worlds."

Sierra hugged him right before he vanished.

Mace appeared in front of his best friend Sweets. Sweets stepped back surprised, then hugged Mace briefly. "What happened to you? Did you escape?"

"Not exactly. They want to help us break free of the assembly."

"Are you crazy? They will kill us?"

"Not if we escape and help them. You should see how powerful they are. We finally have a chance to be free of the assembly."

"You really believe that?"

"Yes. We need to see if we can get others to join us."

"I will get them. Where can I meet you?"

Mace looked at his best friend and wondered for the first time if he could trust him.

"In the human city. Beneath the covered walkway. I'll meet you there in an hour."

"If I don't show, you'll know one of our friends turned me in."

"If you fear for your safety, go to the meeting place and wait."

Sweets nodded his head in agreement. Mace vanished and entered the next safe, dark world. It took some effort to convince them to risk leaving and traveling to another dark world.

Within an hour, he convinced four more worlds to relocate. He appeared outside the walkway and didn't see anyone, so he appeared inside the crowded walkway.

Mace was excited to see nearly twenty of his dearest friends, including Doni.

"Your new friends have created quite a mess for the assembly. They've sent for reinforcements." Doni said.

"We need to hurry and inform the others," Mace said.

One by one they vanished, reappearing in the deserted city. He looked around terrified that he'd been tricked.

Sierra reached out to him to let him know they had relocated beneath the city. Mace moved around the city with his friends, waiting several minutes to make certain that they weren't followed. Confident that they were safe, they joined the others beneath the city.

Mace and the other shiners looked around in awe. They were standing in the center of an underground city, a newly constructed, clean city.

"How did you do this?" Mace asked. "You're human."

"You say that like it's a bad thing," Sierra said.

"I mean no disrespect."

"None taken. I'm glad to see your friends showed up,"

Another group of other worlders showed up, escorted by Dak. They too, looked around in awe.

"Feel free to look around and find a home," Dak said. "You are safe here. If the assembly sends anyone here, they won't find anything."

"Do we have a plan?" Mace asked.

"We're working on one. First, I want to get people to safety."

Mace nodded. "It's a start. At least we have a chance. That's more than we had before."

"Will the other shiners be able to track you," Dak asked.

"Not down here," Doni said in relief, feeling safe for the first time that he could remember. It was an odd, but pleasant feeling.

Mace and the other shiners went off together to explore the city. You couldn't tell you were beneath the surface with the blue sky above them with a sun shining in the distance. They passed a market stocked with food and became excited when they learned they could take whatever they wanted or needed.

"What now?" Dak asked Sierra.

She shrugged and said, "I have no idea. I guess I need to check on the Elders."

"I'll do it. I think they need you to stay close by. You'll figure it out. You always do."

Sierra kissed him. "Thank you. I'm sorry I dragged you into this, again."

Dak laughed. "I think the assembly dragged you into it," he said, kissing the tip of her nose before he vanished.

Chapter Forty-Two

The Assembly

The dark black cloud of destruction ripped through the town, destroying everything in its path. The quaint houses Sierra had admired were leveled.

The forest trees managed to escape the destruction by lying flat on the ground, letting the cloud pass over them, stirring up dirt and debris as it went.

When it reached the city, it unleased its wrath, sending the remains of the town soaring through the air.

The shiners arrived just as the cloud was approaching the assembly building. With dozens of them working together they managed to gain control of the cloud and send it back to its world.

Before they had a chance to take a breath, they were hit by a swarm of bees. Their sting was extremely painful and caused the other worlders that had been stung to scream, trying to fight off the unreal attacks as they ran in terror.

The shiners sent the bees to keep the dark cloud of destruction company. Terrified that the cloud had returned, as another cloud headed their way, they prepared to gain control of it again.

This cloud was different. Lightening flashed, striking the ground, hail rained down on them, painfully striking one of the shiners, knocking him to his knees.

The other shiners came together to contain the cloud. They concentrated their efforts on the cloud's center with little effect.

Theador, the head of the assembly joined them, adding his considerable power to theirs. The cloud started to shrink. The lightning raged within the cloud as it fought against the shiners.

Another assemblyman, Lucy, from a distant world joined in the fight. She possessed the power of fire and ice, and shot ice crystals at the cloud, freezing its water particles.

The cloud grew heavy under its weight and began to drop lower as it turned the water to hail stone, pounding those beneath it.

Shrinking, the cloud darted away and fled through the door, returning to its creator. Ben felt its frustration and created other clouds to assist it. The four clouds returned to combat the assembly.

Lightening rained down on them to be redirected by the shiners. Lucy pelted the clouds, alternating between bursts of fire and ice.

Miranda joined Lucy, sending a tornado at the clouds, sending them swirling through the air. The clouds split up, dumping ice, and lightning across the surface as they fled back through the door where Ben sent them to the dark world of the first cloud.

Lucy dropped down on the scorched ground exhausted. She looked around at the destruction of the burned-out city. Sadness threatened to overwhelm her, seeing their beloved city leveled.

"Who is this human?" she asked breathlessly.

Miranda sat down next to her. "Someone we shouldn't have messed with," she said looking at Theodore. "Did you consider for even one second that she was telling the truth? We had no indication that any of the dark worlds had been breached, until now."

"You're blaming me for this?" Theadore asked, stunned,

"I'm blaming all of us. We had no proof, but thought since she was weaker, we could force her to admit her guilt."

"So, we underestimated her. We need to find out where the man is from that helped her escape."

"And then what?" Lucy asked.

"We find them and destroy them," he said.

"Look around you," Miranda said. "Do we really want to start a war with an entire race of these people?"

"Look around you. We are already at war," he yelled.

Maki appeared before Theodore. "We are transporting the warriors as we speak," he said.

"Please get rid of this mess before they arrive," Theadore ordered.

Maki opened a rip that sucked all the debris through the opening until all that remained were the foundations where the buildings once stood.

"Get the builders here to start rebuilding," Theodore ordered.

"Yes sir," Maki said, disappearing.

"The assembly will convene in the council room, please don't be late."

Lucy and Miranda rose to their feet, dusted off the fine dust from the destruction of their town from their clothing and walked away from the remains toward the residential area.

Lucy and Miranda sat in their seats as instructed as a teams of generals entered the room. The tall, muscled men were dressed in black uniforms trimmed in red. The sheer size of them was intimidating.

General Wayland approached the assembly. "Distinguished assembly. May I offer my condolences for the losses you suffered today."

"Thank you," Theodore said. "We are under attack by a human and her otherworlder husband."

General Wayland frowned. "A single human and her spouse did all this damage?" he asked in awe.

"Somehow, they were able to send one of the dark worlders here. It caused the damage."

What world is the otherworlder from?" General Wayland asked.

"We've never seen his kind before. He must be from farther down the lines," Theodore said. "Don't risk looking for him outside our jurisdiction. We don't need additional conflict."

"What are our instructions?" General Wayland asked.

"There is talk of the dark worlders relocating to plan another rebellion. Find them and put a stop to it. And teach the humans a lesson. Their world should be easy to terrorize."

"Yes sir." General Wayland said as he turned, rejoining his generals, and left the assembly.

"The others will be here later to assist us in protecting our home," Theodore told the assembly members.

"I'm afraid we're making a mistake going after the humans," Lucy said. "There numbers are great, and we know very little about them. We run the risk of causing trouble all down the lines."

"Which could cause war with other factions," Miranda added.

"You heard the ladies. Don't go beyond our borders. Please instruct the general," Theodore told Maki.

"I will let him know," Maki said before he vanished.

General Wayland and his troops of hundreds appeared in a residential neighborhood. Everything was quiet, until the shiners overturned cars, uprooted trees, and ripped the roofs off houses.

They moved on to the first darkened world. Everything was quiet. The setting sun made the already darker world an eerie cast over the burned-out ruins of what was once a thriving city.

"There's no one here," Maki said.

"We will find them," General Wayland assured him.

They moved on to the second world. Sierra and Dak felt them the instant they arrived. Together, they cast another concealing spell just to make sure the shiner couldn't feel them.

The darkness was even worse here, and again, no sign of life.

"They were here," Maki said, "but they are gone now."

Sierra turned to Dak and the shiners and said, "I don't care what you have to do, get the people out of the other dark worlds before they arrive."

"Will do babe," Dak said, kissing her before he vanished.

General Wayland decided to alter his search, and they popped into the last dark world. The moment the inhabitants saw the soldiers, they ran in panic.

The shiners froze them in place allowing General Wayland to question them face to face.

General Wayland approached the terrified young man suspended in midair. His eyes darted around frantically, looking for someone to help him.

Stopping nose to nose with him, General Wayland asked, "Where are the members of the rebellion hiding?" he demanded.

"Rebellion? The rebellion ended years ago," he stammered.

"The new rebellion," he pressed.

"What new rebellion? Look at us, we're barely surviving, how can we start a rebellion?"

General Wayland looked around at the half-starved villagers seeing the truth in his words. "Have you been approached by anyone to join a rebellion?"

"No. We obey the assembly," he cried, terrified.

Gerald Wayland nodded to Maki and released the terrified young man who fell to the ground, scampered to his feet and ran away taking cover in a derelict building.

"Destroy them," General Wayland ordered.

His army moved toward the building, firing at anything that moved.

Dak entered the world just as the shooting began. Taking in the situation at a glance, he hit the advancing army with a gust of wind, knocking them backward.

General Wayland turned his weapon on Dak, firing angrily, infuriated by his sudden appearance. Dak dodged the first bullet, the second one ripped through his shoulder, causing him to stagger backward.

He turned the gun red hot, burning the soldier's hands. He turned to smoke and raced into the burning building and reappeared, and called out, "If you want to live, come with me."

When no one answered, he yelled, "There's not much time. If you don't want to burn to death, run."

Dozens of people came out of hiding behind broken bits of furniture, fallen walls, and dropped down from the ceiling. "How can you help us?" asked the young man interrogated by the general.

Dak opened a rip to the underground city. "Hurry," he said.

"There are others near the river. Please help them," a young woman cried before stepping through the rip.

Dak closed it, turned into smoke as the first bomb hit the building, ripping it apart. The second bomb leveled it to the ground.

High above the destruction, Dak flew in his smoke form, searching for the river. He spotted a green tree line looking for signs of life. He spotted houses and raced toward them. As he descended, he heard popping noises and anger filled his soul.

Hurrying, he landed in human form just behind the shooters. His furry grew as one of them shot a boy no more than ten years old.

A yell grew deep in his throat as he pulled fire from the ground and engulfed the two shooters.

"Are there more of you?" he yelled, racing to the boy's side. "Gather the wounded," he said, picking up the boy. "And come with me."

He opened a rip to the city and urged them to hurry. The ground was covered with the bodies of the dead. What kind of monsters kill for no reason and murder innocent children. Shaking his head sadly, he stepped through the rip, closing it behind him.

Sierra took the child from him, her eyes brimming with tears as she poured her healing energy into him. Seeing Dak's bleeding shoulder she asked, "Are you okay?"

"I healed it. I'm fine." He bent down next to her and whispered, "These people are monsters. They don't deserve to live. They shot that boy without blinking an eye."

Sierra blinked, tears rolled down her cheeks as the boy sat up, frightened.

"I'll be back. I'm going to the other cities to try to save them before the killers show up."

"Be careful," she begged and moved on to heal the next person.

Dak arrived at the next city and tried to rush the reluctant and scared people to leave. Frustrated, Dak yelled, "I just saw the assembly's army shoot a child.

They are on their way here to do the same to you. If you want to live, come with me now."

He opened a rip, and they stared at it in shock. A loud boom rocked the ground beneath them as the army sent a bomb through the rip they'd opened before entering the city. It exploded just yards away from them, knocking some of the scared people off their feet.

They scrambled to their feet and ran through the rip. Dak's fury heated up as he strode toward their rip. He pulled the energy from the air around him and sent it through. When it hit the army, it nearly crushed the men in front and knocked the rest of them off their feet.

By the time they recovered, Dak had walked back to his rip and vanished.

Sierra had never seen him so angry.

"I want to kill all of them," he hissed. "They are monsters."

"Not all of them," she said.

"You can't be sure," he said.

"When Mace returned with a group that had encountered the soldiers, Sierra's anger surpassed Dak's.

Many of them were burnt, over half their bodies, being carried by other wounded.

Mace's clothing was smoldering, but they extinguished the flames.

Sierra and Dak rushed around the wounded, healing those that were worse off first.

"I'm so sorry," Mace cried, holding a child, trying to comfort her as she screamed. "They showed up as we were leaving and set off a bomb before I closed the door."

Sierra frowned. "Why didn't it blow up here?"

"I contained it the best I could, but it wasn't good enough," he cried.

Sierra healed the screaming child and touched Mace, healing his wounds and mind. His pain fueled her anger, and she reached deep down into the earth, pulling at its core and released it.

The fiery energy traveled all along the fey lines shaking them apart. Buildings crashed in on themselves. The ground opened up, destroying anything and everything in its way.

The city of the assembly disappeared into a crater, fortunately for them, they had already abandoned it until it could be rebuilt.

All along the lines, everyone was demanding to know what caused the massive earthquake. The human world near the lines felt a small shudder and instantly dismissed it.

General Wayland feared that his bomb inside a doorway may have caused the quake, but Theodore answered that it was the humans, and the other worlders that were responsible.

The other worlders received General Wayland's account of events with mixed reactions. Some believed that he was responsible and trying to place the blame on someone else, while others couldn't believe a human could cause such damage.

A select few were excited about teaching the human's a lesson.

Chapter Forty-Three

The Human World

Anton approached Ben and Egon reluctantly. "Excuse me sirs," he said, nervously. "I sent messages along the lines letting them know that the humans are to be left alone, and that we can travel the human world if we respect them."

Ben patted Anton on the shoulder. "Good work my man."

"Can I come back?"

"Yes, but I have another favor to ask."

Anton looked around nervously, "What favor?"

"Let me know if you hear of something trying to hurt the humans."

Anton smiled. "I can do that."

"Thank you. I won't forget it."

Anton smiled and hurried away to tell his family the good news. As he hurried along the lines, he felt the ground shake.

He paused until the shaking stopped and hurried on.

On order from the assembly, six black clouds emerged from their world and rose above the clouds, disbursing across the planet. Each cloud took position over major cities and rained down destruction, hurling tornadoes, hail, and torrents of rain.

The spells cast by the Elders tried to block them, but the clouds were too strong. An alarm went out to the Elders, and they raced to each location to stop them.

Ben reached inside the tormented mind of one of the massive dark clouds hovering above Atlanta. He felt sorry for the creature and tried to help it by easing its torment, until it gleefully tried to pull him deeper inside its twisted brain.

Ben resisted its pull and warned it to retreat and never return or he would destroy them. The cloud pulled harder at Ben and Ben didn't resist. He pushed his way deep into the clouds' mind and opened up his own mind, flooding the creature's tiny brain.

It tried to push Ben away, but it was helpless against him until it couldn't take anymore.

Ben withdrew from the creature and watched it drift into pieces and get carried away by the wind.

Afraid, the other clouds retreated back to their world. Ben joined the others back along the lines. "This is getting ridiculous," Ben said. "We need to end this."

"What do you have in mind?" Egon asked.

"Let me run it by Sierra, then I'll let you know."

Ben opened a rip to Sierra's underground city. He was impressed by its construction and the number of people she'd managed to relocate.

Seeing him, Sierra made her way through the crowd of wounded and hugged him. "We can use your help to heal the wounded," she said.

"I need to discuss something with you first," he said.

His tone worried her, and she asked, "What? Has something happened?"

"Yes and no. Everyone is all right, but these things keep attacking. We can't guard the lines forever."

"I know. I'm sorry I dragged you into this."

"You didn't start this, but we have two options. First, destroy the assembly, or second, shut down the lines so they can't enter your world."

"As much as I would like to destroy them, we don't know the ripple effect that would have."

"I was afraid you'd say that." he teased.

"If you block them off, will you trap them in their cities? Some of them depend on other cities for survival."

"I can leave an open area between the doors and your world allowing them to move freely between the lines, but not enter the human world."

"Will I be able to open a rip into their worlds?"

"Yes, but you can't stay."

"I have to. I can't abandon these people," she said.

"So, what is your plan?" he asked.

"I'm not sure yet. They need to fight back against the assembly and retake their lives. They've been imprisoned for too long."

"And you're going to lead them?" he asked even though he already knew the answer.

"I have to."

"What about Pandora?"

"What about it? Is something wrong? I've only been gone for two days."

"How long do you expect this to take? Weeks, month, years?"

"Not years," she replied.

"It's admirable that you want to help them, but you have no idea what could happen. We know nothing about all these worlds. We don't know how long they've existed or how many there are. We need to isolate them."

"I know, but I'm going to help them, then I'll come home," she promised. "Close them off and I'll take care of this as fast as I can," she promised.

Ben helped her and Dak heal the rest of the wounded, then Ben hugged them both and left, returning to Egon.

"Well?" asked Egon.

"I'm going to shut down the lines. They will no longer be allowed to enter this world unless they can open a rip."

"Is Sierra returning home?" Egon asked anxiously.

"No. I couldn't talk her into leaving."

"I'm not surprised."

Ben saw Anton and his family carrying their belongings and waved him over.

"Yes sir," Anton said. "It's okay if we come back?"

"Of course, it is, but things are about to change, and I thought you should know."

"Change how?"

"We're going to block off the lines from the human world. You won't be able to travel between them anymore."

Alton chewed on his lower lip and said, "But I can stay here?"

"If that's what you want."

"It is. It's peaceful here. I like it better."

"Then we're good?"

"Yes, we're good," Anton said, smiling.

"Dad. I need a couple of you to go to the other end of the lines and perform the ancient elder's sealing spell."

"We haven't used that spell in a very long time," Egon cautioned him.

"I know, but it will work."

"Yes, it will. It is a tough spell to get right."

"That's why you're going to do it," Ben said. "These worlds have been here for centuries, hidden from the humans and I'm certain they've interfered with them, and not in a good way."

"I don't doubt that. But remember, we know next to nothing about these places, and we could be bringing more trouble for the humans and ourselves."

"They'd have to break our spell and find us, so I'm good with sealing them in," Ben said laughing.

Egon laughed. "Let's just hope none of them are powerful enough to do either. I'll let you know when we're ready."

Egon opened a rip and stepped through to Ireland. The lines were far more powerful there. He could feel the power in the air. He briefly wondered at the wisdom of what they were about to do but shrugged off his doubts. He didn't see any other way. He reached across the world to let Ben know that he was ready.

Together, they recited the spell, holding their hands out toward the lines. Egon instantly felt something pushing back against him. He pushed forward, repeating the spell.

The resistance grew stronger, but he felt the spell working. He saw nearly invisible threads weave themselves together around the line. The weaves grew tighter and tighter and spread out in front of him. The two sides met in the middle securing the web along the lines.

Egon could feel the power coming from it. He could still feel something resisting the spell. Satisfied that they'd secured the lines away from the humans, Egon and the other Elders rejoined Ben.

Let's check on Sierra and see if we can help," Ben said. Egon and Ben stepped through the rip and joined Sierra while the rest of the Elders returned home.

Sierra hugged Egon, then Ben. "Are the lines secure?" she asked.

"Yes. The human world will be safe," Ben said.

"Unless they use the shiners to move beyond the seal," Dak said.

"What's a shiner?" Ben asked.

"They can open a rip," Sierra said.

"That could be a problem," Ben said, frowning.

"We will have to deal with it," Sierra said. "We have shiners here."

"Do you have a plan?" Egon said.

Sierra rolled her eyes. "I've moved all the people here from the dying cities they were destroying. Next, we start training them how to defend themselves against the assembly's army."

"Would you like some help?" Egon asked.

Sierra smiled in gratitude. "I'd love for you to stay if you can spare the time."

"We can spare the time," Ben said.

"You just got married. Go home to your wife," Sierra said.

"My wife understands," he said. "What exactly started this?"

Sierra exhaled softly. "They think I brought the Destroyer out of a dark world to help him."

"And that's bad?" Ben asked in confusion.

"To them it is. They wanted the people they defeated in the last rebellion to die out, and to help them is a crime."

"That's crazy. How many cities belong to the assembly?"

"I have no idea."

"Maybe that's where Dad and I can help. We can visit them and determine their affiliation."

"And charm them away," Egon teased.

Dak laughed, "Good luck with that."

"You doubt by ability to charm?"

"No. I find you very charming."

Chapter Forty-Four

Reaction

The assembly gathered in a newly constructed building with leaders from twenty other cities along the lines. The massive destruction Sierra caused down the lines had them concerned and talking.

Theodore stood to address the group. "Thank you all for coming so quickly. I hope the shift in the earth didn't cause too much damage to your cities."

"What is the emergency that pulled us away from our homes?" Annalee, a white-haired woman with blue streaks in her long hair asked.

"A human and her otherworlder husband have been helping the survivors of the rebellion to regroup and start the rebellion again."

"A human? Surely, you're mistaken," Tasha said, smoothing back her long black hair.

"How can a human pose a threat? What world is her husband from? He should be punished."

"He will be punished when we locate him," Theodore said, frustrated.

"Do you know where they are gathering?" Tomlin asked.

"We have been unsuccessful in locating them, unfortunately," Theodore admitted.

Tomlin looked around the room at the other city leaders before he said, "Someone must be hiding them. I'm sorry, none of this makes sense. How did a human find the lines?"

"She didn't find them," Lucy said.

"Please explain," Tomlin asked.

"She was brought here to be interrogated," Lucy said.

Tomlin's brown eyes widened in understanding. "Why would you bring a human here? They knew nothing of our world."

"She had to know. She was seen helping one of the creatures from a dark world," Theodore defended.

"If that is true, it doesn't mean she was aware of our world. If the other jurisdictions learn about this, they could seek to punish us," Tomlin reminded him. "My people shall have no part of this. You caused this mess. You clean it up," he said, rising from his seat.

"You can't do that. You are part of the assembly," Theodore yelled.

"Not anymore," Tomlin said, heading for the door.

"If you're not with us, you are against us," Theordore threatened.

Tomlin turned and faced the assembly. "Don't you think you have enough to deal with, without threatening me. If you enter my city, it will be an act of war," he stated and turned slowly, walking away, gently closing the door behind him.

"Are we going to allow him to just walk away," Cadence asked.

"He is part of the assembly and bound by the rules he not only agreed to but helped draw them up."

"You're right, Maki, contain him please," Theodore said.

Maki nodded his head and vanished, reappearing in the blink of an eye to take Tomlin by the arm and deposit him in a cell before vanishing again. He reappeared at Theodore's side with no expression on his face.

Cadence smiled. She was terrified of the assembly unraveling. Her world was much better off under the structure and guidance the assembly provided, not to mention the trading with the other cities representing the assembly.

"Tomlin was right about us not having the time to deal with him," Theodore said smugly.

The assembly leaders laughed, some clapping their hands. They had endured much to bring the assembly together and wanted to keep it intact.

"General Wayland encountered the rebels as they were fleeing with a shiner and as of now, all the cities we defeated in the war have been abandoned."

"Where are they then? The human world?" Lucy asked.

"We don't know, but we will find them."

"Have we tried talking to them?" Miranda asked.

"We left them to die. Don't you think it's a little late for talking?" Lucy stated.

"We left them so they couldn't threaten the lives of our people again," Theodore reminded them. "They wanted no part of us and left us with very little choice."

"And look how well that's turned out," Miranda said. "They are now threatening the lives of cities outside our jurisdiction."

"Which may very well work in our favor," Theodore said, smiling, hoping to put an end to the rebels once and for all.

"We need to secure our hold on the dark worlds. Without them, we could have a hard time ending this rebellion," Cadence said.

"Absolutely," Theodore said. "You can take a team and accompany the shiners to make sure they understand what's at stake for them if they fail to live up to our bargain."

Cadence waved in the direction of half a dozen assembly and again at a dozen shiners as she rolled her eyes at Theodore. He had threatened to make the inhabitance of the dark worlds vanish into whatever was between their world and the next world they passed into.

Terrified of being abandoned into nothingness, they agreed to help them.

⁂ ⁂ ⁂

Fearful for the safety of the refugees, Sierra, Dak, Egon, Ben, and Mace relocated them to a new city below a thriving city. They opened multiple doorways before they arrived at their new location.

"That should prevent them from tracking us," Sierra said. "Now, let's start training these people to defend themselves."

Ben approached Sierra as the people prepared to start training. Standing beside her he asked, "How long do you plan to stay with these people?"

"I don't know."

"You left things unsettled at home. Don't you think you should check on Pandora?"

Sierra sighed heavily. "I'll go home in the morning," she promised.

"Helping these people could take a lifetime or we could fix the problem for them," he offered.

Sierra frowned. "We won't do either. I've only been gone a few days. Given a few more, we can show them how to defend themselves against the assembly. We can capture more of them using the tactics Ambro used against Alexi's people. Once we capture them, they can negotiate terms they can all live with."

"What if they won't negotiate?"

"Then you can scare the crap out of the head of the assembly so we can all go home," she said without turning to look at him.

Ben smiled. "That's my girl," he said, a grin spreading across his face.

Chapter Forty-Five

The Ancient Lines

Agusta looked at the large crack that ran down the center of the white marble floor and frowned. Never in all the centuries of the ley lines had something caused interference. Now the lines were off track, and something was wrong.

For the first time in recent memory, Agusta stepped outside his world and into the human world around him. The noise was deafening, which he silenced with a wave of his hand.

He instantly felt the blocking spell Egon put up and frowned. Who would want to block them from the humans? He saw nothing out of the ordinary as he stared down the lines and returned to Spartan, breathing in the serenity of his elegant Roman style city.

Even though his ancestors were Druids, he preferred Roman architecture. He passed through his city to the next city along the lines and to the next. Nothing except for the large crack seemed out of place.

Frowning, he wondered how many cities had popped up from the fallout of their magic. He hadn't checked in far too long.

He continued along the lines, removing cities that failed to thrive. He found it odd that the use of magic could have such a side effect, but some of the creations to come out of excess magic were useful and interesting.

He frowned when he realized he was entering America. He didn't care for Americans. They were too different from the humans outside his home.

How were there so many new cities, he wondered as he cleared away the empty worlds as he made his way down the lines.

Curious, he entered the world of the assembly. He found the talking trees interesting. The trees eyed Agusta fearfully. His Roman attire stood out imposingly.

He entered the ravaged city with interest, taking note of the large crack down the middle of the city. He bent down and touched it, feeling remnants of strong, unfamiliar magic.

Theodore, Lucy, and Miranda watched the stranger from a distance in fear and awe. They could feel his strength and power and knew he was one of the Ancients.

Agusta looked across the debris strewn street at the three assemblymen. He felt their fear and interest as they watched them.

"What caused this?" he asked. His voice booming out across the city.

Theodore took a deep breath and stepped forward. He didn't know Agusta, but he'd heard rumors of the creators and was terrified.

"We believe it was caused by a young girl."

Agusta frowned. "Where is this young girl."

"We don't know. We have been looking for her. She may have returned to the human world, and there is a spell blocking us from their world."

"You expect me to believe that a human girl caused this damage along the lines? Unbelievable."

"She is accompanied by someone with magic. He may be responsible," he added nervously.

"Where is he from?" Augusta demanded, losing patience.

"We've never seen anyone like him," he said softly.

Agusta glared at him in disgust. "I shouldn't have allowed you aberrations to continue."

Theodore paled. He knew Agusta could wipe them out with a wave of his hand. He murmured, "We're not aberrations."

"You were created from remnants of magic, like discarded garbage," Agusta said with disgust, turning away from them. He searched across the world for any remaining magic from the stranger.

Feeling nothing, he turned away and left them alone.

Shaken, Miranda turned to Theodore and asked, "Who was that? Why does he hate us so?"

Theodore's mind was racing, worried for their safety. "He is from the first city on the lines."

"Is he really responsible for our creation?"

"That is what legends says."

"I hope he never returns," Lucy said.

"As do I," said Theodore.

Agusta moved down the lines as he headed toward home, searching for the source of the strange magic. He felt something unusual and entered a world filled with colorful exotic birds.

The birds flew close to him unafraid. Agusta smiled. Not all the aberrations were bad. He walked through the forest, reaching out to locate the source of unusual magic, but he felt nothing.

He encountered a quaint colorful city. He watched the people move around working together. He felt a peace he hadn't felt in an extraordinarily long time.

Sierra felt a stranger enter the city. A strong source of power poured off of him. She wondered who he was, and why he was here. She was afraid to reach out to him, afraid he would feel her intrusion.

Agusta took one last look at the peaceful city and thought to return another day.

Sierra released the breath she didn't realize she was holding when Agusta left.

"Whoever that was is very powerful," Egon said.

"Are we ready for plan 'B'," Egon said. "I hope it works, because plan 'A' isn't," he teased.

"That's not funny," Sierra said, frowning at him.

"You really want to take Theodore?" He's not going to be pleasant to deal with," Ben said.

"It won't work without him," Sierra said.

"Then let's get to it," Ben said.

Dak, Egon, Sierra, Ben, and Mace opened rips to the assembly, catching Theodore, Lucy, and Miranda by surprise, taking them back to their hidden city.

Theodore looked at them in shock. "This is an outrage," he yelled. "You will be punished for this."

"Unless you want to be consigned to the emptiness you threatened the dark worlds with, I suggest you relax and listen to what we have to say," Ben said.

Theodore paled at the thought of being sent to nothingness. "What do you want?"

Sierra slowly approached the three assemblymen. "We want peace between the assembly and the former rebels. They want to be free to live their lives."

"Are you insane? They tried to kill us?"

"And you tried to kill and succeeded in killing most of them. Isn't it time for peace."

"We can't trust them," Lucy said.

"They don't trust you either," Sierra said.

"We can put a blood spell on all of them," Egon said.

"What's that?" Theodore said.

"It will bind you together and if one of you doesn't keep your word and hurts the other, it will also hurt you."

Miranda's eyes widened in surprise. "Is it safe?"

"Unless you try to hurt them. Any of them," Ben said.

"They won't move to our city, and the three of you vanish and leave us alone?"

"We will leave," Sierra said. "If the others agree."

Sierra left the assembly with Ben and Egon. She asked Mace to join her. The moment the door shut Mace turned to face Sierra. "I want to go with you. Please don't leave me here."

Sierra smiled. "You are free to come with me."

Mace exhaled in relief. "Others will want to come with you. Even if they can't hurt us."

"We will welcome them," Sierra promised. "Let's go talk to them together."

Sierra reached out to all the people she'd brought together. She told them what she'd proposed to the assembly and that they were welcome to relocate to her home, if that was her wish. She would help them relocate anywhere they chose, and she would help them find a new home.

A murmur went up between them. They divided into groups those that wanted to stay in the underground city, those that wanted to relocate to other cities along the lines.

Dak took Mace and the others back to Pandora. He kissed Sierra whispering, "Don't take too long."

Returning his kiss, she said, "I won't," against his lips.

Dak opened a rip to Pandora in a quiet unoccupied neighborhood away from town. He produced keys out of thin air and handed them out.

"You are free to choose any house. The key will work and mold to the lock. There is food, clothing, blankets, and everything you will need inside. It's late, and tomorrow I will come get you and take you on a tour of Pandora."

Mace and the other shiners stepped forward, "Where are we?" Mace said. "We're not on the ley lines anymore, are we?"

"No, we're not."

"This isn't the human world?"

"No."

"Can we move between this world and the Ley cities?"

"Yes. I will show you how. Now if you will get settled for the night. Sierra and I will show you around tomorrow."

Sixty or more people moved through the quiet neighborhood and picked among the elegant two-story houses nestled on tree lined streets, with a soft glow from the streetlights on the two-lane road.

The night air was quiet, and they could see the faint glow of Pandora City. A faint breeze carried the scent of jasmine and honeysuckle across the neighborhood.

Mace entered his new home in wonder and shock. The last few minutes were a blur. He felt truly safe for the first time in his life. He searched through the house and frowned at the television, dishwasher, and microwave. He wondered what they were.

He located the bedroom and fell across the bed exhausted and fell asleep.

Sierra led the three assemblymen to the remaining rebels. She joined hands with Ben and Egon and cast a blood spell on all of them. Egon opened a rip to the assembly room and instructed Miranda, Lucy, and Theodore to return home.

Sierra created a staircase to the surface and created a small town in the woods for those that wished to remain.

Together, they took the remaining rebels and relocated them to cities out of the jurisdiction of the assembly. They provided them with new homes.

They returned to the underground city to bid them good luck and goodbye. Sierra showed Pierce, a shiner, how to open a rip to Pandora in case they needed her.

They told her that they planned to continue training in case they needed it and thanked her for finding a peaceful solution to their problem.

Bidding them goodbye again, they opened a rip home.

It felt so good to be home. Sierra took a deep breath, inhaling the sweet scent of home. How did trouble continue to find her?

Chapter Forty-Six

Alexi

Alexi watched with pride as her Dragons and Dragoneers trained. They were almost ready to teach Rialda not to mess with her.

She retreated to her room and opened a black metal box filled with ingredients she'd gathered from the forest. She gathered a knife, bowl, and heavy wooden spoon. She diced up the plants and placed them in the bowl, sprinkling a dusty white powder over them.

She added several magical powders, a liquid and stirred it together. The plants dissolved and turned into a dark paste. She put the paste in several vials and sealed them tightly.

She dipped her finger in the remaining paste and tasted it. It was tasteless. She carried one of the vials down to the kitchen and added it to the Dragoneers' food. She took another and added it to the Dragon's food.

It would make them stronger and faster. She continued to add it to their food for the next five days, ingesting it herself. The change was slow, but effective. She grew faster, smarter, and stronger.

Alexi couldn't have been more pleased. After training, she retreated to the forest to gather more plants. Unable to find the correct plant she moved deeper into the forest, finally locating them. She cut several clippings for her potion, unaware that a dark spore spewed out of a black flower.

Inhaling the spores, she sneezed, not noticing that they fell into her bowl of plant clippings. She prepared the paste for next week's meals, adding it to tonight's meals.

The change in the Dragons and Dragoneers was immediate. They grew darker, stronger, and faster.

Alexi's eyes grew darker and her thirst for revenge deepened.

She watched the Dragons and Dragoneers train. They were ready to take on Rialda. First thing the following morning, she gathered them together. Climbing on Alton's back, they took flight and headed toward Rialda's mountain fortress.

Their dark clothing and the black and silver Dragons nearly blocked out the sun with their numbers. As they neared the fortress, one of the lookouts raised the alarm.

Rialda called out to the Dragons and Dragoneers to ready for battle. Gnome and human riders raced to their Dragons and took to the air.

Rialda called out to the Gnomes informing them that they were under attack. Next, she called out to Enid. He flew in through the window landing next to her. She quickly climbed on his back, and she raced to the front of her army.

Taking her place in the front of her people, they flew to intercept the incoming riders.

Alexi and her dark riders raced through the air, gliding through the sky effortlessly. Their dark rimmed eyes were bright with excitement as they moved closer to the mountain fortress.

Rialda reached out to her people, reminding them to work together and be careful. The Elfin, Muriel and Firefly flew next to Dragoneer Mac and his Dragon Devil Star. Mac winked at her and gave her a thumbs up.

As the dark cloud of Alexi's army drew closer, Rialda could feel their anger. "Alexi," she whispered softly.

"Something is different about her," Enid said.

"Obviously, she hates me more than ever. I can't say that I blame her."

"You were only following orders," Enid reminded her.

As soon as Alexis' army came into sight, the Elfin and Dragoneers hurled spells across the sky hitting them with blast of binding spells that prevented them from using magic.

The next spell whirled around a dozen of them, blowing them end over end, knocking them from the sky.

Furious, Alexi countered with a freezing spell, encasing Dragons, and riders with ice, sending them spiraling toward the ground.

The Elfin quickly countered the spell, releasing them from the ice. They shook off the remaining ice crystals and hurried to gain altitude, rejoining the formation. They nodded in gratitude to their Elfin brothers.

Alexi's newborn followed her example and blasted them with multiple spells which hit a shield and were reflected harmlessly.

Alexi screamed in frustration and sent out a spell to break through the shield. It weakened it but didn't pass through.

The Elfin and Dragoneers combined their magic and sent a massive gust of wind that blew Alexi and her dark Dragoneers from the sky.

They spun away like gnats hit by a tornado, crashing into one another, spiraling out of control toward the ground, barely regaining control before crashing.

When they tried to take flight, they were hit by multiple spells that prevented them from taking flight.

The same spell knocked the remaining army out of the sky. Frantically, they tried to fly and couldn't.

Alexi pushed aside the panic as she fell from the sky and created a gentle wind to slow their descent, and they gently floated to the ground.

"What do you want to do with them?" Enid asked.

"Nothing. Let them go for now," Rialda said, instructing her army to turn and fly away. As she turned, she cast one last spell, clipping the wing of all the Dragons, rendering them unable to fly.

Furious and defeated, Alexi's army was forced to walk home. Alexi removed the spell that prevented them from flying, but she'd have to make a cure to heal the wounds that clipped their wings.

"They are stronger than we expected," Alton said.

"We will be ready the next time," Alexi promised.

Rialda and her army returned to the mountain fortress in triumph. Rialda landed in the center of the village near the flowing fountain. She reached out to all her people proudly.

"We fought well today. The threat will return, stronger than before, and we will be ready."

Atmos came up next to Rialda and smiled. They were so much stronger together. Today had proved it.

"We need to keep track of Alexi and her army. We will take turns watching her city," Rialda said.

Atmos coughed and smiled at Rialda. "I have an idea," he said.

"Please share, my friend," she said.

"I can teach you all how to open a rip, so the next time they attack, we can use it against them."

Rialda was surprised. She knelt down next to Atmos. "You would trust us enough to do this?"

"Yes. We are one family. I trust my family."

"Excellent. This will allow us to enter her fortress undetected and to fight them. Thank you, my friend, for your generous offer."

"My pleasure. This will allow us to learn about our adversary and predict her next move. Training will begin in the morning."

⁂   ⁂   ⁂

The walk back to Dragon's Pride didn't do much to help Alexi's mood. She couldn't believe that her army was defeated so easily.

"We will do better the next time," Enid assured her. The Elfin's magic mixed with the Dragoneers was powerful."

"Then we will have to be even more powerful," she said angrily.

"Remember, once you go too far, it's a long road back," Enid said.

"You talk in riddles my friend," Alexi said.

"No. I speak a truth you don't want to hear."

Alexi stopped and faced Enid. "Do you want me to stop? Just tell me to and I will give up my quest for justice."

"I just want you to make sure that it's worth the price you may have to pay."

"I've already lost everything. She killed my family, and I will punish her."

"Very well. Your father would be proud."

"If you think he'd be proud, why the lecture to stop?"

"I want you to be sure."

"I'm sure."

Tired and frustrated, they arrived home. Alexi sent her Dragoneers to rest. She could see the disappointment on their faces.

Feeling like she had failed her people, she headed out to the forest to gather more cuttings. The darkness enveloped her, comforting her with its blanket of quiet.

She found the plants close to a stream that was lined with the spore plants. As she cut away the plants for her spell the spores erupted around her. She breathed them in and suddenly felt more powerful than she'd ever imagined. She gathered the spore plants, excited that she'd found something to help her win.

The spores danced around her head as she walked through the dark forest unseen by her, everything started to change.

The forest grew darker and new plants appeared around her. Vines and thick thorn covered trees providing protection for the spores.

As she approached the fortress and walked through the gate, the spores branched out and covered the fortress. The spores sprang up out of the fortress walls and moved up columns supporting the gate. The spore plants spread out across the city, covering everything, and turning it black.

Unaware of the changes and the tiny black spores swirling around her. Alexi moved through the fortress and up to her room. She created a new spell with the spores and added it to their food, as she absently snacked on the paste. The changes in her were immediate. Her skin grew pale as her eyes and hair grew dark. Dark circles appeared around her eyes and her ears grew tiny points on the end of them.

Her senses grew stronger. She could hear crickets chirping outside the wall. The sleeping Dragons grew darker, and their wounds healed as their skin grew thicker.

The changes in the Dragoneers were similar to Alexi's. Exhausted, Alexi climbed the stairs to her room and fell across her bed in a deep restful sleep.

An excited Atmos stood alone in the training room. Never would he have imagined that he'd be training an army.

Rialda surprised him when she gently touched him on the shoulder, causing him to jump.

"I'm sorry. I didn't mean to startle you. I'd like to thank you again for trusting us and apologize again for all my past mistakes. I am so grateful to everything you and your people, our people," she corrected, "have brought to this city."

Atmos laughed. "Who could have predicted this?"

Rialda laughed with him. "I'm ready to learn," she said.

Atmos walked her through the steps of opening a rip. Rialda was a quick learner.

She was able to open a rip to Alexi's fortress and stood outside the eerily dark fortress. Something wasn't right. She quickly returned to Atmos.

"Something is very wrong with Alexi's fortress. There are strange black flowers covering the entire wall."

Atmos frowned and vanished through the rip. He stared at the fortress in dismay. This was powerful dark magic. He feared that they didn't know what they had gotten themselves into. He quickly opened a rip back to Rialda.

"This is very bad. She's discovered an old, very dark form of black magic. This magic can't be controlled by the user. The magic controls the user."

Rialda paced back and forth lost in thought. "How powerful is this magic."

"Very. It will be hard to defeat."

"Then, we need a spell to render it useless, like an antidote. We need to find a way to get rid of it."

"A vaccine against magic. That's brilliant. I will need some spores to make it," he said excitedly.

"Whoa, you have students waiting. I will get the plants. You can get them after class," Rialda said.

Atmos turned, facing a roomful of eager students, smiling shyly, he started teaching them how to open a rip.

His students were eager and excited, learning quickly. He was pleased that they learned quickly and instructed them to practice.

He excused himself and hurried to Rialda's apartment, where she was waiting for him with a complete setup to allow him to create a vaccine against the spores. They both knew it wouldn't be long before Alexi attacked again.

Alexi awoke, unaware of the changes in her and felt better than she'd ever felt. She decided to send Dimitri a message. Maybe he regretted not coming with her.

Excited by the idea of being reunited with Dimitri, she hurried up and dressed, calling Enid. Enid landed next to her with a thud. He was much heavier with his new, thicker hide.

Exhilarated, they passed through the gate to Callis. Slade's men guarding the gate surrounded them, pointing guns at her.

Alexi raised her hands in surrender. "I'm here to give a message to Slade for Sierra. Can I please speak with him?" she asked sweetly.

They stared at the dark unholy pair unsure what to do when Slade walked up frowning at Alexi's changed appearance.

"It's good to see you again," Slade lied, wondering what had happened to her.

Alexi slid off Enid's back and held out a letter she'd prepared. "I'd like to get a message to someone in Pandora?"

Slade took the letter. "I will see that Sierra gets it."

"Thank you," she replied, looking around at Slade's men still pointing weapons at her. They were afraid of her. Why?

She nodded at them and said, "Thank you. I will leave you then." She climbed back on Enid and retreated through the gate.

"They were afraid of us," she said, sadly to Enid.

"Good."

"We need to follow her," Slade said. "Something isn't right."

"You want us to go through the gate?"

"Yes. Come with me," he said and stepped through the gate.

Rialda felt them the moment they entered. She climbed on Alton and met them at the gate.

Slade held out his gun, pointing it threateningly at her.

"I'm not here to hurt you, just to see why you've entered our world," she said.

"We followed Alexi. What did you do to her?"

"Nothing. She did it to herself."

"How? Why?"

"Dark magic. She wants revenge against me. I don't blame her," she said, sadly.

Slade frowned. "My, things have changed."

"Being handed a massive defeat makes you reassess your situation. Please join me at my home. We would like peace between our people."

"This isn't a trick. Why would you want peace with us? We are no threat to you."

"You are valiant fighters, and I have changed my way of thinking. I want to prove that to you and apologize for the pain I inflicted on your people."

"Thank you. We are open to talks of peace."

"Wonderful. The only way to reach it, is by Dragon."

"Wow. Okay. I guess we ride Dragons."

His men looked at him like he'd lost his mind and backed away.

"Okay. I'll ride a Dragon. They will wait here."

Rialda laughed. "You can ride with me." She extended her hand and helped Slade onto Alton's back.

They soared above the forest, and she circled the city so Slade could get a clearer view of their home.

He was impressed with the majestic city below. They landed in the center of the town square, next to the fountain. The city was beautiful. He looked around in awe.

"It's beautiful," he said.

"Thank you. We are happy here. I'm sorry that Alexi can't move beyond our past."

"Sometimes it is very hard to let things go," he said.

"Sadly, I know that all too well. Would you like to see our training facility?"

"I'd like that."

They entered the large training room and the Elfin and Dragoneers were learning a new spell.

Slade watched them concentrating on the words when a flash of light flew from his fingertips. He jumped back startled. "What was that?" he asked in surprise.

Rialda looked at him in surprise. Her mind was racing for an explanation. "Try it again," she said softly.

"What? I didn't do that."

"I believe you did. Please try again."

Slade listened to the spell but was unable to concentrate and stepped back. "See it wasn't me."

"Please concentrate and try again."

Slade frowned, but agreed to try again and within moments, light flashed from his fingertips.

Rialda gently touched him on the shoulder. I think I can explain if you will allow me."

"Yes, please do. This is unbelievable."

"I believe my ancestors escaped to your world during the sickness, trying to avoid it. The only reason you don't possess magic is because of the world you live in."

"You mean, we could all learn magic?"

"Yes. I believe you can."

"This is unbelievable. Would you be willing to teach us?"

"It would be my pleasure. Afterall, we're family."

"So, while you were sleeping, our people prospered?"

"Yes. I'm so grateful that so many of our people survived. You've given us a miracle," she said, hugging him tightly.

"Will we get Dragons?" he asked, smiling shyly.

Rialda laughed. "If that is your wish." It struck her, that it really felt good to laugh and to know that many of their people didn't die because of her. A dreadful weight was lifted off her slender shoulders.

Now she needed to pay her respects to those who lost their lives in their war, then she would finally be free.

Chapter Forty-Seven

The Gnome's Festival

The Gnome's city was alive with activity. Colorful lanterns hung from matching streamers across the quaint town. Games of chance were lined up around the town square.

Simmy was practicing ring toss with shiny brass rings. The sweet smell of cotton candy and caramel apples filled the air.

A large patchwork tent held tight rope walkers and animal tricks. Simmy put down the brass rings and hurried by dunking booth and balloon darts to the front gates, opening them. The Gnomes excitedly took their places.

Lorelie and Drake were the first to arrive on a pair of blue, sea-green Dragons. Lorelie hugged Simmy and looked around the festival with interest.

A Gnome took a seat at a piano and began playing a happy tune. Ocean and Water Fairies hurried around the square taking it all in. They had never seen anything like it.

Skylar waved to her friend leaving them to head to the festival without her. Her and Hawk landed in front of Alexi's fortress. She looked up at the dark walls covered in strange black flowers.

The flowers opened and all together, turned in her direction, releasing their spores. Hawk released a stream of fire, igniting the spores.

Skylar jumped back in alarm, dropping the flyer with pictures of the festival. "What are those things?" she asked.

"Nothing good," Hawk said.

As they watched, the flowers released more spores, which Hawk burned away.

Let's get out of here," Skylar said, climbing back on Hawk.

Hawk circled around the fortress emitting a stream of fire, burning away the flowers. The flowers let out a shrill cry as they burned away.

By the time they returned to the front of the fortress, the flowers were growing back.

"What are those things," Skylar said softly.

"I have no idea, but we should go. There's nothing we can do here," Hawk said.

As they flew away, they didn't see Alexi, dark and brooding, watching them fade in the distance.

Noticing the flyer at her feet, she picked it up and studied it with interest. She called out to Alton. They were going to a festival.

Skylar tried to shrug off the sickening feeling from the condition of Dragon's Pride. She hurried to join her friends who were already enjoying a game of bowling for prizes, while eating a fluffy pink confection.

The Flower Fairies were playing jokes on them by popping up while they were trying to bowl.

The Elfin heard about the festival and Atmos encouraged Rialda and the Dragoneers to attend, and Slade agreed to join them.

They arrived right behind Skylar, who turned and stared at Rialda and Atmos in a mixture of shock and fear.

Rialda smiled and said, "Hello Skylar. It's good to see you."

Skylar was speechless and mumbled, "Hello," before turning and rushing away.

"You tried. They will come around," Atmos said. "If you can win me over, you can win anyone over," he teased.

Rialda laughed, watching her people join in the festivities, when she came face to face with Slaven and Mertz.

"Good evening," Rialda said.

Slaven and Mertz stopped and stared at her in a mixture of nervousness and a little fear.

"Hello," they said together.

"Isn't this amazing?" she asked, looking around at the crowd of Elfin, Fairies, Gnomes and Dragoneers, playing and laughing together.

"Very," Mertz said. "Have you tried any of the games?"

"Not yet. What do you recommend?"

"I'm going to the ring toss," Atmos said, dragging Slade away with him.

"You and Atmos are friends now?" Slaven asked.

"Yes. Unbelievable, isn't it? I hope we can be friends as well," she said hopefully.

Mertz and Slaven were stunned. "I hate to bring this up, but I feel you should know …"

Alexi took that moment to land Alton next to them.

Everyone jumped to get out of the way.

Alexi slid off Alton and stared at Rialda with abject hatred. "How can you talk to her after what she did?" Alexi yelled.

Mertz and Slaven stared at her altered appearance in stunned silence.

Rialda moved between Alexi, Mertz and Slaven protectively. "Your issues are with me. Leave them out of it," Rialda said soothingly.

"Wow. Now you're protecting them?"

"I don't want anyone hurt. It's a festival," Rialda reminded her.

Alexi looked around, her eyes raked over the Elfin and Fairies. When she saw Lorelie and Drake climb on the backs of their Dragons, she was furious. She ignored Rialda and stormed over to Lorelie and jerked her off of the Dragon, spinning her around and yelled, "What do you think you're doing?"

Lorelie was startled by her behavior and said, "Excuse me," in a low threatening tone.

"Are you trying to steal that Dragon?" she demanded.

"Of course not. Why would you think that?"

Alexi looked at Lorelie in disgust. "Your kind don't have Dragons."

Drake moved between Lorelie and Alexi threateningly. He was disgusted by Alexi's behavior and said, "We had Dragons until your kind stole them and killed the rest. This is a celebration and you're causing a scene. I don't know what's wrong with you, but you will leave my wife alone."

Alexi stared at them. "You vial creature. I will not be spoken to in that manner."

Lorelie pushed Drake aside and slowly approached Alexi, stopping inches from her. "You will not ever speak to us in that tone. I used to be a lot like you, and you really don't want to see that side of me," she threatened.

"You think you can scare me?" Alexi asked in disgust.

"No, probably not. You are not that smart," Lorelie said and turned away from her, climbing on her Dragon.

Furious, Alexi reached out with magic to jerk Lorelie off the Dragon, but Lorelie batted the spell away from her and took flight, ignoring her.

When Alexi turned around Skylar, Mertz, Slaven, Rialda, and Atmos were staring at her shocked by her outburst.

"What's wrong with you?" Skylar asked sadly.

"What's wrong with me? You're standing next to a killer."

"And you just assaulted my friend," she shot back.

"I guess you're the fool that gave her the Dragon?"

"You need to pull yourself together. Look at you. Something is terribly wrong with you."

"Nothing is wrong with me. And tell your friend, I'll be coming for the Dragons."

"You attack her, you attack all of us," Skylar said sadly.

"You would defend her over me?"

"Yes. I don't know this, you."

"Fine. Have it your way. You will be sorry," she threatened before climbing on Alton and disappearing into the night.

"She's mixed up with some very bad dark magic," Atmos said, shaking his head.

"How do we cure her?" Skylar asked hopefully. "There are dark plants growing out of the walls at Dragon's Pride. They spit strange spores at me," she added.

"That sounds bad," Slade said.

"Very bad," Rialda said. "I've heard of these plants. Alexi could be in trouble. She will completely lose herself in their poison."

"This could explain why she attacked us," Atmos said.

"She attacked you?" Mertz asked.

"Yes, but I don't think the plants caused that," Rialda said. "I'm the cause of that," she added sadly.

Skylar reached out and gently touched Rialda's arm. "We've all done things we wished we hadn't."

Rialda smiled gratefully at Skylar. "Atmos and I will check out the plants and see if we can at least destroy them, then we can work on a cure."

"I'd like to help," Skylar said.

"So would we," Mertz said, speaking for himself and Slaven.

"Come to our city in the morning and we will get started."

Skylar, Mertz and Slaven exchanged glances and nodded in agreement.

"For tonight, this is a celebration, let's enjoy ourselves," Rialda said, excited for a chance to make peace with Skylar and the others.

"Rialda's right. Let's have fun tonight and tomorrow we'll try to help Alexi."

As they moved through the festival grounds enjoying the games and treats, Rialda and Skylar found themselves competing against each other in a dart game.

The game was evenly matched and coming to an end. Skylar, caught up in the excitement of the game, intentionally bumped into Rialda, causing her to completely miss the board.

Skylar jumped up and down when she was declared the winner, accepting her prize of a sweet spun sugar confection. She turned to face a scowling Rialda.

Skylar's face fell until Rialda laughed and snatched part of the confection and popped it into her mouth and smiled.

Skylar burst out laughing and snatched away her treat protectively, then teased Rialda with it before snatching it away from her.

A crowd of Dragoneers from both cities had gathered behind them watching intently, laughing at the exchange. Skylar and her people walked away laughing.

Rialda turned to Atmos and Slade and said, "I never thought we'd be friendly."

"I told you, it will come," Atmos said.

Chapter Forty-Eight

Alexi

Alexi called her army to action before the sun rose out of the dark ocean.

Her troops numbered over one thousand as they glided through the air. As the army descended toward Lorelie's island paradise, it blocked out the rising sun.

The swarm hit the island as Walan came out of his hut, stretching. He looked up and saw that they were under attack.

He raced for the beach and dove into the water and sank beneath the surface. He quickly swam the distance to the ocean fairy kingdom and entered the great hall and yelled, "We're under attack."

Skylar, Mertz and Slaven met Rialda and Atmos outside Dragon's Pride. The plants had grown even larger.

"Let's get some samples of the plant so we can make a cure for Alexi and her people," Atmos said.

"Then we will destroy the plants," Rialda said.

Atmos filled three linen bags with the dark plants, avoiding the spores they shot at him. Satisfied that he had enough, he stepped away from the plants.

Edin, Moss, Cloven, Hawk and Suri flew around Dragon's Pride burning the plants down to the surface of the wall.

Rialda came behind them, casting a spell to poison the burned-out plants so they couldn't regrow.

Lorelie and Drake raced toward Walan and asked, "Who is attacking and where?" Lorelie asked.

"The island, by Dragons," he said.

"Alexi," cursed Lorelie, calling out to Elkie.

The blue-green Dragon flew through the doorway, shaking off the water.

"Gather the troops," she instructed Drake.

"I'm going to help my people," Lorelie said as she climbed on the Dragon and flew away.

"Lorelie's in trouble," Skylar said.

"I feel it too," said Mertz and Slaven.

"Thank you for your help, but we have to go," Skylar said, racing toward Hawk.

"How do you know she's in trouble?" Rialda yelled.

"We're linked."

"Wait. We can help," she offered.

"Meet us at Lorelie's island," Skylar said before she raced away, followed by Slaven and Mertz.

"Let's go," Rialda said opening a rip to home. She left Atmos to find a cure while she gathered her army. They opened a rip and arrived a few hundred yards before Lorelie's island city.

Alexi's dark Dragons were trying to set the island on fire, but the water and ocean fairies kept putting out the fire while attacking them with water spells, which were useless against the Dragoneers' magic.

For the first time in her life, Lorelie was terrified. The dark magic the Dragoneers were using could easily destroy them. She took a deep breath and told her people to retreat to the ocean palace.

The Water Fairies were stunned. They had never retreated from anyone. They dove into the water and raced toward the palace.

Realizing they were in trouble, Rialda instructed her people to open rips and send Alexi's people back to Dragon's pride.

The Gnomes felt Lorelie's distress and felt powerless, unable to reach her in time. They raced toward the coast, praying that they wouldn't be too late.

Dozens of rips opened around the dark Dragoneers. Having no idea what they were, they passed through them and reappeared at home.

Alexi saw what was happening and screamed out in anger. She saw Rialda and her army closing in on them and instructed her army to intercept them.

Lorelie breathed a sigh of relief that help had arrived and hurried her people off the island.

Skylar and her people arrived and were surprised and relieved to see Rialda's army in conflict with Alexi's.

They quickly joined the battle. Several of her Dragoneers got too close to Alexi and were overcome by streams of poisonous fire.

Skylar paused in flight, stunned to see her friends hurling to the ground, burned beyond recognition and her friend was responsible.

Rialda's army hit them with spell after spell that they'd never seen before, driving them back.

Rips kept opening behind them as they were driven back and forced through them.

Furious that Rialda was so strong, she vowed to get Atmos so she could learn his magic.

All the remaining Dragons spewed out their poisonous fire, and Alexi cast a spell that carried it across Rialda's and Skylar's Dragoneers, burning them wherever it landed.

Alexi and her army raced away in defeat. Alexi's anger grew when she arrived home and found all the plants dead. What was she doing wrong? How did Rialda keep defeating her? She landed on her roof, slid off Enid and went to her room alone to think.

Relieved that the attack was over, Lorelei returned to her island to meet with the Dragoneers.

"Thank you all for coming so quickly. My magic had no effect against her magic," Lorelie said.

"Her magic is infused with dark magic. It was clouding her thinking. She could have destroyed all of us," Rialda said.

"How do we stop her?"

"We've killed the plants that have strengthened her magic, and we are looking for a cure."

"If she's cured, will that stop her from attacking again?" Lorelie asked.

"I don't know. Alexi is angry. Did you do something to upset her?" Rialda asked.

Lorelie laughed. "You could say that. I stole some Dragon eggs."

Rialda laughed. "That would do it."

"Once she's cured, we can try to reason with her," Skylar said hopefully.

"I think she is beyond reason," Rialda said.

"I think Rialda, and her people should join our treaty," Lorelie said. "We wouldn't have been able to defeat her without her help."

Skylar and Mertz exchanged glances before she replied, "That's a good idea. We were lucky they were with us today or the encounter with Alexi may have ended very differently."

The Gnomes came up the beach path relieved that Lorelie and the others were safe. "Sorry we're late," Simmy said. "I think we need Dragons."

Lorelie laughed and hugged him. "You are right on time. We were just discussing adding Rialda to our treaty."

"The more the merrier," Simmy answered. "Who attacked you?"

"Alexi. She's not happy that I took Dragons."

"Her measures were extreme. I'm glad she wasn't successful."

"Me too," Lorelie said smiling. "Thanks to our new friends. If everyone agrees, let's add Rialda."

"We agree," Skylar said.

"We agree," Simmy said.

Rialda added her hand to theirs and Lorelie cast a binding spell on them so they would know if the others were in trouble.

Lorelie produced slender flutes of honeysuckle nectar to celebrate.

"So, what do we do next?" Simmy asked.

"We are working on a cure for Alexi and her people," Rialda said.

"What happens until then?"

"We defend ourselves against future attacks from her," Lorelie said, "But I need to improve my skills. I would love to learn more about your magic if you don't mind."

"We can teach you," Skylar said.

"Thank you," she said, wishing it was Rialda she would be learning from.

"You are all welcome to come to our mountain city to train with us. We've learned a lot from the Elfin."

"Thank you," Skylar said. "I'm glad that we are all on the same side again. You scared the crap out of me."

Rialda laughed. "I'm glad as well. I'm sorry that I was a terrible leader, and I promise that I've learned from my mistakes, and I'll try not to let you down again."

"I'll hold you to that promise," Skylar said nervously.

Rialda nodded in understanding.

Chapter Forty-Nine

Checking In

Sierra opened a rip to Callis and was surprised to learn that Slade was visiting the Dragon world. She didn't know if she should be worried about him or aggravated that he might be in trouble.

She strolled out of the city to the gate and stepped through and reached out for Slade, locating him in the mountains. Opening a rip to his location she found him training in magic. And to her surprise, Atmos was teaching the class.

The moment Atmos saw her, he stopped and stared at her in surprise.

"I'm sorry. I didn't mean to interrupt," she said. "Can I borrow Slade for a moment? I won't keep him long."

Atmos nodded.

Slade followed Sierra outside.

"Please catch me up," she said.

"Well, I've discovered that we are originally from this world and can perform magic, so I'm training with the Elfin and Dragoneers."

"Who've made peace with one another?"

"Except for Alexi and the dark Dragons. They've unleashed a dark spell and Atmos is trying to find a cure for it. He took a break from it to teach this class."

"Rialda isn't giving you any trouble?"

"She's changed. You'd like her now."

"I'm not so sure about that. I'm sorry to hear about Alexi. She's let her thirst for revenge lead her down the wrong path."

Slade patted his jacket pocket. "I have a letter from her," he said, pulling it from his pocket and handing it to her.

"Thank you. I will see that Dimitri gets it."

"Since you are not in trouble, I will leave you to your training."

"You don't want to stick around? They could use your help finding a cure for Alexi."

"Too many people died because of Rialda. I'm not ready to see her just yet without wanting to kill her, but thank you. I will check back with you in a few months."

"Thank you, but we will be fine. We have learned how to take care of ourselves."

"Very well. This isn't goodbye. I will return," she promised.

"I will see you then," he said, hugging her tightly.

Sierra opened a rip to Ben and Iesha's city to look for Dimitri. She found him running the latest Dragoneers through training. He was chatting with an attractive Dragoneer, smiling, and laughing with her.

His smile faded when he saw Sierra striding toward him. The girl glanced back at Sierra before walking away.

"How are you?" Sierra asked, hugging him briefly.

"Actually, I've been very good," he said.

"I'm so happy for you."

"I assume you're here because of Alexi?"

"You are correct. I have a letter from her," she said, handing him the pale envelope.

Dimitri hesitantly reached out, taking the envelope. "Did you see her?"

"No. She left it with Slade."

"How is she?"

"I only know what I've been told. She's using dark magic and has attacked others in their world."

He tore open the envelope and scanned the letter's contents before folding it and putting it in his pocket. "She still wants me to join her. She said she's discovered a new source of magic that she hasn't begun to tap its potential. She's losing herself."

"I'm afraid she has. I'm sorry."

"Me too, but I can't be a part of it."

"I don't blame you. No matter how this plays out, I'm afraid she's going to be hurt."

"I'm sorry to hear that. But I can't let it affect me anymore. So, please, no more letters."

"There won't be. I won't be returning anytime soon. They will have to deal with this alone. I can't continue to run to everyone's aid."

Dimitri laughed. "I bet it's exhausting trying to fix things for everyone."

"You have no idea," she laughed.

"You know that it's only a matter of time before she comes for us?"

"I know. I hope you are wrong."

"I do too."

"What will you do?" she asked.

"I'll protect my home, and she knows that."

"Then we should pray they find a cure."

Epilogue

Sierra surprised Dak on the sun porch, slipping her arms around his slender waist.

"It's about time you came home," he teased.

"I'm not going anywhere, anytime soon," she promised.

"What about your classes?"

"I've decided against that since it didn't work out so well the last time."

"Do you really think the assembly will keep their word?"

"Who knows. I hope we've seen the last of them. How are Mace and the others settling in?

"Very well and excited to be here."

"How were the Dragoneers and Slade?" he asked, pulling her over to his chair and into his lap.

"Seems Slade can do magic. His ancestors were from there."

"That's a weird twist of events."

"Alexi has tapped into some dark magic and has been attacking Rialda, who is now one of the good guys," she said, laughing.

"I didn't see that coming."

"Right. That world has gone crazy."

"What are you going to do about Alexi?"

"I'm going to let them figure it out. It will delay her coming here for Dimitri."

Dak shook his head again. "I'm glad we're sitting this one out."

"Me too. It's time they do this on their own. I just can't see helping Rialda against Alexi."

"That wouldn't feel right."

"We deserve some peace and quiet for a while.

"Amen," Sierra said.

Sierra and Dak strolled hand in hand through Pandora. They were relieved and so proud of their young trainers for defending Pandora against Rialda's Dragoneers. She couldn't believe her baby brother was such a good fighter.

They walked past the new school, bank, library, and dozens of new shops.

"The town has grown so much," Sierra said sadly.

Dak squeezed her hand. "Your children did well in our absence."

She punched him in the arm playfully. "I'm aware, and I'm proud of them. I just wanted to be a part of it."

"I know you did."

They stepped inside a colorfully decorated café and seeing her parents and Adam across the room, they hurried to join them.

Sierra hugged her mom and dad tightly, then grabbed Adam and hugged him. "I'm so proud of you," she said, then punched him in the arm. "Are you crazy? You guys could have been killed."

"Did you want us to let them kill everyone?" he teased.

"No. Of course not."

"Sis. We trained for this, and we are fine."

"I can see that."

"Enough battle talk," Erin said. "Are you home for a while?"

"Yes."

"Wonderful. We've made a lot of progress with modernizing Pandora."

"That's cool. I'm sorry we weren't here to help."

"You can't do everything sweetheart."

"I know. So, how are you guys enjoying Pandora, minus the fighting?"

"It's very different, but we like it, and it's nice to go home on occasion."

"You miss home?"

"Some. This is a lot to adjust to."

"I know it is, but I love having you guys here. I promise that things will calm down."

"At least for a while," Dak added.